Pink Bra
and Black Jacket

also by RAFAËLE GERMAIN

Gin & Tonic and Cucumber

Pink Bra and Black Jacket

by RAFAËLE GERMAIN

translated by DAWN M. CORNELIO

McArthur & Company
Toronto

First published in English in Canada in 2010 by
McArthur & Company
322 King Street West, Suite 402
Toronto, Ontario
M5V 1J2
www.mcarthur-co.com

Published under arrangement with
Groupe Librex Inc., doing business under the name Éditions Libre
Expression, Montréal

First published in French in 2008 as *Soutien-gorge Rose et Veston Noir*

Library and Archives Canada Cataloguing in Publication

Germain, Rafaële, 1976-
[Soutien-gorge rose et veston noir. English]
Pink bra and black jacket / Rafaële Germain ;
translated by Dawn M. Cornelio.

Translation of: Soutien-gorge rose et veston noir.
ISBN 978-1-55278-855-4

I. Cornelio, Dawn M. II. Title. III. Title: Soutien-gorge rose et veston noir.
English

PS8589.R4739S6813 2010   C843'.6   C2010-901135-X

The publisher would like to acknowledge the financial support
of the Government of Canada through the Canada Book Fund and
the Canada Council for our publishing activities. The publisher further
wishes to acknowledge the financial support of the Ontario Arts
Council and the OMDC for our publishing program.

Design and composition by Tania Craan
Cover illustration by Maud Gauthier

Printed and bound in Canada by Webcom

10 9 8 7 6 5 4 3 2 1

To André Bastien and Véronique Forest,
the wind beneath my wings

When I was just a little girl, I asked my mother
"What will I be?
Will I be pretty? Will I be rich?"
Here's what she said to me:
"*Qué será, será.*"

When I was little, I never asked my mother if I was going
to be pretty or if I would be rich. But often, I asked her if
I would find true love someday. And my mother would
literally answer, "*Qué será, será.*" Actually, she would sing
it. "*Qué será, será*": whatever will be, will be. That meant
I had to wait and see where life would take me.

Chapter 1

"I have an announcement," said Stéphanie as she stood up. She glanced around the yard, but no one, except me, seemed to have heard her.

The day had gotten off to a bit of a bad start – I'd woken up at two in the afternoon, slightly surprised to be in my bed, and without the slightest clue of how I'd ended up there. I had a terrible headache, was somewhat nauseous, and felt like I was lying in a fog of alcohol fumes, not to mention the usual collateral damage: dull, dry hair, a piercing sense of guilt and worry about what I could have said and done the night before, and a bite mark of unknown origin on my left thigh. At least there wasn't a stranger snoring in bed next to me. There was at least that bright side about it, as my mother would have said.

After an hour, I'd dragged myself to the kitchen to fry a few slices of bacon, which I planned to wash down with a big glass of Gatorade – fat, salt, electrolytes: the ideal hangover remedy. I'd sat down on the washing machine, looking back and forth between the bacon and the frayed border of my bathrobe, and, prone to introspection as I usually was on mornings like these, I'd thought (sluggishly, it's true) about what I'd become: a twenty-eight-year-old, single (irreparably, joyously and proudly single), researcher and freelance writer, living in a less-than-modern two-bedroom apartment with three cats and a recycling bin full of empty Gatorade bottles – none of these bottles, I must admit, had been consumed in relation to anything athletic.

At four o'clock, I was still digesting my bacon when I got to Stéphanie's, in Verdun, for her damned annual corn roast. She'd decorated the yard in a pretty questionable way, with bales of hay and checked tablecloths – certainly with the intention of creating a "country getaway" that, unfortunately, didn't really match the seedy little street running behind the fence, where a flea-bitten cat was playing with an empty beer can.

Stéphanie must have invited just about everyone she knew: about fifty people were squeezed onto the lawn, each with a beer in one hand and an ear of corn in the other. Laughter was echoing across the yard, corn husks were flying and the conversation was steady – in other words, it wasn't an easy audience for poor Stéphanie, who was still trying to get their attention by coughing.

"A-HEM!" she finally shouted as she raised her glass. She waited a few seconds, made a discouraged gesture signifying to me, the only one listening, that really, nowadays, it was impossible to be heard at your own corn roast without shouting, and then started tapping on her glass with the blade of her knife.

People finally turned around to face her, looking obviously annoyed. I heard a voice behind me ask, "What's got into her?" which was followed by an amused yet inattentive commotion that forced Stéphanie to shout, "HEY! I have a FUCKING announcement to make!" A slightly stunned silence fell over the yard.

"Good," Stéphanie finally said. "I'm glad you're all here tonight." Amused glances were exchanged. Since when did our friend sound like a guest speaker at an orthodontists' convention? "I'm glad you're all here," Stéphanie said again, "because tonight, Charles and I have a very, very big announcement."

Oh my God, I thought to myself. She's pregnant. But she had a glass of wine in one hand, making this explanation unlikely. A new job, maybe? A house in the suburbs?

"Charles and I," said Stéphanie, "are getting married."

WHAT? All eyes turned towards me. Apparently, I'd said

that out loud. I put on a sheepish expression. "I knocked over my glass. Oops." And I leaned over the ground, where, obviously, nothing had spilled.

There were a few seconds of silence, then, in my opinion, an exaggerated explosion of joy, applause and shrill screams from the girls. Why, I wondered, do girls always get overexcited when one of them is getting married?

"Chloé?" I turned to see Charles, who was gently tugging on my sleeve. "You look like you're off in space somewhere," he said to me. "Are you happy for us?" Good old Charles was on the verge of ecstasy. "I can't believe it," he babbled. "I can't believe she said yes."

I gave him a nice smile. Stéphanie and I had met Charles in university – in fact, he'd been our professor, and from our first class, Stéphanie, with her long black hair and innocence, had caught his eye. At first she'd been flattered by the attention this cultivated, older man was showing her, then little by little, she'd been charmed. They flirted shyly and subtly – affairs between professors and students were a no-no – then they started going out, at least according to the official version, when Stéphanie became an instructor herself.

"I can't get over it," Charles repeated. He was forty-nine years old – in other words, twenty years older than Stéphanie. He looked like a real grown-up man, with his round belly, his baldness, and his apparently endless stock of brown sweater vests. This explained why he always appeared astounded when he looked at Stéphanie, and what always touched me about him: even after seven years, he still couldn't believe it and considered himself the luckiest man on earth.

I put a hand on his shoulder. "It's… it's super, Charles. I'm happy for you." I was happy for him. Really. But I didn't have a chance to say any more. Stéphanie appeared next to us and was pulling on Charles' arm.

"Forgot about it, baby. Chloé isn't happy for us. You heard her, didn't you? Shouting 'What?' Chloé won't tell you because she likes us, but she thinks marriage is stupid. Right, Chloé?"

"…"

"That's exactly what I thought. And now, she's just waiting to see Juliette or Antoine so she can talk about us. Am I wrong?"

In fact, she was exactly right. So I settled for giving them a silly smile and muttering, "No, really…" while I waited for her and Charles to move on. They finally walked off, leaving me there with my glass of wine and my hangover. I was wondering if my stomach was going to be able to tolerate corn when I felt a hand on my shoulder.

"Un-fucking-believable, eh?"

I turned around and gave a little shout of joy when I saw Antoine. He was dressed all in black, as usual, and was wearing a jacket despite the heat. He's unbelievable, I thought. Not only does he never look like he's hot, but even at a corn roast, he fits right in wearing a jacket.

"Oh! Hello, sweetie!"

He gave me his little half-smile, the one that had won me over years before. I gave him a kiss on the cheek, thinking that I hardly noticed how handsome he was anymore, with his moderately arrogant air.

"Hey, man," Antoine said, stepping back. "You look like hell."

"Hey, easy, now… I'm in bad enough shape as it is; no need to rub salt in the wound." Antoine never looked like hell, even after spending four days completely drunk in a Val-d'Or motel with a dancer named Belinda.

"Your commentary before was very understated," he said. Then he repeated my "What?" in a mocking way.

"I know that," I sighed. "But still, people shouldn't tell me things like that when I'm in this bad shape."

"Yeah, but what do you expect… They'll all end up getting married. The whole bloody gang. Even Juliette."

He pointed a finger towards our friend Juliette, who was

talking in a corner with her new boyfriend, a big, dopey
twenty-one year old, who claimed he was a conceptual artist
and whose name I could never remember.

"What's his name, again?" I asked Antoine.

"I don't know, I can never remember. Fido? He follows
her around like a purse dog."

I started to laugh, but Antoine gestured for me to stop:
Juliette and Fido were heading our way. They were a
strange-looking couple: Juliette was ten years older than
Fido, and with her short hair and paint-spattered clothes,
she looked a lot more masculine than he did, with his long,
coloured scarves and blond curls. Anyway, Antoine and I
were convinced Fido was gay, which made Juliette furious.

"I don't know why she always insists on having ridiculous
boyfriends when she knows perfectly well things won't work
out," whispered Antoine as he watched them come closer. It
was true enough. Like Antoine and me, Juliette didn't really
believe in true love, but she strung together a series of relationships that never lasted more than two or three months.
I'd done the same thing. My mother called it self-sabotage: by
dating boys that didn't really interest us, we were guaranteed
we wouldn't have to commit.

"Hi there, kids," said Antoine. "How's it going?"

"Fine," said Juliette.

"Cool, man," said Fido.

Juliette kissed my cheeks, and then stepped back, like
she'd just seen a ghost.

"Well, now, would you please tell me what time you went
to bed last night, missy?"

"That's enough!" I answered, as Antoine burst out laughing. "I don't know what time I went to bed. That should
give you an idea of what shape I'm in right now."

"Poor baby," said Juliette, rubbing my back. "You remember Samuel, don't you?" she asked, pointing towards
Fido.

"Samuel!" I shouted. "Of course! Hello, Samuel!"

He nodded hello, looking like an intense conceptual artist, and wanted to know if I was sure the corn we were being served was really organic.

"Excuse me?"

"I refuse to eat food that's not organic, man. It's full of pesticide, nothing but slow-acting poison."

"Your body's a temple, eh?" Antoine asked him mockingly.

Of course, completely serious, Samuel nodded yes.

"Unfortunately," Antoine answered, "the corn isn't organic. But, the garlic dip is made entirely from organic ingredients. You should go get yourself a nice plate of vegetables and dip."

Samuel didn't need to be told twice, and he happily went off towards the table where the raw vegetables were.

"Why do you two always make fun of him?" Juliette asked us when he was far enough away not to hear. She was trying to look angry, but I could see that she wanted to laugh.

"Because he's absurd," Antoine said. "What are you doing with him, anyway?"

"He's nice... and I really like what he does."

"Ohhh, please!"

We'd already been to see one of Samuel's performances. He was standing in the middle of an empty room, completely bound by metres and metres of phone cords that he was trying to undo with abrupt, sweeping gestures, to the sound of dial tones and answering-machine noises. At the end, he was completely naked and gave a long, freeing shout. Antoine and I nearly died laughing.

"Oh, stop making fun of him," Juliette said. "You should be concentrating on Stéphanie. I can't believe she's getting married..."

Stéphanie was on the other side of the yard, surrounded by a group of hysterical girls who couldn't stop touching her, as if they believed that just by coming in contact with her they were increasing their own chances of getting married someday.

"Well," said Juliette, "if getting married makes them happy…"

"They'll be divorced in three years," Antoine went on, "and it'll just be more of a bother and more complicated. Those two have no reason to get married. They both make enough money, and it's not like they were super Catholic or anything like that. They're just doing it to be like everyone else."

"That depends," I said, serving myself another glass of wine. "You could see it as something very postmodern, like, I know it's corny and useless, but that's exactly why I'm getting married. It's like getting a really ugly lamp at the flea market, because, in fact, it's so kitsch it's cool."

"No," replied Antoine. "No one gets married for reasons like that. It would be like having a kid for the same reasons. Ridiculous."

"Personally, I don't have anything against marriage," said Juliette. "I just don't see why it's necessary. It's the twenty-first century, for Christ's sake. Your relationship isn't going to be any stronger, more stable or cuter because you're married. People who say otherwise are just hypocrites."

A little redhead in a pink miniskirt who was walking by looked at Juliette in shock, then, in a particularly annoying tone, she added, "*I* think it's beautiful when people have the courage to celebrate their love. If you're afraid of getting married, that's your problem."

The three of us rolled our eyes and muttered, "Right, right."

"They all say the same thing," Antoine said. "If you don't want to get married it's because you're afraid. What crap!"

I nodded my head enthusiastically to show Antoine I agreed with him completely. But, a little voice hidden deep inside me, was saying maybe it was true, maybe we were afraid. Of marriage, of being with someone, of being a couple, of something we didn't really understand, that was larger than us. And that this was the reason Juliette, Antoine and I made our proclamations of disbelief about love loud and clear.

I quickly chased the little voice away. Doing this had become a habit, in fact. When it started speaking up, whispering things that I really didn't want to hear, I'd bury it. The sneaky little thing would often tell me that maybe I was just a little less happy than I thought I was. That I couldn't go on this way forever, that a person couldn't spend their whole life chasing after nothing at all, after the wind, after the next feeling, simply out of fear of having life catch up with them.

So I never listened to the little voice, it was a matter of principle. The voice was fragile and worried, and it needed love. But, years before, the three of us had decided to be living proof that it was possible to be single AND fulfilled. We decided that it wasn't true that you desperately needed someone else in order to be happy – we, at least, found ourselves to be enough. In fact, our slogan was "Live carefree." No long-term relationships, no worrying about our love life, no being ridiculous, neurotic, single people. Pleasure, complete freedom, lust and gluttony: life lived day to day, and as if each day were the last. It was a tough balancing act, but so far we'd managed to pull it off.

I wondered if sometimes Juliette heard the little voice, too. I was sure that Antoine was completely immune to it – I would have liked to believe otherwise, but I was sure that men resisted the voice more easily than women. And, watching Antoine happily try to pick up the little redhead, who apparently was less principled than she thought, I figured all he must hear was the loud, thundering voice of his own sexual appetite.

"Some dip?" Samuel had come back over to Juliette and me, and was proudly offering us a plate of vegetables in the middle of which regally sat a bowl of garlic dip. Juliette took a carrot, wiped it through the dip, and coquettishly held it out for Samuel, who gobbled it up while giving her a look that was supposed to be overflowing with restrained sexuality, I think.

"Now, go play somewhere else," Juliette said to him. "We're talking girl talk over here."

Samuel smiled at her and turned away, taking his plate with him.

"Why do you talk to him like that?"

"Because I didn't want him to stand there like an idiot with his plate of dip."

"But, Juliette, he's still your boyfriend."

"Of course, but it's not like we're in love," Juliette retorted, emphasizing the word *love*, as if it were something completely ridiculous and laughable.

"I don't understand why you insist on going out with such dopey guys. It would be so much better for you if you'd just get laid. Believe me, it's a lot less trouble. And, I'd like to remind you, that was the first clause of our manifesto, so…"

"Ah! The manifesto!" Juliette interrupted. "The manifesto… Do you still have it?"

"Of course."

Of course. I would never throw away the manifesto, which was lying around somewhere among my old papers. It had been composed five years earlier, during a night of many libations. Juliette, Antoine and I had been in our favourite bar, and, like we often did, we were bitterly ranting about the dim fate our society reserved for single people. ("Nowadays," said Juliette, "the ultimate symbol of success isn't a car, it isn't even a beautiful house with a white-picket fence, it's not even a great career or intelligence. It's love. If you don't succeed in love, you're a pariah.") We'd just ordered three more pints of Kilkenny when Antoine shouted, "A Manifesto! We'll write *The Manifesto of the Single Person*." At the time, it seemed like the greatest idea we'd ever heard in our lives. Juliette had grabbed an old paper placemat and started writing. The result was barely legible, given our secretary's state of intoxication, but it was possible to make out the following items:

Manifesto of the Single Person
We, Chloé Cinq-Mars, Antoine Bernard and
    Juliette Beauchemin, would like to:
Be and remain single.
Re-proclaim singledom as a noble status.
Be perfectly and joyfully self-sufficient.
Reject the dictatorship love wields in our idle,
    jam-packed societies.
Spread the good news that it isn't necessary to be part
    of a couple to be happy.
Regularly honour Casanova's memory.
Defend single people, their rights and their self-esteem.

Everything was going fine until then, but Juliette got a little carried away and added:

Take over the Guinness factory in Dublin.
Sleep with Johnny Depp.

The surprising thing is – with the exception of the last two items, where success unfortunately escaped us – we stayed pretty faithful to our manifesto. Juliette had a boyfriend every once in a while, but, in the end, she was as unattached as we were. We went out a lot, always together, noisily proclaiming our status as fulfilled single people, and supporting each other in this sometimes arid role. To be honest, we thought we were pretty cool and were happy to look down on anyone who was always lovesick and spent their life dreaming about what they'd never have and desperately searching for it in bars, on the Internet, in the street and in ridiculous books with titles like *Learn to Love Yourself, Learn to Love Another* or *A Garden of Love: Does your Heart Have a Green Thumb?*

"Did you really keep the manifesto?" Juliette said as she looked at me. "I can't believe it."

"Why? That manifesto is cool. I like it."

"Stéphanie never liked the manifesto."

"No, she didn't. She even hated it."

As if to prove what I was saying, Stéphanie appeared next to me.

"Are you talking about your ridiculous manifesto?"

"Hey! It's an excellent manifesto, written with love on a paper placemat with hardly any grease stains at all."

"Oh, girls," Stéphanie sighed. "You'll never grow up, will you?"

God she could be annoying when she started acting like a schoolteacher who was strict, but a little touched by her students' stupidity. "At some point," she continued in the same tone, "you have to move on to something else. It's time to open your eyes and realize that, in life, you can't always go it alone. It's not a defeat, it's a victory. Personally, I think it's a lot more mature and courageous to agree to get involved, to be part of a couple, to go beyond your own personal borders. Staying stubbornly single like you is kind of like running away."

She crossed her arms and looked at us defiantly. I had a thousand things to say back to her, but I kept quiet. First of all, because I was too tired, and second of all, because, to my own great despair, I thought what she had said made sense. She said it in an unpleasant way, and her only goal was to bug us, but, from a certain point of view, she was right. Yes, we were running away. And I would have liked to have told her that it wasn't because we were too scared, but because we were free. But I was too afraid I wouldn't believe it myself.

"Is that it?" Juliette finally said. "Are you done?"

Stéphanie started to say something, but in the end, she just settled for a smile.

"Oh, come on, girls. I'm getting married, it's summer,

the weather's nice, there's corn for everyone. Sorry. I didn't mean to be annoying. I would like it if you could just pretend to be happy for me."

Then it was our turn to smile. She was right again. And even though I found the idea of marriage completely absurd, in the end, I was happy for her.

"Yes, Steph, you're right. A toast to your health and happiness!" I said as I held out my glass. We happily clinked glasses and then hugged each other.

"Have you thought about your dress at all?"

"Oh, boy," Juliette, the eternal tomboy, exclaimed. "If you're going to start talking about clothes, I'm getting out of here."

As she walked away, she had a slap on the back for Stéphanie and a wink for me.

"Come on," Stéphanie said. "Let's go eat some corn."

All in all, it was a very nice evening: the corn was sweet and the wine chilled, Samuel had managed to get people to eat all of his dip, Antoine had left with the little redhead, and a delicious, warm breeze was blowing down Verdun. I was sitting on the porch steps with Charles and Juliette when I looked at my watch.

"My God!" I shouted. "Twelve-thirty! I have to go."

"Sorry? Since when do you have to leave at midnight? You're always the last to leave!"

"I'm tired, Juliette. And, um…"

"Um, what?"

"It's not important, it's just that I'm going to have lunch with Luc and, well, I'd like to look half-decent."

"WHAT? You're bailing on us for Luc? Your fuck friend Luc who never sees you at night? WHAT?"

Stunned, Charles looked back and forth between us.

"Who's Luc? What's a fuck friend? What's the problem?"

"Luc's a guy I met at a product launch," I answered. "We sleep together sometimes, nothing serious. That's what fuck friend means. It's a friend you sleep with. Nothing serious."

"Well, if it's nothing serious," said Juliette, "can you please tell me why you have to leave us at twelve-thirty, just for him?"

"Because we're having lunch together at noon, and…"

"Yeah, and that's something else," Juliette added as she turned towards Charles. "He never wants to see her at night. Not because he has a girlfriend or a wife, just because he likes to go to bed early. Personally, I don't see how you can put up with it," she said, turning back to me.

"Well, at least I'm not going out with a conceptual artist who's twenty-one and probably gay!"

"Girls! Girls!" shouted Charles, raising both his hands in the air. "Stop fighting, you're hurting the pacifist in me. If Chloé wants to go, let her go. That being said, Chloé, I don't want to sound like your father or anything, but watch out for your heart, okay?"

"Of course, Charles. Don't worry about my heart. It's nice and strong. Besides, there's nothing in it anyway."

I gave him a kiss on the forehead, and then kissed Juliette on each cheek. She was looking at me half-disappointed, half-mad, and she said, "Hurry, Cinderella! Your taxi's probably already turned back into a pumpkin!" I made a face at her and laughed casually – but as I stepped away from Charles, I prayed for my heart to be as strong as I wanted to believe. Because I knew Juliette was just getting upset because she'd guessed that sometimes, when I got into my big bed all alone, I'd imagine Luc beside me and that would make me smile. It made me mad at myself – I thought it was a humiliating weakness and it weighed on me: I wasn't as strong as Antoine, and I knew it only too well – I would never be as free as he was.

On the way home in the taxi, I thought about my heart again and I tried to tell myself that even if it wasn't as unassailable as Antoine's, it could still take quite a beating. I grumbled a little about Juliette, she knew me so well, and about myself, I really didn't know myself well at all. In fact,

I was afraid of Luc. I thought about Antoine, how he made the little redhead laugh by kissing her on the neck and I grumbled about him, too, just for the hell of it, because I was jealous of how carefree he was. Then I tried to fill myself up with the same carefree attitude and imagined my date the next day was something simple and light, fun without consequences, just to be enjoyed in the moment. But it was a wasted effort: all alone on that back seat, I was smiling, smiling at the thought of Luc falling for me, smiling at a series of slightly silly, romantic images. Too bad for Juliette, I thought. Too bad for me and my childish fears. I have a date tomorrow and I'm going to be fabulous.

Chapter 2

I was in the middle of a big church. The pews were full, and every head was turned towards me, with happy, kind eyes. I was getting married – I was at my own wedding, but there was a problem, well, several problems really. I wasn't supposed to be there, but I didn't know why. My white dress was stretched so tight over my belly that it was ripping in some spots: I was pregnant, very pregnant. Then my fiancé came into the church as the wedding march began to play (it's strange, I thought, isn't the bride the one who's supposed to make an entrance, while the groom patiently waits for her in front of the altar?). I watched him come down the aisle, stubbornly looking down, so I couldn't see his face. He slowly came closer and was about to look up at me when a sharp sound rang out, far off at first, then closer and closer, filling everything…

I awoke with a start. My alarm clock was ringing, with a very unpleasant, electronic ring that I was unfamiliar with. I turned towards it and, to my great chagrin, I could see that it was noon, and it was ringing like that because I put the alarm on when I'd gotten back from Stéphanie's, but I hadn't set the time or the kind of ring. My date with Luc was in an hour. This was, at the very least, a catastrophe.

A lifetime of getting up late had made me quite efficient when the time came to hurry in the morning, but still: an hour to get ready and get to a date was a joke. I jumped out of bed, cursing Luc for his ridiculous habit that forced me to see him at noon, and noon alone. A half-hour later, I'd taken my shower, had my makeup on and was running across my room in a skirt, desperately looking for a bra.

"Ursule, where's Mommy's bra? Hmm? Have you seen Mommy's pink bra?" Sometimes I have an out-of-body experience and I see myself talking to my cats as if they could answer, and I'm always a little disappointed when I imagine myself, eighty years old, sitting on my balcony in my rocking chair with a rifle in my hand and eight cats on my lap.

"Do you think Mommy's going to become the neighbourhood crazy lady, Ursule? The kind that kids are afraid of and who has forty kitties? Hmm?" Ursule, perfectly concise as usual, settled for a short "meooowww," followed by a long yawn. I stroked her little gray head, and gave her a noisy kiss on the forehead. She sneezed and then, obviously annoyed by my kisses, she got up, uncovering my crumpled, fur-covered bra.

All I had left to do was get my hands on my avocado green shoes, which were also nowhere to be found, but with a little luck, they'd be somewhere under a cat, too. Still, after searching fruitlessly for ten minutes and being already rather late, I finally picked up fat, old Siffleux, who was lying on the rug in my room, when I remembered that I'd loaned the shoes to Juliette, because she wanted to use them in one of her installations, some kind of sculpture I hadn't seen yet, but that she'd been talking about for months.

"Shit! Shitshitshitshitshit!" I was desperate: without my green shoes, I had to rethink my whole outfit, which was utterly impossible given the fact that there was absolutely no time left. Worse still, I needed those shoes, they were my power shoes, my magic shoes that always boosted my confidence and put a spring in my step. And this whole situation was really bugging me, mostly because it forced me to realize that I was a lot more upset than I wanted to be and that yes, in fact, I did want to impress Luc, I wanted to enchant Luc, I wanted him to be seduced by my boosted confidence and my springy step, in short, I wanted a boyfriend, me, one of the three signers of the *Single Person's Manifesto*.

I could see the surprised and slightly hurt look that

Juliette had been wearing the night before, when she'd realized how important my date with Luc was to me. I was still
a little mad at her – I was upset with her for knowing me so
well. She's like my conscience sometimes, I said to myself.
Like my Jiminy Cricket. Then I started laughing as I imagined a mini-Juliette with a monocle and her blond hair
tucked up in a top hat, spending her time on my shoulder
and teaching me right from wrong. I thought she'd really
have a laugh if she had seen me, running across my room
like a chicken with its head cut off, hoping for divine intervention or that something like an archangel would come
down and tell me what to wear.

"Utter bullshit," I finally said out loud. "Ut. Ter. Bull.
Shit." And with unusual courage, I put on pink shoes, without changing anything else I was wearing. "Crazy yourself,"
I thought it was appropriate to say to Ursule, as she looked
me up and down particularly impassively. I grabbed my keys,
my purse and my lipstick, and I left as I was trying to imagine
a charming excuse I could give Luc (I had been writing, and
lost track of time? I was completely absorbed in Howard
Bloom's latest book? I was online with Paris? Something
absolutely insane happened, listen, I'll tell you?). In short,
something funny, glamorous, intellectual – irresistible.

"Everything okay?" Luc asked when I arrived, pretending
to be out of breath and trying to look both hurried and
casual.

"I'm fine…" He'd rolled up the sleeves of the light blue
shirt he was wearing and his neck was exposed, a handsome man neck that I had immediately noticed the first
time we met.

"Listen, I'm sorry I'm late, something absolutely ridiculous happened, wait till you hear this…"

"…no problem," Luc interrupted me. "I've only been
here for five minutes. I knew you'd be late, you're always
late. So, I got here twenty minutes after our date was supposed to start."

"Oh? Okay." I was a little taken aback, and gave a ridiculous flirty little laugh that instantly made me want to run away. Luc was looking at me calmly, a mischievous smile on his lips, without saying a word. His attitude was always calm and somewhat detached like that and it made me crazy, first of all because it really bugged me ("What are you thinking?" I always wanted to ask, like a real girl, "What's wrong?"), but also because I thought it was irresistible. He was like a movie star, infinitely cool just by being there, quiet, relaxed with an enigmatic smile and a slightly lewd glint in his eye.

"How are you?" he finally said. He raised his water glass and took a long drink, without taking his eyes off me. It was exciting, but, at the same time, sometimes I would have liked it if Luc didn't necessarily *always* look like he absolutely couldn't wait to get to bed, even in restaurants, at noon.

"I'm okay, I'm okay, a little tired, actually. There was a corn roast at Stéphanie's yesterday."

"Stéphanie?"

"You know, Stéphanie, she's tall and pretty with long black hair, and she has the face of an angel…"

"Oh! Yeah! Hmmm… She really is very pretty. She's going out with kind of a surprising little square?"

"Yes. Well, no, Charles isn't a square."

"Well, he looks like a square."

"Okay, you're right, he does look like a square. But apparently that doesn't bother Stéphanie because, believe it or not, they're getting married!"

"Really?"

Luc was no more surprised than if I'd told him it was going to be cold this winter.

"You don't think it's very surprising?"

"Well… no, people get married every day, don't they?"

I was almost mad at him. His impassiveness, although it was incredibly sexy, usually ended up getting on my nerves – it was so unlike me, so out of character for me – always changing, always on the alert – that I almost had a hard time understanding him: I always wanted to grab him under the chin and shout "Wake up!" And, on top of that, it seemed to me Luc wasn't in a very good position to talk about marriage like the nicest thing there ever was, since he was terrified by the idea of my leaving a toothbrush or a pair of panties at his place.

"You're one to talk," I said to Luc. "You'd be the first one to start getting nauseous if someone was talking marriage with you."

"Me? No."

His voice was as calm as could be and he was looking me right in the eye. For a brief moment – a split second – I thought it was his way of telling me he was ready, not to talk about marriage (that would have made me a bit nauseous, too), but maybe to talk about commitment.

Then I understood. It hit me all of a sudden, as I was watching Luc look up towards a server who was casually waving at him. I looked down at the table, the salt shaker, the pepper shaker shaped like light bulbs, the test tube with a single daisy in it. Luc had absolutely nothing against commitment, or marriage, for that matter. Luc wanted to get married. Luc hoped to make a commitment. Someday. Not right away. Not. With. Me.

I took the blow, I still remember, quite gracefully. It was quick, just the time it took to exhale, that's all, and to catch my breath. Careful not to let anything show. Since Luc only saw me as a temporary lover, I wasn't, absolutely wasn't, about to imply that I saw a boyfriend in him. (Oh! But I had imagined us with our arms around each other in my parents' sunroom watching the rain fall! Bickering good-naturedly while we played all those charming, silly games all people in love play! I'd even imagined us – and no one, absolutely no one, must ever know this – I'd imagined us at Stéphanie's wedding, dancing and laughing while the other women watched jealously – they would have thought Luc was so handsome, incredibly cool).

The server came over, just as I was getting ready to make a cute joke about marriage, to let Luc know he could get married if he wanted to, but, really, I preferred being single and all the pleasures that went with it.

The atmosphere at the table was pleasant as we ate, drank Chardonnay and talked about our work (Luc was a graphic artist – he often designed album covers; it was pretty interesting, he was rather talented, but he talked about it like it was the most important and most complicated job in the world, right after being a cosmonaut, but way ahead of being president of the United States). Luc was making the usual dirty allusions, stroking me with his eyes and running his hands, under the table, along my naked thighs. I'd almost forgotten what had been said earlier, or, to be honest, I'd convinced myself that my pride had been slightly wounded, nothing more.

Luc paid, we finished our drinks, and we walked out of the restaurant laughing. We look like a couple, I thought to myself. Like a real couple. Maybe that's what made me make up my mind – that, or the Chardonnay, or something else, I don't know what got into me, but as we stepped out onto the sidewalk, into the clear, hot summer noon air, I took Luc's hand, and, very quickly, I said, "I want more than this."

He looked at me, speechless.

"What?"

"I want more than this."

"Than what?"

"Than this," I said, gesturing from me to him, then from him back to me.

"What do you mean?" he suddenly looked weary.

"I mean, I don't want to just keep going to bed together. I want more. I want to go to the movies, take walks, see each other at night…"

He interrupted me by kissing me on the mouth. "Come on," he whispered in my ear. "We get along well, don't we?

Things are good like this, aren't they?" He was running his hands under my camisole and kissing me on the neck. For a couple of seconds, I thought about giving in. It would have been so easy, Luc had expert hands. Then I saw myself, at his condo, making love on one of the big leather couches or on the light wood stairs, and then I saw myself, at about six o'clock, leaving the place, kissing him one last time because he liked to go to bed early and spend his evenings alone. "No, Luc. I can't. I'm sorry, but we've been doing this for four months. It's ridiculous."

"But this is what you've always done!" he answered, astounded. "You even said so yourself!"

Of course. I'd even thought I was charming and modern, I'd told him about the *Manifesto*, my wonderful freedom, I thought I was irresistible.

"I know, Luc. But I don't feel like it anymore. I'm sorry, but it's all or nothing."

We were standing in the middle of the sidewalk, and people on their way back to their offices were constantly bumping into us, without saying "sorry." Luc looked at me for a second, looking surprised, and worse, *amused*.

"Well, then, I'm the one who's sorry Chloé, but it's going to be nothing." He gave me a kiss on the cheek, shrugged his shoulders and walked away, without another word, towards Old Montreal.

I stood there on the sidewalk, in the middle of everything. It took a few seconds, I think, for me to understand what had just happened. There was sunshine everywhere. Too much sunshine – noon sun that was overbearing, white, hot and merciless. I was a little drunk, and the light seemed too bright to me; so I crossed the street and went and sat on a stone step, in the shade. A bike messenger stopped in front of me, checked the address and went into the building. I was still there five minutes later when he came out.

"You okay?" he asked. I looked up at him – his bike helmet, his little goatee, his pierced eyebrow – and I realized that I really must look a little strange, sitting on a dirty step, staring at a sewer drain. "Fine," I said in a voice I hoped sounded natural. "My feet just hurt a little." He glanced at my high heels, gave me a little smile and went on his way.

I got up and started walking, with the vague goal of finding a taxi. I was, first and foremost, stunned. I couldn't get over it. I couldn't believe I'd rolled over on my own pride like that, that I'd said such things, and especially, that Luc had rejected me in a way that meant, generally speaking, that he couldn't care less about me. I was humiliated, too, and, after a few minutes, I realized I was hurt.

It can't go on like this, I thought. And the whole time, my surprise was growing, though it was mixed with a sadness that was growing, too. I was surprised I was that hurt, and I was even more surprised that I no longer liked living the life of a "fulfilled single person," no matter how much we'd idealized it. I hailed a cab and, as I sat down, I thought to myself, things have to change. I couldn't say exactly what things – I was embarrassed and tired, and, even if the idea of change seemed instinctively obvious, it still scared me and depressed me. I gave the driver Juliette's address, and I started to cry.

Chapter 3

I was still crying when I got to Juliette's. Marcus, her house-mate, a six-foot-tall Jamaican she'd met in art school where he was a model, opened the door.

"Darling, DAR-ling! What happened?"

"What happened to *you*?" Marcus was wearing a long pink bathrobe, and had a towel wrapped around his head, like at the hair salon, and around his right eye there was a huge blue and purple circle that stretched right up to his eyebrow.

"Oh!" He started to laugh. "Oh, that, darling, is just some makeup." Then, when I looked at him skeptically, he ran a finger along his eyelid and showed me. "See? I was just taking off my makeup. I'm trying a new look for my next number."

"Ohhh…" During the day, Marcus worked as a waiter, but two nights a week he was Grace Jones in a very gay musical revue in a club in the Village.

"I'm a little sick of Grace," he explained. "I want to try something different. Something flashy. A lot of feathers, I think. But come in, come in! Sweetie, you look awful! Juliette! GIULIETTA!"

He went before me into the apartment, shouting Juliette's name and swinging his hips like a model on a cat-walk.

Juliette's head appeared in the distance at the end of the hall. Their apartment was huge. It took up an entire floor of an old factory in Saint-Henri, which had only had a super-ficial renovation, therefore, they paid very low rent. It was both very rustic (cement floors everywhere) and surprisingly exotic (the washroom was the old public washroom of the place, and they'd decided to keep the three stalls and two urinals).

"Oh, it's you?" said Juliette as soon as she saw me. She was holding a big paintbrush in her right hand and seemed a little mad at me, just for appearance's sake undoubtedly. "Did your date go well?" Then, noticing my red eyes and my crestfallen face, "What happened? What did he do? What did that fucking asshole do? Loser!" Juliette never missed a chance to call men bastards or idiots – it was one of her greatest joys.

I followed Marcus into Juliette's studio. The room smelled like industrial glue, and the floor was covered with dirty old sheets and a slightly disconcerting number of mis-cellaneous objects. She was in the middle of painting a mannequin's torso blue, as it arose from a shapeless pile of consumer goods: a hair dryer, a toaster, a portable TV, a teddy bear...

"Hey, is that one of my green shoes there?"

I had my finger on the heel of a shoe that was sticking out between a toilet brush and a cushion in the colours of the American flag.

"Yeah, yeah," Juliette replied casually. "But don't worry, I didn't use any glue on them." When I looked up I could see that the other shoe was on top of the mannequin's head. "I'll give them back, I promise. It's a temporary installation. That's the message."

"What do you mean that's the message?"

"Well, that consumer society is devouring us, but it's very fleeting in the end."

I nodded my head for a few seconds so I looked like I understood, or at least like I was trying to understand, and I sniffled two or three times.

"But all that's not important," Juliette said. "What's wrong? Why are you crying?"

The emergency exit door, which led to the roof, was open and a bit of air and light filtered in. Marcus, still in his pink bathrobe, had sat down on the iron steps that led to it and lit a cigarette. I sat down on a mattress that was lying on the floor and I told them what had happened at the restaurant.

"That jerk," Juliette muttered after I described Luc's reaction to the idea of marriage. "Don't move," she added as she raised her hand to tell me to keep quiet. "I'll be right back." She dropped her brush and ran out of the studio.

"Goes to show," sighed Marcus from his perch, "that all men are assholes."

"Marcus. You're a man."

"A gay man, though, sweetie. It's not the same thing, you know."

"No, of course not... I don't know what I was thinking."

Juliette came back into the studio with a bottle of Calvados and three glasses. "Here," she said, handing me a glass. "It'll be good for you." She poured herself a good amount and handed the bottle to Marcus.

I finished my story just as I finished my Calvados. "What an asshole," Juliette repeated as she refilled my glass. "What kind of moron drops a girl like you?"

It was nice, but a little pointless: "That's not even what bothers me the most," I said to Juliette. "It's just that..." I looked down at the floor. It was ridiculous, I was really ashamed of myself. I thought I was stupid, I felt like a bad student facing their teacher. "...It's just that I really wanted it to work, Juliette." I looked up at her. She wasn't saying anything. Behind me, I heard Marcus' voice: "Well, I'll be..."

"That's the worst part," I continued. "Shit, Juliette, for a couple of seconds I almost called him back. Or tried to catch up with him. It's pitiful."

"What's pitiful," said Juliette, "is that idiot. Can you tell me what got into you? I mean, I could see it if he was Johnny Depp or some great human being, but he's just an ordinary guy! Okay, he's cute, but other than that... in my opinion, a guy who goes to bed at 8:30 and leaves three buttons undone on his shirts..."

"Who are you talking about?" asked a voice behind me. I turned around to see Antoine's shape leaning against the door frame. The sun was shining behind him, so you could just make out his outline – his long legs and his vest. He came down the iron steps slowly, giving Marcus a big kiss on the cheek on the way by. A few years before, he'd gotten into the habit of using the emergency stairs behind the building. It was complicated, dirty, but he seemed attached to using it. It was "his entrance," as he liked to say.

"Hi, sweetie," he said, giving me a kiss. He kissed Juliette on each cheek, and then bent down to pick up a glass on the floor. He gave it a quick inspection, blew in it, and then served himself a healthy dose of Calvados.

"You okay?" he asked. "What's going on? Why the long faces?"

Juliette and Marcus started to answer at the same time – the words *asshole, bastard, heartless* and *fucking jerk* shot through the air around us. Antoine looked at each of us as he tried to understand; I wasn't saying a word – for the first time since noon, I felt like laughing.

"Okay! Whoa!" Antoine finally shouted. "I don't get it. Who's a bastard? Who are we talking about? What restaurant?" Juliette sighed and walked over to Antoine, looking at him like he had a learning disability. "Chloé," she said, pointing her finger at me, "had a date with Luc at noon."

"Luc…?"

"Open-shirt-collar Luc, the guy who was at the bar the other night."

"Oh," said Antoine. "The guy who goes to bed early?"

"Yes. So," Juliette continued, "Chloé (her finger was still pointing at me) had a date with open-shirt-collar Luc. And Chloé (still with the finger), in a moment of weakness, told Luc that she wanted more than just a simple fuck friend. And Luc thanked her for her services and got the hell out."

"Oh!" Antoine seemed to think this over for a few seconds. "Is that all?"

"What do you mean, 'Is that all?'" I retorted.

"Well, it's just that that's nothing new," Antoine said. "You'll be over it in less than a week."

I shot him a look that was intended to be haughty and scornful. "Don't look at me like that," he said. "I should know."

Of course. Antoine and I had met eight years ago, in a bar we went to every night. I was twenty years old and had quickly fallen for the charming Antoine, who tried to pick up everything that moved and went to bed so easily with whomever he wanted it was disconcerting. Yet, to my great surprise (and to my friends' great surprise, which was even more painful), he had set his heart on me.

We'd slept together a few times, and I could already see us walking along Saint-Vincent's deserted beaches, or down rainy London streets. I imagined introducing him to my parents and hearing him tell witty jokes that made the whole family break into a fluty hahahaha as we threw our heads carelessly back (in this fantasy, we were always having tea in pretty porcelain cups, and my mother, my sister and I were wearing big, flouncy hats. Which is strange given that my family never has tea. Neither does Antoine, for that matter).

After a few weeks, Antoine had explained to me, as sweetly as possible, that I was getting attached to him, and that this was a bad idea because he personally had no intention of getting attached to anybody at all. I'd been a little hurt, but it had mostly been a revelation for me. I'd understood that Antoine's charm could be found in the fact that he didn't belong to anyone, he was free as a bird, with no one to answer to and nothing to hide. That's what I want, I'd thought to myself. I wanted to be Antoine. Or at least, the female version of him. And I'd done a pretty good job of it – until now, anyway – and in the meantime, Antoine and I had become best friends.

"No, but, am I right or am I right?" Antoine repeated.

"Yes, you're right! Shit! That's what's bugging me."

"Well then, it's just a passing phase. You'll see, you're just a little tired…"

"No, Antoine. I don't think it's just a passing phase."

"Come on, Chloé…" He sat down next to me on the mattress and started to rub my back.

"Stop! I'm telling you it's not just a passing phase. I've had it up to here, Antoine. I'm fed up, I'm sick of it, I'm at the end of my rope. Christ, I woke up yesterday with a bite mark on my thigh…" I lifted my skirt to show him the spot – the red mark left by two nice rows of teeth. Antoine ran a finger over it, as he laughed softly.

"Who did that?" he asked.

"I don't know! I don't know! And it doesn't make any sense! That's what I'm trying to tell you: this lifestyle's not for me, or at least, it's not for me anymore. I'm not like you."

"Sure you are!" said Antoine. "You're my alter-ego! Don't you remember? Antoine and Chloé, masters of the universe?"

I gave a sad little laugh. It was five years ago, in New York, we'd spent the night in a bunch of clubs drinking and flirting and managing to get into the VIP lounges. The next morning at ten o'clock, as we came out of an after-hours club, we'd gone for a walk in Central Park, shouting "We're masters of the universe!" to the joggers and the homeless people. We were drunk and tired, and completely convinced that we truly were the masters of the universe.

"Oh, I know, I know," I said to Antoine as I leaned my head on his shoulder. "But… it's time to move on. It's like I don't have the stamina I used to have. Aren't you just exhausted sometimes? From always running after the next thrill, the next girl?"

Antoine looked at me as seriously as he could. "No way." I knew what he was thinking, too. "What are you going to do, hmm? Start having ridiculous boyfriends like Juliette?" Juliette kicked him in the shin, as she raised her finger to her lips and made frantic motions towards the hallway:

Samuel, I finally understood, was sleeping in the room next door. Antoine looked a little defeated and Marcus burst out with a loud laugh.

"Seriously," Antoine continued, rubbing his shin. "You know you're not cut out for that. The boring life of couples isn't for people like us." Juliette was listening to us, with her arms crossed. "Antoine's right," she finally said. "And if you think you want someone to play your boyfriend, find yourself a harmless guy like Samuel. But don't start getting wrapped up in relationships with guys that are moderately interesting just because you're going to be thirty and that's what everyone does when they're thirty. You know as well as I do you'd be bored to death. Right?"

She nudged my foot with her own, repeating, "Right?" Next to me, Antoine had started to elbow me. "Right?" he said, too. They were both smiling – I think they were thinking that I was going to wake up and give myself a shake, like someone coming out of a trance.

"No, you don't understand," I said. "I'm serious. We proved it's possible to be single and fulfilled. I had fun, lots of fun. But, despite that, staying single on principle is ridiculous. I know deep down that I wasn't in love with Luc. To be honest, I don't really like him. He's pretentious and has no sense of humour."

"Good," said Antoine, as if I was making progress.

"But that's not the point! Luc was just an excuse. If I fell for him, it's because I really liked the idea of being with someone, and of not running all the time."

Antoine frowned.

"Stéphanie was right," I added for Juliette. "It's time to move on to something else."

I was shocked by my own words. I thought I was pushing it a little, but at the same time, it seemed critical to make them understand that I really was serious, and that it wasn't some passing weakness.

"Chloé," Antoine finally said in a voice that was now so

solemn it made me want to laugh. "Listen to me. You know very well that you don't really believe what you're saying. We've talked about this a thousand times. It may not be easy for you to be single, but you should realize it's harder, and a hundred times more thankless to try to find love like some crazy woman, just because someone gave you the idea that that's what you should be doing."

"That's right," said Juliette. "And, on top of that, it's not worth it. I've been in love once in my life, and it nearly killed me. Cripes, it's been ten years and I'm still not completely over it."

I rolled my eyes. The story of Juliette's unhappy relationship was a legend for us, one of the two founding myths of our universe. It had been told to us so often that it was more familiar and even more relevant than *The Odyssey* or *The New Testament*. We knew every last detail, along with its moral, and the lessons it taught us: love is something vast, mysterious and extremely cruel, and it's better to keep your distance.

"What are you going to do?" asked Juliette. "Start looking for true love?"

"When I was little," I said, lowering my head as if I were about to confess something, "that's all I dreamed about."

"Oh, come on!" Juliette shouted. "When I was little I dreamed of marrying Billy Idol. That doesn't mean a thing! We all dreamed of true love when we were little!"

Antoine thought it would be a good idea to correct her. "Not me," he said.

"Anyway," Juliette went on, "you see what I mean. At some point you grow up. And you figure out a couple of things. True love exists. And if you ever find something that you think is close to that, well, there's a good chance it will be taken away from you and that you'll end up nice and alone and a lot more unhappy than before. One way or another, you'll end up disappointed, hurt and bitter."

No more than you, I felt like saying, but I stayed quiet. "It's a myth," said Antoine. "Love, true love, is a big conspiracy.

They make us believe it exists and that we should all be searching for it. Bullshit. You might get a helluva kick, but passion like that doesn't last. What lasts are the plain, little relationships that two people lock themselves into because they're afraid to be alone. Little things that get comfortable like an old pair of shoes and that…"

"…oh, will you both be quiet!" Marcus suddenly shouted. He stood up, proud and dignified in his long, silk bathrobe, and came over to the mattress. "*I* think you're right, Chloé. Don't listen to them. They're just a little bitter and they're scared. If you want to find true love, go for it!"

"Oh, for God's sake!" Juliette shouted. "Marcus, you change boyfriends like you change shirts! There's not one guy who's lasted more than three weeks. Don't try to tell us you believe in true love!"

Marcus looked offended. "Well, excuse me! At least I'm trying! I'm a hopeless romantic, Juliette, you know that. I know my relationships never work out, but at least I try." With a slightly ridiculous gesture, he pulled the top of his robe closed and added, "I believe it every time."

He turned on his heel and walked out of the studio with his head held high and his hips swaying. We looked at each other for a moment – I thought Juliette or Antoine would start to laugh, but no one opened their mouth. There was something in Marcus' expression when he said "I believe it every time" that was too sincere.

"Anyway," Juliette sighed, "do what you want, but really…" I wanted to tell them lots of things. Platitudes about love and solitude, clichés, commonplace things. But I settled for shrugging my shoulders and falling back onto the mattress. Antoine tapped me lightly on the thigh. "Everything will be fine, princess. You're just tired."

I didn't say anything else. Maybe I was too tired. I really didn't know. But I didn't feel like hearing them say the same stupid things about love again and again. I knew those stupid things by heart. They bored me.

"Have another drink," said Juliette, as she came towards me with the bottle.

"No, no, I'd better not. I have to be at my sister's in an hour."

"Oh boy," Antoine shot me a worried look. "Are you really in any state to face your mother right now?"

"And your sister?" added Juliette, and rightly so, in my opinion. I released a long sigh. "Yes, yes. I suppose."

Then I thought of my mother, hysterical as always, and Daphné, my little sister, my infinitely-perfect-never-does-anything-wrong-married-and-mother-of-two-children little sister. "Oh! God! No, frankly, I'm not sure I can take them."

"Have another drink," Juliette said, full of concern, since she knew my family.

"No, really, I think it'll be even worse if I'm drunk when I get there. It'll open the door for my sister to start in on one of her lectures..."

"Your mother will be drunk," Antoine interrupted.

"My mother's always a little drunk. Never completely drunk, but always a little drunk. It's her motto," I added with a laugh.

"Oh my God," Juliette suddenly said. "Are you going to tell them?"

"Tell them what?"

"Well, that you've gone crazy, and that you decided to start looking for love?"

"No! No. My God, no."

I imagined my mother, bent over hysterically after my announcement; my sister's look saying "I knew it!" and my father going from one to the other, looking surprised and asking, "What is it? What's going on? What did I miss?" and I repeated, more for myself than for Juliette. "No. No, really."

Juliette raised her eyebrows and cocked her head to one

side, as if to say she didn't believe a word I was saying – she knew I could never hide anything from my mother or sister. I held her gaze, repeating to myself the whole time, "She's right. She's completely right." And, naïve as I was, I just kept hoping that it wouldn't be too painful.

Chapter 4

In the taxi on the way to my sister's, I took out my little mirror and wiped away the mascara that had run under my eyes. I looked in the mirror for two or three minutes, trying to see if there was something that had changed in my eyes, to see if anything in my face gave away the agitated state I was in. It wasn't bad, really. Except for the bags under my eyes that were a little bigger than usual – and I could always chalk them up to one or two very late nights – I looked the same as always. With a bit of luck, maybe my mother wouldn't notice anything.

The taxi stopped in front of Daphné's house – a devastatingly boring bungalow, which could only be distinguished from her neighbours' by the location of the garage (on the right instead of the left! Unbelievable!) and its green shutters (the neighbours' were blue! How daring!).

"Thirty-two-fifty," said the driver without turning around.

I sighed. Paying thirty dollars to go to Laval always made me kind of sick. It was like spending three hundred dollars on a vacuum cleaner instead of a pair of shoes. I walked around the house, and I opened the little white wooden gate to get into the yard. It was still really hot, even though it was almost six o'clock, and Daphné was in her above-ground pool with one of her twin girls (to my family's great chagrin, I still couldn't tell them apart – I don't think anyone could, but they all pretended to recognize them at a glance, and always looked offended when I asked Daphné which was which). I was going to make my entrance when, from above, I heard, "Well now! WELL NOW!"

It was my mother, perched on the balcony and leaning

over towards me, waving wildly, as if it was possible for me
not to notice her.

"There's the straggler!" she said.

"Yeah, sorry. I was…"

"Tut, tut, tut, you're certainly not going to apologize to
your old mother for being late. The only one it bothers is
your sister."

It was true: my mother was always late, and she was
strangely proud of that fact. As for my sister, she liked to say
things like, "Punctuality is the politeness of kings," which I
always thought was unbearably stupid, even if it was a quote
from Louis XVIII.

"How are you, sweetheart?" asked my mother.

"I'm fine, but… what did you do to your hair?" She'd
wrapped a purple silk scarf around her head, knotted it at
her neck and had the ends trailing down her back.

"Oh, this?" she answered coquettishly. "It's a new look."
I came closer and noticed that her eyes were heavily made
up, too, with a shadow that looked a lot like kohl.

"A new look?" I said. "Mom, you look like Francine
Grimaldi!"

"Don't be ridiculous, Chloé. It's a very seventies look.
Think of Valentina Cortese in *Day for Night*."

"Oh… and I guess the martini is part of the costume,
too, right?"

"Exactly. Glamour, Chloé, glamour."

I laughed and gave her a kiss. I understand why my
friends always thought my mother was "so cool." She was
funny, lively and completely different. She was also half-
crazy and often unbearable, and she went around with
purple scarves on her head, but I always figured that was
part of the package.

"Where were you?" she asked me, with a look in her eyes
that said she'd already figured out that I was hiding something. With her scarf and outlandish makeup, she looked a
little like a gypsy fortune-teller.

"At Juliette's. We were having a drink with Antoine."

At the mention of Antoine's name, my mother closed her eyes and said, "Mmm… Antoine. How is that handsome boy?"

"Fine."

"You tell him that if I were twenty years younger, I'd eat him right up. I don't understand why you don't go out with him, Chloé. He's absolutely gorgeous."

"Mom, I already told you…"

"I know, I know. Neither of you wants to settle down. You already told me the whole story, with that declaration of yours…"

"Manifesto."

"Manifesto, declaration, it doesn't matter. You make me laugh. You think you're so modern because you've decided to stay single. Remember, my generation came up with the idea. In the sixties, when I was starting out as an actress, no one settled down. We flitted around quite freely, and we weren't stingy with our favours…"

I let go a long, exasperated sigh, but I still couldn't keep from smiling. My mother had been a stage actress in the beginning of the sixties, and had been popular for a little while in a ridiculous 1970s TV show. She hadn't acted since 1973, but she'd retained a frightening quantity of memories from that short time – each of the stories was more ridiculous than the last, and I knew them all by heart.

"Anyway," she said. "I'm not going to bore you with all that…" She waited for a second, hoping that I'd say, "No, no" and encourage her to continue. Obviously, I didn't say a word, and pretended to concentrate on the cedar hedge around the yard. I was thinking about what she'd just said, "You think you're so modern…" It bugged me to admit it, but she was right. We thought we were so modern, so wild… I could suddenly see us for what we were – young, naïve, and lacking insight into ourselves. Really, we couldn't see any farther than the tips of our noses, happy just to believe we were different from everyone else.

I looked at my mother for an instant. She was still waiting for me to protest, and it occurred to me that, in the end, she really was a lot more modern than me. It was literally the most unpleasant thought I could have had. My mother? Modern? A stubborn teenage reflex was telling me that by definition a mother could only be old-fashioned.

She finally turned towards me, obviously resigned to the fact that she wasn't going to be able to go on with her little story, and she leaned towards my ear, "Can you believe we have to sit through another barbecue in Laval?" she whispered in a conspiratorial tone. I shrugged and tried to look powerless. It was a tradition with us to laugh at Daphné's suburban life. Five years earlier, when my sister had announced she was moving to Laval, my mother almost choked on her martini – to her, the suburbs was a place for people with no imagination who just wanted to settle down and lead "tiny, tiny, tiny lives" (I pretty much agreed with her). The fact that Daphné chose to live here was seen as a kind of betrayal – but my mother had learned long ago that her youngest daughter would never be like her, and it never ceased to amaze her that *she* had raised someone who was so sensible and settled.

"Hey! Chloé!" My father waved at me from the other end of the yard, where he was talking with Stéphane, my sister's husband. He always looked surprised to see me – in fact, he always looked surprised, period. It was as if he lived in another dimension that allowed him to keep an eye on ours and its surprising customs. He was wearing a shirt and tie, despite the heat – sometimes I suspected he slept in a tie, and even that he had possibly been born wearing one, which would have been quite a shock for the doctor who'd delivered him.

"Stéphane's showing me their compost," he said to me. "It's very interesting. I think I'll start composting at home."

"You don't have a garden, Dad."

"Yes, that's true... but maybe I'd like to start one. It would be a good hobby."

"Another one?" My father had about ten thousand hobbies, which, in my eyes, were all infinitely boring. He played golf, he painted, he did a bit of cabinet-making, he collected old books and restored them himself – he had even tried to get into building ships in bottles and calligraphy on silk. "I don't know where you find the time. With working on top of it."

He shrugged his shoulders. "Well, you know, it's a myth that lawyers work all the time. Well, yes, you work a lot in the beginning. But by the time you're my age..." He laughed. "We make the young ones work for us! They can take it. At that age, they're full of ambition... right, Stéphane?"

Stéphane, who was rocking the other twin on his shoulders, nodded in agreement. "That's right... it's not unusual for me to work fifty or sixty hours a week." My God, I thought. Stéphane was a gastroenterologist, who spent fifty or sixty hours a week concentrating on people's intestines.

"But when you like what you do," he added, successfully convincing me he was just a little masochistic. I had a hard time imagining him, in his white coat, considering a rare disease of the small intestine. His patients did, too. He was thirty-one, but he looked like he was about seventeen, so when they had their first appointment, worried people always asked if he'd finished med school.

He came over to me and leaned over slightly so that the twin perched on his shoulders would be at my height.

"Will you give Aunt Chloé a kiss, Rosalie?" I smiled at Stéphane. He always made it a point to say the girls' names when I was around, before I had to ask Daphné. Rosalie stretched her arms out towards me with a happy laugh. The twins adored me, something that made me unreasonably happy – I always felt like I was "chosen" when a child showed me any affection, as if only "special" people could be appreciated by creatures who were so lacking in hypocrisy.

"The girls are really crazy about you, eh?" said Stéphane. "They're always so happy to see you."

"That's normal, she's not their mother," answered Daphné's voice from behind us. "For them, you're just fun, never discipline." She was holding the other twin (deductive reasoning said it was Mya) in one arm, and twisting her hair with her free hand.

"Can you go get her dressed?" she asked Stéphane, as she handed him the little girl who was shouting words I didn't understand at her sister. "They have a kind of coded language. The pediatrician said it happens quite often with twins."

"Really?"

Enviously, I watched them for a moment. That must be really handy, I thought. I imagined Juliette, Antoine and I sharing a language that only we knew. It was almost true, in fact. Often, the three of us would be in the middle of a crowd, in a bar or at a party, and our conversation would become so private that other people would have a hard time following.

"Chloé!" My mother was pulling on my hand, waving her empty glass in front of me. "I need a refill. Do you want one?"

"With pleasure."

She walked off towards the kitchen, but she stopped halfway there, and came back towards me. "What's going on?" Not already, I thought, before I answered, "Nothing, why?" She squinted at me and pulled my chin up with two fingers. "Hmm… I know you Chloé Cinq-Mars. I'm the one who made you, don't forget. And you're hiding something from me… You've got nothing to lose by waiting, sweetie. But you're not leaving here until you tell your old mother what's going on." I know, I thought to myself. I know all too well.

Daphné elbowed me, and waved her chin towards me as

if she, too, were saying, "What's going on?" I motioned for
her to drop it, and I looked towards the kitchen, where my
mother was distractedly making a martini – it was such a
routine gesture for her that she did it almost without thinking about it, like other people brush their teeth.

Daphné gave me a wink. It was one of the few things we
agreed on: when she wanted to, our mother could be one
of the most unbearable people in the universe. Even when
we were little, we'd already developed a bunch of ways of
letting the other know she was in one of her moods, and to
steer clear.

"Come with me, I have to change," Daphné whispered
to me. I followed her into her big bedroom where everything was beige or cream. She took off her bathing suit in
front of me – as usual, I turned my eyes away when I noticed
the scar the Caesarean had left along her lower abdomen.

"Stop it," she said, "I'm not a monster, you know."

"I know, sorry."

I looked back up at her and watched her for a moment
– this little sister who was so different from me. She was drying her hair with a towel – the colour was indistinct,
between blond and brown (exactly the same colour mine
would be, I thought, if I had been dying it for fifteen years).

"So?" she asked me. "What's going on?"

"Are you going to tell Mom?"

"No, but you know she'll end up dragging it out of you."

I sat down on her bed. "Oh, I know... it's nothing, really,
it's just that I had a date at noon and it didn't go very well."

"So? Seems to me it's not like you want a boyfriend,
right?" There was a note of reproach in her voice. Daphné
disapproved of my lifestyle, my choices. Daphné disapproved of a lot of things.

For a few seconds, I thought about lying to her. Because
her attitude bugged me and because I always liked to con-
tradict her and make her frown and remind myself I was a
lot more unconventional than she was. Then I remembered

what Marcus had said at Juliette's – I could picture him in his bathrobe, somewhere between being ridiculous and noble, saying, "Go for it."

"Not anymore," I said to Daphné.

"What?"

"I mean… maybe I do want a boyfriend. After all." I was looking at the floor. I was too scared to look at Daphné's expression – I was sure she'd be looking triumphant. But she sat down next to me, in her simple, practical underwear, and she leaned her head till we were looking each other in the eyes. Her big eyes. They were so dark you almost couldn't see the pupils, just like our father's. She rubbed my back (she's the big sister, I thought) and smiled at me.

"Well. I don't believe it…" And she crossed her arms on her chest. "Mom's going to go absolutely crazy if you tell her that."

"I know."

"Mind if I ask what got into you? What made you change your mind?"

So, as Daphné got dressed, I told her about my day, about Stéphanie's announcement of the day before, all the dreams and naïve, outrageous desires I'd been keeping secret for years. I hadn't felt close to Daphné for a long time. But, because she was my sister maybe, and because, when we were little, we'd imagined hundreds of love stories with us as the heroines, I told her everything I hadn't dared tell Juliette and Antoine. Long walks on wild, deserted beaches, shared looks deep enough to get lost in, intimate laughter – love, like a torch, brandished against the world, between it and me, like a shield.

Daphné listened to me carefully, smiling from time to time. When I finished, I was a little surprised by the whole thing, she said, "Yep."

"Yep? That's all you have to say?"

"No… it's just… be careful, Chloé."

"Careful of what?" I couldn't get over it – she'd been

waiting for this moment for ten years. And now that I'd come around to her side, she was telling me to be careful.

"It's just that… I don't want to sound like I'm lecturing you, but love, well, it's not often fireworks and walks on the beach. That doesn't last long."

"I know that! I'm not an idiot, after all."

"No, no, I know you know that. I've been married for five years. You've never been with the same guy more than three months."

"Yeah, but…"

"No, not 'yeah, but.' When I say you don't know, it's that no one *ever* knows. Everyone always thinks it'll be different for them. That's normal. But when you realize after a year or two that the fireworks are more or less over and that all that's left is a few butterflies in your stomach once in a while, I swear it's… it's not awful, it's not the end of the world, but… it is something."

She laughed. "Sorry. I'm not saying what I mean. I just want to warn you not to be looking for an unrealistic kind of love that will knock you off your feet. That may exist, but most of the time, love is made up of little things that aren't very exciting. And that's okay, too, but you have to be ready to accept it. It didn't take me long to figure out that Stéphane and I, especially since we had the girls, well, we're first and foremost a team. We work together. Of course, there are still times when we tell each other we love each other to death, but honestly, they're rare. And it's okay like that. We appreciate those times when they come up. Plus, honestly, I wouldn't have the time or the energy to play Scarlett O'Hara all day long."

"Scarlett O'Hara?"

"You know what I mean! Scarlett O'Hara, Emma Bovary… superpassionate women who refuse to accept real life. Look where they all ended up!"

"But Daphné! I…"

I really didn't know where to start. Because, while

Daphné's speech had been depressing, it also made sense. I
knew that in the end, if you looked at things objectively, she
was right. But I was still pretty naïve, undoubtedly because
I didn't have kids, but also because I'd forbidden myself
from thinking about true love for so long. And now that I
was daring, I wanted it to be true, completely true, and wild
– like a big gust of wind sweeping everything out of its path.

"Daphné…"

"I know, I know. I'm talking with my head, not my heart,
blah, blah, blah… That's easy to say, Chloé. You don't have
any kids, you don't have a mortgage to pay, a relationship
to maintain, a family to feed. Think about it for a couple of
seconds: do you really think it's possible to keep up the passion fest when you have to remind your boyfriend to pick
up a bottle of April Fresh Downy?"

"April Fresh? Don't they know that the month of April
literally smells like crap?"

"Chloé… be serious for a minute."

I thought for a moment. I so wanted to say something
brilliant and sincere that would make her change her mind,
but I know my sister: she'd never really been a big fan of
passion. When we were little, she always laughed at my
romantic, impossible dreams. She played with her little
Fisher-Price kitchen, pretending to be the mommy, while I
was running around outside in the yard, imagining I was
being carried away by a great winged horse.

"Okay, passion is a lot more attractive than reason,"
Daphné finally admitted, "but believe me (she really
emphasized those two words, 'believe me,' as if they were
of the utmost importance), it doesn't get you very far. Deep
down, I need a partner, not Prince Charming. A Prince
Charming isn't good for much. You see? That's why if you
just dream about fireworks and passion, there's a good
chance you'll have to come in for a pretty bumpy landing."

I was going to reply that I wasn't that naïve (which, to tell
the truth, was a big lie – all I did dream about was fireworks

and passion), when we heard my mother, in the hallway,
"Hey, what are we out here, chopped liver? What have you
been doing in there for an hour?" We'd been in Daphné's
room for half an hour at most; our mother had always exaggerated so much that I ended up believing she had to be living
in another time and space.

"Your martini is ready, Chloé!" she finally shouted.
Daphné and I shared an amused glance and I put my finger
to my lips, to remind her not to say anything. She closed her
lips with an imaginary zipper, and I left her room. To my
great surprise, I was amazed by what I'd just heard. I was
thinking that after all, if she was right, it wasn't really worth
it. Why would I give up a carefree life of pleasure for a
responsible life of April Fresh Downy?

Unfortunately, I didn't have much time to think it all
over: I was barely out of the bedroom before my mother
grabbed me by the arm. "What were you talking about?
Hmm?" I jumped. She really did look like Francine
Grimaldi.

"Nothing... Daphné was showing me her bras."
"Oh my! They must be in shades of beige and drab!"
"Pretty much."
"I don't understand that girl. It's so wonderful to feel like
a woman. Personally, two days after I had you two, I was
back in my lace and negligees. It drove your father crazy. We
couldn't make love, you see, I'd just given birth, but we still
managed to give each other pleasure."

Too much information, I thought. Way too much information. Stéphane was in the yard, lighting the barbecue
under the watchful eye of my father, who was giving him
bits of completely worthless advice (What you have to do is
get a good fire going – it was a gas barbecue).

I was just about to step outside when my mother stopped
me. "Don't think I don't know you were talking about
something more important than bras." She cocked her

head. "What? It shouldn't surprise you that I figured out
what you were talking about, I am your mother after all."
I smiled.
"You finally decided you want a boyfriend?"
"Mom! Were you listening at Daphné's bedroom door?"
"No, silly. I just know you, that's all. I knew it would hap-
pen someday."

I took a drink of my martini – actually, it was pure vodka
with an olive at the bottom – and my mother did exactly
what I was afraid she would: she went out into the yard, waving her glass, and shouted, "Everyone! Chloé's looking for
true love!" I heard Daphné burst out laughing behind me.

Two seconds later, I'd finished my martini. My mother
was hugging me wildly, Stéphane was congratulating me as
if she'd just announced I'd discovered a vaccine against
every kind of cancer there was, and Daphné, despite our
many differences, knew exactly what I needed, and was fix-
ing me another drink.

The situation was bad enough, but leave it to my mother
– she leaned towards the twins and happily exclaimed, "And
who's going to get a new little cousin? Hmm? Is it Rosalie
and Mya?" as she shot me knowing looks. My father opened
another beer and, looking shocked, asked me how long I'd
been pregnant.

Exasperated, I downed my second martini, smiling in
response to my family's excited comments. I was torn
between two completely irrational desires: either telling
them I regretted everything I'd just said and I was swearing
off love for the rest of my life, even if I had to join the
Carmelites, or having an absurd coming-out party, where
I'd admit insightful things like, "I want a Prince Charming
who'll be good for something."

I hesitated for a moment, before I simply opted for a
quick escape. I placed my empty glass on the synthetic
resin table, and I went inside, on the pretext of going to

the bathroom. Once I was out of my mother's sight, I sat down on the first chair I came across and heaved a sigh that surprised even me.

Of course, my mother's reaction bugged me beyond belief. But not as much as what Daphné had said. Next to the barbecue, I could see the little pink walkie-talkie that transmitted everything that happened in the twins' room to Daphné and Stéphane. "It's too depressing," I thought. "Too depressing." I was thinking about the nights Juliette, Antoine and I had spent together – whirlwinds of lights, faces and music, light years away from little pink walkie-talkies. Was there a happy medium? Somewhere was there love that would have the intensity of my life so far along with the sweetness I was dreaming of?

I was still asking myself these questions, when, out of habit I grabbed my phone to check my messages. It was a single person's habit and I hated it – I check my voicemail twenty times a day. Distractedly, I heard the monotone recorded voice tell me I had Two. New. Messages. The first was from my downstairs neighbour, an unpleasant bachelor man who wanted to know if I was going to sign the renters' petition to protest the new mailboxes the landlord had installed because, for a reason I didn't really understand, they weren't "regulation."

The second was from Antoine: "Christ, Chloé, I can't believe you're at your sister's. Call us as soon as you get home. We're at Juliette's. You won't believe what just happened."

Chapter 5

"Oh, man, I really can't believe it. I can't believe it."

"I told you you wouldn't believe it," said Antoine as he lit a cigarette. He was still laughing. Juliette was sitting on her bed with her knees pulled up under her chin, and she was giving us dirty looks.

"Yeah, that's right, laugh at me on top of everything."

"We're not laughing at you, Ju," Antoine said to her. "We're laughing at…" He stopped to laugh some more. "It's just… I mean, what irony!" Juliette made a face at him and slumped down on her pillow. "You could at least pretend to have a little compassion," she said.

"Oh, Juliette… if we can laugh about it, it's 'cause we know you're going to get over it, you know. It's not that bad!"

"Sure, but it's not funny either!"

"Okay, first of all…"

I weakly agreed, as I tried to choke back another laugh. No matter what Juliette said, it was pretty funny.

I'd finally gotten hold of Antoine the night before, after feverishly calling Juliette every fifteen minutes, as my mother came over to me every thirty seconds to ask me what I was doing and tell me the sausages were ready. Antoine had eventually answered his cell, and he told me what had happened.

He'd left Juliette's a little while after me, to go "work a little" (which, in his language, probably meant reading the latest *Wallpaper*). An hour later, Juliette had called, hysterical, telling him that after he'd left, Samuel had woken up and announced he "needed to talk to her." There followed a long monologue on what he'd been going through, his life

as an artist, his spiritual and emotional needs, at the end of
which he admitted, "Listen, I think my relationship with
you has opened my eyes: I realize I'm gay. Thank you."

Antoine was hiccoughing with laughter as he repeated
that last sentence. Motionless, I stood there with one hand
on my cheek and said, "Oh. My. GOD. Antoine! It's our
fault!"

We had indeed pronounced Samuel gay as soon as
Juliette had introduced him to us. I don't think we really
believed it (after all, she claimed he made love to her twice
a day), but we did agree that we could see he had a number
of personality traits and several mannerisms that were a little suspicious (the fact that he often told us that the most
beautiful word in the world, out of all the languages, was
homosessual put a bug in our ear, even if he insisted that it
wasn't the meaning of the word he liked, but rather its
"sweet musical sound").

I'd repeated, "It's our fault" at least ten more times, then
I burst out laughing myself. Juliette, on the other hand,
according to what Antoine had immediately told me, was
not laughing so much. She was beside herself, humiliated
by Samuel's leaving her, and mortified that we'd been right.

"Poor thing," I sighed between laughs. "I'll go see her
tomorrow; I don't have too much work." That was totally
false, of course, I was running late on a number of projects.
But Juliette's destiny (and the delightful prospect of a little
drama to iron out among friends) immediately pushed
them farther down on my list of priorities. I went back out
into the yard, where a pyramid of sausages and saucy comments from my mother where waiting for me, and I
promised not to laugh, the next day, and especially not to
bug Juliette with statements like, "We told you so."

But despite all my wonderful promises, twenty-four
hours later, I still wanted to laugh uncontrollably.

"I know it's dumb," I said to Juliette as I had my face

behind my hand, "but... you didn't really like him deep down. In a couple of weeks, you'll laugh about it, too."

"Laugh about what? The fact that I'm a fucking idiot who always falls for stupid guys who are either impotent, manic-depressive or gay?"

I made a little face. I had actually forgotten that before Samuel, there was one guy who was impotent and another who was more depressed than manic. There was also a masochist who'd wanted Juliette to straddle his back and shout, "Giddy-up, you nag," while she whipped his butt, but I thought to myself that this probably wasn't a good time to bring him up.

"Christ," shouted Juliette. "I know I sound like a 'girl' when I say it, but what's wrong with me? What the hell's wrong with me?"

"Juliette, come on," said Antoine, sitting on the edge of her bed. "It doesn't have anything to do with you... you've been a little unlucky, that's for sure... really unlucky... sorry!"

And he started to laugh again. Expressionless, Juliette looked at him for a second, and then she turned over fast and pushed him off the bed with her legs. Antoine landed on the rug with a thud, and I could still hear him laughing. This time, even Juliette laughed a little.

"Seriously," she finally said, "it's not normal. Is it karma, or what? Cripes, I chose Samuel because I figured that even if he wasn't the love of my life, well, while I was waiting, he was nice, he wasn't bipolar, he looked normal. And, in fact, he is normal, but, oops! He's gay! Just that minor detail. Jesus Christ."

"What's going on?"

I looked at the bedroom door, where Marcus, who had obviously just gotten up, was standing. He still had on half his makeup from the night before and was almost completely naked, except for a teeny-tiny, form-fitting pair of red briefs. It was quite a sight. Not only did Marcus have a body that would make just about any male model jealous, but his skin, which was so black that in certain lights it looked almost like it had blue glints in it, was absolutely, divinely soft. "My God," I said. "It's really awful that you're gay, Marcus! You've got a helluva body!"

He smiled coquettishly, and spun around, laughing with his arms in the air. When he was facing us again, he looked down at Antoine, who was still lying on the floor, and then he again asked Juliette, "What's going on?"

"What's going on? What's going on is that Samuel is gay, goddammit."

"Oh," Marcus said, looking indifferent. "Sweetie, I could have told you that. It was so obvious! Nobody noticed?"

I thought Antoine was going to explode. I was pursing my lips and wildly rubbing Juliette's hand, just so I'd have something to do.

"Excuse me?" shouted Juliette, jerking back her hand and looking annoyed.

"Come on, sweetie. It showed! God! You didn't even have to be gay to notice. The way he moved – it was so obvious. And that little thing he always did with his scarf? No, really, I can't believe you didn't realize it... I figured maybe he was bi... Why is he laughing?" He was pointing at Antoine, who had one hand across his face and was choking with laughter.

"Because, apparently," Juliette shouted, "everyone on the fucking planet except me knew he was gay! What's wrong with me, Marcus? Why do I always attract guys who are fucked up or confused? Am I an idiot or what? What's wrong with me?"

"Oh, Giulietta..." Marcus came over to the bed, leaned over and gently put his arms around her. He was huge and she looked so tiny next to him. "Giulietta... I hope you don't think you're the one with the problem! Sweetie, that guy was obviously fucked up! How else would you explain the fact that he was gay and sleeping with a girl? He didn't know who he was! And besides," he said, raising Juliette's chin with two fingers, "it means you're really pretty hot, no? Don't you think?"

Juliette looked at him for a second without saying anything. I looked at Antoine, on the other side of the bed. He wasn't laughing anymore – he did look curious about how Juliette was going to respond. I knew he was jealous of Marcus sometimes, the way he always came up with THE magic word, the exact thing someone needed to hear.

But Juliette just shook her head sadly, as she gently patted Marcus' hand. "That's nice of you, Marcus, but... okay, maybe Samuel was confused, but that's the problem. I always attract guys like that. Guys who are weird, or deviants, or at best, confused... why?"

"Because that's what you're looking for," Marcus answered.

There was silence in the room. Antoine was now leaning up on his elbows and looked absolutely absorbed in the conversation. I was shocked, too, not only by Marcus' audacity (if Antoine or I had said such a thing, she would have thrown us out), but also because Marcus was certainly right. The whole time I'd known Juliette, she'd only had lame, complicated relationships, and each man she got involved with was worse than the one before. And the most horrible thing about it all was that, and I could read it on Antoine's face, too, was that we had never thought of it.

I could see my mother in my mind, and, again, I had the unpleasant feeling she'd been right about the whole thing. Not only were we far from being as modern as we thought, we were just three little idiots who didn't know anything about love, and the way we justified this was by saying we just didn't care about it.

And that's when, to my great surprise, Juliette said, "I know, Marcus. I know." Antoine got up abruptly and we exchanged a flabbergasted glance.

"Excuse me," said Antoine.

"No, no, Marcus is right," sighed Juliette. "I'm not a moron after all. The guys don't come looking for me, I go after them."

"But why? Are you a masochist?" I rolled my eyes – sometimes Antoine's tact was amazing.

Juliette didn't even turn towards him, and she simply said, "No, I'm not a masochist, you jerk, it's just that I'm too scared to get my heart broken again, so I always manage to find a relationship that's completely ridiculous and won't go anywhere."

"But why?" Antoine repeated. "Why don't you just sleep with them?"

This time, Marcus turned towards him, and in his most serious voice, he said, "Okay, I think it's time for you to shut up, now, Tony Boy."

Antoine looked at him with an offended air, and leaned against the wall, with his arms crossed over his chest, like a pouting child. "Tony Boy," I heard him murmur. But Marcus had again turned his attention to Juliette.

"I understand, sweetie. You know, yesterday, when I said I believed in true love every time? Well... I suppose that part of me wants that... but at the same time... I'm not crazy, you know. I know there's a reason I always end up with ass-holes. We're afraid of love, Giulietta. We're afraid of love."

He took her in his arms, and this time, she started to cry. "But I'm so tired..." she moaned.

"I know," said Marcus. "I know." And he started to rock her gently. They made quite an odd picture, the tall, half-naked Jamaican man wearing makeup, and the little blond woman, lying on her unmade bed in her old pyjamas.

"You never told me that," I said to Juliette, more to break the silence than anything else.

"Oh, I know," she said, in a pitiful voice. "But I really have a hard time admitting it to myself. It's not very strong!"

Then, with a sad little smile, she added, "I did sign the *Manifesto*, didn't I?"

I smiled and smoothed her hair. We really were naïve, I thought. Kids pretending to be grown-ups.

"It's just that… it's so hard for me because of Benoît," Juliette continued. Benoît was Juliette's legendary first boyfriend, true love, original sin.

Tony Boy, who visibly couldn't keep still any longer, came closer to the bed. "But what does that have to do with anything? One guy breaks your heart and you want to throw in the towel?"

Marcus and Juliette looked up at him sharply. "You've never been in love, have you?" asked Marcus, in a tone that was almost aggressive. I walked around the bed and stood next to Antoine.

"Antoine. Shit. Shut your mouth instead of saying stupid things like that."

"What? What stupid things? You think this makes sense?"

"Well…"

I thought for a minute. Of course, it didn't make "sense." But it seemed perfectly understandable to me. It wasn't the absolutely strangest way to behave – Juliette was neither the first nor the last person to act like that. What was harder to understand, though, was that we'd taken so long to figure it out. We were either blind or the worst friends in the world.

"See?" Antoine said to Juliette, as if my silence had confirmed his theory. "Your thing isn't making any sense." Juliette was staring at him, with an indefinable expression – I think she was wavering between complete indifference and indignant anger. Antoine looked at her, and then he turned towards me, then, finally, towards Marcus. "What?" he finally shouted. "*What?*"

That's when I understood. Antoine was one of the only people I knew who'd never been in love, who never planned to be, and, above all, who had never been hurt by it. Even when he was little, at elementary school, he'd been the darling of his class. He'd never had to court the prettiest girl in the school. She came to him, just like the most popular girl

in high school did (along with her best friends), and the
pretty Spanish girl who started *cégep* the same time he did.
And he really went to town at university, where he was one
of the few boys in the communications department (this,
however, didn't keep him from making a couple of incursions into the departments of art history, anthropology and
French studies, along with the law school).

Undoubtedly, it was a fine résumé. And it hadn't stopped
there – it had continued at the ad company where he
worked, at the bars he went to, with the pretty dental assis-
tants he managed to charm, who knows how, as they flossed
his teeth. How could he ever understand Juliette's attitude?
Antoine had never sighed as he hoped for a smile or a
glance. He'd never wrung his hands as he cried and wondered why he wasn't being loved back. In fact, he had never
wanted to be loved. He settled for being adored and desired,
and for picking up whomever he wanted.

He stood there for a minute, his arms spread wide, waiting for a reply.

"Antoine," Juliette finally said.

"What?"

"Forget it."

"What?"

"You can't understand. And, anyway, you're not interested." Antoine crossed his arms.

He looked insulted, almost hurt. "What do you mean I'm
not interested?"

"Because!" Juliette shouted at him. "Did you see your
reaction yesterday when Chloé started talking about love?
It was like she said she wanted to be a nun!"

"But you reacted exactly the same way I did!"

Marcus leaned in towards Juliette. "He's got a point
there, sweetie. You were in complete agreement, it seems to
me..."

"Okay, okay!" Juliette said. "I know... it's just that... oh,
shit!"

"What?"

"I hate talking like this! I feel stupid, small, like a real loser... That's why yesterday... I just wanted to say, 'Chloé, don't change a thing! Stay just like you are! Stay safe!' But it would have seemed stupid... I don't know how to talk about things like this."

She threw her arms into the air. "I never learned how to talk about my feelings," she said, emphasizing the word *feelings*, as if it were something sappy and trivial. We didn't talk about that stuff at my house. The only person I ever opened up to was Benoît. And look what happened! He broke my heart!"

She turned towards Antoine, and, in the meticulous tone of someone who wants to be certain they're being understood, she said, "He broke my heart, get it?"

Antoine shrugged his shoulders. "I guess... but... but still," he added cautiously, "I wonder... can't you just forget that? I mean, tell yourself, 'Okay, I'm going to put it away, I'll have sex, I'll going to have fun, but I'm keeping my heart to myself.'"

"It's not as simple as that, Antoine," I said to him.

"What do you know about all this?"

"Maybe I've never had my heart broken like Juliette, but my heart has hurt because someone didn't love me back. You, for example."

"Me?"

"Yes, you! Back in the day, you know, way back when... of course, I knew it would never work, but... I really would have *loved* it if it did."

I looked away. I'd never admitted that to Antoine before. I supposed he had either figured it out or maybe he didn't even care – we'd gotten to the point in our friendship where it seemed useless to me to remind him that at the base of it was a feeling that was a little like love.

Antoine wasn't saying a word. "I figure you're going to brag about it now, right?" He looked up at me, and then quickly lowered his eyes. "No," he answered, running a hand through his hair. "I'm not going to brag. I didn't know... I just really didn't know." He raised his head again and looked at me, directly in the eyes this time. "I didn't know," he repeated. He had the soft, surprised tone of someone who's been hurt by their own indifference.

"Anyway," I said, trying to look detached, "do you get it now? That's why we thought the manifesto was such a good idea, I think. That's why you, your whole life, your attitude were so attractive to us. You were never in pain, your heart, your soul never suffered. You were safe from all that."

"Above all that," Juliette clarified.

"That's not true," said Antoine. "I'm not above all that."

"You're not?" asked Marcus. "Then why don't you understand what Juliette is saying?"

"I..." He looked upwards, as if he were searching for his words. "I don't understand why you get caught up in vicious circles. If you know... why do you keep chasing after guys who aren't worth it? And you, Chloé, why do you want any part of the whole mess, if you know that you might end up with a 'broken heart'?" He made air quotes around the last two words.

"You can't escape the mess," said Marcus. "That's why everyone goes back for more."

"Bullshit. No offence, Marcus, but I think that's what you tell yourself to justify the fact that you always end up in lousy relationships. It's possible to turn your back on the whole mess. Look at me. I'm not above it all, as you say... but I don't play the game. That's all."

"You're right," Juliette said to him. "You're completely right."

"Okay, you don't have to insult me, on top of everything else."

"I'm not insulting you! It's true. I think it's easier said than done, but you're right. Maybe you have a gift for indifference and that makes it easier for you." Antoine frowned when he heard the word *indifference*, as if he'd been hurt, but he didn't say anything. "You know what? I'm going to give it a try myself."

"Try what?"

"Keeping my heart for myself, like you said."

Antoine, Marcus and I looked at Juliette in disbelief. "Giulietta…" Marcus sighed.

"No, I'm serious. I'm stuck in these lousy vicious circles, and, let me tell you, there's nothing fun about it. I don't need those men."

"Exactly," said Antoine, elatedly, as if he'd just converted someone. "You just have sex, without getting your heart mixed up in it."

"No, no," Juliette said. "I think we have clearly established that I can't do that. Even if I wasn't in love with Samuel, I still ended up hurt."

"So what are you going to do?" Marcus asked.

"Well, nothing. I don't need it, really. I can do quite nicely without it. As far as affection is concerned, to tell the truth, you're all I need."

"You think you can do without it?" Antoine repeated, stunned.

"Yes. You may not be aware of this, Antoine, but as far as sex is concerned, the less you have, the less you want. And, in my case, it's not worth the trouble it comes with. I prefer to manage on my own, if you know what I mean, rather than end up with a guy who, at the end of the day, is going to hurt me. From today forward, I have just one motto: self-reliance."

Antoine was staring at her, with wide eyes. "Well, good for you, kiddo, if you can pull that off! I could never do without sex, but…"

"We know, we know…" we all said together.

"…but," Antoine continued, "you're right about the rest. You don't need jerks like Samuel. All you need is yourself. And us."

"Exactly." For the first time since I'd gotten there, Juliette seemed happy. Marcus was looking at her, grinning. "You're crazy, girl. But if that's what you need, not to end up crying in your bed, well, go for it." He kissed her on the forehead and jumped up. Antoine, who's nearly six feet tall, looked short next to him. "Oh well," said Marcus. "I'm out of here, kids. I have to get dressed."

"You should take off your makeup, too, while you're at it," Antoine said to him. Marcus touched his face and burst into a resounding laugh. "Oh my God! I'm still wearing makeup! That's too fuuunnny!" He laughed even harder, and walked out of the room, swishing his hips.

I was sitting next to Juliette. "Are you really serious?"

"Completely."

"Well, listen..."

"It's been quite a week, eh?" said Juliette. "You decide you're going to conquer love; I decide to cross it off my list."

"You're both crazy..." Antoine said. "But if those are your decisions, ladies, well, we may as well celebrate them. What would you say to a little champagne?"

"Oh! You know us. We'll use any excuse to have a glass of champagne."

"That's what I thought. I'll go to the liquor store and I'll be back in ten minutes. Juliette, I expect you to be out of bed, dressed, and with a smile on your face."

"Don't ask for too much!"

Antoine gave her a wink and backed out, smiling at her.

"Are you sure you know what you're doing?" I asked Juliette after Antoine was gone.

"Yes, I'm telling you. I don't know if I'll be able to do it, but it makes me feel better just thinking about it."

"Okay..." We were quiet for a moment. "Tony Boy... Wasn't that the funniest thing?"

Juliette started to laugh. "Not bad, really."

"He must think we're both fucking nuts, eh?"

"I don't know," Juliette answered. "I'm not sure about that."

"Yeah, what was he talking about, 'I'm not above all that'? There's no one in the whole universe who's higher above all that."

"It's still weird," Juliette said.

"Come on!"

"I'm telling you. Deep down, he's not as far above it as we think. Than even he thinks."

I shot her a disbelieving look. "I don't know if it's because you're kind of upset, love, but really... really, I doubt that. If anyone is immune to love, it's him."

"I don't think so," Juliette protested. One day, he's going to wake up and realize he's in love. And he'll be the most surprised of all, but I'm sure it'll happen. I don't know, he's so... excessive. In everything. Some girl's going to turn his head, and he's going to fall face first."

I nodded my head. "Maybe. But, my God. Antoine in love? There'll be an earthquake, the tectonic plates will shift..."

"...and New York will be swallowed up by a tidal wave."

"Exactly."

That was a recurring theme with us – in all our catastrophe scenarios, no matter how absurd they were, New York always ended up being swallowed by a tidal wave, like in bad disaster movies.

"Anyway," said Juliette, "I think it's going to happen sooner than we think."

"The tidal wave?"

"No. Antoine. In love."

"Oh, I wouldn't count on it, Ju. Honestly..."

I stopped: the front door had just slammed, and we could hear Antoine humming. I motioned to Juliette that I thought her theory was wrong, and she signalled something that meant, "Someday, you'll see."

Chapter 6

"You'll see, you'll see… hmmf. Nonsense. Right, Puce? We know Antoine, don't we?" Puce was a tiny black cat that Antoine had found in his alley one sleet-filled night, who literally slept on my head (she needed the affection – when I wasn't around, she slept on Siffleux, who weighed close to twenty pounds and was almost three times heavier than her). I had regular, long conversations with Puce. I'd talk to her, she'd look at me with her tiny, intelligent eyes, and I read her answers in them. An undeniable sign, Juliette often pointed out to me, that I was turning into a half-crazy old maid.

That night, when I'd gotten home from Juliette's, after drinking too much champagne, I decided to consult Puce for her wise opinion. After all, she'd lived at Antoine's for a month, during which time she'd slept in his bed every night – much more than anything any woman who'd been through there could claim. "Really," I added, "do you believe it?" Puce stared at me, motionless, and then she blinked and ran her tongue over her nose. "That's what I thought… Nonsense!" And I fell asleep, without getting undressed.

I woke up the next morning with a serious headache. Puce, as usual, was lying on my hair. She stretched and sat up on her hind legs, while Siffleux stomped around on me trying to tell me he was hungry. I'd dreamed of Antoine: he was selling flowers, which he kept in the trunk of his car, and refused to sell me the ones I wanted. "Orchids aren't right for you," he kept repeating. And he insisted I buy a branch of cherry blossoms.

I turned towards Puce, "Oh boy, Mommy has a headache.

Oh, man. Antoine in love…" I'd watched him, last night, trying to imagine him holding a girl by the waist and lovingly
caressing her face, and I absolutely couldn't see it at all. We'd
toasted at least twenty times, screaming that love didn't exist
– Antoine, even more than Juliette, seemed joyfully certain
of this fact. "No, I'm telling you, Puce, Juliette couldn't be
more wrong. It's a good thing we're around, isn't it? She
looked at me and – what a surprise – sneezed. It was a very
cryptic message. But I still said "Bless you" and got up, trying
not to step on Ursule who was running towards the kitchen,
and making figure-eights around my ankles.

I grabbed a Gatorade from the refrigerator, and then
called Juliette. A dying voice answered.

"Mmmmhhhhhmmmm?…"

"Were you asleep?"

"No, not exactly… My head is pounding too hard. Dude,
how many bottles did we drink?"

"Five. Between the three of us."

"Five bottles of Veuve Clicquot? Man, that must have cost
Antoine a bundle."

"Two hundred and eighty-five dollars. I think he repeated it at least ten times."

"How are you?"

"Oof. I have a headache. Ju?"

"Yeah?"

"I thought about what you said. Antoine? In love? Christ,
didn't you see him, yesterday…?"

"Oh, just drop it, Stretch."

It was a habit that was born from our long friendship;
Juliette called me "Stretch" even though I'm only five-foot-
three, and I called her "Chubs" even though she was skinny
as a rail.

"Maybe I'm wrong, maybe not. We'll see, won't we?
What made you bring that up again?"

"I just don't think your theory makes any sense."

"You know what I think?" Juliette asked. I could feel her smiling from the other end of the phone line. "I think you'd be terribly offended if Antoine fell in love with some girl."

"What?"

"That's right. Even if you don't like him that way anymore, even if you turned the page eight years ago, I'm sure you'd be offended."

I thought about it for an instant: she was completely right. I started laughing. "Okay. Maybe a little. Just on principle. But anyway, and I'm not saying this because I'm afraid of being offended, but I'm sure you're wrong. I talked it over with Puce…"

"Chloé, you can't talk things over with a cat."

"Not just any old cat. I'd never try to talk to Siffleux. But Puce is very smart."

"Chloé… I have a headache."

"Anyway, yesterday Puce and I were thinking you might be right, but this morning, we're more clear-headed and…"

"Have you ever told anyone else besides me that you ask a cat for advice?"

"Why?"

"Because someone's going to lock you up someday, Chloé."

"Lots of girls talk to their cats, I'll have you know."

"Now that is sad."

I hung up and told Puce that Juliette was just jealous of our beautiful friendship, and I walked towards my office, with the firm intention of doing some work. After just barely an hour, I realized I was really far behind and it was going to take a week of being locked up and doing nothing but working to get caught up. "I'm going to be serious," I said to Siffleux, who'd come to lie on my desk under my lamp. "I'm going to work hard, go to bed early and not go out."

Which would have been easier to do if Juliette hadn't called me three hours later begging me to bring my laptop over. "I absolutely have to email some pictures!"

"Why don't you come over here?" I asked.

"Because I have to take pictures of all the paintings I have here! And I don't know what I want to send. A gallery owner might be interested, but he needs material, and plus I'd also like to have your opinion at the same time and..."

"Oh, shit, Ju! I have work to do! Why don't you ask Antoine?"

"His laptop is broken."

"Oh, crap."

"Pleeeaaase?"

"You're such a baby, aren't you? You really could come here."

"Yes, but I need your advice! Your marvellous advice!"

"Okay, okay, I'll come. But I'm not going to stay long," I said.

"Oh, you're absolutely fantastic!" shouted Juliette. I replied with a "yeah, yeah," and I hung up, secretly happy for the excuse to get out of the house.

I was a little late getting to Juliette's. She was in her studio with Marcus and Antoine, who'd brought over his digital camera. "Hey, Tony Boy!" I shouted. He made a face at me. "You get recruited, too?" he asked me with a smile – and we started looking at the paintings Juliette was showing us.

It took two good hours just to choose the paintings that were worth taking pictures of and sending to the gallery owner.

"Why doesn't he come over here? Will he really be able to judge the quality of a painting on the computer?" Antoine wondered wisely.

"He did come," Juliette answered. He looked at a few things and now he wants me to send him some pictures of examples of my work, so he can keep them in his database. They do that all the time. Like a digital portfolio."

"You should set up a website," answered Antoine.

"Too complicated."

"And you think what we're doing now isn't complicated?"

Juliette laughed, and she started taking photos – at least twenty of each of the paintings we'd selected.

"Okay!" she said when she was done. "We can go into my room, to plug the computer in." One after the other, the three of us followed her.

"So," Marcus asked me as we crossed the wide hallway. "Have you found true love?"

"Marcus, it's been four days…"

"But is it still what you want?"

"I don't know, Marcus…"

Walking in front of us, Antoine turned around and grinned. "You don't know?" he asked me.

"Oh, listen, you two. I don't feel like talking about this, okay? Anyway, I know what you both think. So, when I figure things out, I'll let you know."

"Okay, don't get all offended," Antoine said.

"It's not that, I'm just sick of talking about it. It's so girly," I added, squeaking when I said the word *girly*.

I hated things that were "girly." I put the computer on the desk, and opened it up, unveiling a desktop covered in a wonderful collage of a bunch of photos of Aragorn in *The Lord of the Rings*. Antoine sighed. "And you don't think that's 'girly'?" Nobody answered him, and Juliette nudged him out of the way to get closer to the screen. "Beautiful…" she murmured dreamily.

Juliette and I often imagined the wonderfully delicious moment when Viggo Mortensen would wildly take us on a bed of branches. He was, of course, always wearing the Aragorn costume, which caused quite a logistical problem: the armour, which, while it was virile and the true source of the fantasy, risked being uncomfortable, or even painful. Juliette suggested it be removed, we spent way too much time talking about it, and we always ended up deciding that, really, it was essential.

"Oh, Christ," Antoine sighed. "This is disgusting. Nobody but nerds and pimply little guys like that kind of movie. You girls should really be embarrassed. Honestly, you know the first two movies by heart!"

He was right: we both had the DVDs of the extended version, and we must have seen them each at least ten times. They were "our" films, the source of countless running gags, quotes we were constantly repeating, and a lasting fantasy.

"You're just jealous," I answered.

"No. First, I'll have you know that's not a very original fantasy… and, next, I don't see how I could be jealous of a guy who spends his life chasing after orcs and sleeping on the ground. And on top of that, he must be dirty."

"Hmmm… a *dirty* Viggo…"

"Okay, you're absolutely ridiculous."

He sat down on Juliette's bed, next to Marcus, who'd been following the scene and laughing.

"Didn't you used to have a Kandinsky painting as your desktop?" Juliette asked me.

"Yes… sometimes I do feel a little bad about putting my baser instincts before art, but, well… it puts me in a good mood every time I start up the computer, so…"

"Personally, I don't understand," Antoine muttered. "I don't see what's so hot about that guy. Brad Pitt, on the other hand, I could understand. But him…"

"Brad Pitt?" Marcus interrupted. "Darling, he's so nineties." Juliette and I burst out laughing.

"What?" said Antoine.

"Brad Pitt," Marcus repeated. "He's just so nineties. Totally out!" He got up, gave a little curtsey and left the room.

"What's he talking about?" Antoine asked when Marcus was far enough away.

"Antoine," Juliette answered, "that's Marcus. He refused to drink Cosmopolitans in 2001, because it was 'so 1999.'" He didn't drink any until 2004 because by then it was 'retro.' So, there's no reason to be surprised now."

"But that's completely absurd! And really gay, if you want my opinion."

"Of course it's gay! Marcus isn't just gay, Antoine, he's SuperQueen. Have a little respect."

"SuperQueen?" Antoine looked like he was asking us if we really had gone crazy.

"Yeah! Like Superman."

"What?"

"Okay, listen."

Juliette pulled her eyes off my computer desktop and turned towards Antoine. "Think of Superman. He has all the characteristics of an ordinary man, but multiplied by ten, right?"

"Yesss," Antoine answered, visibly worried about what was going to come next.

"Well, Marcus has all the characteristics that are usually associated with gay men, but multiplied by ten. So, he's SuperQueen!" Juliette raised one fist in the air, and held the other near her face, in an imitation of Superman's flying posture.

"SuperQueen, eh?" Antoine repeated.

"Exactly."

"That's the most ludicrous theory I've ever heard in my life."

"We have some others, if you want to hear them..." Juliette said, tapping her finger against her temple.

"Thanks, no need. But, does he know you call him that?"

"Yeah, of course? He thinks it's absolutely hilarious, and, I think, kind of flattering. The guy's a drag queen, Antoine. He's out of the closet. I even made him a cape once – a pink sheet with a sequin *F* on a yellow and purple triangle, like Superman's logo. And he wore it."

She'd barely finished her sentence when we heard Marcus' voice: "Giulietta! I can't find my bra with the pearls! Did you take my bra with the pearls?"

I burst out laughing again. Antoine looked at me, smiling and nodding, as he dropped back onto Juliette's pillows. "What a circus. What a fucking circus. Someday, a donkey

or a baby elephant is going to come out from under the bed,
Ju, and I won't even be surprised."

He paused for a minute while I was explaining to Juliette
how the software worked, then he went on, "And if I were a
Super, what Super would I be?"

"SuperMacho," Juliette and I both answered together.

"Pshhh... Not likely. SuperMacho is Italian. Everybody
knows that."

"Uh, no," I said. "That's just a cliché."

"Maybe," said Antoine. He looked like he was thinking,
then he added, "SuperMacho, eh?"

"You want me to make you a cape?" Juliette asked him.

"No. Thank you. Really."

We sent Juliette's pictures pretty quickly, while Antoine
looked at an old newspaper and made useless comments
every other second. ("*Ferdinand*... can you tell me WHO
laughs when they read that comic? It's one of the great mys-
teries of my life. The guy who figures that out should get a
Nobel prize.") I was listening to him and laughing, and
thinking that maybe Juliette was right: maybe there was a
way to settle for what we had. Between the three of us, we
generated enough mutual love to not need to go looking for
more elsewhere. I wished that were the case, in fact. The
three of us, together, carefree and self-sufficient. And, as I
listened to Antoine's pointless jokes and Juliette's childlike
laugh, I realized that I'd believed it until now.

I ended up staying at Juliette's until pretty late, as usual.
She and Antoine tried several times to get me to talk about
what I wanted now, but I didn't give in – I was vaguely
humiliated by all the questions I was asking myself: it
seemed to me there was nothing more "girly" than spending
your time torturing yourself and worrying about relationships that didn't even exist yet. "To tell the truth, it's very
Eve-Marie," Juliette pointed out. I could only agree.

Eve-Marie was a researcher I worked with from time to
time – the prototype of the "girly" girl that Juliette and I

hated so much. Bridget Jones, but less funny and more straight. Eve-Marie wasn't a bad person. She was even pretty nice. But when she started talking about love, she could turn off even the biggest romantic – forever.

Yet, for some unfathomable reason, Eve-Marie adored me. Maybe because, unlike other co-workers, I still felt like I had to at least pretend I was interested in her troubles. The result was that she rushed over to me whenever she saw me, and that I ended up getting sucked into a vortex of questions and stories that were all punctuated by a series of "So then I said…" and "Then, he said…" that gave me a headache.

I didn't want to become Eve-Marie. In fact, that possibility was one of the things that weighed most heavily on me when I wondered if being in love was worth it. I was terrified by the idea of turning into Eve-Marie overnight, and of spending my days languishing on the phone and harassing my co-workers by constantly asking, "Yes, but did I make the right decision? Hmmm?" or by saying, dead seriously, "In the end, what I learned is that I have to listen to myself. Me first." I also knew it was a thin line, and that once you set foot in Eve-Marie land, you rarely came back.

So, a few days later, I wasn't really surprised when I got a call from a producer we both worked for, who, as she invited me to the meeting, added, "Oh, and Eve-Marie will be there. You better fasten your seatbelt, I saw her last week and, apparently, she's going through a rough patch in her love life." I rolled my eyes. All Eve-Marie ever went through were rough patches in her love life. Eve-Marie *was* a love life in a rough patch.

The next Monday, I was sitting in a conference room, completely numbed by Eve-Marie's stories, which she told as she both cried and shouted simultaneously. The rest of the team had fled like a bunch of cowards, leaving me alone with her, as usual.

"So then, he said to me, 'Eve-Marie, you're a great girl, but

I don't think we're at the same place.' Can you believe it?" she was saying to me, "Can you believe he did that to me?"

"No..." I lied.

What I couldn't believe was that her boyfriends didn't all run away screaming in terror. On occasion, we'd worked near each other and I'd hear her talking about them all day long. She must have driven them half-crazy with her worries, her demands and her spontaneous – and inevitably over-intense – declarations of love.

"Everything was fine," she was crying. "I was sure he was THE guy, the man of my dreams!"

"How long were you together?"

"Three months. But that doesn't mean anything. It's a matter of instinct."

"Of course."

"And then, out of nowhere, he says I'm 'too much'!"

"Too much what?"

"I don't know!" shouted Eve-Marie. "Too much of every-thing, apparently. Too intense, too emotional, too passionate."

A very good judge of character, I thought to myself.

"He said I loved him too much!" she went on. "You can't love too much!"

"Eve-Marie... honestly, I think you can."

"WHAT?" She looked up at me, horrified, like I'd just pronounced some unforgivable heresy.

"I just mean... it's not a matter of loving too much, but of not doing it right. You suffocate your boyfriends, Eve-Marie."

"I can't believe you're saying things like that to me! You can't measure out love, you know! When I'm in love, I'm in love all the way, with all my heart and all my soul. And you think because my love is so big I scare men?"

"Eve... sometimes, you..." I was weighing my words. I didn't want to insult her, but I couldn't keep holding her hand and pretend she really was the victim of heartless men.

"Sometimes what?" she asked.

"Sometimes, I think you're more in love with love than with the guy. Lots of times, I've seen you with guys who really weren't very interesting that you said you loved… you jump into every relationship as if it were true love. Why don't you try taking things a little slower?"

She was staring at me, her eyes overflowing, as if I'd just told her she may as well become a nun. "But how?" she finally murmured. "How? How do you want me to take things slower?" I watched her for an instant. She didn't look insulted – she didn't *understand*. At all. Evidently, what I'd just said was a complete aberration to her. "How do you expect me to do that?" she repeated.

I didn't know how to respond. "You let yourself get carried away too quickly," I tried. "Maybe you could… I don't know, weigh both sides, let time do its thing, not get involved body and soul after just two weeks…"

"But, did you hear what you just said?"

"Um… yes."

"Chloé! You're asking me to put the brakes on my emotions!"

"No, I'm telling you it might be better for you if you listened to your head sometimes. You'd see that, very often, your feelings aren't as strong as you think."

"And you think I'd like having less intense feelings?"

"Well, you should! If they're supposed to become intense, they will. But is it necessary to talk about true love after just twenty-four hours? Eve-Marie! You just got broken up with again because of that! And you're in as much pain as if you'd been together for years! Don't tell me you really don't see the connection!"

"You're really heartless, aren't you?"

"Oh, Eve-Marie, shit…"

But, for just a quick second, I was afraid she was right, that I was heartless, and that I'd never noticed.

"No," Eve-Marie continued. "I don't want that. So, you

can go ahead and laugh at me, you can say I'm too romantic, you can say that's why I keep falling on my face, well,
then, fuck it!"

I jumped. Eve-Marie never swore. "I'm going to keep
falling on my face and making people like you laugh at me."

"Listen…"

"No. What do you want? For me to be like you – always
thinking with my head or my hormones?"

"Hey!"

"What, hey? That's what you do, Chloé. I've known you
for five years, and every time I've seen you with a guy, you've
said, 'It's just for the sex.' Except for that friend of yours,
um, Alain."

"Antoine."

"Whatever. How long are you going to keep it up, Chloé?
Protecting your heart by making yourself think you don't
feel anything. You know what you remind me of?"

I didn't answer.

"A hibernating animal."

"Okay. That's enough now. I don't mind listening to
your stories, Eve-Marie, but I'm not interested in letting you
insult me just because I'm not like you. So, keep falling for
guys who aren't interested, and give me a fucking break. You
like what you're doing; I like what I'm doing. But honestly,
I don't think I have anything to learn from you."

I picked up my files and walked out of the conference
room, biting my bottom lip. I wanted to cry, just like I
always did when I was angry. I found an empty office and
I called Juliette.

"Helloooo!" answered a cheerful voice.

"Marcus? It's Chloé."

"Oh, how are you darling?"

"In a bit of a hurry. Can you put Juliette on?"

"She's not here. She's out running some errands."

"Shit."

"You want to leave a message?"

"No. Thanks, Marcus."

"Bye-."

I hung up quickly, before he could get in the other "bye," and I dialled Antoine's number.

"Antoine Bernard."

"Antoine?"

"Hey, sweetie."

"Since when do you answer the phone like that?"

"I don't know, two or three days. Very businesslike, don't you think?"

"No. It's ridiculous."

"Of course. But if Viggo Mortensen answered 'Viggo Mortensen,' I bet you'd find it unbelievably cool…"

"Shut up, Antoine."

"Oh my God. Everything okay, Miss Sunshine?"

"Not really. I just told off Eve-Marie Saulnier."

"Who?"

"You know, the girl I work with who's always in love?"

"Oh, right."

"Antoine, I think I was really mean."

"Why?"

"Well, because she was being such a pain in the ass! She was going on again with her ridiculous stories. I told her it might be good for her to take things more slowly, and quit throwing herself at a guy like white on rice, and then, she went nuts, and started telling me I was like a 'hibernating animal,' that I was heartless… Antoine, do you think I'm heartless?"

He started laughing. "Chloé, you're not going to believe what an emotionally challenged crazy woman tells you, are you?"

"No, but it's true, Antoine… there's no doubt she's unbearable and her idea of love is completely unhealthy but… what the hell am I doing? I don't feel anything, Antoine!"

I started to cry. "Or else I feel something because of a jerk like Luc, and it barely lasts a few days! Don't you ever wonder if you're the one who's not normal? Always gliding along the surface of things?"

"Chloé... don't cry."

"But how long is this going to last? Always being in the grey zone? Some comfortable space where there's no risk? That's what she said to me, and it... hurt me so much!"

And I sobbed even harder.

"Chloé. Chloé. You're the most extraordinary girl I know. You let yourself get hurt by what a poor bitter girl tries to feed you! You're strong and independent, and, to tell you the truth, your heart's as big as the whole city."

"You're just saying that so I'll stop crying."

"Sure, but that doesn't mean I don't mean it. Chloé, unhappy girls are biased to think everyone should be obsessed by love."

"Yeah, but don't you think there's a happy medium? Somewhere between Eve-Marie and me?"

"You're exactly where you're supposed to be, my dear."

"No! You're just saying that because you want me to stay like I am! Because, for you, as long as Juliette and I keep on refusing love with all our might, it justifies you! It means you don't have to wonder what the hell you're doing with your life."

Silence came from the other end of the line, during which I rubbed my forehead.

"I'm sorry," I said.

"No, no. If that's what you think..."

"Antoine..."

"No, it's a possibility. Anyway, if I had to worry about what other people think of me, I'd never leave the house."

I didn't say anything: in his own way, Antoine was obsessed by other people's opinions. His obsession came down to one thing: looking like he couldn't care less – but it was all for show.

"I just meant that maybe it's time to move on to something else," I added. "For me. You can do what you want.

You know what you want, right? I just said that because I was mad. Sorry."

"It's okay."

But I could tell he was hurt. "Chloé if you really think you need to start chasing after love to be happy, then I'm not going to stand in your way, just because I need to justify myself, or for any other reason."

"Okay, okay…" I wanted to tell him that I really was sorry, that I didn't actually believe a word of it, but somehow, it wouldn't have been true. I knew he needed us, because he couldn't pretend to be independent all alone. "I have to go, Antoine."

"That's fine."

"Do you think I should apologize to Eve-Marie?"

"Hmpf. If it'll make you feel better."

"I don't know. I'm going to go see if she's still here."

"You want to grab a drink tonight?"

"No… I still have stuff to finish for next week."

"Right. What part of *Lord of the Rings* are you going to watch?"

I laughed. "The end of *The Two Towers*."

"That's what I thought," Antoine said, laughing now, too. "Okay, have a nice night, princess."

"Bye, Antoine."

I came out of the office a little less sad than when I'd gone in. I knew I'd hurt Antoine a little, and the idea hurt me in a strange way. I looked for Eve-Marie, but she was already gone. So I left the building, and that's when, on boulevard René-Lévesque Ouest, on the last day of the month of August, I met Simon.

Chapter 7

In fact, to be honest, I'd met Simon before that. We'd been in the same class in grades 9 and 10 at high school – Simon, a young Anglophone from Kingston, had come in the middle of the school year. His French was pretty bad, but he was gorgeous and, apparently, quite a bit more brilliant than the rest of us. After a few months, he was near the top of the class, except in French, where he was still a little behind.

But, at that time, I had braces, and I was the kind of girl who sent her picture to magazine *Fan Club* for the "Pen Pals" page, with a note that said, "Hi! I'm Chloé! I'm a thirteen-and-a-half-year-old girl, who likes music and cute guys. If you're crazy about NKOTB like I am, and you think Kirk Cameron is superhot, then write to me!" (Apparently, I was fat, too. Antoine's the one who pointed that out, when he came across a photo of me at fourteen. With his legendary tact, he'd said, "My God, Chloé. You looked about as feminine as the drummer from Metallica. And, am I wrong, or were you fat?") The strange thing is, I had no memory of being fat. So I called my mother, and, she confirmed, I'd been "a little chunky" until I was sixteen.

So I was doubly surprised when Simon recognized me, without my recognizing him. I'd just gotten out into the street, was thinking about what I'd said to Antoine, and was distractedly looking for a taxi, when, right beside me, I heard someone say my name. I turned around, and there he was, exactly as I remembered him. Tall and thin, very blond, with a delicate face and huge blue eyes, so blue they almost looked black if he wasn't directly facing a light source.

In a few seconds, it all came back to me, our old school colours, the poorly heated rooms, the big gym with its wood floor, the cafeteria with its naïve paintings on the wall, the cool kids smoking – and shivering – outside in the winter. I could see Simon in the bomber jacket he always wore, and all the girls hovering around him because, "Even if he is a little nerdy, he's so cuuute!" And me, filling up entire pages of my diary with "I love Simon Markovic" or "Chloé Cinq-Mars + Simon Markovic = Love." According to my memory, Simon had barely even known I was alive.

"Simon?" I finally said, squinting like I was nearsighted, just to be sure it was really him.

"Yes! How are you, Chloé? Long time, no see, eh?"

He gave me a big smile and I had to hold back from saying, out loud, "Simon, I'd forgotten how handsome you are." Then I started to laugh, for no reason, and I answered, "I'm fine, I'm fine," clapping him on the shoulder like we were two baseball players and I was congratulating him on a great pitch.

"What have you been up to?" he finally asked, with an accent that was more French than English.

"Um, I'm a researcher. For TV."

"Really? Cool." He's teasing me, I thought. But no, he was smiling nicely and looking at me with visible interest. Simon Markovic thought the fact that I worked in television was really cool.

"What about you?" I asked him. "Didn't you go live in France or something?"

"I did. You've got a good memory." Good memory, if you only knew, I thought to myself. I remember what colour your shoelaces were. "We went to live there after I finished my third year of high school, and I stayed there to do *terminale* – it's like *cégep*. Then I travelled around for a while, and finally I went back to Lyon to go to school."

"And what are you doing now?"

I expected him to say something like oceanographer,

photographer for *Natural Geographic,* or Doctors Without Borders, but he answered, "Chef."

"What?"

"I'm a chef." Then, when he saw how confused I looked, he added, "You know, a chef? In a restaurant?"

"No! I mean, yeah, I know. No, I'm just a little surprised. I don't know, I thought you'd be doing something more... less... I don't know." I wanted to say more important, but I remembered I'd already insulted two people today and that I was a researcher – it wasn't exactly like I was saving lives on a regular basis.

"I love cooking," I added. It seemed less compromising, and, on top of that, it was true. "For fun, of course."

Simon smiled at me. I think I smiled, too. I was, in fact, almost petrified – I didn't really know if it was because I'd idealized him so much after he left for France, spending years imagining his triumphant return and his declaration of love, which, of course, he would have made in front of our class, at a reunion or some other event like that. He would come towards me, ignoring girls who had been popular, and say something very sappy, like "Chloé, I've always loved you, and now that I've made my fortune as an oceanographer/climber of Mount Everest/Doctor Without Borders, I've come to get you and take you away with me to London/Paris/Bali/Rio." And I'd fall into his arms and we'd leave as everyone applauded and watched us jealously.

It must have been that. The memory of my teenage passion, like a Pavlovian reaction. Maybe it was because of the luminous beauty radiating from Simon and the fact that he was smiling at me – *me* – and looking me right in the eyes. But nonetheless, there, on boulevard René-Lévesque, on the last day of the month of August, I felt like I never had before (except, maybe, that distant night when I met Antoine). I was overexcited and terrified, and I felt like I had a sun where my heart should have been.

"It's incredible how much you've changed," said Simon.

"I know! I can't believe you recognized me. The last time we saw each other I had braces and brown hair."

"And you were, um… you know." He put one hand next to each hip, at a bit of a distance from his body.

"Yeah, I know, chubby."

Was it really that bad? Simon laughed, a little uneasily, then hurried to add, "But now… you look fantastic, Chloé."

For a brief instant, I wondered if I wasn't going to start laughing like a little girl, or simply run away. On top of everything, he had spoken with an ease that was absolutely disarming, like there was nothing more natural than telling a former classmate she looked fantastic. Most of the men I knew didn't compliment women without having a specific goal in mind – you could almost always tell there was something hidden behind their words – or they did it mechanically, to be polite or out of habit.

He looked at me for an instant, still smiling, and then he said, "Hey, do you want to get a cup of coffee?"

"A cup of coffee," said Juliette. "He invited you for a cup of coffee."

"Yesss."

Juliette and I never had coffee. We had drinks, cocktails, beers, binges, but coffee? It was kind of like getting invited to watch the boats or going to the races. Weird, even old-fashioned, but a little exciting.

"It's sweet," said Juliette, after a moment.

"I know… but well, there's no reason for us to go crazy, everybody has coffee."

"Except us."

"Yes. And Antoine."

"Yes. And Marcus. Marcus never has coffee. But he drinks tea, I think."

"Yes. Except us, Antoine and Marcus. And my parents. My God, my parents are so not the type to 'go get a coffee.'"

"Stéphanie has coffee, though," Juliette pointed out.
"And so does her sister."

"Yeah… and Simon…"

Juliette grabbed my arm. "Yes! Simon! So!"

"So what?"

"Well, you went for coffee… then what?"

"Well…"

I paused, remembering everything. I wanted to tell Juliette everything that had happened, everything I'd seen, heard and imagined, how I'd felt, what I thought I'd seen in Simon's eyes, which were a dark velvety blue.

Surprisingly, I'd hesitated an instant before I accepted his invitation. I think I was afraid of something – realizing perhaps that he was less handsome when he wasn't out in the sun, or finding out he wasn't interesting. But I'd said yes, and we ended up in a small, soulless café on rue Saint-Catherine – the tables weren't level, the lighting was ugly, and the pastries looked sad and dry on their Plexiglass shelf.

But I was delighted. By Simon, by the conversation, by the fact that we'd bumped into each other by chance, and that without such a chance, I probably would never have seen him again. I quickly learned that after he finished training in a restaurant in Burgundy, he'd gone back to Kingston, where he'd opened his own restaurant, which had been pretty successful for three years. Then, bored by the routine (and I could guess that, even if he didn't say it, by Kingston in general), he'd decided to give it a try here. "The competition is awful," he'd said, "but people from Montreal love good food. And they know how to tell the difference."

"Of course," I'd answered coquettishly. I was flattered, I realized. Stupidly flattered because Simon had said that people from Montreal "knew how to tell the difference." People from Montreal were refined, sophisticated and just picky enough. And, consequently, I was, too. It was a thing, I'd later learned, that Simon had learned from his old boss in

France: he knew how to flatter people indirectly, without looking like he was doing it.

We'd talked for almost three hours, and, the whole time, I sipped on the same cup of disgusting coffee. After an hour, I'd ordered a piece of chocolate pie that tasted strangely mouldy. I'd put it to the side, and didn't even complain to the fat server who was noisily chewing gum behind the counter. I couldn't care less. The only thing that I was worried about was how to make Simon fall in love with me, as quickly as possible.

"You didn't go too far, I hope," Juliette asked me.

"Me? Really! I'm a pro at picking people up, girl, you should know that."

Juliette settled for giving me a look, with a mocking smile on her lips. I tried to look mad, but I wanted to laugh, too.

"In fact," Juliette said, "you're not half-bad. I've seen you with men you liked, and you almost always manage to charm them. The problem is keeping them."

"I can do it!" I shouted, as indignant as a child facing the challenge of tying shoelaces.

"You've never tried," said Juliette.

I opened my mouth, but I didn't add anything. Had I ever tried? I wasn't too sure. With Antoine, maybe, but still. I was too proud. Once I'd realized he wasn't interested, I'd given up. I've always refused to work at it, to make an effort to get a man to be interested in me. It seemed unsightly.

"Really," I said to Juliette, to change the subject, "I don't think I went too far. I don't know... I felt so good being with him! Well, from the moment I stopped being terrified, everything was... natural. I felt good, that's all. Like with you or Antoine. I wasn't self-conscious, you know?"

For me, it had been a revelation. After leaving Simon and jumping into a taxi, I realized that, for three hours, I hadn't thought of myself, not for a single second. And, right after that, I realized that had never, ever happened before. I was always self-conscious. Of my words, the image I was projecting, my gestures, what other people saw when they looked at me. But with him, nothing. Just Simon, and our conversation, the taste of burned coffee, which, I already knew, I would remember from now on with a certain pleasure.

"You know?" I repeated. "It was like... like everything just let go. Like my whole body just relaxed. I wasn't self-conscious!" I added, placing one hand over my heart.

"Yes," said Juliette. "I see one hundred percent." She looked at the ground, then at the table, and some place between the bottle of wine and the plate of snacks. I couldn't have said if she was lost in thought, sad or a bit of both, but I felt bad for talking so much about myself, when she had just barely decided to give up on love. Obviously, I had rushed over to her place right after I'd left Simon. She'd opened the door and barely had the chance to say, "What's going on?" when I burst into the kitchen piling one on top of the other stories, sighs and descriptions of Simon. I didn't even ask her how she was.

"What about you?" I finally said, while she was still look-ing at the edge of a snack, "You okay?"

She smiled at me, and served us each another glass of wine. "I'm okay. I'm not super great, but I'm not super bad either. But that's not interesting. I didn't meet an angel on boulevard René-Lévesque." She smiled again – it wasn't meant to make me feel bad or guilty. It was simply a sad observation.

"Oh, Juliette..." I couldn't go on. Marcus came into the kitchen with about ten grocery bags in each hand, and, very loudly, asked, "Who met an angel today?" Juliette didn't say anything; she just pointed at me.

"And whooooo was it?" Marcus sang as he put his bags on the huge island that took up the centre of the kitchen – it was the thing I was most jealous of in their apartment: since it was an old factory, the kitchen was industrial, huge, light, and very well equipped, with stainless-steel appliances we hardly knew how to work. Juliette had replaced the neon fixtures with softer lighting, and the results were amazing: it looked like both a fancy restaurant kitchen and an avant-garde dining room.

The owner had told them that, just because of the kitchen, he could have charged twice the rent they were paying. I pretty much agreed. But Juliette had pointed out the leaking pipes, the windows that didn't open anymore, and the awful noise the plumbing made (not to mention the Ville-Marie Highway, which ran right above them), and he hadn't said another word.

"So?" Marcus repeated, taking at least a ton of food from his bags (including a ten-kilo bag of rice). "Who is it?" He was stamping his feet impatiently. I described Simon to him, and told him how we'd bumped into each other, without going into too many details. He was listening so attentively that sometimes I wanted to laugh – he looked like a teenage boy who was listening to his best friend tell him about his first French kiss.

"Oh my God!" he squeaked, at the end of my story. "It's so exciting! He's the one! He's the one! No? You don't feel it? Chloé, girl, you don't think he's the one? Omigod, it's so exciting!" He was jumping up and down, with a pineapple in one hand, and moving his arms wildly. Watching him, Juliette was doubled over laughing.

"It's so exciting…" he repeated for the umpteenth time, and finally put his pineapple on the counter. I was listening to him, a little stunned – he was so excited that, actually, I was becoming less so. "Yeah… it's super," I said. "But we still shouldn't get carried away. You never know. We'll see. No reason to get excited."

"Excited? But, sweetie, it's too late!" And he gave that big laugh of his, got around the island in one leap and stood next to me. "He doesn't have a gay twin, does he?"

"No… unfortunately…"

"Nuts. All handsome guys should have a gay twin, shouldn't they?"

"Why not," Juliette said. "That would mean Samuel would have a straight twin. That would be a better match for me."

She'd smiled as she spoke, and we all laughed. Marcus tousled her hair, as if she were a little girl, "What did I tell you, Giulietta? No more talking about Samuel. Except to say bad things." Then he leaned over to pick up his big bag of rice.

"Will you tell me why you buy rice in ten-kilo bags?" I asked.

"Sweetie." He looked at me like I was a little slow. "I was born in Jamaica, remember? Creole food. Gumbo. Jambalaya. It's all rice. It reminds me of my nana's cooking."

"And he doesn't even get fat," Juliette said to me. "He eats a kilo of rice a day, and he doesn't gain a single gram."

"Hey, that's the advantage of being black, baby. Besides, tonight, I want you to put aside your worries about weight, girls, because Uncle Marcus is going to make a Jamaican feast!"

"What's the occasion?"

"Whatever you want, Giulietta. Does a man need an excuse to make a meal for the women he loves?"

We both smiled. I'd planned to go home, but it didn't take long for me to change my mind. Marcus was whistling as he put away the fruit, Juliette was opening up another bottle, and the traffic noise just above our heads put me in a good mood that night.

An hour later, we'd finished the bottle and Marcus had prepared everything he needed for his feast. On the island, there were cubes of onion, pineapple, pepper, carrot, celery and chayote, an entire, finely minced bulb of garlic, okra, and sliced sausage, six big tomatoes cored and sliced, crumbled bacon, peeled shrimp, half a salted cod – sliced, some cleaned clams, Jamaican pureed pepper, a de-boned chicken, two big cans of black beans, a full bowl of sweet peas that Marcus had shelled himself, and a bunch of spices that smelled like the sun.

"Marcus?" Juliette asked.

"Yes, dear."

"You must have enough there to feed at least twenty people."

"Oh, yes. I like leftovers. You'll see, sweetie, it'll get eaten. You should invite your Simon," he said, giving me a wink. "I may not be a chef, but I'm not bad. You'll see."

He looked around at all his ingredients and said, "All right!" as he clapped his hands together before he started getting out his pots and kettles.

"Juliette," he said. "We need drinks."

"Oh! Right! Sorry!"

Juliette laughed, and she went to get more wine from their "cellar" – really nothing more than an old, out-of-use service elevator, though it stayed relatively cool.

She was barely out of the kitchen before Marcus came over to me. "So?"

"So what?"

"Oh, you don't need to pretend with me, Chloé. I know Simon's all you can think about."

I smiled, helpless. Simon wasn't "all" I could think about, but he was there, in each of my thoughts, like a presence that you don't really see, but whose shape you can make out. It was strange and, ultimately, not necessarily pleasant. I wasn't used to having all my thoughts coloured by the image of someone else, and I didn't know if it was love at first sight, a weird obsession, or, simply, that I'd spent part of the day with him.

"It's strange," I finally said.

"But of course it's strange! It's love!"

"Marcus, it's only been barely six hours since I met him."

"No, you met him fifteen years ago!" He held his hands wide apart, as if it were the most obvious thing in the world, and started mixing a variety of ingredients in a big ceramic bowl.

"You know what I mean, Marcus. It can't be love. I don't know, it's as if…"

I thought for an instant, trying to find the right word, or at least a good comparison, but the best I could come up with was, "It's as if I'd looked directly at the sun, and now, no matter where I look, I see spots."

"Aw…"

"Okay, I know it's kind of a sappy metaphor, and on top of that, I think it was in *Cyrano*, but you know what I mean, don't you?"

"Yes, that Simon is like a sun!"

"No! Well, yes, he's like a son, but I mean that even if I don't think directly about him, he's there, somewhere, in my thoughts. Like an imprint."

"Like a spot you see after you looked at the sun!" shouted Marcus triumphantly, as if that wasn't the exact same thing I'd just said.

"Okay, okay, okay," said Juliette's voice behind us. "Simon has the same effect on you as the sun?" And a sardonic little smile played across her lips.

"It's the only metaphor I could come up with," I answered pitifully.

"Good job, Danielle Steele!"

"Edmond Rostand," I corrected. Juliette put the bottle on the island and looked at me mockingly.

"Oh, come on, Juliette," said Marcus, turning around, and continuing to stir the concoction he had in his pan. "Don't rain on her parade. We all have the right to use sappy metaphors when we're in love."

"It's not love, Marcus," I repeated.

"No? What is it then?"

I had no idea. But in my universe, in my cosmogony, it was impossible to fall in love with someone in just barely three hours, whether they'd been the object of an adolescent crush or not. And I didn't dare talk to Juliette about it, because I thought the idea was too ridiculous and pathetic, but I wondered if I hadn't gotten so interested in Simon simply because I wanted to be in love, and because Eve-Marie's words were still ringing in my ears. That would have been just like me.

"Well, I think there's something there," Juliette said as she looked for a bottle-opener under a pile of pineapple skins. "You just don't know what it is yet, that's all. But you felt like it clicked, right?"

"Oh, yes!"

"For both of you?"

I smiled coquettishly. "Without wanting to be presumptuous, yes."

"I know you," said Juliette. "You're different. But I think you should stop trying to figure it out," she said, "more for Marcus, than for me. Let things, and your feelings, follow their own course. Okay?"

I could see that she wanted to change the subject. I could have talked about Simon for hours, but I preferred to give in – she wasn't wrong, in any case. It did no good to dissect my feelings – one way or another, they were bound to change.

Marcus, who seemed to have finally understood what Juliette was getting at, turned around quickly, a large dish in his hands, and asked, "Salt cod fritters, anyone?"

Juliette and I quickly dipped into the plate, and before Marcus could warn us it was very hot, we'd both burned our tongues. But Marcus' fritters were really worth it: they were tender and juicy, and so tasty that, for an instant, I closed my eyes. "Simon has to taste this," I thought. Then I felt ridiculous for thinking that, as if Simon and I were already together, as if I could allow myself to dream about a daily life we didn't yet share.

"Marcus, you're a genius!"

"No, no. I just copy what my nana did. You need good ingredients, patience, and a lot of loooooving." He swayed his hips lasciviously when he said "loooooving," and Juliette and I burst into laughter.

"Well, then," said Juliette, raising her glass, "here's to your nana, then. A wonderful cook!"

"Wait till you see the rest," Marcus said as he toasted.

Before I even had a taste, I could tell that everything was going to be delicious. For an hour, Marcus kept busy over the stove, sautéing vegetables, meat, rice, peas and beans, one after the other, then mixing them all together. He was constantly adding some ingredient or another: bouillon, pepper, spices, lime juice, and each time he tasted, he closed his eyes halfway and raised one finger in the air.

He was getting ready to serve us, when Antoine appeared in the doorway, "Smells good in here," he said. "What's for dinner?" He'd come in through the emergency exit, like he always did. When I saw him, I don't know why, I had a weird feeling in my heart. He was standing there, with his hands in his pockets, in a black jacket and shirt, half smiling. It was the same Antoine I'd met eight years earlier, and that I'd seen almost every day since. But I felt funny, and it seemed like I was blushing. It's because of Simon, I thought. I felt like a student who'd betrayed what her teacher had taught her, or had failed her final exam, despite the great hope placed in her. I glanced around to make sure my reaction wasn't too obvious, but Juliette's back was turned towards me. Only Marcus had seen me. He was looking at me, with a dish in one hand, his right eyebrow raised.

"Oh, Chloé! I came over here just to talk about you." I turned towards him, telling myself I had no reason to feel bad, that it was completely ridiculous. I shook my head, imperceptibly, and crossed my arms, "What do you mean, to talk about me?"

"Because you were very unpleasant this morning. On the phone." He was smiling, but I knew him well enough to know he was half-serious. "I'm sorry," I said. "I felt bad all day long."

"Yeah, right!" shouted Juliette.

"What?"

"Chloé is in love!" said Marcus. She doesn't want us to use the word *love*, but trust me, it's looooove..."

Antoine lowered his head towards me. "Is that true?"

For a second, I wanted to slap Marcus. "No, it's not true..." Then I thought of Simon. "I'm not in love. I just bumped into an old crush." I realized I was smiling.

"Oh, well, good, then!" said Antoine as he came closer to the stove. "That's what you wanted, isn't it?" He leaned over Marcus' pan. "Mmmm! That really smells good!" He sat down and ate a fritter. "Oh, really good, Marcus. That makes me feel better. I really had a shitty day."

"What happened?" Juliette asked.

"Well first, our friend here insulted me," he winked at me. "Then, and please excuse me if I make any bad jokes here, but I worked my ass off for an absolutely ridiculous toilet paper ad that some little moron screwed up, and now we have to do the whole thing over again."

"What was it?"

"Listen to this: you see a bunch of people in a big office full of cubicles, and they all look disappointed. They're fidgeting on their chairs like their butts hurt or something, and, of course, they're not working. Then, you see this one guy who's very dynamic, grinning from ear to ear and working. Why?"

"I'm dying to know," Juliette answered.

"You figure it out when you see, on this guy's desk, a roll of Cottonelle toilet paper!"

Marcus, Juliette and I all looked at each other. "That's not really that clear," said Juliette.

"And that's the problem," Antoine replied, dropping his arms back down to his sides. "The idea is that this one guy is happy because he wipes his ass with Cottonelle, and all the others are sad 'cause they use cheap paper. My problem is that I don't know how to bring in the cheap paper. You'd have to see the company washrooms, but that means I have to bring in another shot, and it kind of spoils the effect…"

"That's totally ridiculous!" shouted Juliette. Marcus and I were elbowing each other and laughing.

"I know it's ridiculous," said Antoine. "I already told you that!"

He took another fritter. "Sometimes, I swear to you, I think I have the stupidest job in the world." Juliette nodded. Marcus and I elbowed each other once more. "Lucky it pays well," said Antoine. "Besides…" He went back out into the hallway, bent down and picked up a bag he'd hidden there. "I brought over a couple of bottles that shouldn't be half-bad…"

And we ate and drank, and ate some more. Marcus' recipe, which he called "Nana's Rice," was an absolute delicacy – literally, an explosion of flavours. We each gobbled up three plates, even Antoine, though every time he ended up with a piece of okra, he spit it out, stuck out his tongue and said, "Yuck… sticky…"

I felt good with them. So good. I again wondered if I really needed someone else. I had so much already. But I could see Simon, and the bluish burst of his eyes when the sun hit them (like the purple shine at the bottom of a glass of Bordeaux, I'd thought when he was sitting opposite me), and I felt myself lean towards him, almost instinctively.

We were cleaning up the kitchen, which looked like it had been hit by a hurricane, when Antoine took me by the waist, "So all this about love, eh? A guy from Kingston. Really, Chloé. Do you really think it'll go anywhere? Do you really think you need it?"

I looked up at him. He was drunk, just a little, and dark locks of hair were falling across his forehead. He was frowning slightly as he looked at me, a permanent smile on his lips. I was right, I thought, thinking of the conversation we'd had that morning. He wants me to stay the way I was forever. He needs that. He wants me to say it's nothing but a fling like the others.

I looked down, and I said, "I'm seeing him again Sunday."

Chapter 8

At seven-thirty, the next Sunday, I was awake. It might as well have been five in the morning – I was never up before nine, and the fact that I was up already struck me as a little funny, like I was someone else, an athletic person, for example, who got up with the sun to go camping, or someone who was really dynamic, the kind of person who started their day at 6 a.m., with a black coffee and the *Financial Post.*

"My God," I said to Puce, "it's not even eight o'clock." Puce raised her head and looked at me, blinking. At my feet, Siffleux lazily rolled over on his back, with a happy little meow. Normally, he would have been up with Ursule, next to my head, staring at me and making long, hungry whistling sounds. (Which is where his name comes from – Siffleux = Whistler in French. When he was particularly annoyed, he made a strange sound that was more like a whistle than a meow. As a result, according to Juliette, of his being obese.) I looked under the bed, and there was Ursule, with her head resting on her paws, sound asleep. Even my cats couldn't believe I was up so early.

I gave a long stretch, and vaguely considered going back to sleep. But I was too wired. "It's ridiculous," I said out loud. "I have butterflies in my stomach." So, I closed my eyes and stayed in bed till nine, thinking about Simon. I imagined our date a thousand and one different ways, the conversations we'd have, the way he'd kiss me, the instant just before that – with time suspended and me, motionless and perfectly conscious.

Then I had the completely absurd idea that if I imagined something, there was a strong chance it wouldn't come true

– unless of course, I had a gift for seeing the future, which would have been both very surprising and rather upsetting. I made myself stop thinking about Simon, out of fear of building up some terribly romantic scenario that, due to that very fact, had no chance of actually occurring. Then I started to laugh. There was no doubt this was the stupidest reasoning in the world. The kind of problem, I thought, Eve-Marie must have to face several times a day.

I was about to get up, when the sound of the phone made me jump – though not as much as the cats, who all got to their feet, with tired eyes and attentive ears. There's no point in saying my phone never rang before ten o'clock, since my friends and my parents all knew my habits. I hurried, thinking it might be Simon, and cooed a perfectly grotesque "Hello?" into the phone.

"Hello?" answered a surprised voice on the other end of the line.

Slightly shocked, I looked at the phone. "Daddy?"

"Chloé?"

"Yes…"

"Chloé? I…"

He started to laugh, obviously quite amused, as if he'd made one of his famous puns that bored everyone to tears, but that always absolutely delighted him. "Chloé! What a surprise! I meant to call Daphné! I must have woken you up…"

"No, no. You call Daphné at eight in the morning?"

"Sure. Quite often."

"Why?"

"To chat!"

"To chat!" I repeated, annoyed.

I almost added, "You never call me to chat," but then I remembered I didn't call him either. When I was little, I'd been very close to my father. He called me his accomplice and took me with him to the office. Then came the teenage years and their conflicts, and something disappeared. We'd always had a warm, affectionate relationship, but I stopped spending hours reading books to him, looking up from time to time to talk about this or that, things like love, happiness, wisdom which, at the time, seemed terribly important to me. Daphné was the one who now had long, serious discussions with him. When she was thirteen, she'd ask him about law and jurisprudence, and often asked him to read her his arguments.

"Who else would you have me chat with at this hour?" my father asked me. "Your mother never gets up before eleven. I often say mornings are my grace period!" He laughed again, the same as before. "I use it to do some of the little things I like, just to have some quiet time. But now, for instance, I've been working on my crossword for almost two hours…"

"The one in *Figaro*?" My father adored French crosswords.

"No! Didn't Daphné tell you? I have a new hobby."

"No, really?"

"I'm a *verbicruciste*."

"A *verbicruciste*."

"Yeah, the opposite of a *cruciverbiste*, someone who likes to solve crossword puzzles, the *verbicruciste* creates the crossword puzzle. It's like the author."

"A crossword puzzle author, eh? And who solves your crosswords?"

"Yeah, well, that's the problem. Your mother hates crosswords, Daphné has no time, and I don't think my colleagues are interested."

I started to laugh. "You can bring them to me, if you want."

"Really?"

"Yes, really. I like crosswords."

"Oh! That makes me very happy, Chloé."

"Me, too, Daddy."

I laughed, and so did he. "So?" he asked. "By what miracle are you up at the crack of dawn?" I rolled my eyes. He must have been the only person in the world to regularly use the expression, "the crack of dawn."

"I can't sleep." I answered.

"Why? You're not still overstressed, are you? We Cinq-Marses are not overstressed people. Well, your sister is overstressed, but she gets that from your mother's family. And as far as your mother is concerned, with that new style of hers, I'd say she's more overdressed!..."

He must have laughed for a good thirty seconds, until I started to laugh myself – there was something comforting about my father's bad puns. They were like a childhood memory, like the big house on rue Hartland, where I grew up, and still like to visit.

"No, I'm not overstressed," I finally answered when he'd finished laughing. "Well... maybe a little. You're going to think I'm silly... but..." I stopped. I couldn't believe I was about to talk to my father about my love life. This is what it's like in the morning, I thought. Before nine o'clock, the world is a parallel universe where things are exactly the opposite of what they are in reality. Cats aren't hungry, I laugh at my father's puns, and I'm ready to confide in him.

"It's just that... I have an engagement, tonight, and it's got me a little on edge."

"An engagement?"

"A date."

"A date with someone special?"

"Well... I suppose. I don't know if he's someone special yet, but it's definitely not going to be a business meeting. Although, it could just be as friends."

"No, no, it's not as friends if it's got you riled up. Right? In fact, you hope he's going to someone special. And that's exactly what's got you on edge."

I was amazed: as far as I knew, it was the first time in his life that my father showed any insight at all.

"Aren't I right?"

"Well, yes. You are. Since when do you know anything about this kind of thing?"

"Come on, Chloé... I'm sixty-five years old. I've been around the block once or twice. You and your little friends make me laugh, always thinking you've seen it all and that you have something to teach us! Your parents had a life, you know! I've never understood how young people automatically believe they know more than older people. When you think about it, it's not very logical."

"No, it's not very logical, but... times change, and sometimes your references are not exactly..." I didn't want to insult him, "up-to-date?"

"Chloé. Love never changes. It seems to me that you should know that at your age. We imagine love differently maybe. But, at the end of the day, we're thinking about the same thing."

"What?"

"I mean, it may be true that when I was twenty our idea of love and marriage was very different from yours. But, deep down, when you're in love, you're in love. Like our ancestors, like you, like your children will be. It doesn't seem that complicated to me."

"No... that's true."

"You always see love like something that's terribly complicated. Something convoluted, nerve-racking... Would you believe me if I said there were probably fewer codes in my time than today? But when I fell in love with my first girlfriend, it wasn't complicated: I courted her, I told her I liked her, and that was perfect, because she liked me, too."

His first girlfriend. I'd always known my parents had had other loves – they'd met when they were over thirty, after all. But I just couldn't imagine them with anyone else. For me, they formed a single, indivisible, eternal unit.

"But," he continued, "it seems like... you wallow in complications."

"Sorry?"

I glanced at the cats, who'd all gone back to sleep in strange, touching positions. I wished there was someone else here, someone I could tell: "My father just declared that 'we wallow in complications.'"

"I don't see any other way to explain the lengths you go to to complicate your love lives," my father answered. "The other person can never know you're interested, then you have to court each other without it being noticeable, you make love with people you don't know, and you're friends with people you love… I'm telling you, Chloé, you're an odd generation."

"Well, excuse me, but where are you getting all this information?"

"I've watched you, sweetie. It was like a crash course for a worried father."

I smiled silently, as I remembered his reaction when I had my first boyfriends – at first, he valiantly tried to be permissive and tolerant, but I didn't make it very easy for him: at barely fifteen, I already knew what was what, and I always liked "bums" (or the closest thing you could find to a bum in Outremont). And my father, despite his best intentions, was worried. He started with little reprimands, then tried to give me advice, then he got mad, once twice, ten times, but, obviously, the more authority he showed, the more I rebelled – I was a pretty predictable teenager. And when I came home one night at 1 a.m., after a party at the home of a certain Pierre-Olivier Beaugrand-Champagne, a twenty-one-year-old cégep student who sold hash on rue Bernard, he exploded. And I'd exploded, too, screaming that I'd slept with Pierre-Olivier, that no, he wasn't the first, and he certainly wouldn't be the last – words a father like mine didn't deserve.

I sulked for a long time, and so did he, for that matter: he left it to my mother to get me back under control. He didn't say anything after that, and I kept thinking he preferred my sister, who was so perfect, didn't have a boyfriend and never went out. Our mutual sulking lasted a long time. We would talk, we would even laugh sometimes, but there was still a chill, a gap that still needed to be closed. It took me almost two years to understand he'd been right, and at that point I gave him a long, sincere apology, which had touched him more than he'd wanted me to know. I still hadn't settled down, but he had faith in me, and I'd learned to deserve it.

"A crash course," my father repeated, laughing. "My first daughter, and bang! You were something else, Chloé! I saw you go from one boyfriend to the next, though you were always with boys who didn't really interest you much, or that you fell for, but for what? A month, two months? Then there was Antoine – you were different when you talked to us about him."

"Antoine?"

I didn't remember that. I knew he was the first one who'd really gotten to me, but I didn't think I'd shown it.

"Oh, yes. You looked at him differently."

My parents had met him after I'd only known him a few weeks, the four of us just happened to bump into each other at the same restaurant. I was mortified, but Antoine had smiled, cool as always, and we'd eaten together. Antoine had flirted with my mother, and had a friendly discussion with my father, and they'd left the restaurant, thinking I'd met the man of my dreams.

"We thought he was the one," said my father. "But, no, it was over. He may have been a skirt-chaser, he may still be, but your mother and I don't understand what…"

"Dad…"

"I know, all those things of yours, your principles." And he laughed gently. "For a while, I thought you and your friends were the only ones who were that complicated, but then I saw it, in that TV show, what's it called… *Sex and the City*. Those girls must burn two thousand calories a day just worrying about love and…"

"You watch *Sex and the City*?"

Honestly, I would have been less surprised if he'd told me he'd once had a homosexual relationship.

"Sometimes, yeah. It's pretty well done. I like the tall red-head. She's the only one with a head on her shoulders, if you want my opinion. And even that one, she's what, thirty-five, and she acts like a child. And it's an attitude that gets glori-fied, like it's the 'hip' thing to do. It looks like you're afraid of love, Chloé."

I was flabbergasted. Not only did my father watch *Sex and the City*, but he was talking about love in such a natural way that it was absolutely disconcerting, as if we always had such conversations. And, what was even more disconcerting was that our conversation, surprising as it was, seemed rather educational.

"I know, Dad. I'm just a little mixed up, I'll admit it. I went to school with this guy. I had a crush on him back then."

"Oh, right! The guy whose name sounded a little Eastern European?"

"Pardon?"

"Oh, sweetie. Your mother used to read your diary. When you were fourteen, you were head over heels for a boy in your class. His name ended in 'itch.' Or in 'scu.'"

"Markovic! Simon Markovic! My God! Mom read my diary?"

"That surprises you?"

"Um, no, not really, in fact, but, my God! That's not right!"

I felt a little like laughing. At the time, I would have been devastated, but now, it was almost funny – I imagined my mother going through all my adolescent prose, desperately looking for a passage about her.

"So?" said my father. "This Simon Malovitch?"

"Markovic? I bumped into him, and we're going for a drink tonight… and I don't know. That's what's got me on edge."

"Do you want it to work?"

"I just don't know!"

"Chloé..."

"Okay, yes, but I'm afraid..."

"Chloé?"

"What?"

"What have you got to lose?"

"..."

"You don't have anything to lose, sweetie. You're young, you have your whole life ahead of you. Take a chance, Chloé."

"You want me to take a chance."

"Right. It's not complicated. Take a chance."

Take a chance on who? Simon? Myself? I had a thousand questions to ask him. I finally hung up, a little confused about what he'd just said, and because it had been almost fifteen years since I'd had a conversation like that with my father. I also felt unusually light – I was happy, I think, almost relieved to realize the two of us, the two rue Hartland accomplices, could still talk as if no time had passed at all.

I looked at the time. It was eight-thirty-nine – I immediately thought I still had to wait ten hours and twenty minutes before I met Simon, and this idea was both unbearable and reassuring. I got up, and I walked slowly towards the kitchen, thinking about what my father had said, "Take a chance." On what? Then I swept my hand through the air: too many questions. I'd just have to wait and see. Maybe, over at his own house, Simon was wondering if he was going to take a chance.

When I got to the kitchen, I looked around. Something was off. I went towards the counter, I opened the refrigerator, I walked towards the window, and then I got it: there weren't three hysterical cats underfoot, nearly making me stumble with each step. I waited for an instant, and then I pushed the button on the coffee grinder. The result was immediate: a mini stampede could be heard in the hallway, and I was quickly surrounded by sharp meows, whistles and uncoordinated purring.

I fed them, and then I stood behind them for a moment, watching them, with a silly smile. My babies, I thought. Then I wondered if a girl who loved her cats so much was considered touching or just pathetic. I couldn't come up with an answer, but I thought it best to hold off for a while before I told Simon I talked to them on a regular basis, and that I thought of them as my children.

After all, I had to make a good impression. Without really looking like I was trying to, of course. Despite what my father said, I had to look moderately interested. Not desperate. Not Eve-Marie. The idea was to be both cool and sparkly, and to make Simon see that, even if I really liked him, I still had twelve other potential lovers just waiting in line. Simon had to feel like my presence was precious. Like I could have been somewhere else, but I'd chosen to be with him. When he was with me, he had to forget about time. The bottom line was that I had to be like Antoine. Antoine, who'd spent the whole evening gently making fun of me, my date, and love, making me feel a little weak, despite myself. I pushed him out of my head with an irritated "tsk" and, out loud, I said, "Cool, relaxed and fabulous."

I spent the rest of the day in a state close to hysteria. I didn't know what to wear, I didn't know how to act or what I wanted, and I was terrified. I didn't even know what scared me most: having Simon not be interested, or having him be interested. If he was, it would open the door to the possibility we'd sleep together, which was rather exciting, and that we'd develop a relationship, which completely petrified me.

At six-forty-five, I was in a taxi, and astonishingly calm. In fact, not really astonishingly, because my calmness could be explained quite logically by the Margarita I'd made myself before I left. I was a little mad at myself for that, but after I'd weighed the pros and cons, I'd concluded that having a bit of a buzz was certainly better than being intensely nervous, and all the foot stamping and excited laughter this would entail.

I'd tried to call Juliette all day, but she and Marcus weren't home – I'd left at least eight incoherent messages on their voicemail, the last of which was my own personal version of "Crazy in Love" by Beyoncé Knowles. Then, I'd practically run out of the house, completely ignoring my downstairs neighbour, who'd opened his door to talk to me about camaraderie among renters, and the fact that I really should get more involved in the mailbox matter.

We'd almost arrived when my cell started ringing, or, rather, playing an unbearable version of Beethoven's *Fifth*. I took the phone out of my bag, irritated and amused: it was one of Antoine's running gags – always changing my ring tone. Once, a wild *Cucaracha* had played while I was making love with Luc; another day, a kind of rhythm that sounded like porn-film music was heard during a meeting. The joke was certainly tired, but if Antoine had stopped, I would have worried.

I finally found the phone under the countless items that my handbag inevitably held. It was Antoine.

"Hey," I answered. "Beethoven's *Fifth*. That's fun. Pretty."

"I thought you'd like it."

I heard him light a cigarette.

"What do you want?" I asked him.

"I wanted to wish you luck."

"Luck?"

"On your date. Isn't it in five minutes?"

"Oh, Antoine… please…"

"No, I'm serious! If you want it to work, well, I want it to work. I want you to be happy, princess."

"Antoine, you teased me nonstop the other night. And the only purpose was to make me feel cheap."

"Okay, maybe a little. But it's going to take time for me to get used to your new vocation, that's all. I'm going to try hard though, I promise."

"Okay, I guess…"

"What? I'm saying this sincerely."

He took a drag on his cigarette, and then exhaled. I heard a woman's voice say something, then Antoine's voice, far from the receiver, saying, "Two minutes."

"Where are you?" I asked.

"Hmm? Oh, at home. I'm going to go get something to eat. But before that, I wanted to wish you luck, sweetie. Honestly."

I wasn't sure he was serious – judging from his tone of voice, though, he was. But I could hardly believe it. On top of that, I didn't want that. I didn't want Antoine to wish me luck.

"Antoine?"

"Hmmm?"

"I have to go. I'm here."

"Okay. Have fun, sweetie. And don't think too much about me."

"Very funny. Bye, Antoine."

"Bye…"

I closed my cell with an irritated gesture, and I looked out the window: we were indeed here.

I immediately saw him in the little bar where we were supposed to meet. He was sitting at a table, with his chin on one hand; he was reading a book. The late-day sun was coming in through the big windows – Simon was bathed in it, and I remember thinking it was a good thing, that it would let me see the blue sparkles hiding in his eyes. I also remember noticing that when I saw him I stopped being nervous. Automatically. I stood in the doorway, just for a second or two, and he looked up. He saw me and smiled. I noticed his high, elegant cheekbones, and his eyes, which were almond-shaped, like a cat's.

Then, I walked towards him, he got up, and everything was fluid and natural. We laughed, exchanged a couple of enjoyable pleasantries, and I pointed at his book, Douglas Coupland's *Microserfs*. "It's good, isn't it?"

"Have you read it?" he asked, obviously charmed.

"Yeah, two or three years ago. It's a good story, isn't it?"

"Yeah, until now though, I preferred *Generation X*. But this seems more…" He looked for the right word. "Layered? How can I put it: richer, maybe. More real."

"I understand exactly."

I wasn't lying: I knew exactly what he meant. We were still standing. He gestured for me to sit, and I settled down.

"You'll see," I said, "the end is fantastic. To tell you the truth, I cried. It's borderline sappy, but it's just… perfect."

"I always liked that about you."

"What?"

"At school. You were always reading. In math class, with Mr. Lambert, I remember, you had *Voyage au bout de la nuit* on your lap."

I started to laugh. "My God! That sounds like such teenage intensity, when you think about it now."

"It's still a wonderful book."

I wanted to run to the washroom, call Juliette and shout into her answering machine that he was not only more handsome than I remembered, he also read books! And he liked the same ones I did! And he had a little beauty mark next to his right eye.

I don't remember the rest of the evening very well. Well, I remember we left the bar, then went and ate in a tiny Italian restaurant he adored on the Plateau, and everything was delicious. But I don't really remember what we said to each other. We talked about books, France and Kingston, Dubrovnik – where his father was from, and which he'd visited the year before. We talked about me, too, about Juliette and Antoine, and even about my cats.

In fact, we must have laughed more than we talked. Not because everything was funny, but, I think, because we were happy. Happy to be happy. At least, that's how I felt. I couldn't believe I'd found Simon Markovic, after all this time, and that he was even more handsome, nicer and more cultivated than in my teenage dreams. And, on top of that, he seemed to think I was the most delicious person he'd ever met.

Still, I remember wanting the night to go on forever, wishing that nothing would change. At one point, Simon got up to go to the washroom, and I looked at the little table, the softly burning candle, the nearly empty wineglasses and the second bottle we'd just ordered, three-quarters full. There were crumbs on the table, and a big red wine stain next to my plate. And I remember this because I said to myself, "Don't forget anything, not a single thing." And Simon came back, and when he sat down opposite me, it felt like my heart was exploding, gently, and flowing out, everywhere, within me, and around us.

We walked for about an hour after we left the restaurant. We wandered around the neighbourhood, along quiet streets, and busier roads, still talking easily and laughing. Finally, at one particularly busy intersection, we stopped. We were standing facing each other. I moved my hands, but I don't remember exactly what I did. Simon leaned forward, slowly, and took my face in his hands.

"Come here," he said.

Chapter 9

"And then? AND THEN? Did he kiss you? What did he do? Tell meeeee!" For an instant, I thought Marcus was going to explode. If I leave right now, I said to myself, without telling him about the rest of my evening, he might have a heart attack. I liked to keep Marcus on the edge of his seat with my stories. He was, without a doubt, the best audience ever.

I was in his room, a surprising sanctuary where nearly every imaginable shade of pink was present, and where there were a lot, I mean really a lot, of feathers. There was a huge ostrich feather fan on one wall, at least twenty multi-colour boas scattered here and there, and, on the overcrowded dresser, a frightening number of headdresses – some were 1920s-style, others Carnival in Rio, but there were so many that all you could really make out was a shapeless mass, with a few elegant peacock feathers sticking out. But all that was nothing next to the wall behind the bed, where Marcus had hung two huge white wings that he'd made himself with real feathers, and that he'd worn the year before to the *Bal en blanc*. The effect had been striking, to say the least.

My date with Simon had taken place two days earlier, and I was supposed to eat out now with Juliette and Antoine. Juliette had told me to come over first for drinks, but I'd cheated, and I'd gotten there earlier than expected, just so I could be alone with Marcus. I was dying to talk about Simon and our night, but I couldn't force my story on Juliette; though I knew she would listen politely, I was afraid I'd hurt her. There was no changing Antoine: the next day he'd simply called to find out if "I'd scored."

Marcus, on the other hand, was on the verge of having a fit. As soon as he'd opened the door, he'd started clapping his hands like a little girl. "Juliette told me! Simon! But she didn't know anything! No details! My God, Chloé, come in. Come in. Go wait in my room, I'm going to get us some drinks." And he'd rushed towards the kitchen, where I heard his voice shouting, "What are we having? Martinis? Black Pearls? Beer? We have beer, you know! Ooh! Do you want a Salty Dog? I can make Salty Dogs!" I hadn't answered, and he came in a few minutes later with two cocktail glasses and a shaker full of Margaritas. "They're good for stories," he'd explained, though I didn't understand why.

But one full shaker hadn't been enough, and Marcus had had to run back to the kitchen to make a second one. I started telling my story, and I was really enjoying myself. He liked details? Perfect. I must have spent at least twenty minutes describing Simon's clothes – quite a feat, since he'd just worn jeans and a white tee-shirt. But Marcus was a good audience. He asked all the right questions. The exact ones that a girl in love wanted to hear. He asked, "How did the tee-shirt fit?"

And then I spent some delicious minutes describing Simon's pecs – which were just barely visible, his loose shirt, the cotton sleeves that came to the middle of his solid, tanned forearms, the collar that bared his neck. His neck! Just thinking about it, I'd had to stretch myself out on Marcus' bed and exhale a long sigh, exactly like when I was fourteen and was talking about Simon to Daphné, who couldn't have cared less, and shrugged her shoulders as she looked at me.

I'd finally gotten to the first crucial moment of the evening, and I wanted to tell it perfectly. I didn't want my story to be boring – a couple kissing on a street corner, after all, isn't all that unusual. I wanted Marcus to understand, I wanted him to feel the importance and the purity of the moment, just like I'd felt them. I knew it was my story and that this was the one and only reason I thought of it as important and pure. But the idea of not being able to get it across, of not at least being able to do it justice made me sad.

"So…" I said to Marcus. I didn't know what words to use. I couldn't think of anything but empty metaphors, words like *stars* and *breath* and *light* and *time stopping*. And, anyway, that wasn't it. I hadn't seen any stars. I hadn't felt time crystallize around us. I was somewhere else, and, at the same time, I was ultra present.

"I don't know, Marcus. I don't know how to describe it to you. Of all the kisses I've given or received in my life, it was, by far, the most incredible. No comparison."

"Not even with Antoine?"

Sometimes I suspected that Marcus had a crush on him. He looked at his butt way too often, and he wasn't always kidding.

"The first time I kissed Antoine, I was completely drunk. So, yes, no comparison with Antoine. And besides… I don't think I ever felt like this about anyone, Marcus."

"Nooo?"

He couldn't control himself anymore.

"No," I said with a laugh. "It was… Sometimes when I kiss guys I really like, I can see both of us. As if a camera was slowly zooming out from our faces. But with him… I remember my heart pounding – sooo hard – and his face, as it came closer. Like in *À la recherche du temps perdu,* when Marcel thinks he's going to kiss Albertine for the first time.

"Sweetie, all I know about Marcel Proust is that he was gay!"

"Oh! Well, in that case, it's just that in *À la recherche,* the character of Marcel draws close to Albertine's face – he'd desired her for a long time; so he watches this face draw near and he dismantles it, he deconstructs it. He sees every part of it. I saw Simon, and then I didn't see him anymore. I could see his eyes, his eyelashes. Then, before I closed mine, I saw his mouth. Everything in slow motion."

"Okay, not a zoom out, but slow motion."

"Yes... then. Oh, then, the first thing I thought of was, 'My God, his tongue is so soft!'" Then he gently stroked my cheek, and I've always loved that... and then, I just... melted. In his arms."

I stopped without even bothering to hide my big, silly smile. I had literally felt like I was melting, dissolving. I'd never let myself go like that before. Had I taken a chance, like my father had suggested? I didn't know. But I hadn't held anything back. That was something in itself

"And then?" Marcus asked. He was sitting on the end of the bed, tapping on his thigh with a little peacock feather fan. I knew he wanted to hear all the juicy details. He was dying to know exactly how big Simon's penis was. But I wasn't going to tell him. For the first time in my life, I felt almost modest. I wanted to talk about Simon, not about us.

Because, obviously, we'd made love. At his place, on the big, white king-sized bed. I'd stroked his skin, soft as a woman's, and I'd watched him give me long kisses, everywhere. In the beginning, there had been the slight awkwardness that comes with first times, but it quickly disappeared. Simon wasn't a wild, passionate lover. He was a magical lover. There was something graceful in his gestures, in the slow, sure movement of his hips. As we wrapped ourselves around each other on the big white bed, I thought about the rhythm of the ocean.

Marcus looked at me with his head cocked, a wicked sparkle in his eye. "You naughty girl. You don't want to tell me anything, eh? How mean! Naughty, naughty, naughty," he said repeatedly as he waved his fan in front of me.

I brought my hands to my chest, made a face of exaggerated innocence. "Okay," said Marcus. "Don't say anything. Marcus knows. Marcus perceives all, and Marcus can see quite easily that it was gooood." Marcus was drunk, too. There was a sign that was never wrong: when he started talking about himself in the third person, it meant he'd had too much to drink and thought he was Andre Leon Talley. It really made me laugh. I opened the second shaker of Margaritas: it was empty, and I hadn't drunk a drop.

"Oops!" said Marcus. "Marcus drank it all. Your stories were too exciting, Chloé. Shall I make another?"

"No, that's okay, I'll wait for Juliette."

"Oh, that's right. Leave Marcus all alone!"

"Marcus…"

"All right, all right…"

He crossed his arms and pouted. I threw a pillow at him, with a laugh, and he counterattacked with a lime green boa that hit me right in the face. At the same instant, we heard Juliette; as she came in she called, "Honey! I'm hooome!"

Marcus and I looked at each other, then we started to jump and shout like little girls whose mother has just caught them up to some mischief.

When Juliette came into the room, I had three boas around me, and Marcus was hiding behind his bed, and laughing his head off. Juliette put her hands on her hips and, trying not to laugh, she said, "Okay. You're both ridiculous." Then she looked at the shaker, which had fallen onto the ground, and added, "And drunk."

"I'm not," I said. "Just Marcus." That's when he'd jumped up, shouting, "Taaaadaaaa!" and "Marcus is so drunk!" He was still laughing, showing his beautiful white teeth. Juliette shook her head and asked, "You think you're up to having another drink? I bought a little rosé that doesn't look bad. Before the summer's over, it'll be nice, no?"

"Sure, no problem. Just let me get out of these pretty boas." I was laughing, too. I wasn't as drunk as Marcus, just a little buzzed, pleasantly buzzed, like when I'd smoked my first cigarettes, outside, hiding under the living-room window.

Marcus waved his hand. "Go on, girls. I have work to do." Juliette and I exchanged an amused look – whatever work he was talking about, we had no idea, and personally, I preferred it that way.

We crossed the big apartment to the kitchen. Juliette was wearing an inside-out beret, and capri pants, with flats that made her look a little like Jean Seberg in *A bout de souffle*. "You look cute," I said. She smiled. She would have rather died before she admitted it, but Juliette liked it when people said she looked cute.

She turned her head and, staring at the floor, declared, "You really look happy, Chloé. It's been a long time since I've seen you like this." Then she looked at me, and added, "I'm happy for you." That was enough. She wasn't going to say anything else. And I didn't want to, either. I put an arm around her shoulders and we went into the kitchen.

"Have you spoken to Antoine?" she asked as she opened the bottle.

"No... in fact, he left me a message at noon on Monday because he wanted to know if 'I'd scored.'"

Juliette shook her head. "What a jerk... I think this whole thing makes him feel uncomfortable."

"What thing?"

"Well, you and Simon. Love. You know. That you decided to go looking for love and maybe you found it. So fast. It's as if he didn't have enough time to get used to the idea."

"What idea? He's funny. That's what he said to me the other day on the phone, 'I'll get used to it.' But it's my business after all."

"Yes, but you know Antoine... I think somewhere deep down, he would have liked it if the three of us all stayed the same, forever, as if we were frozen in the time when we wrote the manifesto."

"Oh my God! Juliette, that's exactly what I told him!"

"When?"

"On the phone! I can't believe I forgot to tell you about it. The day I met Simon, I had a hell of a conversation with Eve-Marie."

"Eve-Marie…"

"You know, that girl I work with sometimes and who always has these ridiculous relationships…"

"Ah yes. Emotionally challenged."

"Right. Anyway, I had quite a conversation with her – she accused me of being heartless, of being afraid of love…"

"No!"

"Yes, really! And it got to me. I mean, I wondered if she wasn't right somehow."

Juliette gave me a critical look.

"Listen," I went on. "I'm not saying she was right. I just wondered. And I wanted to call you, but you weren't home. So, I called Antoine, and I don't know how we got there, but I told him that deep down he needed us to stay the same just so he could justify what he was doing."

"And?"

"And he didn't take it well, dude. He seemed hurt. I don't know, it was really strange. I felt like I'd really hurt him. Then, on my way out of the office, I ran into Simon, and I forgot all about it… can I have some wine?"

Juliette poured me a glass.

"He's something else all right, that Antoine of ours. I always thought there was more going on in that pretty little head of his than he let on."

"Maybe," I said. "But if you want my opinion, he doesn't even know it himself. What I mean is, he's not hiding it on purpose, if you know what I'm saying."

Juliette nodded.

"It would be so great if we could have all of him. If we could have all of Antoine. He's great the way he is, for sure, but if he…" She was looking up, choosing her words carefully. "You know, I'm sure Antoine thinks he's the freest guy on earth. In his head. He doesn't see any barriers, or limits. When I met him, I thought the same thing, too. I said to myself, 'That man is completely free.' And I'd never seen anything like it."

"I know… and it's really attractive, too. That's what makes him charming, I think."

"Yeah, well, he's not ugly, either," Juliette added with a mischievous little smile. "We don't notice anymore, but still."

"No, that's true. But if he wasn't always so cool… whether it's completely true or not, he wouldn't be as irresistible as he is. Because, well, that's something else we don't notice anymore either, but I can see it when he starts talking to a girl. Like the first time he came up to me. At the time, you think to yourself that there's nothing more desirable than being above everything like that. Cool, with a big smile, and above everything."

Then I had an idea. I crossed my arms, and I looked sideways at Juliette, questioningly. "Did *you* ever have a crush on him?"

She waved the idea away dismissively. "Nah… Antoine was always… yours."

"What?"

"You know. I always told myself, even after you stopped seeing each other, that Antoine was off-limits."

"Come on!"

Juliette put her hands on her hips, "Oh really! So it wouldn't have bothered you if I'd slept with him?" I briefly pictured Juliette and Antoine happily in bed – it was like a slap.

"Why are you asking me that? Did he ever come on to you?"

I sounded almost aggressive. Juliette started to laugh.

"You see?" she said. "I always knew it would bother you. After all, it would be normal. No one wants to know their best friend is sleeping with their ex."

I was immediately grateful to her for saying it was normal, and that anyone would have the same reaction.

"And, just to put your mind at ease," Juliette added, "no,

he never came on to me. In case you never noticed, Antoine likes superfeminine girls. Tomboys are not his thing."

I bumped her with my hip. "But what if he'd wanted to?" She gave a coquettish shrug of her shoulders. "Hey, I always said I'd try everything, at least once." We both started to laugh.

"Anyway," said Juliette. "You know what would help him?"

"No, what?"

"A girlfriend. I'm sure that would change him. He'd have no choice."

"A girlfriend? But Antoine can't have a girlfriend. It's like... it would be against the laws of the universe. It would foretell the apocalypse. I swear to you, if Antoine had a girlfriend, it would start raining toads, or grasshoppers, or whatever, and the next thing you know, the earth would open up, and a tidal wave would swallow New York."

I pointed the finger of the hand that was holding the wineglass towards Juliette. "I'm telling you."

She rolled her eyes. "You both make me laugh. You're as bad as he is, deep down. You both want the other one to stay the same forever. You're not making much progress, you know."

"No way!" I stopped. She was completely right. "Okay, okay," I said, taking a sip. "Maybe. But really. Antoine? With a girlfriend? My God."

"It would indeed be something else," said Juliette. "But I'm convinced that's the only thing that would open him up. And, honestly, I'm more than a little curious about what's hidden behind that façade of his. Aren't you? I'm sure he's absolutely incredible."

I thought for a moment, and I think I smiled. "He'd be incredible."

"Because I'm not incredible all ready?"

Antoine came into the kitchen and Juliette and I both screamed. "How long have you been here?" shouted Juliette.

Antoine gave a little smile, "Long enough."

"What did you hear?" I asked him. Oh my God, what if he'd heard what we'd said about his charm. And when I'd almost strangled Juliette when she'd insinuated she could have slept with him. I looked at Juliette and I could see she was only thinking of one thing, Oh my God, what if he'd heard me say I'd try anything at least once.

Antoine slowly walked around the island. He poured himself a glass of wine, leaned his elbows on the counter and looked at us with that same little smile. "I heard quite a bit," he said.

But he always refused to tell us what. In the taxi on the way to the restaurant, we took turns elbowing him. "Did you hear the part where we talked about the fact that we're lesbians?" Juliette asked.

"And when we said what we really wanted was to have you as our slave, and use your sperm for reproduction?" I added. The three of us were sitting in the back seat, Antoine was in the middle. He raised his arms and slipped one behind each of us. I smelled his aroma, a light, sweet scent I liked and never smelled anywhere else. "Tonight," he said, "we're going out like in the good old days."

The good old days, I'd have to say, weren't really that old. To be exact, the last time the good old days had been the good old days was only a week and a half before. But okay. Antoine seemed to believe that, now that I was close to having a boyfriend, they were almost over. But we'd all been passionate about those times, so Juliette and I gave in, and we went out, the three of us, just like the good old days, just like always.

This obviously meant that after a long meal where we tried to solve all the world's problems, we ordered one, then two bottles of wine which we drank leisurely, at the table where we always sat in the back of our favourite restaurant. I felt fine, perfectly fine. I would think of Simon, and feel rich, then I'd come back to our conversation, and I'd felt like a millionaire.

Antoine and I were sitting on the banquette – I was leaning against him, like always, with my legs tucked up
underneath me, and Juliette was opposite us. In front of her,
the paper tablecloth was covered with drawings. As she
talked to us, with a pen or one of my lipsticks, she drew tall,
tired figures, with outstretched hands.

We were talking about my mother's birthday, which we
always celebrated in my parents' big house. Six years earlier,
my mother had been feeling really sad a little before her
birthday, for apparently intense and unfathomable reasons,
and I'd had the idea of organizing a little dinner for her. And
since her friends all seemed extremely boring to me, and
because the only sensible reason for her sadness was a recent
argument with her brothers and sisters, I'd invited my sister,
her husband, and my friends.

It had been a great success. Mom had stopped being sad,
everyone had a great time and got along perfectly. Since
then, every year, around my mother's birthday, my sister
Daphné and I put together a big dinner with our mother
and father, Daphné's husband, Juliette and Antoine. In six
years, the only addition had been my sister's daughters.

"Are you going to invite Simon?" Antoine asked me.

"Simon? No, I don't think so…"

"Oh, come on," Juliette said. "You have to invite him,
Chloé."

"What? No… my mother's birthday is in a month. Even
if everything goes well with Simon between now and then,
it might be a little soon, I think."

"Oh, come on!" Juliette insisted. "You can't tell me your
family's not dying to meet him!"

"I didn't tell my family about Simon! I'm not crazy, you
know. If I told my mother, she'd probably send over a squad
to see what he looks like."

"That's for sure," Antoine said, laughing.

He adored my mother, and always flirted with her, which
delighted her. He turned towards me. "Seriously," he said,

"you should invite him. We'd like to meet him, too. Right, Ju?" Juliette nodded her head enthusiastically.

"Oh! I don't know," I sighed. "Seems a little soon to me..."

"May as well do it while it lasts," said Antoine.

I gave him my most unpleasant look. "Why do you say that?" He lit himself a cigarette. "Chloé... you know what I think of this whole thing." He pointed a finger at me. "And spare me your ridiculous theory about how I need Juliette and you to always stay the same, so I don't have to 'wonder what I'm doing with my own life.'" He used a nasal voice at the end of his sentence. I glanced towards Juliette. He remembered the exact words I'd used.

"Listen," I said to him. "You can think what you want. I know it's not your thing, I know that you'll never believe that love can be a goal. I'm not trying to change you." Maybe it was the wine, but I thought I was being magnanimous, altruistic, even. "The other day I was mad at Eve-Marie and I took it out on you. It wasn't right. I have no right to judge you. But, on the other hand, you don't need to conclude that I'm completely blind because I decided I want to be in love. Shit, it's not the most unusual idea on the planet; everyone wants to fall in love." Then I realized who I was sitting with, and I added, "Almost everyone. The only thing you can hold against me is that I'm not very original."

Pensively, Antoine took a drag on his cigarette. "That's not true. It's not true that almost everyone wants to fall in love. People *think* they want to fall in love."

Juliette sighed and looked discouraged. "Okay, that's another story," she said.

"In your opinion, oh God's Great-Observer-of-the-Human-Heart, what do people really want?"

"People want... everybody just wants... to be surprised." He looked pleased with that idea. "That's right," he said. "Everybody wants to be surprised. What you think of as love, Chloé, is surprise. You get surprised by someone you like, someone who makes you feel different, who stirs things up when you thought nothing would ever shift again. But, by definition, the surprised effects don't last."

"No? How do you justify relationships that last?"

"They get along well. It's sincere, friendly closeness. The fact that, often, both partners recognize that they will probably never be surprised again."

Juliette listened to him and slowly nodded her head – obviously, she thought that Antoine had put his finger on something. I was shaking my head no, "Bullshit, Antoine."

"No, you wish it was, but I know deep down – he pressed a finger above my left breast – you know I'm right."

"No! And I never did think that either, Antoine. Even before Simon. I didn't necessarily believe in true love, but I believed there were happy couples. Shit, look at my parents. My sister and her husband. They're very happy."

"They've stopped believing they can be surprised."

He smiled triumphantly. Antoine liked to make me mad. And I was. I was because I didn't believe him. I knew Antoine better than anyone, and I knew he was lying – he'd come up with an idea that was relatively plausible and that he liked himself. He liked to see himself that way, casually constructing slightly shocking theories. But I knew he didn't believe a word of what he was proposing.

And that was Antoine's problem: he didn't believe in anything. Not in theories, or principles, or infallible truths, or inevitable reactions of the heart. At the most, he believed in the present, what was tangible, what was here and now. He believed in the volatile nature of people and things. So theories meant very little to him. His one and only goal in saying all that was to provoke me.

So, instead of making him happy by getting mad, I shrugged my shoulders. "Say whatever you want, Antoine. Personally, though, in my immediate family, there are two really different couples, but both of them are happy."

Antoine drew in close to my face. "I'll make a bet with

you," he said. "At your mother's birthday, I'll pick her up."
He seemed to think for a second, and then smiled. "No, that
would be too easy. I'll pick up your sister."

And into my drink, because I was certain that Antoine
was showing off, and because I was completely stupid, I said,
"Okay, what are the stakes?"

"A night with you."

"PARDON?"

Even Juliette turned towards him, like she'd just gotten an
electric shock. "What did you just say?" she asked Antoine.

"That I'm going to pick up her sister, and I'll win a night
with her."

Juliette and I traded an absolutely flabbergasted look. We
both wanted to laugh, but I don't know if it was from nervousness, or if there was really something funny about the
situation.

"Who do you think you are?" Juliette finally said.
"Robert Redford?"

Antoine started to laugh, and signalled to the waitress to
bring over three more glasses. "Chloé?"

"What?"

I realized my heart was beating really hard. I glanced
quickly at my shirt – I was afraid they could see the fabric
rise and fall as it pounded. I was both completely horrified
and completely excited by Antoine's idea. I never would
have admitted it to anyone, but that totally macho and pretentious sentence "I'll win a night with you" was the sexiest
thing anybody had ever said to me. Oh my God, I thought.
I want him to win the bet.

It was disastrous. After all, I bragged about being a free,
modern woman, and, by definition that kind of macho, vul-
gar behaviour should have disgusted me. I should have
slapped him, or laughed at him, or wrapped myself up in
noble indifference. Something Anaïs Lin had said, and that
I'd read years ago, crossed my mind, "As an artist, I do not
mind standing my ground. But as a woman, I want to be

pursued, possessed, and fucked." Mygodmygodmygod. That was exactly what I was thinking, right there, sitting against Antoine, who was looking at me with a smile and an amused glint in his eye. But I was neither an avant-garde artist nor a self-sufficient intellectual, and I couldn't strike the balance. Fucking Anaïs, I thought. Fucking Antoine.

I shot a desperate look at Juliette, who signalled with her head she was just as stunned as I was. "I can't believe you just said that," she said in a flat voice. Antoine raised a hand, so she would be quiet, but he continued to look at me. Juliette pulled her head back, and then grabbed his hand, forcing him to look at her. "Hey," she said, more energetically this time. "Are you completely drunk or what? I hope you're completely drunk, Antoine, if not…"

Antoine pulled his hand free and slowly turned his head back towards me. "Chloé?" he repeated.

"What, Chlóe?" I was too stunned to say anything else. "Shake?" He extended a hand. I heard Juliette sigh in disbelief.

"Shut the fuck up!" she shouted at him. "Really. Shut the fuck up!"

Then, I exploded, too.

"Are you nuts? Who do you think I am! Really, what the fuck! You're an asshole, Antoine. You're an asshole and a jerk, and, for your information, I have neither the intention nor the desire to go to bed with you. I have a nice, charming, respectful guy who can satisfy me quite nicely, thank you." I paused. I was way too mad. And it wasn't very subtle. "And, beside that," I shouted, "if I see you touch my sister!"

"Exactly," Juliette echoed.

Then Antoine looked almost as surprised as I did. He put one hand on my shoulder and said, "Chloé. Christ. It was a joke. I'm not a bastard, you know."

"Pardon?" I was totally stunned. Juliette started to laugh, saying, "Holy shit! You're either drunker or stupider than I thought."

"Chloé," said Antoine. "You're my best friend. You and Juliette are the two most important people in my life. The only two people in the world I'd make sacrifices for. Do you really think I'd mess around with your sister and make you ridiculous propositions just when you seem to be happy?"

I didn't say anything. He looked serious. Serious and something else, but serious nonetheless.

I hid my face behind my hands. "Oooh... I'm sorry!" I peeped out between my fingers. "Sorrrrryyyyy." He gave a little smile. "It's okay, it's okay. It might have been in bad taste."

"Very bad taste," said Juliette, who was now smiling, too.

"Okay, okay, okay... but it's not the first time, right?"

He put out his cigarette and gestured for me to make room for him to get up. I stood up, he did the same, and just before he headed off towards the washroom, he stood in front of me and winked.

I sat back down. "Je. Sus. Christ," I said to Juliette. "He just winked at me."

"Of course he winked at you, he's Antoine."

"Juliette, I'm not sure it was joke."

"Do you wish it wasn't a joke?"

I muttered "shut up" under my breath. Juliette half-opened her mouth and then started shaking her head. She looked at me with a bit of smile. "Oh boy..." she sighed.

"What, oh boy?"

"No, nothing."

"What?"

"No, no."

"Juliette! Shit!"

She sat back on her chair.

"You wish it wasn't a joke."

I didn't say anything. Juliette leaned on her forearms so she'd be closer to me. "Am I wrong?"

"Juliette. Stop it. Really."

She straightened back up. "Whatever you say. But, for your information, I think he was half-joking."

"What?" I motioned for her to hurry up. Antoine was going to be back any second.

"I think there was a little truth in it. Antoine is a little territorial, after all. But I believe him when he says he'd never want to hurt you. I think he said it as a joke, because he needed to say it, if you know what I mean."

It was confusing, but I did understand what she was getting at.

"And besides," Juliette added, "he was coherent."

"With what?"

"His theory."

"What do you mean?"

"You know what he just did?"

"What?"

"He surprised you."

She was right. Which meant Antoine's phoney theory had at least a grain of truth to it. Because, joke or no joke, I'd been... stunned. And, my God, how I liked to be stunned! I let out an unending sigh and, as I saw Antoine heading back to the table, I prayed that the rest of his stupid hypothesis was right and that, in fact, the effects of the surprise wouldn't last.

Chapter 10

The days following that dinner were unbearable. Despite my efforts and my (more or less) sincere intentions, I started elaborating absolutely ridiculous daydreams involving Antoine, which I tried – even more ridiculously – to control. Antoine came to my house late at night and when I opened the door, he gave me a fiery kiss, laid me down, took me, stunned me – it didn't matter what you called it, he left me exhausted and satisfied, and full of delicious regrets. The next day, I'd see Simon, and it wouldn't come up again. That's where I was practising control: my Antoine-filled daydreams were never about love and happiness (well, sexual happiness, sure, but that was it) – they couldn't be.

Besides, I wasn't sure I wanted them to be. Having fantasies about my best friend was kind of troubling. I had wanted to sleep with Antoine, *really* wanted to, but that was eight years ago. Since then, we'd gotten so close I thought of him as a brother. It seemed like there was something morally reprehensible, not to say unhealthy, about trying to remember what he looked like naked, and imagining him making love to me on the dining-room table. It was almost kind of upsetting. But so exciting. It was unbearable.

On top of that, I was spending most of my days alone, which didn't help. Simon worked a lot, and I wasn't supposed to see him till the next weekend. He called, was funny and charming, and, while I was talking to him, I'd kind of forget about Antoine and the dining-room table. I wanted to see Simon. I needed to see him and see that he was marvellous, brilliant and handsome as a god, and totally capable of stunning me at my front door, too. In the meantime, I was rattling around my apartment, leafing through old issues of *Vanity Fair* without reading them, and constantly asking Puce for advice, though she seemed a little out of her depth in this particular situation.

I wanted to see Juliette, too, but she was in the clutches of an intense attack of creativity, and she was spending all her time in her studio. She only came out to eat (and even there, Marcus told me, sometimes he had to go get her and say stupid things like "You need more beta-carotene to work better," in order to entice her into the kitchen).

After five days, I called Antoine. I thought about it for a long time first, before I came to the conclusion that talking to him might put things back in perspective, and also remind me that Antoine was my best friend, a terribly macho man I adored and who told me sex stories to make me laugh. I picked up the receiver, and immediately wanted to put it back on its stand. Out loud, I said, "Really!" Then I added, "I'm talking to myself, this is ridiculous" and "fuck" and I dialled Antoine's number. After it rang four times, I figured he wasn't there, and a rather intense wave of relief went through me. Then he answered, "Hello?" He sounded like he was in a hurry.

"Antoine? It's me."

"Oh! Hey…" I could feel he was glad and that, suddenly, he was less hurried.

"How are you?" he asked. Then before I could answer, he added, "I was afraid you were mad."

"Why?"

"The bet, of course. The one from the other night. It's not like me, Chloé, but I felt bad about it."

"Oh! Come on now!" I made a sound that was supposed to sound like a laugh, but it was more like a sniffle. "Don't worry about it, Antoine. We were drunk."

"Yeah, I know. But it wasn't right. I don't understand why I said it."

"It doesn't matter." I was a little insulted by what he'd

just said. I would have preferred to hear, "I said it because I want you more than ever, and I can't do anything about it."

"So you're not mad?" Antoine asked.

"No, why?"

"I haven't heard from you in five days."

"You didn't call either."

"No, because I was afraid you were mad."

"Ah. But, no, I'm not mad."

"Good," said Antoine. "So? What have you been up to?" Hmmm. Could I tell him I was moping around like an idiot, looking at my vibrator ten times a day without ever picking it up, out of fear of thinking of him at the critical moment?

"Oh, not much," I answered. "I did some reading."

"What?" Fucking Antoine. I glanced around me, looking for any title at all.

"Um… I read *Politique*, by Adam Thirlwell."

"Mmm… kinky…"

"Pardon?"

"I said 'kinky.' There are lots of erotic passages, aren't there?"

"Oh. Yeah. Right."

"Did you like it?"

"What?"

"Um… *Politique*?"

"Oh! Yes. No. It was okay." I'd only read the first chapter, months ago, and I hardly remembered anything, except a botched scene of sodomy, and an overly pronounced resemblance to Kundera.

"I liked it," said Antoine. "He copied…"

"Kundera!" I interrupted him. I was happy to have at least one reference to the book.

"Exactly," Antoine continued, "but he had some good ideas. It's crazy though. The little son-of-a-bitch who wrote that was born in 1978. It's insane. Exactly ten years younger than me. It drives me nuts. When I see people who can do stuff like that at that age, I feel old. It's unbelievable, eh?"

He was laughing as he talked. He was in a good mood. Therefore nothing had changed. Antoine and I could still talk, like always, about everything and anything. It wasn't a surprise, after all, all that had happened was a stupid joke and a wink, but I was relieved. As I listened to him, it felt like I was getting him back. He was no longer the unknown, shiny object of my desire, but rather just Antoine. If I'd known it would be this easy, I thought to myself, I would have called five days ago.

We talked for almost two hours, like always. I got up to get a glass of white wine from the kitchen, and he went to open a bottle of red. I could hear him lighting cigarettes and, through the window, I was watching the sun set behind the red-brick buildings. Soon, I thought, the nights are going to be longer than the days again.

"So?" Antoine said. "How's it going with Simon?"

I pursed my lips. I was always uncomfortable when Antoine talked to me about Simon, and it made me mad at myself. "Oh, it's fine," I answered. "We've talked every day, but I haven't seen him again yet. He works in a restaurant from noon till 2 a.m.; it's a little crazy."

"Why don't you go see him at the restaurant?"

"Yeah, I thought of that, we even talked about it, but he's really superbusy when he's there. He'd feel bad about leaving me sitting there, so it would bother him more than anything else."

"You want to go together?"

"What?"

"Tonight. If you're not doing anything, we'll go. That way, you can see him, plus you're with someone so he won't have to feel bad if he doesn't have time for you. It could be nice, no? Besides, I'd like to meet him."

I tried to think at about two hundred miles an hour. Potentially, that was the worst idea on the planet. But, only in my opinion. From anyone else's point of view, it would be a pretty good idea. A nice idea. Plus, I wanted to see

Simon. And Antoine. Maybe I wanted to compare them a bit. Just a bit.

"Chloé?" asked Antoine.

"Yes! Yes, sorry. I... Siffleux was coughing, I was afraid he was going to be sick on the rug."

"So, what do you say?"

"Well, I don't know, Antoine. Why not?" I made a face.

"Okay!" he said, sounding happy. "Shall I pick you up in an hour?"

"No! No, don't come over here. I'll come to your place."

"No, that would be silly. His restaurant's in the gay village, isn't it?"

"Yes."

"Well, then, I have to drive right past your place to get there. No, no, I'll come by."

"NO!" Antoine was the worst driver in the world. He always drove too fast and, from where I was sitting, had never even heard of the rules of the road.

"No, it's not a good idea," I repeated more calmly. "It'll be like every time we have dinner out, you'll end up having to leave your car there, because you're going to be too drunk. Then you'll get another ticket. No, no. If you want to pick me up, take a taxi."

"Yeah... Maybe you're right. Okay, I'll be outside your place in an hour. I'll call you."

"Cool."

"See you soon, sweetie. Are you going to wear your little blue dress?"

"What blue dress?"

"The silk one with the flowers. It's got a nice, low neckline."

"Antoine..."

"Hey, if I have to eat opposite you, I may as well have a good view."

"See you in a bit, Antoine." I hung up with a smile. He always did that when we were going to see each other. Are

you going to wear your red sweater? Your white skirt? Why
don't you wear the dress you had on the other night? I made
it a point never to listen to him, but it made me smile every
time. Tonight in particular.

Forty-five minutes later, the doorbell made me jump,
and, consequently, I applied a generous layer of mascara to
my left cheek. "Fuck," I muttered as I went to open the door.

It was Antoine. For a second, I thought he might give me
a fiery kiss, lay me down, take me, knock me down – it
didn't matter what you called it, but I remembered that,
according to my infallible theory, since I'd imagined it, it
couldn't happen.

"What are you doing here?" I said, sticking my head out
the half-open door.

"I came to pick you up."

"You said you'd be here in an hour! It's only been forty-
five minutes!"

"Sure, but that doesn't matter."

"Is the taxi waiting downstairs?"

"No, I ended up taking my car."

"Shit, Antoine."

"But it's more practical."

I looked at him without saying a word. "Can I come in?"
he finally asked, exasperated.

"No! I'm just in my bra."

"So?" It really was a pretty weak argument: not only had
Antoine already seen me completely naked, in the last eight
years, I had already been in just a bra in front of him at least
a million times, whether, like now, he was waiting to go out,
or on the roof of his condo, in the summer, during one of
our impromptu tanning sessions.

"Okay. Come in." I opened the door, and he followed me
into the apartment.

"I like what you have on your cheek," he said. "Is that a
new trend in makeup?"

"I jumped, you moron."

"Did you call Simon?"

"Yeah, he reserved us a table." I turned back towards him and smiled, "He was happy."

He came into my room and nonchalantly sat on the pink chair. "Have you managed to speak to Juliette lately?" I could see him in the mirror I was using to put on my make-up. As usual, he was wearing a black jacket and a button-down shirt he hadn't tucked into his pants (he always left his shirts untucked, because tucking them in would be, according to him, "the epitome of bad taste"). He looked around and started playing with a bra that had been lying on one of the chair's armrests, spinning it lightly around one finger.

"No," I said. "I talked to Marcus, though. Apparently, she's 'in the clutches of an intense attack of creativity.'"

"Oh boy," sighed Antoine.

"Yep, oh boy. The last time she had an attack of creativity, she came up with the series of crying faces."

"Yeah, I know. I think it's better when she works under normal conditions. Every time she has one of these so-called attacks, we end up with these completely fucked-up pieces – and they're not even necessarily pretty. Did she sell many of those crying faces?"

"Oh, no. Not really. She'd made a series of fourteen paintings, and she sold two. But, shit, Antoine, it was scary."

He started to laugh. "I know. I know. I bought one." I turned to face him, and I was laughing, too. "Pardon?"

"Yeah, I'd gotten to the opening just after it started and she was so nervous. She said they were superimportant pieces for her, and all that, so I bought one before I left. I thought it might bring her luck for the rest of them. But I guess it didn't work."

"Where did you put it?"

"Um… in my office."

"There are no paintings by Juliette in your office."

"In the closet, there is."

"Oh! Antoine!" I tried to look a bit outraged.

"I know! It's crazy, but when I got home with that thing… Where did you expect me to put it? On my bedroom wall? You said it yourself – it's scary. My goal in life is to coax girls into my room, not make them run the other way."

"She never said anything about it?"

"Wait, at the beginning, when she'd come over, I'd hang it up. Then, one day, I forgot. I don't know, I think at a certain point she realized maybe they weren't her best paintings."

Laughing, I nodded my head. "I'm happy with mine though." I had a series of three little paintings Juliette had done almost ten years earlier. Three bright boats – the colours were warm and unreal, it was pretty, almost Fauvist. Not really innovative, but I liked them a lot.

Antoine suddenly bent over and then stood up, sharply, with Puce in his arms. He was holding her over his face and rubbing his nose on her little tummy. "Ha! Ha!" he said. "I got you! Cutie…" He hugged her close and she arranged herself in a ball in the crook of his arm. Puce liked men. To tell the truth, she liked everyone, but men especially. She raised her head and started nibbling on Antoine's chin.

"Look at that," said Antoine with a laugh. "I'm telling you, she's crazy about me."

"Don't let it go to your head, Tony Boy, she loves every guy she meets."

"Okay, that's enough with the Tony Boy!"

"Oh! I thought that was pretty funny!" I pulled back my hair. "I'm ready, Tony Boy."

"Okay, that's enough…" He gave Puce a little kiss on the top of her head and gently set her on the ground. "Sometimes I think I should have kept her," he said as he headed towards the door.

"No, no. You're never home. She would have been lonely. She needs company."

"I know, I know. She's much better off with you."

He opened the door and motioned for me to go ahead.

We got to the restaurant in less than ten minutes. Antoine had done about 70 kilometres an hour along the little streets of the Mount Royal plateau, and he went the wrong way down two one-way streets. I'd thought I was going to die, we'd nearly run over one cat and two pedestrians, and I wanted to kill him. But, at least on the drive over, I'd stopped thinking about how the night was going to go, which worried me more than I cared to admit. And what if I realized that I wasn't really interested in Simon? This question had me slightly anxious, but it had been blotted out by a more pressing question – my short-term survival.

"You are the worst driver in the world!" I said as I got out of his car. "You're a danger to the public, Antoine."

"No, I'm not…"

"Yes, you are! You almost hit two people!"

"No, I didn't. I saw them. I've never run over anyone, I'll have you know."

"Don't care. I'm *never* getting in your car again. And I'm not far from turning you in, I'll have you know."

"Yes, yes…" He smiled and opened the restaurant door for me.

It was a small place, with about twenty tables. It was warmly decorated – when you walked in, immediately at your right was a big polished wood bar, and behind it there were dozens of bottles of all shapes, leaning against the brick wall. There were little lamps scattered all over the restaurant, with little orangey shades that gave off soft, warm light. Most of the tables were already taken – the atmosphere was pleasant, filled with laughter and voices.

I was amazed: I would have expected a place with very minimal, very chic décor, like most new restaurants. But, in fact, it was a pleasant, and welcome, change. A heavy server in a black shirt came towards us with a friendly, "Good evening," in a very heavy southern French accent.

"Good evening. I... we have a reservation, I think, in the name of..." I didn't know if Simon had reserved the table in his name or mine, and I didn't really want to just say, "I'm sleeping with the chef." Antoine stepped forward. "Is Simon here?"

The server looked at me. "Oh! You must be Chloé. Yes, excuse me, Simon told me you'd be here around eight. Sorry. Come, let's get you to your table, I'll go get the boss." He led us to a little table near the back wall. We sat down, and Antoine said, "It's... warm."

"Okay, go ahead and say it, you don't like it."

Antoine liked places that were very "design" – minimalist décor where everything was black or white. At his place, the walls were white, the furniture was white, black, grey or ecru. Only two very red armchairs, in the living room, echoed a painting hung above the fireplace.

"No, really," he said. "It's not my style, but it's warm." At the same instant, I saw Simon coming from the kitchen. He was in jeans, but still had on his white chef's jacket. He came towards me with a smile, with one hand behind his back, and, to my great relief, I felt my heart expand. I smiled, and he leaned towards me. He placed one hand on my face, as he kissed me, delicately, very gently.

"Hi," he said to me.

"Hello." I felt like a little girl, and I was afraid that I was fidgeting in my chair. "This is Antoine," I finally said.

Simon turned towards Antoine, and they shook hands energetically, as they both smiled. I watched them say hello and exchange a few pleasantries ("Chloé's told me about you," "Yeah, me too," "So, you went to school together"...). The comparison was almost too easy: the blond in the white shirt and the brunette in the dark jacket.

They were both very handsome, but each in a very different way. In terms of basic form only, Simon was the more handsome of the two. He… glowed. I looked at them and realized they looked like there were about fifteen years between them – if I hadn't known Simon, I would have said he was about twenty. But Antoine – with his square face and his eyes which always looked like they saw more than other people's, and the little wrinkles he got around them when he smiled – had a kind of casualness about him, a kind of natural grace that Simon didn't have, at least not yet.

"I brought you a little something," said Simon, as he placed a bottle of champagne on the table.

"The whole bottle?" asked Antoine.

"All you want from the bottle," answered Simon. "At least have a drink with us."

Simon glanced towards the dining room, went to say something to the kitchen, then came back and sat next to me. "Two minutes," he said.

I looked at him, and I smiled. I was happy to see him, happier than I would have thought. And I was happy because Antoine had been nice to him. I watched them talk, and I wondered why I had ever been worried about it.

"So, you work in advertising," Simon said to Antoine. "You like it?"

"Yeah, it's not bad."

"But um… just out of curiosity, do you have to sell your soul to the devil before you start in that profession, or does it happen little by little?" He said it nicely, with a touch of humour, which I knew Antoine would like.

Indeed, he smiled, and answered, "In fact, now that you mention it, I remember my first day, almost fifteen years ago, a guy in an Armani made me sign a paper in my own blood. I thought it was a little strange at the time, but now I think I'm starting to understand…"

They both laughed, and Antoine took a look around the

restaurant. "You've done a nice job with the place," he said
to Simon. "It's quite warm."

"Yes, I wanted a bit of a change. Around here, the restaurants are usually really into design... It's nice, but... I don't
understand why people would want to eat in a place that
looks like it's straight out of *Wallpaper*. *Wallpaper* is super
and all, but it's not very... appetizing."

Antoine laughed. "No, you may be right."

"Plus," Simon continued, "I wanted to recreate what I'd
seen in France. There are lots of little places where you eat
divinely, though they don't look like much. The idea is that
the food is more important than the rest, you know?"

"Makes sense," Antoine answered. "And it's going well?"

"So far, I can't complain. I didn't even think it would
happen this fast. We opened four months ago, and we
already have to turn people away on Friday night. There's
been some good word-of-mouth, I think. But I'm going to
have to find another sous-chef, because Frédéric, the guy
who's here now, and I are working way too much. I like my
work, but not that much. What about you?" he added, turning towards me, "How are you?"

"Well, I'm really good. I'm happy to see you."

He smiled at me, "Not as happy as I am, believe me. It
was a great idea to come."

"Antoine's the one who thought of it."

"Really? Well, then, I owe you one," Simon said as he
held out his glass. We all clinked glasses, then Simon looked
at us, one after the other, "Where did you two meet?"

I was stunned. He only had two minutes, and of all the
questions he could ask us, he had to choose that one. I sat
there, with my nose in my glass, and didn't say a word.

"In a bar," Antoine answered, like it was no big deal. "I
was trying to pick up her friend Juliette. Has Chloé told you
about Juliette?"

"Yeah, your friend the painter?"

"Right," Antoine continued. "Juliette and I went out for a couple of months. Nothing serious." He just barely shifted his eyes towards me, just enough to give me an unnoticeable wink.

"Cool!" Simon said. He emptied his glass, and apologized, "I'm sorry, but they're waiting for me. Oh! And don't order anything. If you don't mind, I'll take care of everything. Is there anything you don't like?"

Antoine said, "Okra," and I shook my head. "Perfect," said Simon. "I'll get started on it for you."

Then he disappeared towards the kitchen. I waited till the door closed, and then I leaned across the table.

"Why did you say that?" I murmured through clenched teeth.

"Because I saw you were about to fall into your glass. And since he asked the question, I figured you hadn't told him *exactly* how we met."

"Yeah, well, I wasn't going to tell him we met each other in a bar and ended up screwing in a washroom! I don't think I even knew your name!" The memory of our first time made me, and Antoine, laugh.

"Yeah, you could have left out the part in the washroom," he said. "My God, that was uncomfortable, eh? Shit was it ever narrow! I think they had the smallest sink in the world."

"It's obvious you're not the one who was sitting on it."

Antoine laughed. He looked at me over his glass of champagne. "Look," he continued, "it doesn't bother me, but why didn't you just tell him we used to go out together?"

"We didn't go out together, Antoine. We had sex."

"You could have told him we'd gone out together."

"I know, I know, but… I don't know how to tell you this without it going to your head, but guys… guys react to you, Antoine. You make guys jealous. If you were ugly, maybe I would have told him. But I was afraid he'd get jealous when he met you, and start thinking that we… you know…"

"Still sleep together?"

"Something like that."

"Silly." He smiled at me lovingly. "You really could have told him. Now, we're going to have to get Juliette involved, and you know us, there's a good chance we'll get mixed up in our lies."

"I know! Why did you have to talk about Juliette?"

"I couldn't think of anything else! You had your face in your glass, and I wanted to say something natural."

"You could have said we'd met in a museum."

"A museum?" He looked both incredulous and amused. "A museum?" he repeated.

"Yeah, you know."

"No! I don't know!"

"I'm sure there are people who meet in museums."

"Sure, people who work in museums. What kind of person tries to pick someone up in front of a Picasso?"

"That sounds like you."

"Ah, no, no way! I only try to pick people up in front of Renoirs. They attract silly romantics and Americans."

I crossed my arms: "I get it; you've already tried it, haven't you?"

"No, but it's not a bad idea. Honestly, Chloé, you might be on to something."

I threw my napkin at him. "You're a jerk."

The food started coming soon after. Simon brought everything to us himself and explained almost lovingly what he was serving us. As an appetizer, we were treated to a poached quail egg, served on a potato blini, with Témiscamingue caviar. Then there was a cold cauliflower and truffle-oil soup, a shrimp and roasted-lemon salad, lightly grilled halibut cheek on an absolutely divine sea-urchin sauce, tuna tataki, a small portion of risotto on radicchio lettuce, and a rice and fig dessert. No theme, the food wasn't "French," or "Fusion" or "Nouvelle Cuisine." But it was great cooking. I was delighted. Not only did I have a divine meal, but Simon was a genius.

Even Antoine was impressed. "It's crazy," he kept saying. "He's only twenty-nine? It's unbelievable." Every time Simon came to see us, we showered him with sincere and joyful praise. The wine was good, too, and abundant, and Antoine was in a good mood – he was talking to me about his lovers, a married woman he didn't want to see anymore because it was too complicated and because she spent all her time complaining about her husband, and the receptionist at the place he worked who was, according to him, the sweetest and stupidest girl he'd ever met.

"Her dream is to become a singer. She doesn't have a good voice, but she's an optimist, because, apparently, it's written on her star chart that she's destined to become a great artist. But she's so nice. And she's got quite a body! I mean, quite a body!" He drew curves in the air. "And plus she's nice. No, really! Why are you looking at me like that?"

"Oh, I don't know."

"I'm telling you she's nice."

"Okay, okay. Antoine?"

"Yes?"

"Why don't you ever have a girlfriend?"

"Christ, Chloé! If there's one person on this earth who should know why, it's you."

"No, seriously, Antoine. Okay, you want to have fun, you don't want to be tied down, you don't believe in being exclusive, but really: isn't there a reason? Something?"

He smiled and took a drink of wine before placing his arms on the table. "Chloé. Chloé. Chloé. Chloé." He was looking at me with something like tenderness, a smile on his lips, and he was gently nodding his head. "I don't know, princess. Honestly, I don't know. I don't want to be tied down, that's for sure. But is it because I'm afraid? Is that what you want to hear?"

"No... well..." It was the first time Antoine had insinuated that there might be another reason behind his stubborn singleness besides an unshakeable vocation for pleasure.

"I never thought about it," he continued. He smiled when he saw how surprised I looked, and pointed at me with the two fingers that were holding his cigarette. "Because of you."

"Me?"

"Yes, I already felt, Chloé my dear, I already thought…" He looked like he was searching for his words. "Let's say maybe it already occurred to me that… you know."

I knew it. I knew it, but I couldn't believe he was telling me here, now. So I answered, "No, Antoine. I don't know."

He laughed. A little laugh directed at himself. "Listen. There was a time when…" He looked all around. In the air, on the table, next to him. It only lasted a couple of seconds. I was waiting, without moving – I was barely breathing. I wasn't nervous, I wasn't excited, I wasn't happy, I was in suspended animation. Antoine finally raised his eyes and stared at me. "I'd never met anyone like you, Chloé. And I know too well I won't meet anyone else like you. So you see, when you realize that kind of thing, you think it would be kind of stupid not to do anything. Well, I didn't do anything."

"Why?" For just a second, I thought I was going to dissolve in tears.

"I don't know."

"You don't know?" I didn't feel like crying at all anymore. I wasn't angry either, which amazed me, just because I still had room to feel amazed. I didn't understand. I didn't understand, and that annoyed me. Antoine was telling me something terribly important, something I'd dreamed about for a long time, even after I stopped being interested in him, and I was annoyed. What a waste, I thought. And waste is stupid, it was a pity, it was too bad. Not heartbreaking or touching. It was – shit – it was a pity.

"No, I don't know," Antoine said. "And I've tried to understand, Chloé." And he laughed again, in the same way. "Can you believe it? Me? While we were writing the *Manifesto*, I was trying to understand. And I came up with pretty unsatisfying conclusions, and they were even more unsatisfying because I was thinking they might be true."

"Like what?"

"Like everybody, I don't know… I'm afraid of being bored, with just one person, I'm afraid I can't do it, of failing – that idea came up a lot. I would think, 'Well, I'm so good at what I'm doing, sleeping around here and there, and being about it all, why should I go to any trouble trying to be a good guy?' The problem, Chloé, was that I *did* care about you. If I hadn't I might have tried. But you? Nah…"

He took a drink of wine, then, as if he'd just remembered something, he added, "Oh, and what you said the other day, in Juliette's room?"

"What?"

"That… how did you say it? That you 'really would have liked to'? Well, princess, it was all new to me."

"Oh, Antoine, come on!"

"No, I thought about it afterwards. I thought maybe I was the one who didn't want to see it. But no, I may be a coward, I may be a bastard, but I know you. It's not that I didn't want to see it. You didn't want to show it."

"You're not being honest, Antoine."

"No, it's true, if what you said in Juliette's room is really true, you made sure I didn't ever know it." He served us both some wine. "Bottom line, sweetie, you are as scared as me." And he raised his glass. I refused to toast. "Why are you telling me this?"

"Because. I'm a guy, Chloé. Sometimes I'm not very subtle. And you, and your cutie pie here, who makes great food and who, if I may, is charming, it… I don't know, you were right, it bugs me that you're not going to be single anymore, that we won't be like we were, that you won't always be beside me, that I won't be able to think to myself, even if I know I'd never do anything, that someday, I could, if I felt like it."

"What, you're not trying to get me to believe that…"

"No, I can't believe it! I'm not subtle, but I'm not retarded either. Besides, Chloé, it's all in the past, isn't it?"

"Pardon?" Of everything he'd said in the last half-hour, it was the first thing that really hurt me.

"It's in the past. Years ago. Yes, I'd like it if you stayed single forever, but just because that's how I am, call it whatever you want. Love and all that stuff, all those ideas, it was so long ago. Honestly, we're better the way we are, aren't we? You've found the kind of guy you were dreaming of. I can't change, and, really, I don't want to. So, to come back to your question, why don't I have a girlfriend? In the end, after thinking about it long and hard, I can say it's because I don't want one. However, I wouldn't say no to a harem..."

He started to laugh. I looked at him, with my eyes wide as saucers, and my mouth open. "You know what, I can't believe I told you all that either," he said, still laughing. "Maybe I'm becoming more open with age…" He winked at me just as Simon approached our table.

"Hey!" he said. "I'm almost done. Well, not exactly, but I decided to delegate a little tonight." He sat to my left and looked at me with a tender, happy smile. I ran a hand along his cheek. This guy is a miracle, I thought. He came back from Lyon, and Kingston, and our second year of high school, and here he is, because I bumped into him, and he looks like an angel. Or maybe an elf. Anyway, he's fantastic. We were, indeed, better off this way.

I turned towards Antoine, who was in an excellent mood. But for a few seconds, I suspected he'd waited to admit all that to me here and now because he knew we wouldn't keep talking about it for hours, and that I wouldn't be able to ask him all the questions I wanted to. He also knew that if we didn't talk about it at this exact time, we probably never would.

"Okay, then," he said, "I have to leave you now."

"Won't you have an after-dinner drink?" asked Simon.

"No, thanks, I already had quite a bit to drink." I rolled

my eyes towards the ceiling. In Antoine's case, "I've already had quite a bit to drink" was the worst excuse imaginable. He saw me and smiled. "You work like mad, Simon. So, if you have a bit of time to spend with the lady, take advantage. And seriously, the meal was divine. You're a genius, my boy."

They shook hands – Simon didn't insist, and neither did I. Antoine then leaned towards me. He kissed me on each cheek, and just before he straightened back up, serious, he looked me in the eye, "Hey, don't think about it. Have fun, that's all."

Then he squeezed my shoulder, and he left. I watched him cross the street. You can count on me, I thought. I wouldn't lose a second thinking about it. And I turned towards Simon.

Chapter 11

"Not a single second?" Juliette asked me. She looked at me through lowered lids, just like she always did when she wanted to make me admit something. We were at a little diner, not far from her place, where she'd finally agreed to meet me, "but for no more than an hour." She was still in the clutches of her attack of creativity and didn't want me to come over, even if I promised not to try to see her work. "Besides," she'd said, "I have to eat. And I feel like poutine."

So with a poutine in front of each of us, I told her about my evening at Simon's restaurant with Antoine. She listened without saying a thing, sometimes smiling, but never looking surprised. "Not a single second?" were the first words she'd spoken in a half-hour.

"Listen," I answered. "Sure, I thought about it once in a while, but honestly, not that much. I saw a lot of Simon, and that helped."

I smiled when I thought of Simon. We'd spent two whole days together, without leaving his house, making love and watching movies – *24 Hour Party People*, *Nashville*, *Le Père Noël est une ordure* (and, obviously, we spoke each line before the actors, which, with a few drinks in us, we thought was an absolute riot) and *Dumb and Dumber* – I knew all the dialogues to that one, too, and that made Simon a little depressed.

Then I went to see him at his restaurant almost every night. I realized I was falling in love. I was learning to recognize his gestures, intonations and looks, and I liked them. He told me about himself, and I told him about myself, and I was delighted at the idea of having someone to discover.

Someone whose whole life was unknown and accessible to me. What was he like when he was five? What had the women in his life looked like? Where had he travelled? I wanted to get to know him little by little, so that there would always be a little something to discover.

"So, that's why I haven't thought much about it," I told Juliette. "In fact, I think about it, but rationally. It's funny, isn't it? As Antoine was telling me all that, I kept thinking, 'This should be knocking me off my feet, it should make me see red,' he's telling me he was wondering about all this, and that he didn't do anything, but, at the time, that's all I was hoping for, that very thing – listen, I would make up stories, ridiculous scenes, I could see us kissing on the *Pont des arts*, laughing as we ran through the rain, in London, having tea with my family, making polite jokes…"

"Tea with your family?" Juliette repeated, laughing.

"And that's only the half of it," I said.

"That makes you look pretty silly!"

"Pretty much, yeah." And I laughed myself. "So, I was thinking to myself, 'it's really unbelievable, at the time when I was imagining scenes worthy of a Harlequin romance, Antoine was wondering if he might be in love with me. Or something along those lines. And here he is telling me all this now!' It seems like I should be frustrated by the irony of life, but I don't know… I look at Simon, what I have with him, what it could become, and I think that Antoine must be right and that we're better off the way we are."

"And, there's no guarantee Antoine would have made a great boyfriend."

"Right. Exactly." I stopped talking for a second. I tried to imagine Antoine as a boyfriend. Not a man running in the rain or making women laugh at high tea. No, simply as a boyfriend, a man who sleeps next to the same woman every night, who watches television with her, who some-times eats breakfast without saying a word, who makes plans together for winter vacations down south, who tries to find *the* right gift for every birthday, who says, "I love you" and believes it, forever. It was hard to picture.

"I knew it," Juliette said.

"Pardon?"

"I always had a feeling there was something between you and that it wasn't just coming from you. I can't believe you never noticed it, Chloé. Antoine looks at every woman in the world in a certain way, but he looks at you in a different way."

I shook my head, smiling despite myself – too many revelations, too few days. "So why didn't you ever say anything?" I asked Juliette.

"I don't know. I didn't want to get involved, I think, and because somehow, selfishly, it hurt me."

"Why?"

"Because sometimes I'd think to myself I was sure that you two would end up together and I'd be left all by myself like a ninny. You know how you told Antoine he didn't want you to get a boyfriend because, deep down, he wished we'd all stay single forever, you were right. But not only about him. I wish time stopped five years ago, too, when we didn't have anything to worry about, when we thought we could do anything, and it was just the three of us, and we didn't know anything about anything, but we were so happy."

"We thought we'd figured it all out," I added.

"We were happy, weren't we?"

"Yep. We were happy."

"We'll never be that happy again."

"Why do you say that?"

"Because," said Juliette, stirring the solidified remains of her poutine. "Because even if we end up with perfect lives, we'll never have that innocence again. Now, I tell myself, okay, maybe we will be happy, but… there's the outside world, the fact that we know for sure now that it won't last

forever. That's kind of why I liked the idea of our lives staying the same. That way, I could still convince myself that
nothing would ever change. Pretty silly, eh?"

"No, it's not silly. We all miss those days. Sometimes, I
think about it, and I don't even know how we managed to
function: we were going to university, we had ridiculous little jobs, we drank beer every night..."

"...while we played darts."

"While we played darts. But I don't know, I think we've
come out ahead in the deal."

"We know that's what you think..." Juliette thought I
was an incorrigible optimist – which, coming from her,
wasn't a compliment. Still, I wasn't that much of an optimist, but, next to her, I was a happy idiot. Juliette had
perfected a rather unique mix of cynicism and pessimism
(when we were visiting western Ireland, and I was delighted
by each hill and each clover, Juliette had announced "it's
so bucolic, it makes me sick"). When Antoine met her, he'd
nicknamed her the Ambassador of Despair.

In fact, her despair was superficial: Juliette was often sad,
and she had a tendency to lack self-confidence, but she was
happier than she let on. There was a kind of flirtatiousness
in her attitude. She liked to be the dark, melancholy one in
our group. It flattered her artistic temperament.

"I'm telling you we came out ahead in the deal," I repeated. "There's an urgency now which is... very healthy."

Juliette crossed her arms and gave me a look that said,
"Don't push it."

"You know what I mean," I went on. "It colours everything we do. Okay, sure there's something bittersweet about
it, but, Juliette, you know as well as I do that if we were still
playing darts and telling ourselves there would never be a
tomorrow, you never would have started painting again."

She shrugged her shoulders. "Yeah, I know."

"Besides, how's it going?"

She couldn't hold back a smile. "I'll call you when it's

done. Chloé, I think I might have found the reason I was put on this earth." I thought it would be wise not to mention the crying faces. "I'm telling you," Juliette continued, "I can feel it. I'm beat, I hardly eat, I work sixteen hours a day, but I think I've got something."

"That's great!"

"I hope so." She laughed a little, coquettishly, and added, "I'm actually pretty sure."

"You think you were inspired by your relationship with Samuel?"

"Partly, maybe. Actually, it just released something. But it's true I tend to be inspired when I'm feeling sad. It sounds like a cliché, but what can I say, it's true. Art becomes therapeutic."

"When do you think you'll be done?"

"Soon. Very soon. In a week or two, I think."

"That's quick."

"Yeah, I know. But like I said, I'm working sixteen hours a day."

"And what medium are you using, exactly?"

"Eight canvases. Medium-sized. You'll see. But, getting back to Antoine..."

"No, no, there's no need."

"I just have one question."

"Okay, what?" I crossed my arms to signal I was ready for anything.

"Do you love him?" Juliette asked.

"Pardon?"

"Do you love him? I've wanted to ask you that for years. Him, too. But I was afraid you'd tell me to get lost."

"Well... uhh... I did love him, sure. In a way." Then I thought for an instant. "No, in fact, I just loved him. Period, end of story."

"And now?"

"Juliette! I'm falling in love with Simon!"

"So you don't love Antoine."

"Of course not! I mean, I…"

"You can't say no, can you?"

"No. I mean yes. I am completely capable of saying no."

"And of saying, 'No, I don't love Antoine'?"

"What are you doing, Juliette?"

"Playing devil's advocate. I think the question you should ask yourself is why you can't say no. I know you love Simon. But why can't you say you don't love Antoine?"

"I am completely capable of…"

My cell started ringing – a hellish *Macarena*. I dove into my purse, as Juliette said, "Saved by the *Macarena*, eh?"

"Hello?"

"Chloé! It's your mother! Remember me? Your poor old mother who you never call?"

"Oh, Mom…" She was right, though. I had been totally neglecting my responsibility as a daughter the past few weeks. And her birthday! I'd forgotten her birthday, which was in two weeks and for which Daphné and I had to organize our traditional festivities.

"No, it's okay," my mother went on. "I know you've gotten into the habit of chatting with your father in the morning now…"

"Mom… it happened once."

"So when were you going to tell me you have a boyfriend?"

"How do you know that?" I covered the receiver with my hand and whispered to Juliette, "She knows I have a boyfriend."

"I have my sources," my mother answered. Who? Who? My unbearable downstairs neighbour? The heavy server from Marseille who worked in Simon's restaurant? Puce? Neither my sister nor my brother knew about it. It was a catastrophe: my mother had found out I had a boyfriend from someone other than me. She was going to think I was trying to hide him from her (which was true, of course: I wanted to wait a few weeks). I was going to hear about it for months. No, years. But who… Suddenly I had an idea.

"Hmph! Antoine!" I shouted. Opposite me, Juliette went, "Hmph!" too.

My mother giggled into the phone. "It's not important. At least some of your friends are loyal to me." When Antoine had an afternoon to kill sometimes, he'd stop by my mother's and have a martini with her, while he listened to her stories from "when she was an actress." They liked each other a lot, which had always made me happy. But not right now.

"Boy, he's got a big mouth!"

"Oh, sweetie, you can't blame him. Your father told me you had a date. So, you can see, since you weren't calling me, I decided to grill Antoine when he stopped by yesterday and that…"

"Mom! Someone's calling on the other line!" I awkwardly pushed the buttons on my tiny phone.

"Hello?"

"Hey, it's me. I just wanted to tell you that I went and had a drink at your mother's yesterday and that…"

"You, you son-of-a-bitch!"

"She grilled me, Chloé! She made me three martinis. Ten ounces each!"

"Yeah, well, she's on the other line! I'll call you back!" I saw Juliette who was silently saying, "I have to go." I motioned for her to wait, I took a deep breath, and I switched back to the other line.

"Yes, Mom."

"Was it your boyfriend?"

"No, your spy."

"Oh! Antoine! What a sweetheart! Chloé, that boy gets better with age. I don't know what your boyfriend looks like, but…"

"Mom, I know it's been a long time since I've called you,

but can I call you back later? I'm with Juliette and she has to go."

"Okay." She tried to sound mad. "That's okay. In fact, I just wanted to know if you'd talked to your sister."

"No, no I haven't talked to her either. Mom, the boyfriend's brand new. That's why I haven't said anything. And that's why I neglected you a bit, too."

"Yes, yes, I know, sweetie." Her tone reassured me immediately. She really did know. That didn't mean she wasn't going to bug me about all this for weeks, but, at least, she knew. "Personally," she said, "when I met your father, in the beginning, we never went out at all. We made love eight hours a day."

"Ew! Mom!"

"What? Your father is an amazing lover!"

"Mom! A thousand times, ew! Stop!"

"Oh, come on. You can be such a prude sometimes, sweetie!" She was laughing. She loved to tease me with that kind of comment, which I never got used to, for reasons that seem quite justified to me. "But anyway," she said. "Your sister Daphné's not feeling well."

"What do you mean?"

"She doesn't want to tell me. Apparently, I gave birth to two secretive girls." She giggled again, proud of herself. "But I can feel it. She's not doing well. So, I was wondering if you had any news."

"No. But I have to call her."

"Right, for my birthday, which is coming up."

"Yes, for your birthday. Mom? Really, can I call you back in an hour?"

"Of course. I love you, sweetie."

"Me, too, Mom."

I hung up. "Son-of-a-bitch!" Juliette was laughing. "Antoine opened his trap?" she asked me.

"Mmmm. But she says she grilled him. And he said the

same thing. He said something about three ten-ounce martinis."

"That's a good one. And it's just like your mother. Really, I don't think you should be mad at Antoine. If he and your mother both say she basely bribed him with alcohol, it sounds more than plausible to me."

"Yeah, I know… but don't you think it's just a little strange? That Antoine and I had that particular conversation and one week later he ended up at my mother's?"

"Oh, I don't know." She started putting on her coat. "It doesn't really surprise me, if you want my opinion."

"Hmmm." I glanced at my plate, looking for a little piece of cheese, but there wasn't any left. "Maybe you're right," I said. "Maybe I'm seeing cause and effect where there's nothing but coincidences."

"That could be part of it, it's true. It's just that Antoine is territorial, too." She got up. "But he was still honest enough to admit it bothered him that you weren't single anymore."

"Yessss. That's what surprised me. It's not like him to be introspective or admit his little character flaws."

"Ah, he's growing up. On the other hand, if I were you, I'd watch out: he might just start peeing all around you or your apartment."

We both laughed, and we left the restaurant. The air was cool and damp, and I wrapped my arms and my coat tighter around myself.

"Fall's here, eh?"

"Yep." We gave each other an amused look. Every time the season changed, we had the same unending conversation about the temperature.

"It's like there's a bit of a north wind," said Juliette.

"Yep, feels like winter."

"Oh, but we've still got some nice days on tap."

"That's for sure."

"Still, every year, we say the cold weather comes too early."

"Every year."

We turned down rue Notre Dame, where a wind that didn't feel exactly like winter was still blowing. "Seriously," I said, "I hope it'll be nice for Mom's birthday. You remember three years ago? We celebrated on October 6th and we ate outside."

"Yeah, it was cool. Antoine went through the screen door..."

"Ha! That was pretty funny. I think it took him a minute to figure out what had happened." It was like a scene out of *Drôle de video*: Antoine was sitting near the French doors, balancing on the back legs of his chair, with a glass of champagne in one hand. I was talking to someone when I heard a big ripping noise – when I turned around, all I saw was Antoine's legs in the air, and then he was saying, "What happened? What just happened?" Stéphane, my sister's husband, was laughing so hard he almost choked.

"Why did you keep saying 'ew' before?" Juliette asked me.

"Hmm?"

"When you were talking to your mother, you were saying, 'ew.' What was that for?"

"Oh! Ew! She was telling me about her sex life. She said, and I quote, 'Your father is an amazing lover.' Jeez!"

"Oh, come on," said Juliette. "It's cute!"

"Please. Would you like it, if your parents told you all about their sex life?" Juliette looked at me with raised eyebrows. Her parents had had her later in life – her mother was now almost seventy and her father almost eighty, and, since a recent accident, he'd been in a wheelchair.

"Okay, yeah, it's not the same," I continued. "But you know what I mean."

"Yeah, but your parents are young," said Juliette. "And

they're cute, together. They give each other kisses, they snuggle. When I met them the first time, I thought they were a little weird. Parents who snuggle? It was beyond me. But now I think it's cool. You should consider yourself lucky."

"Okay, but I don't need to know that, on top of everything, they're doing it. It's... no. Really? Ew."

"Okay, okay, okay." We'd arrived back at her place. "I won't ask you up," she said.

"No, I know... I'll call you to confirm when Mom's party's going to be. You'll come, won't you?"

"Yes, yes, of course." I gave her a kiss on each cheek, and when I was getting ready to leave she said, "Hey, Chloé? You really were saved by the *Macarena*, eh?"

"Oh, stop. No, it's just that... it makes me sad to say I don't love Antoine anymore. It's something that was part of me for a long time. Even after I stopped dreaming about him, it was still kind of there. He was... I'd convinced myself I didn't really believe in love, you know, but my fantasy of love was Antoine. So, telling you I don't love him anymore makes me feel weird. It's like you said, deep down, things have changed forever. Life goes on."

"So, you don't love him anymore?" I looked at the ground. I wondered why she was insisting so much on this question. I felt like answering something stupid like, "I'll always love Antoine," but it wouldn't have been true. I thought about Simon, his apartment, his voice and his body, his laugh, when he was repeating, "*Mais qu'est-ce que c'est que cette matière? C'est de la merde?*" from *Le Père Noël est une ordure*, and I answered, "No, I don't love him anymore. Not like before."

She slowly nodded her head and she went inside, without my being able to determine if my answer made her happy or sad. Personally, I was surprised, surprised and sad at finally admitting it, and I went back towards rue Notre Dame, my arms wrapped around me.

On the way home, in the taxi, I called Daphné. She answered right away, in a soft, tired voice I wasn't familiar with.

"Daphné? It's Chloé."

"Oh, hi, Chloé."

"How are you?"

"Okay."

"Daphné, Mom told me you weren't feeling well."

"What? Oh, come on, since when do you believe what Mom says?"

"Well, um, since forever. No matter what we say, her instinct is never off. So, what's wrong?"

"I told you, nothing!"

"Well, I'm telling you that, I have a pretty good instinct, too, when it comes to knowing how my sister is."

"I'm just tired, that's all. I can tell neither of you has twins. I'm tired. All I do with my life is take care of my girls…"

"Of course, my love. It's normal. You take on so much, Daphné, always wanting your life and family to be perfect."

"My life isn't perfect."

"Come on now, Daphné! You have a wonderful family, a handsome husband, a beautiful house!"

"But I'm a slave to all that! Shit, Chloé. Sometimes… sometimes, I'm jealous, I'm so jealous of how you live, you don't even know, it makes me cringe." My mouth dropped open. It was the first time she'd ever admitted I could have something she wanted. And it wasn't a doll, or a skirt or a later curfew – it was "how I live." She'd said it sincerely, without the little hint of scorn she usually slipped into that kind of remark.

"Daphné. Really. You're just tired."

"No…" She paused. I couldn't hear anything, not even her breathing, on the other end of the line. After a few seconds, I understood she was crying.

"Dadi!" I hadn't called her Dadi for at least ten years.

And, I thought to myself, she hadn't cried in front of me in just as long.

"Come on, what's wrong, Dadi? You're not just tired, I know."

"Oh, Chloé!"

She was sobbing.

"It's awful!"

"What? What is it?" A long shudder went through me. Could something have happened to one of the twins? No, that was impossible. Daphné would certainly not have tried to convince me nothing was wrong. I thought for a few seconds, and then I shouted, "Oh my God, Stéphane didn't leave, did he?"

"No… but…" It suddenly occurred to me that Daphné didn't have any friends, except the other moms in her neighbourhood she sometimes went for walks with.

"Chloé?"

"What?"

"Can I come over tonight? It hurts so much."

"What is it?"

"I'd rather tell you about it in person, okay?"

"Of course, of course. Come whenever you want. I'm just getting home now. I'll be waiting for you."

"Okay."

She hung up without saying another word. I ran up the stairs four at a time, and I went into the apartment wondering if I should call my mother right away. Then, I thought, no, whatever it was, it was obvious Daphné didn't want to talk to anybody else about it. I sat on the couch and started tapping my foot. Even if Daphné left right then, it would be at least a half-hour before she arrived. I was reaching for a book, when the phone rang – of course, it was my mother.

Chapter 12

I looked at the call display for a few seconds before I decided to answer. Then, it occurred to me that if I didn't, my mother might give me the cold shoulder, and that was always a long and painful process, so I picked up the phone.

"Yes, Mom!" If I managed things right, I might be able to make her believe that I hadn't talked to Daphné, and also get off the phone before my sister showed up.

"Well, I'm calling you since you didn't call me back."

"Mom…" I sighed in exasperation. "I was waiting till I got home. I just got in." I was happy: it was the truth. So far, I hadn't had to lie to her. Given that, ninety-nine percent of the time, any lies, even little white lies, that I told my mother always came back to bite me, and I was very conscious of the need to keep the damage to a minimum – my future serenity depended on it.

"So?" she asked. "Did you talk to your sister?"

"Mom, I just told you I just got home." Technically, I still hadn't lied.

"Okay, but try to call her tonight. Chloé, I talked to her twice this week and she seemed really upset. In my mind, I could hear Daphné's faint voice saying, "It's awful."

"Maybe she's just tired," I offered.

"No. No, no, no. I can feel these things."

"Yes, I know."

"I can feel it when my daughters are hiding things from me." I gritted my teeth: was she doing it on purpose? Did she suspect something? It was exhausting.

"And," she went on, "every time I told her that I could feel something wasn't right, she'd say, 'Come on now.' But she didn't get mad. And you know your sister, that was very suspicious."

"That's true." My sister was the kind of person who couldn't stand people asking how she was. When we really insisted, she'd curtly answer, "Why are you asking me that?"

"I'd like it if you called her, Chloé."

"I promise."

"Today?"

"Um, hmm, I don't know, Mom, Simon's coming over." I smiled despite myself: that was a good one. Not only had I just come up with an alibi for not calling Daphné right away, it was also the perfect excuse for hanging up soon.

"Simon?" my mother asked.

"Yeah, you know, Mom. The new…" I hesitated before I said it out loud. It was like a magic word, a word which, as soon as it was uttered to my mother, could never be taken back. "…the new boyfriend."

"Oh! Ohhh!" She seemed curious and amused. "Will you please tell me why you didn't tell us about him?"

"Oh, I don't know, I know it wasn't nice, but… I just wanted to wait a little, you know. To be sure. I felt like, if I talked about him, I was going to jinx it all."

My mother laughed at the other end of the line. "I understand, sweetie. I'm like that, too. Listen, if you're happy, I'm glad for you. Can I ask what he's like, if it's not too much?"

"It's okay. He's nice, he's sweet as anything, he's smart… " I realized I was smiling as I was talking. "For the moment, it seems like he's everything a girl could want."

"Here's hoping it lasts!"

"Yes, here's hoping it lasts! But it seems it's on the right track to last. I think it is. I hope it is." I didn't want to go too far. It was too fragile, too precious; I didn't want to make this barely opened blossom close back up with words that were too sudden, too presumptuous. It had to be cared for, fed, gently coaxed out with the proper, discreet attention. I remembered my conversation with Marcus, and the strange yet pleasant modesty that inhabited me when it was time to share certain details.

"Is he handsome?" asked my mother.

"Oh, is he ever! Mmmm... He's blond, with blue eyes, he's... oh! But, Mom, you know who it is!"

"What do you mean?"

"Because! Daddy told on you!"

"Told on me about what?"

"My diary! You read my diary when I was younger."

"Oh! He told you that!"

"Yes, he did."

"Oh, but Chloé, you were so young. It was harmless. All mothers do that, you know, so they can know their daughters better."

"If you say so." It was unusual, and quite amusing – my mother seemed uncomfortable.

"It doesn't matter," I said. "It doesn't matter." To tell the truth, I was almost happy she'd read it, because it gave us the chance to talk more about Simon, to bring it back to that time, to create a beginning for us.

"You remember," I went on. "In my diary, I was always talking about a boy."

"Oh, yes! Yes! What was his name again? His name was Slavic or something."

"Markovic. His name is Simon Markovic."

"Of course!" My mother was delighted, and as excited as a teenager. "I can't believe it! How funny! Tell me every-thing!"

So I told her. I was happy and proud of having someone to describe to my mother, someone nice, handsome and smart, and who seemed to like me.

"And his restaurant?" my mother asked. "Is it good?"

"It's fan.tas.tic."

"You should tell us where it is. I'll go with your father."

"Yes, yes, I'll tell you." I imagined my parents showing

up in Simon's restaurant – my mother shouting, "Where's the young man who's giving my daughter goosebumps?" and my father, visiting the kitchen, going "Mhhmm, mhhmm, verrrry interesting… What's that there? A blast furnace?…" and I felt a little sick.

"We'll go together, Mom."

"Oh, yes! Yes! It'll be great!"

"But before that, we have to think about your birthday party. I'll talk to Daphné about it. What day would work for you?"

"Whenever you want, whenever you want. For me, the Friday after my birthday would be perfect. Check with Daphné though, because of her husband's schedule. Sometimes he's at the hospital until late on Friday nights. You check with her. And Chlóe?"

"What?"

"Will you bring Simon to meet us?"

"Oh… I don't know, Mom… We've never invited other people to these parties…"

"But, sweetie, don't be ridiculous! If he's your boyfriend, he's welcome, of course! And Antoine told me he's charming!"

"Antoine said that?" I had no idea why, but that made me mad.

"Yes, he really liked him."

"Well now." I felt like saying it wasn't any of Antoine's business. "That's good," I finally said.

"So?" my mother asked.

"So, what?"

"Are you going to bring him or not?"

"I'll see, Mom. Friday nights are a little complicated for him. That's a big night at the restaurant. But listen, I'll see."

"Promise you'll put a little pressure on him?" In my mother's language, a little pressure meant threats that approached the limits of legality.

"Yes, Mom. I'll put a little pressure on him." I answered with a smile. At the same instant, the doorbell rang.

"I have to go, Mom! It's Simon."

"Ooh! Have fun, sweetie! Don't do anything I wouldn't do!"

"Yeah, yeah!"

"And, Chloé, you'll call me as soon as you talk to your sister?"

"Yes, Mom. Love you! Bye!"

I threw the phone down on the couch and ran towards the door. I barely had time to congratulate myself on the way I'd handled that situation, and to think that a new boyfriend was really a wonderful diversionary tool, when I found myself face to face with my sister, who was looking at me in silence, with eyes that had darker rings than ever.

She was standing in the doorway, in a little beige dress, and a jean jacket, and worn, flat sandals that seemed inappropriate for a cool, rainy day.

"Aren't you cold?" I stupidly asked.

She shrugged and simply stepped around me to get into the apartment. I followed her into the living room: she was standing there in the middle of it, with her back to me.

"Daphné?" She slowly turned to face me, still not saying anything, with an expression that was so sad I almost started to cry, myself. Indeed, she looked desperate – and weak.

I walked towards her, and asked, in an imploring voice that even surprised me, "What's wrong?" Then I saw her chin start to tremble, and I rushed over to her. She dropped her purse and threw herself into my arms, and we both fell onto the couch – I was holding her tight, and I didn't understand what we were doing, my sister was sobbing, and I didn't know what was wrong, but I was crying too, because I could never keep from crying when I saw her cry.

After a few minutes, I took her by the shoulders and gently shook her.

"Okay. That's enough now. What's going on, Daphné? You're scaring me."

She looked at me for a moment. Her eyes were red and

swollen, her nose was running and strands of hair were stuck to her cheeks, soaked with tears. She opened her mouth, and then she smiled. I was staring at her, speechless, and I truly did not understand anything that was happening.

"Why are you smiling?"

"Because you're crying…"

I ran a hand under my nose, and I smiled, too: "You know I always cry when you cry." That made her laugh a little, a sad, memory-filled laugh. She slowly ran her hands under her eyes, and took a deep breath. "Okay," she said in a decided tone. Daphné had never been able to let herself go for very long.

"Okay. Well…" she breathed again. "Well, I'm pregnant."

I was sitting opposite her, my eyes still full of tears, and I was completely taken aback. "Okayyyy…" I was sure she wanted more children, she'd said so herself. For a few seconds, I thought maybe it was just hormones and that, after all, everything was okay.

"Um… you're pregnant?…" I finally asked, motioning for her to go on.

"Yes."

"And is that… a good thing?"

"Yes… no… I don't know!" And she started to cry again, and then stopped right away. What control, I thought. Really.

"Daphné," I said. "You're going to have to explain it to me. Because, right now, I'm not sure I follow you."

"Stéphane doesn't want any more children," she answered, so quickly, it sounded like a single word, some kind of magic formula – "stéfanduzntwantanimorchildren."

"But wait," I said, "the other night, at your place, he said, yes, he'd like that someday."

"I know," she was holding her throat with one hand, as if she wanted to block her sobs. "But when I told him I was pregnant…"

"First of all, when did you find out?"

"A week after the party at my house, when you came with Mom and Dad, and we ate merguez sausages in the yard. So I told him, and at first he seemed disappointed. Then he said he was sorry, and said, 'It's just that it's a little soon, the twins aren't even two yet.' And, well, I agreed. I think it's a little soon, too. And then we didn't say anything more about it, but then last week, he came to me and said – at least he was honest, we have to give him that! – he was sorry about how he'd acted, but he was really worried, he was afraid he couldn't do it, and he was panicking and... oh, you should have seen him, Chloé, he was crying and calling himself every name in the book..."

"But what did you say? What are you going to do?"

"At the time, I tried to reassure him – I mean, he was really panicking. But I was mad, Chloé, I was thinking that really I'm the one who does everything anyway, I'm the one who takes care of the kids, I'm the one who gave up the possibility of a career... Anyway. We talked for a long time, and, of course, he said it was my decision, but well... and then I thought about it more and more..." This time she couldn't keep from sobbing, and she started to cry again, holding her head in her hands.

"Oh, Chloé! I'm not sure I'm capable of having another child either!"

"What do you mean, not capable?" I felt like I was thousands of kilometres away from Daphné. Her problems were serious and complex – it was a question of life, morality and heavy responsibilities. Mine were simple and light – they were made up of frequent daydreams and charming desires.

"I'm tired, Chloé. Totally exhausted! The twins, you know... sometimes, it seems like it's so much work, I realize I think of my daughters more as a full-time job than my family. Do you get it? I spend so much time looking after them, I hardly have time to love them."

"Oh, Dadi..." I looked at her, and thought, this is my little sister, after all, my little sister, who's only twenty-six. Sometimes, every once in a while, I could still see the little girl inside the woman, the mother, the wife. She placed one hand on her belly, and I thought about what was there – this child who already seemed so heavy and fragile.

"So, you can imagine," Daphné went on, "a third child. If Stéphane had been excited by the idea, I'm just saying, maybe I would have found the energy somewhere, but now… every time I think about it, I feel dizzy."

"But what are you going to do?" I'd almost said, "Are you going to get an abortion?" In my head, I knew, it was simpler. I couldn't understand. Despite my best effort, I couldn't grasp that it was an impossible decision to make. A sudden wave of stupid satisfaction at the fact that I didn't have to understand washed over me. I was far from all this, protected from this very sad, serious moment. I could still be carefree.

"That's just it," said Daphné. She wasn't sobbing anymore, but tears were still streaming from her big, black eyes. "That's it. I beat myself up every day. Every day. I feel like such an idiot! Such an idiot for letting it happen! Can you believe it! We stopped being careful six months ago. I just thought, if it happens, it happens. And now I realize, maybe it shouldn't have happened…" She was having trouble saying certain words, as if they were sacrilegious, so she said them in a very low voice. "But what am I going to do?"

I looked at her, sad and stunned – she knew as well as I did that I had neither the expertise nor the right to answer.

"I can't have an abortion," she finally said.

"Why?" I dared.

"I can't," said Daphné. "I just can't. I may have gone to plenty of pro-choice rallies, but I can't. I can't!" She repeated, "I can't!" a few more times, rubbing her eyes and crying.

"Oh, my God…" I took her hand, and I didn't say anything else. No matter how you looked at it, it was a no-win situation – in fact, I already knew she'd keep her baby. She did, too, really. But she was going to do so without joy, at least in the beginning – I wanted to believe that she'd eventually find some joy in it, in her belly as it swelled, in the tiny body of the child she would, of course, love in the end.

So, since the unnecessary still seemed appropriate to me, I said, "It'll be all right. It'll be all right. You want a drink?"

She looked up at me; this time, a little smile was playing around the edges of her mouth. "You're unbelievable, you know that?"

"Oh! Oh, oops! Sorry." I slapped my forehead. "No, sorry, I'm ridiculous. You're pregnant. Obviously. But, um…"

"Of course, go make yourself one."

"Do you want something? Juice? Water?"

"What have you got?"

I thought about the contents of my refrigerator for a second. I had cranberry juice, to make Cosmopolitans, pink grapefruit juice to make Salty Dogs, Clamato for Bloody Caesars, and Gatorade for the mornings after.

"Cranberry, pink grapefruit, Clamato," I answered. "Or Gatorade." Daphné smiled. "I'll have a Virgin Caesar."

I went to the kitchen, cursing my stupidity, and wondering what Marcus would have said – he always knew what to say, he had words full of compassion and understanding, words that are like soothing lotion. He'd ask her questions, I thought. Marcus always asked sad people questions. He made them talk about what was hurting them; he forced them to know it, to tame it.

So, when I went back into the living room, with a Virgin Caesar in one hand and a Bloody Caesar in the other, I sat right up against Daphné, who was pensively petting Ursule, and I simply asked her how she felt.

"What?" she answered. "Well… well, I really don't know. Not very good, that's for sure."

"The first word that comes to mind."

"Guilty," said Daphné. "Terribly guilty." Then, she added,

"And confused. I don't know what I want, Chloé. And that doesn't happen to me very often – we both know that."

"Yes, I do know that." And we both smiled.

"Oh, and on top of everything, it doesn't make sense!" she went on. "For the last week, I've been racking my brain, I've been making lists of the pros and cons, and…"

"What's on your lists?"

"I brought one with me. If you don't mind." She leaned towards her purse, and as she removed a neatly folded paper, I felt an uncontrollable wave of affection, and a desire to protect her – something I'd repressed for a long time.

"Here," she said. "You'll definitely think it's stupid, but that's what I came up with."

There were two columns on the sheet, separated by a long line she'd drawn with a ruler. I couldn't keep from smiling. Daphné, my little sister whose school notebooks had always been flawless, and who was still taking the time to use a ruler to make up a list she'd had to write in a moment of distress.

On one side, she'd listed the cons:
- Stéphane doesn't want any more children.
- I'm tired.
- I already have my hands full with the twins.
- The timing is bad (too soon).
- It feels like I'm making a mistake.
- I'm afraid I'll become a bad mother if I have another child.

Then, on the right said, were the pros:
- A baby.

I looked at the paper and pointed at "a baby." "Is that all?" I asked Daphné. Her voice cracked when she said, "I couldn't think of anything else."

"But, at the same time, there's no doubt 'a baby' is a lot."

"I know." She was still petting Ursule, who had rolled over on her back and was purring like a little motor.

"Daphné…" I stopped. I felt stupid and awkward. "Why did you say you can't get an abortion?"

"Because…" She shook one hand, like an Italian caricature. "It's psychological. I mean, I already know I can't do it, just like I couldn't have my arm pulled off. It's not a question of morality or ethics. No, morally, I don't have a problem with it. That's the ironic part. But anyway… I don't know if I *want* to have one either. Yesterday morning, I was in a good mood, I was giving the twins their breakfast, and I was imagining them, at two and a half, with their little brother or sister, and I thought, 'If we hired someone three or four days a week, it could work,' and you see, I imaged my baby, and I thought about how nice it would be to breastfeed again."

"Oh, boy…"

"I know! You can say that again! It's a no-win situation! See, when I talk about it like this, I get all mushy and I think, 'Okay, I'll keep it,' and I'm very happy for, what, four minutes. Then I think about it some more, and I see Stéphane wandering around the house looking pitiful and mopey, and I think, it makes no sense. No sense, Chloé. If I wanted this baby with all my heart, I'd tell Stéphane too bad, and I'd have it. But… I understand why he's panicking at the idea of having another one, shit, I'm panicking, too."

She started to laugh, "It's ridiculous! Completely ridiculous! And I think to myself that if I really didn't want it, I wouldn't have such a visceral hesitation at getting an abortion. And I would have asked you to put at least eight ounces of vodka in my drink."

I laughed, too. "Talking about it makes me feel better," she said.

"But I'm such an idiot, Daphné, I really don't know what to tell you."

"No, just talking about it. Just listening to me. For weeks, I've been on my own, thinking about it – I don't dare talk to Stéphane, he looks so helpless it drives me insane."

"Mom thinks something's going on."

"Oh, I know! She called me twice this week, and I tried my best to act normal, but you know her…"

"Why didn't you talk to her about it?"

"Just like that, on the phone? No, I couldn't do it. And I wanted to talk to you about it first."

"Me?" I felt proud.

"Of course," said Daphné. "You know, with the girls, I don't see my friends much anymore. And anyway, you've always been the person I felt closest to."

"Me?" I felt flattered, but also a little ill at ease: I didn't feel close to Daphné at all. At least, not in years and years. At one time we'd been close – sisters, really – but time had passed. Today, I knew my friends better than my own sister. I loved her, a lot, but I felt there was a distance between us. I looked at Daphné and I had nothing to reply. She'd become serious, she'd pulled back, curled up on herself. One day, I'd stopped making her laugh, and she'd started locking her bedroom door. I kept it up for a while, I remember, and then I gave up. I must have been fourteen, Daphné barely twelve.

There had been another time, too, in the courtyard of our secondary school, where Daphné had come to see me – she'd just started her first year and didn't know anybody. I'd curtly told her to go away because I didn't want to be seen hanging around with little kids. She'd turned around, and didn't say a word to me for a month. When my parents tried to reason with her she said, "She's the one who doesn't want to talk to me." But she never told them about what had happened at school – a gesture that baffled me completely and that I was unable to understand. I didn't say anything about it either; I was sad, and mad at myself, but I was too proud to apologize.

After a while she'd started talking to me again, but never like before. Our relationship was civil, cordial and automatic. I'd go into her room, tell her about the boys in my class, she'd answer, but without any real enthusiasm. Sometimes, she'd tell me about her dreams (she wanted to be a lawyer or a gymnast) and her (very rare) crushes, and I'd listen. We'd watch *Lance et Compte* together, eating Duncan Hines cake mix that I'd barely baked, which drove our mother nuts, but delighted us, especially when our father came and stole a few mouthfuls. I loaned her dresses, and she'd try them on secretly in her room, without ever letting us see how they looked.

These were all far-off, very distant memories. I often thought that if Daphné hadn't been my sister, I wouldn't have had any kind of relationship with her. Not because I didn't like her, just because we weren't made to have a relationship. That's the way I interpreted things – two people linked by genetic chance, two people that didn't know how to know each other.

That's why I repeated, in a tone I hoped would seem pretty harmless, "Me? I'm the person you feel closest to?"

"Yes, you. I know you have friends and all, and plus I'm not very demonstrative, but… you're my big sister." The little girl again came surreptitiously to the surface.

"Anyway," she said. "That's why I wanted to talk to you before I talked to Mom. She's always so intense about this kind of stuff. You're so cool. Although it is pretty hard to be cooler than Mom…"

I laughed. "Yes, that's true. But, speaking of Mom, what am I going to tell her? She won't leave me alone."

"Yeah… do you think you could keep it secret? At least until I make my decision?"

I took a big drink of my Bloody Caesar. I liked vodka and its gentle effects. I felt a little soft and honest. "Daphné, honestly, haven't you already made your decision?"

She lowered her eyes. "Until I'm less confused, then. I can't face Mom with all this doubt and worry, Chloé. It would be too hard."

I took her by the arm. "I know exactly what you mean.

Not. A. Word." Then I thought about our mother: "Anyway, I'll try my best." Daphné laughed. She knew what I meant.

"Oh, by the way," she added, "when Mom called me this week, she wanted to talk about your b-o-y-f-r-i-e-n-d."

I smiled widely. "My b-o-y-f-r-i-e-n-d, eh?"

When we were younger, Daphné and I had thought *boyfriend* was a fascinating, terrifying word that should only be uttered when necessary. The rest of the time, we talked about our b-o-y-f-r-i-e-n-d-s, as in, "The guy you went out with yesterday, is that your b-o-y-f-r-i-e-n-d?"

"Maybe. A potential b-o-y-f-r-i-e-n-d."

"So," said Daphné, "tell me about it!"

"No, no, there's nothing that exciting about it."

"Pardon? It's totally exciting! My big sister has a b-o-y-f-r-i-e-n-d! I haven't heard you use that word in twelve years!"

"Yeah, but, Dadi, you're not feeling well, and…"

"It would be very nice if you would get my mind off it for a minute or two."

"Okay, okay… It's Simon Markovic."

"No!" shouted Daphné, slapping her thighs. "I can't believe it. You must be so happy! You drove me nuts talking about him for what, three years?"

"At least."

She laughed, with her hands in front of her face, like a high school student. I wondered if, sometimes, she regretted growing up so fast.

"Well, tell me!" she said.

"Are you sure? When we were little, you hated it when I talked about him."

"Oh, no… I just wanted to look like I was in control of things. I don't know why I reacted like that. Maybe it's 'cause I was a little jealous that you looked like you were having so much more fun in life than I was. So, I said to myself, 'I'm going to be the superserious girl, the one all the adults will think is mature and interesting and wise beyond her years.' It was my way of being different. From Mom, as exuberant as she was, and from you."

"Really?" I was more than surprised. "You did a good job, Daphné, because I always thought you were wise beyond your years. A little too wise, in fact."

She shrugged. "I know. In fact, since I had the twins, I don't really need to pretend." A shadow passed over her face. "You must think I'm pretty boring, eh?" She asked me.

I looked at her for a moment, in her little beige dress, with the same "practical" haircut she'd had for years. I thought about when she was little, doing all her homework on the big dining-room table, and then helping my mother set the table as she said she didn't want to be interested in boys at least until she finished university. About her room, which was always tidy, with her books and her gymnastic trophies. She was so serious.

"No…" I answered. "But… but I don't understand you, Daphné. I have a hard time figuring out how someone can spend their whole life doing what's reasonable. Now, there's no doubt about it, you have the girls, you have responsibilities, but even before. Jeez, you were so reasonable!"

We didn't say anything for a few seconds. She was thinking about her baby, and so was I.

"So," said Daphné, after a little while. "What about Simon? Tell me about him, really. I'm going to go crazy if I don't think about something else."

"Okay, then, here goes…" The story was short, and, for the moment, relatively simple. But for Daphné's sake, I found details and comments, funny moments, and a bit of suspense. I could see she was happy, and I was thinking it was stupid just to be doing this now that we were grown-ups – well, at least she was, and I was, sort of.

"That's great," she said when I was done.

"Yeah, I'm happy. Really happy."

"You think he's the one?"

"Daphné, it hasn't even been a month!"

"Doesn't matter. You can feel that kind of thing. When I met Stéphane, I knew right away. And I never had a single doubt."

"Even now?"

"Yes, even now. So? Is your Simon the one?"

I made a little face. I'd never thought about what "the one" could be. The father of my children? The man I'd spend the rest of my life with? These ideas were completely beyond me. I just wanted love, after all. That was enough for the time being.

"Seriously, I don't know, Daphné. But when I think about him, I feel satisfied. I wouldn't want to be without him, and I wouldn't want to be with anyone else in the world."

"Nobody else?"

I looked around the living room, the rain falling outside, the purring Ursule. "No."

"Then he's the one," Daphné said.

"Stop it. I don't like those kinds of words."

"You'll get used to it…" She paused, and then started to laugh. "I sound like your old auntie!"

"No… just a young auntie." She laughed heartily and gave me a little tap on the arm.

"Oh, by the way," she added, "what are we doing for Mom's birthday?"

"Right… I was going to call you… the Friday after her birthday would be good for her."

Daphné counted on her fingers. "So that would fall on October 8th," she said. "Stéphane is only working during the day, so that would be perfect. Do we have a theme?" Every year, we organized the party around a more or less serious theme: Italian trattoria, Bordeaux banquet, *comida mexicana*, Thai cuisine, powwow (which, surprisingly, had been quite a success) or sugar shack (a monumental flop).

"I don't know," I said. "We'll have to see."

"Okay. But shall we book the eighth?"

"Yes. I'll call Dad tomorrow."

"And will Juliette and Antoine be able to make it?"

"Of course, no doubt about it. They wouldn't miss it for anything in the world."

"Good! I'm anxious to see them."

"Oh, come on, Daphné. You don't even like them." I was convinced that she wasn't at all fond of them. Antoine didn't help his case at all, he winked at her as he flirted with our mother, and Juliette and she had so little in common it had become a running gag.

"That's not true," Daphné said very seriously. "I like them a lot." I could see in her big eyes that she wasn't lying. Really, I thought, she'll never stop surprising me.

"Well, that's even better, then," I said. "That makes me happy." That was true. Daphné looked at her watch. "Oh, I'm going to have to go. Stéphane is all alone with the girls."

"And? You're always alone with the girls."

"Stop. I know, I know. But I have to go."

I didn't protest. Daphné hated it if anyone expressed an opinion on her relationship with her children and what my mother called "insane devotion."

"You going to be all right?" I asked her.

"Yes, yes." She was back to using the distant, energetic tone she always did.

"No, Daphné." I took her by the arm. "Really."

She sighed and looked me right in the eye before she answered. "It'll all work out okay, Chloé."

I hugged her. "Call me whenever you want, okay? Any time. I mean it." She smiled – I had obviously made her very happy.

"Call me if you need anything at all. Promise?"

"I swear."

"Cross your heart?"

"And all the rest." We hugged each other again. She was about to leave when she turned towards me, "By the way, you're bringing Simon to meet us, right?"

"When? Where?"

"To Mom's party, silly."

"Oh, I don't know…"

"Chloé, it's not open for discussion."

"I'll see… Mom mentioned it, too. If he's not working, okay."

"You know he'll work it out."

"Yessss, I suppose…" In fact, I was terrified at the idea of him meeting my family, and I couldn't accept the idea he was now going to be "one of us." And I was more than aware that my worry was ridiculous and childish.

"Yes," I sighed. "He'll be there."

Daphné smiled and hugged me around the waist. "It'll be a nice evening, Chloé. A really nice evening."

Chapter 13

When the day of Mom's birthday came, I wasn't at all sure anymore, I mean not at all, that we were going to have a "really nice evening." Everything was going fine, though. I'd been at my parents' since noon, and Daphné and I had been busy in the kitchen preparing the items on our "Moroccan Kasbah" menu. There had been a long debate concerning the nationality of the Kasbah: did it have to be specifically Moroccan? Couldn't it be Algerian or Tunisian? "But was the word *Kasbah* explicitly Moroccan?" my father had wondered. Since we didn't have any idea, we thought of maybe a Maghrebi Kasbah, then Daphné pointed out that our tagine recipe was typically Moroccan, so we'd simply come back full circle to the Moroccan Kasbah, and she promised to slap anyone who made any comments.

Daphné still hadn't "decided" anything yet, but I suspected she'd gotten used to the idea of another baby and had finally found some joy in the whole thing. Since she'd been to my house, we'd talked almost every day – something that hadn't happened since I'd moved out, ten years before already. She was still sad and fidgety, but I felt her soften little by little. The day before, we'd gone shopping together, and she'd been funny, almost light, two words I applied to her only rarely. I didn't say anything to her, but the last time I'd seen her like this was when she'd been pregnant with the twins.

The guests were supposed to arrive at around seven-thirty, and my mother at about eight. She always insisted on making an entrance. It wasn't seven o'clock yet, we'd set the table, the tagine was cooking, the dessert was ready, and there were only a few little things to finish up. My father had just opened a bottle of wine and poured me a glass – he was sipping his as he walked debonairly around the kitchen, lifting the lids off pots and, as a general rule, dipping a finger into everything he discovered.

I had no reason to be nervous. And I knew it. But what I really wanted to do was knock back my wine in one gulp and then throw myself voraciously on the bottle we were working on, before I opened another one. Once in a while, Daphné passed by and gave me a little pat on the head, saying, "Everything's going to be fine…" My father sat down at the kitchen table and asked, "But why wouldn't everything be fine, eh?" And I repeated to myself, "Exactly. Right. Why wouldn't everything be fine?" but I didn't believe a word I thought.

First, you had to consider my mother's agenda. I was not going to be able to make her keep believing Daphné hadn't wanted to tell me what was going on – the past two weeks, I'd heroically managed to keep her secret, but I was convinced that it was going to be totally, absolutely, undeniably impossible to keep up the act in front of her. I was clinging to a very faint hope that the presence of people from outside the family would keep her from making a scene, but I knew full well that after her third martini, she was going to pull me into a corner, look me straight in the eyes, and say, "Come on, spill it," leaving me the choice to either spill the item in question and thereby give rise to a most unpleasant scene (my mother freaking out, my father having no clue, Daphné crying, the twins screaming because their mother was crying, and Stéphane being held responsible for all the evils in the world); or, I could jump out the window.

Simon's impending arrival also had me terrorized – obviously he had gladly accepted the invitation, even if I had only asked him a few days before, after spending a long time thinking about not mentioning it to him at all and then telling my parents he was busy. He'd immediately offered to help us with dinner (he was so nice, an angel), but I'd refused. First, because I thought it was too much to ask so soon, and because, according to family tradition, Daphné and I had to prepare the meal on our own. It was one of those useless traditions that I clung to stubbornly, without knowing why – it seemed like not living up to it would have been an unforgivable sacrilege.

From time to time, I looked at the clock and thought, "There's still time." Maybe someone's going to call from the restaurant and tell him there'd been a catastrophe. Maybe his mother's going to call from Kingston because his father had an accident (nothing serious, of course – a temporary injury that would be completely healed by the next morning, a false alarm). Maybe he's going to call right now and tell me he has a terrible migraine, or an unbearable cramp in his left leg that's keeping him from walking (again, nothing serious, a passing problem whose only consequence would be keeping him from coming).

It was stupid of me – totally idiotic and childish. I had no reason to worry about Simon. My family and friends were marvellous. They were funny, spontaneous, amusing, entertaining, and as loveable as anything. And, obviously, they were going to love Simon. He was perfect. Honestly, I was in the middle of an amazing, progressive discovery of Simon's perfection. He was perfect. Absolutely perfect. It was intoxicating, and vaguely unsettling. He was funny, cultivated, curious, handsome, gentle and generous. He was good at making love. He liked to eat. He was interested in everything. He knew how to make me want him, he knew when to step away and when to be there, he knew how to give me little surprise gifts to make me fall even more for him. And, besides that – and it was as I noticed these details that I began to believe something was going on – he knew how to let himself go and do nothing.

Juliette, whom I had told about this perfection on the

phone, had said, "Maybe he's really an elf. Have you checked his ears?"

"What do you think? That's the first thing I did. They're not pointy."

"Hmmm. Maybe he had an operation. Wait till this winter. If he walks on top of the snow, you'll have your answer. Or else, get into a fight with him. If he fights with the grace of a dragonfly and the strength of a lion, you won't have to wonder anymore."

"Stop. I wouldn't even be surprised."

"Okay," said Juliette. "I have to go. I still have work to do. I'll see your Lothlórien prince at your parents' house."

The day before my mother's party, as we were quietly having dinner at his place, Simon had said, "I can't wait to meet your family." And, since I could tell Simon everything, and I felt perfectly comfortable with him, I'd answered, "I'm a little worried about it."

"Why?" Simon had asked, serving me more pasta.

"I don't know. All those people are so important to me, and... you, you are even more important to me than..." I had realized that there were still certain words that made me uncomfortable. I'd coughed, "You're the first person in my life to be as important as they are. This has never happened to me before."

He'd come closer and said, in an indefinable tone, "Chloé... I think I'm in love with you." Then he'd smiled, pulled back and added, "No, to tell the truth, I'm pretty sure."

I'd stopped eating – I was so disconcerted that I didn't know how to react. I took his hand and we just sat there, without speaking, with our fingers entwined. I hadn't said, "Me, too." I didn't want a "me too." I wanted my first "I love you" to be entirely mine.

And despite all that, barely two hours before he was due to arrive, I was completely nervous, so nervous in fact, I was

ELE GERMAIN

wondering if I was going to start smoking again. So I decided to go find Daphné, who was arranging flowers in the living room, so I could think of something else and put my problems in perspective.

She was sitting on one of the couches, placing flowers in a big crystal vase, and humming softly. I watched her for a few seconds; she pushed one lily in a micrometre, pulled another out a bit, imperceptibly spun a big red flower I didn't know the name of.

"Hey," she said when she saw me. "How's it going?"

"Okay, why?"

"Oh, I don't know, because you look nervous, maybe?" And she laid a long green leaf on the table. "Chloé. What are you afraid of, really? You know we're going to like him. Are you afraid we're going to make a bad impression?"

"No! No! My God. I'm not worried about that at all. So not worried."

"So, what's going on?"

I sat heavily down on the couch next to her, conscious of my selfishness and uselessness. Daphné was going through something dramatic that was frankly beyond my ability to understand, and I couldn't help but dwell on a worry that I had completely fabricated all by myself.

"I don't know..." I said. "It feels like bringing Simon here implies so much..." Daphné looked at me with a concern-filled expression, which actually reminded me of a mother listening to her young daughter's meaningless difficulties. It was, I thought, utterly appropriate.

"That's normal," she answered. "Jeez, it's the first time you've brought a boy home to meet your family. Except Antoine, but that's not the same."

"No, it's not the same." Nothing was ever the same with Antoine. He was unpredictable, and I was always proud of being one of the only people who could, occasionally, predict what he was going to do.

"I know what you're afraid of," said Daphné.

"What?"

"Promise you won't get mad."

"Why would I get mad?"

"Because what's bothering you is that if Simon comes here, it'll be the end of one era and the beginning of another. Part of you was still a teenager, Chloé, and…"

"Oh, come on! I'm twenty-eight years old, Daphné. Just because I don't have a house and a husband…"

"Hey! I said, 'Don't get mad.' *There* is a part of you that's very much a teenager. And that's the exact part I'm jealous of. Today, you're leaving something behind. It's not just your family, your friends and your life with no strings attached. Your circle is growing. And of course, it's a little nerve-racking."

I looked at my feet. "Shit, you make me sick."

"Pardon?"

"Because you're right, you pain. I'm really ridiculous, aren't I?"

"Oh, stop." She put her arm around my shoulders. I thought about Juliette, wanting time to stand still, and I felt almost nostalgic. Happy and nostalgic at the same time. I was twenty-eight years old and I'd just figured out that you always lose something when you move forward. Really, in my case, you could say, I'd heroically put off the fatal moment as long as possible. It was time, I said to myself.

Daphné rubbed my arm gently, "Come on, you little stinker." If she said something like, welcome to the grown-up world, I thought, I'm going to feed her those lilies one by one. But, all she added was, "Besides, if I know you, you're going to love having nostalgic little moments for 'how it was before.' It's really fun, it's sweet and it hurts just enough to let you wallow in self-pity… it's really great. I always thought it gave me a little buzz like alcohol, you know…"

I looked up at her, and, for the first time in my life, I said to her, "Daphné, you're incredible." I don't know if it was the fact that she had kids that had given her this new skill, but she'd managed to tell me the truth about myself without hurting my pride, and she taught me something without making me feel like an idiot.

She smiled – there was a joyful sparkle in her eyes – and, pretending to be condescending, she said, "Oh, it's nothing... you'll understand when you grow up."

I laughed, pushed against her with my shoulder, and said, "Get lost," though I was thinking she really was right.

At the same time, my father came into the living room and dropped down in his chair, sighing, "Oof! Now I'm done." Confused, Daphné and I looked at each other.

"Done with what, Dad?" I asked him.

"Wrapping my gift." He was holding some kind of block, wrapped in what looked like banana leaves, and on top was a spectacular multicoloured ball, with little coloured picks sticking out of it.

"What is that, exactly?" asked Daphné.

"Origami. You know, I did origami for a while." He pointed at the ball. "There are exactly eighty-three sheets there."

Daphné and I nodded, both looking way too impressed. "And the block?"

"I didn't really know what to do with that. So, I took the leaves from your bouquet, Daphné. I thought they went with the origami."

"That's right," I said, though I didn't believe it in the least. "And what's the gift that's inside?"

"The ball? It's empty."

"There's no gift?"

"Of course there is! The gift is up against the block."

There was a moment of silence. "And what is the gift?" I finally asked.

"Tickets to Vienna," Dad answered.

Daphné and I cooed in delight. "Oh that's so nice!" said Daphné. "For when?"

"For New Year's. We leave the day after Christmas."

"That's great," I said. "New Year's in Vienna. That must be so…"

"…sooooo romantic!" Daphné sighed. I remembered that when she was ten, she'd seen Sissi on TV and was then devoured by passion for her – for the next four Halloweens she'd even dressed as Sissi, in an old dress of my mother's, with an oversized crinoline sewn in underneath.

"Why don't you come with us?" our father asked her.

"Oh, no. How could I, with the girls."

"A week! I'm sure you could leave the girls with Stéphane's parents for a week."

I saw a shadow cross Daphné's face. "No. Really. It would be a dream, but no…"

"Come on, Daphné…"

"Dad! I said 'no'!" Her reply was a little too aggressive. My father shrugged his shoulders and said, "Okay. Your loss, then!" He hadn't noticed a thing. If Mom had been there, she would have already started her investigation.

"It's really a wonderful gift," I said, to create a bit of a diversion, even if no diversion was necessary for our father, since he could be distracted by a fly, a cloud or a gust of wind.

Dad smiled. "Yeah. I'm happy. We've never been to Vienna together. I can't wait." He looked like a dreamy young man. Daphné and I looked at each other, "Isn't he cute?" Daphné said.

"Yep, he's pretty cute, all right."

"Okay, that's enough," Dad said. "You're going to make your old Dad blush." He played with the knot on his tie and pointed a finger at me.

"Another drink, Chloé?"

"Of course."

"Daphné, come on, have one. The guests will be here in less than an hour." There was a moment of silence that seemed interminable to me, and I wondered how Daphné was going to justify not even having a glass of wine the whole night. At least she didn't usually drink a lot. If I was the one who had to try to hide a pregnancy at a party, there would have been a serious problem.

"Okay, I'll have one," Daphné finally said. Dad headed off towards the kitchen, and I turned towards her.

"What are you doing?" I whispered so softly I could hardly hear myself.

"What do you want me to do?" She was whispering, too, and I could see us, in my room, before we were even ten years old, when she'd sneak into my room after my parents had put us to bed – we'd whisper so we wouldn't get caught, but she always ended up falling asleep in my bed, which made all our efforts completely futile. We knew it, but there was something about whispering under my pink quilt that was so wonderful that we wouldn't have passed it up for anything in the world.

"Did you decide not to keep it?" I asked.

"No! I don't know! I don't know, and time is running out."

"Daphné!" I looked worriedly towards the kitchen door. "Don't be silly. I can see it in your face, you're very happy. I don't want to put words in your mouth, but it looks to me like you've already more or less made up your mind to..."

"I'm not ready yet. And Stéphane is still half-crazy."

"But you can't drink!"

"I know…" She said between clenched teeth. "But it's going to be damned suspicious if I keep refusing to have anything. And believe me, I don't want it coming out tonight."

"Lord, no."

"So I'm going to pretend. I'll just sip my drink. Even if I end up drinking half of it all night, it won't be the end of the world."

"But Mom will notice! Why don't you say you're taking antibiotics?" Daphné raised her eyebrows and gave me a look that said, "Are you serious?" I thought about our mother and I shook my head. "No," I said. "You're right, that doesn't make any sense. What are you going to do? Chuck your drinks out the window?"

"No. I'll finish them."

"How?"

"That's where you come in."

"Daphné, I can't finish your drinks on top of mine, I'll be dead drunk. Anyway, Mom would notice that, too."

She gave me a hangdog look. "Chloé…"

"But it's a completely stupid plan!"

"We can try…"

"I'll have to get Antoine in on it."

"Pardon?" she said out loud.

"Shhh… Antoine knows."

"WHAT?"

"Shut up…" The week before, I'd gone to see Antoine at his office to have what was supposed to be just one drink at the bistro across the street. The one drink had turned into at least ten, and we'd ranted till two in the morning like a couple of sorry cases. So the cat was out of the bag, and in quite spectacular fashion, I'd ended up telling Antoine everything, including my own editorial comments as an added bonus.

"Can you believe it?" I'd said to Antoine. Stéphane doesn't even look after the twins: Daphné's the one who does everything! He's talking about the financial implications!" I'd slammed my hand down on the table. "Financial implications, my ass! He's a doctor!"

"Maybe he's worried about other things," Antoine had said.

"Like what?"

"Christ, Chloé, bringing a child into the world isn't something to sneeze at! And he already has two on top of it!"

He motioned to the server to bring us two more drinks. "Don't get caught in the trap, Chloé."

"What trap?"

"Of immediately pointing a finger at people who don't want children. If it's a woman, you say it's not natural, when it's a man, it's because they're scared. Stéphane may have plenty with two, that's it. That's no reason to make him into a villain."

He leaned towards me, "Besides, do you want them?"

I didn't know what to say. The idea of having children had always been in the back of my mind: it was a simple, unavoidable fact – you went to school, you grew up, you got a job, you had kids. But it had never seemed real to me, and I'd never really tried to make it real either. "Someday," I'd say to myself, that was all, and it was enough. Like, "Someday, I'll have grey hair": it was such an obvious fact that I didn't even think about it anymore, except sometimes when I imagined myself as a strong, gentle mother with a little cherub in my arms, and a calm, angelic smile on my face. I could see myself, pregnant, in Pucci dresses, like Kate Moss on the Croisette in Cannes. (There were also a few scenes of family bliss involving Viggo Mortensen or Johnny Depp, or even a magnificent Afghan professor of French literature at Oxford – I auditioned more than one candidate.)

"I... yes," I'd finally said to Antoine. "I don't know. It's still too far off."

"You're not getting any younger."

"Hey! Take it easy!"

"You're twenty-eight, sweetheart."

"Exactly! I still have time."

"How old do you want to be when you have them?"

"I don't know... thirty."

Antoine nodded his head.

"That's only a year and a half away."

"Okay, thirty-two. Or thirty-four. I don't know, Antoine."

"Simon would make a good father."

I'd jumped. "Antoine, please. We've only been together

for two months." Then I tried to imagine Simon and me, smiling over a cradle. It wasn't unpleasant, but it was completely unreal.

"All I mean," Antoine had continued in a more instructional tone, "is that, if you want kids, you'd better make up your mind pretty soon." I'd replied with a shrill, drunken "I know!" He was right. I really did know it, but I'd never given it much attention, and it was an observation that really depressed me.

"No kidding," I'd said to Antoine. "You don't have to worry about that issue."

"What do you mean?" I was stunned. He'd smiled. "I don't know. I like kids."

"That doesn't have anything to do with it."

"No, I know."

"Antoine, to have kids, you need a girlfriend. And stability."

"Yeah, I've heard about that," he'd answered. Then he'd shook his head, "No, you're right. I suppose it's not right for me. Anyway..." He took a big drink of wine.

"Anyway, what?"

"Anyway," Antoine had said, "I don't think I'd ever have the courage."

"The courage?"

"Oh, come on, Chloé. At least I'm honest. If someone somewhere can say having a kid doesn't scare them, well, they're either crazy or a damned liar. Personally... " he gave a long whistle, "...it would terrify me."

I'd thought for a moment, and then I'd added, "Yeah. Me, too, to tell the truth."

On the couch, Daphné was still looking at me, with one hand on her face, looking totally devastated. "You told Antoine?" she repeated, at the edge of despair.

"Listen. I didn't want to tell you about it because I didn't want you to worry, but..."

"Because you didn't want me to worry? Christ, Chloé, Mom will finish him off in one bite!"

"Mom is certainly not about to start interrogating Antoine about your moods. If she decides to grill someone, it's going to be me. How could you even imagine she'd think he'd know?"

"Yeah… but, shit, Chloé, you know how he is when he's drunk!"

"If you tell him to keep his mouth shut, he's quieter than a grave."

She shot me a desperate look. "Oh, Christ, Chloé! Why did you have to go and tell him?"

"Oh, I know… I'm so sorry, but what's done is done. And *he can* drink your drinks on top of his own. And, he can also drink them without Mom noticing."

She nodded her head, looking doubtful.

"Believe me, Daphné. If there's one person who can do this, even drunk, it's Antoine."

Daphné put her head in her hands and made a sound that resembled a moan.

"Come on! Trust us!"

She looked up. "I don't have any choice, do I?"

"No choice about what?" asked my father as he came in with our drinks.

"Her bouquet!" I shouted. "Leaving it the way it is, since you took her leaves."

"Oh. Sorry," said Dad. "It's beautiful the way it is, sweetheart." He handed a glass to each of us. His eyes met mine for a second, and I thought I could see in them that he surely knew we hadn't been talking about flower arrangements. He was less gullible than he looked, I knew. But how much less? He smiled at me sweetly and I thought to myself, "If he thinks something's going on, he won't say a word. To anybody. Dear old Dad."

It was six-fifteen. No one was supposed to show up for another forty-five minutes, I was the only one already being devoured by worry. In fact, I was getting calmer and calmer, no doubt because Daphné was getting more and more nervous, and other people's nervousness has a strangely calming effect on me. From the magazine rack, Daphné picked up the previous week's expert crossword puzzle, which my father hadn't touched yet (since he'd become a verbicrucist, he'd remarked that Hannequart's puzzle had become much too easy for him and, indignantly, he refused to do it).

As Daphné focused all her attention on the puzzle and wildly tapped her right foot, my father was telling me about Vienna and its museums, which he'd seen, years before, when he'd visited with his mother, who'd always dreamed of seeing the Danube.

"It's a little selfish of me," he said. "I want to bring the love of my life where I first went with the woman who gave me life." He laughed dreamily. "Ideally, I'd have to bring you two as well. All the women in my life in Vienna. Wouldn't it be wonderful?"

"A fucking Swiss cheese!" shouted my sister.

"Pardon?" Speechless, we turned towards her.

"A Swiss cheese, in nine letters. The third one... no, the fourth is an *e*."

"Oh," I said. "Appenzell."

"What?"

"Appenzell. A-p-p-e-n-z-e-l-l."

Daphné bent over the puzzle and checked two or three things.

"How did you know that?" she asked.

"I did it on Saturday."

"Hmmm. Then you must know what the 'plant' is. I hate it when they put 'plant' or 'symbol' or 'mollusc.' Could they be any more vague?"

I was going to answer her, when someone knocked on the door. "Hmm," said my father. Someone's early." He got up to do open the door, and I was watching him, lovingly, when Daphné said, "Maybe it's Simon."

I jumped up, and I caught my father by the arm.
"Tututut! I'll get it!" I gave him a good push so he'd sit back
down. Not already, I thought to myself. Not already. At the
same time, maybe it would be better if he got there early,
discreetly, without anyone even noticing.

Needlessly, I pushed a rebellious lock of hair behind my
ear, and I opened the door.

It was Antoine.

"Oh, my God," I sighed. "Oh my God, am I ever happy
to see you." He was standing in the yard, with two bottles
of champagne in one hand, and, in the other, a nicely
wrapped potted flower. He smiled. "Ah, women always say
that!" I wasn't listening to him – I was thinking of Daphné,
and about how we were going to let him in on our scheme
as soon as possible. "You're early – you, the one who's
always late."

"Yeah, sorry…"

"No! No! It's great!" I took the bottles of champagne and
I put my other arm around him. "You have no idea how well
this is going to work out." I felt him give me a soft kiss on
the neck, and I closed my eyes for one second, two seconds,
then I raised my head and I motioned for him to wait before
he went in.

"Okay, listen carefully."

"What's going on?" He looked amused and a little disconcerted. I looked behind me, to make sure my father
wasn't there.

"Okay. You remember what I told you about Daphné?"

"Yes, yes, listen, no problem, I won't say a word, don't
worry."

"We're going to need your help."

"What?"

"Listen to me. Stop asking questions and listen: Daphné
can't drink, okay, because of the baby."

"So she's going to keep it?"

"Listen to me… No one knows. So, they can't notice

she's not drinking. And when we have the champagne toast, she won't be able to refuse, it would be too suspicious. So, she's going to slowly sip her drinks. But, from time to time, so my mother doesn't think anything's up, her glasses are going to have to be emptied."

"Okay…" It was obvious he still didn't know what I was talking about.

"Well, she can't spend the night running to the bathroom to dump them in the toilet. So, I'll sit you next to her and you can take care of her drinks."

He was looking at me, with a smile on his lips, without saying a word. "Are you kidding me?" he finally asked.

"Shit, Antoine…"

He started to silently laugh. "Unbelievable. It's unbelievable. That's the worst scheme on the planet."

"You have a better idea?"

"Yeah, Daphné just has to say she's taking antibiotics."

"Shit, Antoine, you know our mother; there's no way she'd swallow that excuse. Come on. She's already suspected something's up with Daphné for the last couple of weeks, and then Daphné suddenly shows with the old, 'Oh, I just have a urinary infection' excuse? Come on!"

"And you think we're going to manage to be passing drinks around right under her nose without her noticing I'm the one who's drinking them?"

"Antoiiiiiine!"

He was still laughing. "Okay, okay, I'll do it."

I wagged a finger under his nose. "Antoine, no one can notice."

"Nobody will notice. Now, do you think you could let me in?"

I turned around, and he followed me into the house. My father was standing between the living room and the entryway. "What took you so long, Chloé? You carrying on with your boyfriend?"

"No, it's Antoine. We were just talking."

Antoine stepped around me and set his gift on a little table.

"Hey!" my father said joyfully when he saw him. "Antoine! My boy!"

Antoine opened his arms, and shouted, "Mr. The-Fifth-of-March!" and they gave each other an exaggeratedly virile embrace. Antoine had lost his father in a car accident when he was only four, and he and his two sisters had been raised by a somewhat depressed mother who was often absent – which, in my opinion, explained his machismo and his relationships with women in general, as well as a touching, unfailing affection for my father. On the other hand, my father often said it was nice to see "a real guy" once in a while, since he was always surrounded by women. Of course, that was a rather insulting remark to make as far as Daphné's husband was concerned, but it always made me very happy.

"Hey," said Antoine, stepping back and noticing Daphné. "How are you, beautiful?" Daphné got up and went to give him a kiss. She hated being called "beautiful" and I knew it. She kissed him and smiled, and I noticed, from the corner of my eye, that Antoine took her arm and said, "Everything will be fine." His back was to me, but I could see Daphné's face and her supremely doubtful look. They stayed like that for a moment, looking at each other, and I saw that Daphné was relaxing – she was starting to have confidence.

I knew how he must be looking at her. I knew Antoine's looks; the ones that were meant to be irresistible and the ones that really were, the ones that were supposed to be understanding and reassuring – it must have been one of those, when he looked at you with warmth and conviction and could make you believe anything, but, above all, that he was there, for you, and that everything would be all right, forever.

Slowly, Daphné's face relaxed. I couldn't get over it: he'd done it. He turned towards me and gave me the traditional wink.

"Wow, what's that?" he asked as he picked up my father's gift.

"That's Dad's gift," Daphné answered. "In fact, the gift is on the block. The ball is more a…"

"An expression of his creativity?" I offered.

"I was going to say an example of origami," said Daphné, "but that works, too."

"And what's on the block?" Antoine asked.

Daphné clasped her hands together and sighed, looking like a dreamy little girl: "Two tickets… to Vienna!"

"Oh…" said Antoine, turning towards Dad. "Excellent move."

"Yes," answered my father. "I think it'll get me a few points."

"That should get you two or three indulgences."

"At least three," said Dad, laughing. "Will you have a drink, my boy?"

"With pleasure."

My father didn't even have his back turned before Antoine was reaching for Daphné's glass. "To you, beautiful," he said, taking a good drink.

"Finish it," Daphné whispered.

"No, no. We have to go easy." He tapped a finger against his temple. "I know what to do with this kind of ridiculous plan. Leave it to me."

Daphné sighed, and she dug into the couch, looking resigned. I gave her a little pat on the shoulder.

"What did you bring in the flowerpot?" I asked Antoine.

"A Potinara Beaufort Gold."

"Pardon?"

Antoine raised one finger in the air and repeated, very clearly, "A Potinara Beaufort Gold. It's an orchid. A hybrid. Normally, it's an epiphyte, but you can grow them in pots, too. Flowers for three months. Very easy. Verrrrryyyy beautiful."

"Since when do you know anything about orchids?"

"Since I've been sleeping with a florist."

"I see… I should have figured it out."

"In fact, I planned to buy a cattleya. Because I know your mother likes Proust and she thinks she's Odette. But Julie…"

"Julie?"

"The florist."

"Oh."

"So, Julie told me that, for the most part, cattleyas are pretty common. So. One thing led to another… Ah! Thanks." He took the glass my father offered him and went on, "One thing led to another, so, and well, Julie turned out to be an excellent florist."

Daphné looked up at him, seeming slightly disgusted. "Do you sleep with all the salesclerks you meet?"

"Only if they're pretty."

"You're such a jerk, Antoine." And she went back to her crossword puzzle.

"You're sleeping with a florist," asked my father.

"Oh! Dad!" I shouted in unison with Daphné.

"What? I just want to find out, that's all!"

Antoine nodded yes, and they both clinked glasses, giving each other a knowing look.

"So?" said my father. "What about work?" They sat down together and started to talk and laugh very loudly, the way men do when they get together.

A little after seven, someone knocked on the door again. Daphné and I jumped at the same time. I was still nervous, but it wasn't the same pale, worrying nervousness from earlier. It was now a kind of excitement mixed with expectation and doubt: it was either going to be smooth sailing, or we were about to have an absolutely memorable evening.

I got up to go open the door, and I saw Antoine, standing next to Daphné, switch their glasses in a single quick, subtle movement. He raised the one in his hand in my direction and said, "Showtime."

Chapter 14

Later, Simon would tell me that if he hadn't already been in love with me, the night of my mother's birthday would have made him fall. That night, I'd seen him fall in love with my family and friends – he was like a thirsty man who finally got something to drink.

Fifteen minutes after Antoine, Stéphane arrived. When I'd opened the door, he was standing there with one twin in each arm – like always, I wondered how he managed to get around like that with two thirty-pound girls in his arms. On top of that, with two fingers of his right hand, he was holding a bag from the liquor store.

"Hey," he said to me. I could see he was uncomfortable. Of course he knew that Daphné and I had been talking for a few weeks, but he didn't know what had been said. Maybe he'd been portrayed as a heartless, career-oriented man who didn't understand anything about women. Perhaps I'd turned my sister against him.

"Hey!" I answered a little too casually – I didn't want him to think we were mad at him, or that I'd judged him. The situation was a lot more complex than that and, after all, it wasn't really my business. Not directly, at least.

He looked relieved, and gave me a big awkward smile.

"Give me that," I said, reaching for the bag, but the twin sitting on the same side immediately leaned towards me, with her arms open.

"Oh! Come here…" I looked at her for an instant – at her big, very blue eyes, like her daddy's, her pink cheeks, her tiny nose, and her little – eternally moist – mouth. I hadn't seen them in a month and, nonetheless, for the first time, it

felt like I recognized them. "…come here, Rosalie." I looked
up at Stéphane, and he nodded, looked impressed, and said,
"Bravo!" We smiled at each other, more naturally this time.

"I finally get it," I said. "Rosalie is the one who looks the
most like me."

Stéphane raised one eyebrow. "I don't want to hurt you,
Chloé, but I think they get their blue eyes from me, not
you."

"No, not the colour of their eyes… Look at her. Rosalie
is always smiling, just like her old aunt. Right, Rosalie?" It
was true – well, not that I always smiled, but Rosalie smiled
a lot more than her sister.

"You see?" I said to Stéphane, as the little one grabbed
my nose and laughed. "This child has a charming disposi-
tion. Just like me." Stéphane leaned towards me. "You sound
like your mother," he murmured, which made me laugh.

We went in, one behind the other, each of us with our
big, thirty-pound package (more like thirty-five, I thought)
in our arms. When she saw the girls, Daphné got right up
and came towards us, with a radiant smile on her face. I was
always a little jealous of the way mothers looked at their
children. I said to myself that even if I tried with all my
might, I'd never be able to copy it. It was something unique
and inimitable – you had to be part of the In-Group.
Daphné, my little sister, was part of that group.

With a nimble, flexible movement, she took Mya and lifted her into the air before she held her close, as I struggled
under Rosalie's weight, and I wondered who I could pass
her to. Stéphane shook my father's hand (formal, polite),
then Antoine's, and he said, "How are you?"

"Good," said Stéphane. "I just finished a ten-hour shift.
I'm a little beat."

"Hmmm…" sighed Antoine. "Operations?"

"No. Just routine. Colonoscopies. I had four patients
who…"

"Right!" said Antoine, raising one hand. "No need for details. Right. You want a glass of wine?"

"Please."

"Red? White?"

"Red," answered Stéphane, gazing anxiously towards Daphné. "But, honey, what are you…"

"Stéphane!" said Antoine. "Come choose the wine you want. There are lots of bottles."

"No, but…"

"No, really, go on," I said, giving him a little push.

It was ridiculous. We had no chance of getting through this elegantly. No chance at all. I sighed, muttered something like *alea jacta est* to myself, and finished my drink. If I wasn't going to be elegant, I may as well do it with panache.

My father was relieving me of my adorable burden when someone rang the doorbell again.

"It's your b-o-y-f-r-i-e-n-d," said Daphné, standing by the big window in the living room. Smiling, I rushed towards the door, and when I saw it was Simon, my nervousness evaporated and was transformed into sweet, solid confidence. He was wearing a turtleneck, something I always hated on men, but it looked fantastic on him, even if the colour was indefinable – I would have said it was something like ochre or burnt sienna – as I hugged him, I was thinking about the colouring crayons I had when I was little; they had names like "spring green" or "brick red," names that still came back to me today when I had to identify a colour.

He kissed me and, with one hand still in the small of my neck, said, "You okay?"

"I'm okay. You're here. You're not nervous?"

"No, why?"

"Because some people get nervous at the idea of meeting their… their in-laws."

"My in-laws, eh?" He was smiling.

"Come on," I said. "Come in."

Everyone was in the living room, except Daphné, who, I noticed, was in the kitchen, leaning over one of the pots. She looked up, noticed Simon, and her face opened up. She quickly came towards us, and I could see her again, that twenty-six-year-old little girl, excited about meeting her sister's new boyfriend.

My father was the first to step forward. He was holding a glass of wine against himself and he stretched out his other hand saying to Simon, "Delighted to meet you, Mr. Markovic. Really delighted."

My God, I thought. Don't let him start saying stupid things like, "It was about time Chloé brought a boy home to meet us." He said, "Did you know you're the first boy Chloé has ever deigned to introduce to us?" I rolled my eyes and I gave an exasperated sigh, exactly like a fifteen year old. "Daddyyyy…" Simon laughed and took my father's hand. "Really, Mr. Cinq-Mars, the pleasure is all mine." I saw Daphné, behind his shoulder, mouth the words "He's handsome."

"Simon," I said, placing a hand in the small of his back, "let me introduce my sister, Daphné. He smiled at her, took the hand she extended, and kissed her lightly on each cheek. Daphné cooed something, and I thought she was the one who should be with Simon, she deserved the perfect boy more than I did. For the last little while, I'd been feeling vaguely like an imposter when I thought of Simon and me – I was a joke, a girl of many faults, someone who was irremediably ordinary. I was unstable and changeable, like a weather vane or a stream; he was solid and upright – sometimes I thought of him as a beautiful tree, a strong, calm tree, in whose branches I was just a gust of wind or a flapping bird. Daphné, who was so serious and thoughtful, so attentive and conscious of other people, deserved someone like that. Anyway, I'd always thought that Daphné deserved more than I did, she worked so hard to accomplish what she

thought was right and fair, and all I did was wait. She planted, and I reaped.

"Wow," she whispered, as Simon introduced himself to
Stéphane. "He really looks like a great guy."

"Not bad, really. Not bad." I watched him and wondered
what I could have ever been worried about – as far as I could
see, he was comfortable, without being too casual. Antoine
approached him, looking happy, and they gave each other
a warm handshake. There they are, I thought. The two
prodigies everyone loves. It was the only thing they had in
common, and it wasn't insignificant. But, in everything else,
they were leagues apart from each other. If Simon was a
beautiful tree, Antoine was a flame – a big fire. I smiled at
the idea and I looked at them tenderly, until Antoine pointed a finger at Simon and said, "You need a glass of wine. I'll
go get you one."

"Oh," said Simon. "And I have this, too." He raised a red
bag that a champagne bottle was sticking out of.

"Give it to me," I said. "I'll put it in the fridge."

"There's a little something for your mother, too," he
added.

I reached into the bag and pulled out a small jar of
Russian caviar.

"I have contacts, because of the restaurant," explained
Simon, as if to imply it was no big deal.

"You're unbelievable," I said to him with a smile, before
I joined Antoine who was opening a bottle of white wine in
the kitchen. "We'll have to put some bottles in the freezer.
There aren't any cold ones left." He'd taken charge of the
situation and, oddly enough, this was completely reassuring.
I watched him for an instant – his eyes were lowered and I
could see the long black lashes I envied so much, the same
ones all women commented on when they met him for the
first time – it was their way of telling him they thought he
was handsome, without coming right out and saying so.

He looked up at me. "What?"

"Nothing." I thought about the fact that I couldn't conceive of a world without him. "Nothing," I repeated, and I put Simon's bottle in the freezer. The doorbell could be heard once again, and my father shouted, "I'll get it!"

It was Juliette. Behind the square of my father's shape (or I should say my father's mass – he hadn't had much of a shape for several decades now), I could make out her little beret. I shouted for joy, and I ran towards the entryway to give her a big hug. I'd only seen her once since the beginning of her "attack of creativity," and as I hugged her thin shoulders, I realized that I had missed her terribly.

"Did you finish?"

"All of it. It's all fucking finished."

"It's about time," said Antoine's voice from behind me. "Christ! A month and a half, Juliette! I was really getting bored!" He took her in his arms and lifted her slightly off the ground.

"You've lost weight!" he cried.

"You try painting sixteen hours a day and only eating bits of carrots and drinking coffee."

"Oh! The life of an artist!" said Antoine as he kissed her. She snuggled up against him and reached her arms towards me. "Shit, am I ever happy to see you two!" she sighed as she hugged us both tight. We were in the middle of the entryway, a little island that had been sufficient unto itself for quite some time. "Anyway," said Juliette, "tonight, I will not be living the life of an artist."

"When are you going to let us see it?" asked Antoine.

"Whenever you want."

"Tomorrow?"

"Tomorrow," answered Juliette. Then she noticed Daphné and went "Heeeyy!" as if they were the best friends in the world. They hugged each other (Daphné was a little surprised but happy, Juliette was contagiously cheerful) and Juliette turned towards Simon, who was chatting with Stéphane. "Hi," she said, extending her hand. "I'm Juliette."

"Finally!" Simon shouted. "I've heard so much about you!"

"Me, too!" said Juliette, giving him a little wink.

"Did I really see what I just saw?" whispered Antoine, leaning close to me.

"Yep."

"She winked at him."

"She winked at him," I repeated, and we both laughed: it had been literally years since Juliette had seemed to be in such a good mood.

"Oh, Chloé," she said as she turned back towards me. "Look what I found for your mother." From her backpack, she removed a frame wrapped in bubble wrap. "I didn't wrap it," she explained to my father and me, "I wanted you to see it first." She took off the bubble wrap and showed us the frame. It was the face of a woman, with long red hair; the painter had added flowers to it, and it was floating around her, as if she were lying in water. She was looking to the side at something we couldn't see. The painting was rather ugly, obviously done by an amateur. I was about to ask Juliette what it was, when Daphné cried out, "But... that's Mom!"

I stepped closer, and at the same time, my father and I said, "Son-of-a-bitch..." It was indeed my mother, at about the age of thirty. The resemblance was far from perfect, but it was there, and unmistakable once you'd noticed it.

"Where did it come from?" asked my father.

"You'll never believe me," said Juliette. "My friend Florent found it for me." Antoine and I exchanged a tired look: Florent was an unbearable prig, an unsuccessful artist who compensated for this by annoying everyone he met and whom Juliette liked, inexplicably.

"Don't make faces, you two," Juliette said to us. "I was at his place, and he was telling me about this guy he met at an opening, a kind of loser who shows up at all the openings for the free wine." (Antoine and I looked at each

other again, smiling this time: a few years ago, thanks to
Juliette's contacts, we used to do exactly the same thing.)
"So," Juliette continued, "this guy claimed he used to be a
pretty popular artist in the seventies, and he said he'd painted several celebrities, including the entire cast of *Le Grand
voyage.*"

"No way!" Daphné exclaimed. *Le Grand voyage* was the
TV series my mother had been in. It was also the source of
at least half of her stories.

"So," said Juliette, "I found the guy. He's sick. He lives in
a three-room apartment, surrounded by all his old stuff. He
couldn't understand why I would want to buy his painting.
Finally, I promised to invite him to my next opening, and
he agreed."

"How much?" Antoine asked.

"You won't believe that either."

"How much?"

"Seventy-five dollars."

"Seventy-five dollars!" my father exclaimed. "But that's
not much!"

"Mr. Cinq-Mars," Juliette said as she placed one hand on
his arm, "with all the respect I have for your wife... the
frame is worth more than the painting. And the frame is
worth about $3.95. But the price isn't what's important. I
thought that the sentimental value was pretty amazing."

"I mean it, kids," said my father. "You have a gift for finding incredible gifts."

"So do you," I added.

"What did you get her, sir?" Juliette asked.

"First of all," said Dad, "you're going to stop calling me
sir, young lady."

Juliette blushed: my father had told her that at least
twenty times, but she seemed physically unable. "What are
you giving her, Mr. Cinq-Mars?"

"A Christmas trip to Vienna."

"Oooh!" Juliette cooed. "The land of Sissi."

"I knoooowww!" my sister sighed. It appeared they had at least one thing in common.

"Let's go into the living room," I said, "we're standing around in the entry like a bunch of clowns; it's not very sophisticated." So we settled into the chairs and sofas – Daphné was on the floor, next to her daughters as they played with coloured rings; I was on a loveseat next to Simon; Juliette was on the rug, at Antoine's feet, as he and my father reigned over us from two grotesque leather armchairs. Like always, Stéphane was standing next to the fireplace, one arm casually leaning on the mantle, which was at my eye level. He looked like he belonged to another time, a time of drinking scotch slowly after getting home from work, a time of fedoras and big mahogany radios. He wasn't saying much, and I was thinking that he must be living with the weight of this as yet unmade decision, which wasn't his to make.

Juliette was in the middle of every conversation, something she couldn't stop apologizing for ("Oh, just tell me to be quiet, I must be a real pain, but I haven't seen anyone in month"). She wasn't a pain, she was funny and lively, and she was talking about art and Marcus, who woke her up when he came home to go to bed at six in the morning, by covering her with his feather boas.

"Marcus?" asked Simon.

"Oh, you have to meet Marcus," said Antoine.

"He's my flatmate," said Juliette. "He's Jamaican. A drag queen. Flashy and flamboyant."

"Flashy and flamboyant," repeated Simon, looking amused.

"Honestly," said Antoine. "I think those two words were invented just for him. He's…"

"An inspiration," I said.

"An inspiration?" asked Antoine.

"Hey! When I said I wanted to find love, he's the only one who encouraged me, I'll have you know. And I did the right thing listening to him instead of to you two."

Daphné gave a tender "ahhhh," and I placed a tiny kiss on Simon's hand, which was close to my face. It was the first time I'd done anything like that in front of my family and friends.

At eight-fifteen, we heard my mother's key in the lock. "She's unbelievable," said my father, "she knows it's not locked; she just did that so we'd know she's coming in." We were all looking towards the entryway, silent, like a bunch of idiots. She finally made her entrance (theatrical as always, she was in a long, sea blue kimono, its back and sleeves covered in complicated, colourful embroidery – it certainly was surprising, but it was also superb. And, as I'd suspected, she had been to the hair salon, and was looking like Zelda Fitzgerald. Out of the corner of my eye, I saw Simon, who seemed completely stunned – he probably would have been less surprised if Zelda herself had showed up in our living room).

"Surprise!" we all shouted, out of habit, even if it wasn't a surprise, and to give my mother the pleasure of saying, "Oh no! I don't believe it! Oh! You're so nice!" She suddenly stopped, brought one hand up to her cheek, and said, "Oh! You must be Simon!" Then she crossed the living room, came over to us, and, without even looking at me, took his hand. "Hello," said Simon. "Happy Birthday!" He was smiling in disbelief – I imagined he must have been thinking there was a camera hidden somewhere, and that we'd hired a crazy woman to play a prank on him.

"Thank you," replied my mother, who was giving him what was supposed to be a burning gaze. "You have wonderful eyes, you know."

"Mom," I said. "Could you wait two minutes before you try to start charming him?" She didn't even turn around.

"Where are you from again?" she asked Simon. "Your family is Serbian, no?"

Simon was still wearing the same smile – from what I could see, he couldn't quite get over it, but he was also enjoying the show. "My father's Croatian," he explained. "My mother is Irish."

"Mmmm," said my mother as if he'd been talking about *crème brulée* or chocolate fondant. Then, after a few seconds, her face was transformed: she changed from a nymphomaniac brothel owner into a warm mother. "I'm very happy you came, Simon. Welcome to our home!" She kissed him on each cheek, and then she gave me a long hug and whispered, "He's as handsome as an angel!" Then she turned around, with her eyes wide open, to greet everyone else.

"My God," Simon whispered in my ear.

"Yeah, I know... sorry..."

"No, really, she's extraordinary."

"That's true, she's sure not ordinary."

"How old is she?"

"Fifty-nine."

"Wow."

"Two facelifts."

"Oh." He watched her for a moment. "But it's not just that, though. She's got... a kind of energy... you're really lucky to have a mother like that."

I watched her. She'd open her arms, hug people tight, lean down to kiss the little ones. I even heard her whisper to Antoine, "You're still number one on my list," and I replied to Simon, "Yeah, I know." Then I asked, "What's your mother like?"

"My mother?" he said, as if I might have been talking about something completely different.

"Yes."

"Oh..." He looked at Mom. "She's just... sad."

"Sad?"

"Yes. My mother is sad." Then everyone started talking at the same time, and he seemed to forget about his mother.

For the first few hours, I thought that, contrary to all expectations, we'd manage to pull it off. We spent the first hours in the living room, drinking champagne and eating

the olives, baba ganoush and mouhamara that Daphné and
I had made and which we were exceedingly proud of. Mom
opened her presents, delighting in each one, giving little
shrieks when she saw the frame from Juliette, and immediately hugging her as if she'd just given her the moon, licking
her lips for what I thought was an unnecessarily long time
when she opened the caviar, and taking advantage of the situation to kiss Antoine on the mouth to thank him for the
orchid, a pink and orange explosion of petals whose shape
was somewhat erotic, which prompted me to say that Julie
must indeed be an excellent florist.

My father gave her his present last – she gingerly lifted
off the origami ball and placed it on the fireplace mantle,
then she slowly unwrapped the block. Finally, she noticed
what looked like an envelope, opened it and said, "Oh! My
God..." She went over to my father and sat on his lap, whispering, "My wonderful love..." Everyone was smiling wide,
we looked like a perfect, united family, an American
Christmas card – I wouldn't really have been surprised if
someone had started singing a carol.

This whole time, Antoine moved with ease around the
gifts and the chairs, serving champagne as soon as the glasses were even a quarter empty. From time to time, when my
mother wasn't looking, he'd take a big drink from Daphné's
glass. He was obviously enjoying himself, but Stéphane on
the other hand, who was attentively watching the whole circus, looked like he was on the verge of depression.

As I went back and forth between the kitchen and the living room, I could see him looking towards Daphné, pursing
his lips. He seemed angry with her, maybe because, unlike
him, she was having fun, or maybe because he never could
stand lies and secrets. I would have liked to talk to him, reassure him a bit, but I didn't know how to broach him. I was
afraid I'd attract my mother's attention to the situation –
and that was precarious enough as it was. On the phone, I'd
managed to heroically keep Daphné's secret, and she, too,

had pushed back a number of my mother's incursions, saying, "Nothing's wrong, I'm just really, really tired," but face
to face with my mother, I couldn't promise anything.

"If she comes to talk to me," I said to Daphné, "I don't
know if I'll be able to hold out."

"Everything'll be fine," she answered. She was calmer
than me. "Everything'll be fine. Anyway, Mom is too busy
being the belle of the ball to think about it."

But just before we sat down to eat, she came and found
me in the kitchen, where I was putting the final touch on
the first course (stuffed grape leaves) with Daphné and
Simon.

"Chloé?" she said. "Come here a minute." I gave Daphné
a worried look, but she replied with a confident wink. I
smiled to myself: Antoine had managed to reassure her, too.
Then I thought about the bet he'd come up with more than
a month before: "At your mother's birthday, I'll pick up your
sister" and I wondered if he could have done it. I also
remembered that, somehow, I'd hoped he'd win his bet. I
saw him by the living-room door; he was holding Mya in his
arms and making her laugh by touching her nose and chin.

"I'll be right back," I said to Daphné, who gave me a
smile. I heard her ask Simon, "Do you think we should cut
one of the rolls?" They had taken an immediate liking to
each other, and Daphné was talking to him with the ease
she normally reserved for people she knew well. Simon was
funny and nice to her – he knew what was going on, of
course, but was too tactful to say anything about it to her.

"What's up?" I asked my mother, who was waiting outside the kitchen.

"Don't you think Stéphane looks a little sad?" Oh shit! I
thought. Another layer of difficulty. If she decided to try and
get Stéphane to confess, we were done for.

"Oh, I don't know," I muttered. "He must be tired..."

"You know what I think?" my mother continued. "I
think Daphné's hiding something from us. I think the two

of them went through a rough patch, and that's why she wasn't feeling well this last little while."

"No, Mom, Stéphane is tired, that's all. Besides, look at Daphné, don't you think she looks better?"

"That's true," said my mother. "That is true. But Stéphane, really… I asked him what was wrong earlier and he said he was tired. But…"

"But that's all it is, there's nothing else! He worked ten hours straight today, Mom. So quit analyzing people like that."

She shrugged. "I'm telling you there is or was something going on."

"Mom…"

"You'd have told me if Daphné had let you in on a secret?"

I couldn't lie to her. Hiding the truth, maybe, but outright lying to her face, no. So, I simply repeated, "Mom…"

Because she was in a good mood, and had already had three glasses of champagne, she rubbed my arm and said, "What counts is for everyone to have fun, right?"

"Exactly."

"Thanks for what you're doing, your sister and you both. Every year, you put so much into it. It's a wonderful gift."

"It's because we love you," I said, snuggling tight against her.

"Oh, and can we talk about Simon for a second?"

"He's a good one, eh?"

"He's fan.tas.tic."

"You say the same thing about Antoine."

"Oh, it's not the same thing. They're both exquisite, but Antoine… he has a devilish side I looooove."

"A devilish side?" I couldn't wait to tell Antoine. He was going to loooooove it.

"Yes, devilish. But that Simon. He looks like an angel. And not just physically."

"I know, Mom. He's… perfect."

"Really?"

"Yes. It's kind of stupid."

She assumed the attitude of someone who's been around the block a time or two. "That's not easy – living with someone who's perfect."

"No, but he's not a pain in the ass about it. He's just perfect. That's all."

"That's what I said. It's not easy. You'll see."

I didn't want her to go any further. I didn't care, anyway. I wanted him just the way he was, complete with the perfection she wanted me to watch out for. So, to change the subject, I put my hands on my hips, and said, "Are you insinuating I'm not perfect?" My mother laughed and took me in her arms. "My God!" she answered. "You? You're perfection personified." And we both laughed, as if we'd wanted to make fun of perfection, any perfection, and remind ourselves that both of us were above all that, free and proud of our flaws.

In the kitchen, Daphné and Simon had finished plating the food – obviously, it looked like it was straight out of a restaurant: on each dish, there was one stuffed grape leaf on its side, and another cut in two and nicely leaned against the first. Simon had drawn a circle of olive oil around them and added what looked to me like chopped black olives.

"I wanted to add a little piece of pepper, for colour, but Daphné said it would be too much."

"People would have thought we had professional help," Daphné added with a laugh.

"Right you are." I picked up two plates, and we followed each other into the dining room. Everyone was still standing, deciding where to sit. My mother, of course, would sit at the head of the table. "Antoine," she said authoritatively, "come sit next to me." He faked a bow and hurried over to her. Daphné quickly set down her two plates and rushed over to Antoine's right, where she gave him a nervous smile that was out of character for her. Juliette elbowed me.

"What's going on? He's not really trying to pick her up is he?"

"No, no! Shhh! Sit next to me." We took our seats – I was between Juliette and Simon – and I started telling Juliette the whole story. Dumbfounded, she listened, nodding her head. "But you're completely crazy," she said. "It'll never work." She took a drink of wine and added, "You know it'll never work, right?"

"Not necessarily. Look."

I pointed my chin towards Antoine. He was talking to my mother and, with one hand, he was pulling Daphné's glass closer to his dish. Then he quickly placed his glass, which was nearly empty, next to her dish. My mother, without noticing a thing, continued to talk to him in a lively way. Juliette gave an astonished little laugh.

"On top of it all, he likes it, eh?"

"What do you think? He figures he's James Bond."

"Oof…" said Juliette. "I don't think James Bond ever had to go up against your mother."

"No. Way too risky. MI6 never would have allowed it. He is their best agent, after all."

"That's when Antoine comes in to save the day."

"Exactly."

"He's so brave," Juliette cooed. "And what charm!"

"I know. I heard Miss Moneypenny wasn't interested in Bond anymore."

"That was to be expected."

Simon leaned forward and said to Juliette, "Were you and Antoine together very long?"

Juliette didn't even have time to say, "Pardon?" before I gave her left thigh a ferocious pinch.

"Ouch!" she shouted.

"Antoine and I? Hmm? Oh. Pfff. What… a few weeks? Nothing serious. I… hmm." She looked mad, "Chloé! Why did you tell him that? You know it's still a little… touchy for me." I almost burst out laughing.

"It wasn't me," I said. "It was Antoine."

"Yes," Simon explained. "I asked him how he and Chloé had met, so he told me. But he didn't go into details, so don't worry."

"Oh. Okay," said Juliette. "Because I still have some trouble going into the details." She was pinching my right thigh, without looking at me. She must have wanted to laugh as much as I did. It was awful, obviously: I'd completely forgotten that ridiculous, rather unbelievable lie. I thought to myself that, in a few years, we'd all remember this as the Night of Stupidly Concealed Lies and laugh a lot.

"How's it going?" I asked Daphné when we were alone in the kitchen getting ready to serve the tagine.

"Like a dream. Chloé, I can't get over it. That guy has an incredible talent for this kind of situation."

"Yes, it's called duplicity," I said.

"Oh, he's not like that…"

"When he wants to be? Better than anybody." I thought about the bet and thought, if I hadn't reacted, if I had encouraged him, he might be trying to pick you up tonight.

"Daphné," I said as I took the meat out of the big pot and put it on the porcelain platter. "Why are we all doing this?"

"I don't know. Because I'm like a chicken with its head cut off?"

"Daphné…"

She looked at me. "Chloé, I don't know where I'm going. I don't want my mother on my back, telling me where to go and how to get there on top of it. It won't help."

"You can't take months to decide, Daphné."

"Okay. If there's anyone here who knows that, it's me."

"I know. Sorry."

"No, really. I'm having fun tonight. I can think about something else for a little while. Couldn't we just pretend there's no problem? Just tonight?"

"Whatever you want. But it seems to me that Stéphane doesn't exactly look like he's having a ball." An hour earlier, he'd gone to put the girls to bed and had stayed upstairs almost forty-five minutes, claiming the girls wouldn't go to sleep. But I'd gone up and seen him, sitting there in the dark room, with the twins fast asleep.

"Just tonight?" Daphné repeated, as if she hadn't heard what I'd just said.

I took her by the waist and kissed her, "Of course, Dadi. In the meantime, give me your glass."

"Your cheeks are starting to get a little red."

"Hey, take a look around the table – it's the Red Cheek Festival."

"That's true. Dad's more like a whole red apple, I'd say."

"Yeah, it's more uniform with him."

Simon came into the kitchen. "Can I help you, girls?"

"Okay, here's the chef!" shouted Daphné.

"Sous-chef," said Simon. "Tonight I'm just the sous-chef. And that's it!" Daphné smiled.

The sous-chef, nonetheless, had the idea of adding honey and grilled almonds to the tagine – it was a rich idea, and the result was splendid. Daphné and I were showered with praise, which we underhandedly accepted, without giving any credit to the sous-chef, who'd already warned us he wouldn't accept an ounce of it. It was now an indisputable fact: the Moroccan Kasbah was our greatest success since the powwow!

It happened at dessert – a semolina cake, flavoured with rose water: Stéphane got up and said he was going to wake up the girls and go.

There was a surprised, inebriated silence around the table.

"What are you doing?" Daphné asked him. "The girls are sleeping here, you know that. And I'll stay with them." And, very slowly she added, "Like always."

"Yeah, well, that's just it," said Stéphane. "It's not really like always, is it?"

Motionless, Antoine and I looked at each other. Then, my mother asked, "What's going on, Stéphane?" And he said, "Daphné's pregnant, and we don't know if we're going to keep the baby." Just then, I finally understood the full scope of the expression "the shit hit the fan."

For the next five minutes, the scene around the table was a chaotic jumble of indignant protests, recurring questions, and insults, and, on top of all that, my mother's voice repeating, "And you didn't tell me?" When she found out that not only I had known, but also that Antoine had (along with Simon and Juliette), she looked astonished and just said, "Okay." Then she and Daphné went into the living room. Stéphane hadn't moved and was still standing in the same place, and I was wondering who was going to be the first to say, "Nice job!" – and it turned out to be my father.

"Stéphane," he said in a tired tone. "You couldn't wait? We couldn't have talked about this tomorrow? Now, they're all upset," he added, pointing to the living room. "And drunk. At least my wife is. I could have told her more elegantly, you know."

"You knew?" I asked Dad.

"I had a pretty good idea. When I came into the living room, and you were trying to make me swallow that story about the flower arrangement. And then there was your little game with the glasses. Nice work, really, Antoine. Good effort."

"You saw, did you?" Antoine asked, smiling.

"You all don't pay any attention to me," my father answered. "Nobody thinks about the old man. But the old man..." he tapped the side of his nose, "can still smell a scheme."

I took my head in my hands. "We're ridiculous, Dad, I..."

"No. I understand. Your mother does, too. She's up on

her high horse, but it's mostly because she's mad she wasn't let in on everything sooner."

"Yeah, but Daphné didn't want me to tell her…"

"I know, sweetheart. Oh my. Antoine, will you give me some more wine?" He turned back towards me. "Honestly," he went on, "I didn't know the exact nature of the problem. Then I understood when I saw your face, my poor boy." He indicated Stéphane.

"But how's Daphné?" he asked.

"Better," I said.

"No," said Stéphane. "I'm the one who lives with her."

There was another silence. Antoine went behind Stéphane and put a hand on his shoulder.

My mother came back into the living room. I was expecting the worst, but she took a drink of wine and came over to kiss me. "My poor sweetie," she said. "You were in a pretty absurd situation, weren't you?"

"Between a rock and a hard place."

"Scylla and Charybdis," my father said.

"Sorry, Mom."

"No, no…" My mother always exaggerated everything, but sometimes it was impossible (and useless). She had turned back into the warm, attentive mother who had given Simon that kiss earlier in the evening. "Daphné explained to me why she didn't want to tell me about it. Honestly, I'm still a little insulted…" Oh, there it is, I thought. "But I'll give you the cold shoulder later. For now…" she looked up at Stéphane. "What are you going to do?"

"Don't know," said Stéphane, indicating the living room where Daphné still was.

"I think she wants to keep this baby," said my mother.

Stéphane didn't add anything. He must have been feeling terribly alone, standing there like that behind his chair, without our flamboyant mother on his side.

"Stéphane," said my father. "No one's mad at you. Not even Daphné."

"Well, *I'm* mad at myself."

"Of course, that's normal," my mother said to him gently, rubbing his back. Why can't she always be like this, I thought. Understanding and sensible. Stéphane seemed to be wondering the same thing I was: he seemed surprised by my mother's sudden cordiality, but he also seemed infinitely relieved. He gave a long sigh, and motioned vaguely towards the living room.

"Anyway, it's her decision."

"She won't make it without you," said my mother.

Stéphane shook his head. "I think she's already made her decision."

"She still needs you, my boy."

"I know," said Stéphane. He looked down at the ground, and said, "I'm sorry." Lively protests sprung up around the table – I don't know if it was because of the alcohol, or because we were really feeling compassionate towards him, but everyone was repeating "no, no," and shy Stéphane smiled.

"I just have to get used to the idea," he said, with his eyes still glued to the floor. "I have to find the joy in it."

"You have to talk to Daphné," said my father.

"I know," Stéphane sighed. "We hardly talk to each other anymore. Well, lately anyway."

My mother gave him a nice smile and nodded at him, and he got up to go to Daphné in the living room.

"So?" said my mother. "Isn't there any more champagne? My glass is empty, guys!" Everyone smiled. I stroked Simon's thigh and whispered, "Sorry," but he shook his head – "No, you have nothing to be sorry about."

Antoine stepped towards my mother with a bottle of Veuve Clicquot – she grabbed him by the arm and said, "Got you, you little sneak…" Antoine fell to his knees beside her chair, "Have pity! If you only knew how hard it was for me to go behind your back! It was torture! It's all Chloé's fault! Everything is Chloé's fault!" He laid his head on my mother's arm. "What can I do to earn your forgiveness?"

"Hmmm… I don't think I can answer in front of my husband."

"Oh," said my father, with a tired gesture. "You better not count on me tonight. You have my blessing. Antoine, listen to my wife."

We all started to laugh – we were relieved, and, I thought to myself, happy to just be on the edge of the drama that was unfolding in the living room. My mother didn't look worried – she must have figured out something I still didn't understand, perhaps that everything would work out okay. I felt reassured, and all warm inside. I leaned against Simon, and said to myself, "Everything is good." They're all here, and I'm with them, and with Simon. I could see us, like parts of a stage set, each one in the right place, where they belonged, even Daphné, even Stéphane. And, out loud, I said, "Everything's going to work out okay," and my father agreed, "You know what? I think so, too."

Chapter 15

I was right up against Simon, in a rather inert state, in the back seat of the cab that was taking us back. We were both pretty drunk, but not too drunk, just enough to feel good, a little loose, and a little naughty. I kissed him on the neck and he said, "Are we going to your place, or mine?" We lived near each other, and we'd given the driver an intersection between our two apartments.

"My place," I answered. "I miss my kitties." Simon smiled and gave my address to the driver. Simon didn't really like cats that much, but, as he often told me, he liked mine (I chalked that up to Puce's irresistible charm).

"Your family," he said, "is… my God. I didn't know it, but that's exactly the kind of family I always dreamed of."

"Come on, now."

"Chloé, they're so… alive."

I didn't say anything. I thought about my family and tried to see them through someone else's eyes.

"You said your mother was sad," I reminded Simon.

"Yeah. Sad and… half-asleep. My mother is half-asleep. I don't think she feels much. And my father is like a big boulder. He's heavy and hard, and has lots of sad stories about Croatia and the war and how things were before that."

"It's true that there are a lot of boulders with stories about Croatia." Simon smiled and held me close. "You're silly," he said. Then he added, "If you want to, we can go see them."

"Who?"

"My family. If you want to."

"Of course, I want to." I had an almost anthropological curiosity – I wanted to know Simon's family, so I could understand him better, no matter how sad and half-asleep they might be.

"This weekend?" Simon asked.

"Already?"

"My mother's already been on my case for three weeks to bring you to Kingston."

"Why didn't you say anything?"

He shrugged his shoulders. "My family's not really a source of joy for me."

"Oh." I didn't add anything – I thought I was lucky and was a little mad at myself about it. Simon was looking out the window, and I was looking at his handsome profile – mostly his mouth, which I always wanted to kiss.

"Antoine never went out with Juliette, eh?" Simon asked. He'd turned back towards me. There was no blame in his eyes, no jealousy either. Just a bit of amusement and surprise – it was the same expression he'd been wearing most of the night: cheerful curiosity. I dropped down across his thighs.

"No… they never went out together." I turned over – now I was lying on my back, across the seat, with my head on Simon's lap. As he looked at me, he was smiling and shaking his head. "You're all unbelievable, you know that? What was that all about? Why did you have to tell ridiculous lies and then get caught up in your contradictions?"

"I know, I'm starting to think it's a reflex…"

Distractedly, he played with my hair.

"What went on between you and Antoine?"

"Hmm?" I sat back up.

"Chloé. For fuck sake. I knew it the first time you mentioned him to me. And then I saw him… hell, even I'd sleep with him."

"Okay, very bad mental image."

"Figure of speech," he said laughing. "But why didn't you tell me?"

"Pure stupidity. I was stuck, and then that idiot came along with his ludicrous story and it was too late. I'm sorry."

"No, no." He was sincere, he wasn't mad at me. Any other guy, I thought to myself, would have had a lot of questions about the whole thing. Simon seemed to think it was all pretty funny. His self-confidence was solid, and I found that terribly sexy.

"You two…" He rubbed his thumb against his finger, like he was looking for an exact, subtle expression. "There's something there, between you two."

"No!" I protested.

"No, no, not that. But there's an invisible thread. Something. As if, in a room, a person could find one of you just by looking at the other."

I smiled in spite of myself. It was a nice way of looking at things.

"Are you jealous?" I asked him. He smiled. He was so, so, so handsome, with that smile and those dancing eyes.

"A little," he answered.

"Don't be."

He kissed me on the hair and said, "Okay."

But, in the semidarkness of my room, just as we were about to fall asleep, all wrapped up in love, with the cats curled up bitterly at the foot of the bed, disappointed because someone had taken their places next to me, Simon said, "What is Antoine to you?"

I stared at the dark ceiling. Just above me, there was a single fluorescent star that Juliette had stuck there years before. Antoine? I thought. I almost answered, "My best friend," but I thought Simon deserved better than that. So I said, "He's the rest of me."

"The rest of you?"

"I know, it's confusing. How can I explain it… A lot of times I feel like he's a continuation of… of me. Of my being. Even though we're completely different." I waited. I didn't

know how Simon was going to react, but I was happy that
I'd told him the truth.

Then Simon spoke, "He answered almost exactly the
same thing when I asked him that question." I turned
towards him. "Pardon?"

"He's a great guy, you know. We were chatting, before,
and he was talking about you, so I asked him, 'How would
you describe Chloé?' And he gave me that funny smile, and
asked, 'Honestly?' and I said yes, and I think he was a little
drunk and he answered, 'She's the part of me I'm not able
to be.'"

"He said that?" I was a little miffed at Antoine, at the fact
that he'd said that to my boyfriend before I had. But I was
also in the clutches of an intense, moving joy: I wanted to
call Antoine and shout, "We said the same thing! We said
the same damned thing!" and then make ridiculous promises about solidarity and unconditional love.

Simon put one arm around me, just above my breasts.
"You two are unbelievable. Just like your family. I've heard
about people who tell the truth with such self-assurance."

"Are you making fun of me? We spent the night trying
to keep our cathedrals of lies from caving in on themselves."

"Our cathedrals of lies?"

"Okay, maybe they were more like barns of lies."

Simon laughed and I could feel his breath against my
temple. "Chloé," he said just before he fell asleep, "you're
opening up doors all around me."

When I woke up the next morning – well, morning's not
exactly the right word, it was almost noon – Simon was
already gone, but he'd left a note on his pillow: "Gone to
work. Call me. S. xxx." Beside me, the triumphant cats had
reclaimed their respective places. I felt above my head and
found Puce, who softly said, "mrroo?" when I stroked her.
At my feet, Siffleux stretched shakily and sat down. He

looked at me, as if to ask what I was waiting for, and finally, he let out a long, helpless, famished whistle.

"Okay, okay…" I got up and went to feed them. Two pairs of yellow eyes and one pair of green eyes were staring at me so intently I started to laugh. "Well now. Since you haven't eaten anything in months, right?"

"Meeeooooowwww!"

I give them three little portions (normal size for Puce and Ursule, diet size for Siffleux, who was still gaining weight nonetheless) and I got a Gatorade out of the fridge.

"Ahhh… Gatorade…" I said. Then I took a big gulp, with my head flung all the way back, like the supposedly top athletes in the commercials, and I made myself laugh. In my own way, I was a top athlete, too.

Leaning against the sink, in my bathrobe and slippers, I thought about what Simon had said the night before. What Antoine had said, and then the statement, "You're opening up doors all around me." Once again, I felt a kind of sun in the centre of my chest. I didn't deserve someone like him. I didn't understand why he was so interested in me – I didn't know exactly how I was opening those doors. I was afraid he'd wake up one day and be disappointed. I went back towards my room, and I picked up the phone.

"Hello!" answered Simon's voice.

"Heyyy. How are you?"

"Good. A little hung-over. Usually, when I'm hung-over, my idea of fun is not doing the shopping for a restaurant. I'm checking out calves' livers. You want details?"

"Simon. I'm still at the Gatorade stage."

"That bad?"

"Nah… it's not that bad, to tell you the truth. But it'll help. Poor baby, what time did you get up?"

"Nine o'clock. You were sleeping like an angel, you stinker. Oh. Just a minute." I heard him bargain for a couple of things and then he came back.

"I swear to you. Twelve dollars a kilo for wholesale calves' liver? Who the fuck are they kidding?"

I took a big swallow of Gatorade. "Yeah! Who the fuck?"

Simon started to laugh. "I had a fantastic night," he said.

"Really?"

"Fantastic."

"Simon? What I said – about Antoine…"

"Anybody else would have made up some stupid story, Chloé. You told me what you thought."

"Yes, but…"

"There's no but. Stop."

"Because I love you so much and…" There it is, I thought. I waited all this time, and I ended up saying "I love you" to a guy who's checking out calves' liver.

"Chloé…" He was laughing happily. "…I'm not going anywhere."

"You're not?"

"No. But honestly, right now, I have to go negotiate on some calves' liver. Can we get together tomorrow? Tonight's going to be crazy at the restaurant."

"Sure. You know where to find me. I'll be waiting for you."

"And this weekend? Still ready to go to Kingston? Because if I call my mother to tell her we're coming and then we don't show up, my God. Hell hath no fury."

"Yes. Sure. No problem. Kingston it is."

"Okay. I have to go."

"Okay. Bye."

"Chloé?"

"What?"

"Back in high school, would you have believed we'd end up like this?"

"Baby, that's exactly what I was hoping for."

"I love you."

"I… me too." I hung up and I laughed, all by myself, in

my bedroom, because I'd just said "I love you" and "Me too" like a little girl. I put down my Gatorade and I floated down the hallway leading to the bathroom.

I was drying my hair with a towel, when someone rang the doorbell. Simon? I thought. Coming by to steal a kiss between the negotiation of the price of calves' liver and the purchase of eighteen bunches of garlic? I grabbed another towel, just in case (I didn't exactly want to come face to face with the letter carrier in a bra and panties), and I opened the door a crack. Antoine was leaning against the wall, looking distractedly at the stairwell.

"What are you doing here?"

He turned around and smiled at. "Shall we go see Juliette's paintings?"

"Um… okay, sure." I opened the door wide.

"Geez, I'm going to start thinking you have a camera hidden in here and that you always manage to arrive at the exact moment when I'm just in my bra."

"Fuck. You blabbed my secret." My back was towards him, but he grabbed me by the waist and pulled me close, to give me a kiss on the neck. I stopped breathing – he still had an effect on me, an unbelievable, stunning effect that wasn't always apparent. Sometimes it would hibernate for quite a while, and then it would come back, like a wave, a tidal wave. And just why did it have to come back now, just when I had Simon and his "I love yous"? I figured it had to be that – I was excited by what was suddenly forbidden, and I thought how stupid and predictable I was.

With my right hand, I tried to move his arm, but he squeezed tighter. "Shit, Antoine." He let go, and I took a few steps. I finally turned around – I still had my towel around me, but Antoine pointed his finger towards my left breast, which was exposed, revealing the pink lace of my bra. "Pretty," he said.

"Fuck you."

He looked surprised – pleasantly surprised – and smiled. I made an unconvincing "pfff" sound, and walked off towards my bedroom.

"Not too wrecked?" I said as casually as I could.

"No, not bad."

"Of course." I wondered exactly what it would take to wreck Antoine.

"You?"

"I'm okay."

"Really?" He pointed to the Gatorade on my nightstand.

"Okay, well, not fantastic," I answered, "but I'm okay."

"I didn't know if you'd be here," he said. "I took a chance. I'm really anxious to see Juliette's stuff – she's sure been working on it long enough… poor thing. She really put herself into it! And did you see her yesterday? She really seems to think this is it… I don't know… I think it's making me nervous."

"Me, too. I can't stop thinking about those damned crying faces."

"I know," said Antoine laughing. "Oh, I hope it'll be as good as all the hard work she's put into it… Come on, get dressed, let's go!" He was leaning against my bedroom door frame, with his hands in his pockets. I slipped a sweater on over my jeans, and, holding my breath like I was about to be in an accident, I said, "Simon told me what you said."

"What?"

"About me. That I was the part of you you're not able to be."

He looked at the tip of his shoe. "You know that I could sue him for breach of confidentiality. It's Paragraph 3 on Conversations between guys."

"Mhhhmmmm."

"It's true, you know. I don't know, it's like I hadn't really realized it. Then the guy asks me a question, and I look at him and say to myself, 'He deserves an honest answer,' and that's what came out."

"Is it cold out?"

"Pardon?"

"I don't know what shoes to wear. Is it cold out?"

"Not really, no."

I chose a pair. Everything inside was shouting for me to keep quiet, but I added, "I said exactly the same thing."

"About what?"

"He asked me the same question. He asked me what you were to me."

"What did you say?"

"The rest of me."

I didn't know why I'd just said that. But I couldn't have done things any other way. I was looking at him, he was looking at me, right in the eyes – I had a shoe in my hands, and I was standing next to my bed, waiting.

Antoine finally smiled, a sweet, little, hardly noticeable smile, and he turned around.

"Simon told me he was in love with you."

"I know." I wanted to throw myself into his arms and just stay there, against him, against the rest of me, standing there without moving, wrapped in his strength and his smell. Simon has nothing to do with all this, I thought. I love him, but he's outside. We are on the inside.

"Do you love him?" Antoine asked me.

I thought about it. "I… think… so."

"I know," said Antoine, smiling. "I love it." So then I smiled, too. I walked over to him, and he opened his arms, and I tumbled into them, completely, my head was against his chest and he lightly kissed my hair.

"When he said it," I continued in a shaky voice that surprised me a little, "I was so happy!"

Antoine didn't say anything, but he took me by the shoulders. My eyes were watering.

"What's wrong?" he asked. He almost wanted to laugh.

"I don't know!" And I started to cry and laugh at the same time.

"Oh, it's the hangover." Antoine was laughing.

"Shit," I said. "It's just fucking great to find out we're in the same place. It gets to me."

"You also cry at the end of *Big Daddy*, when it's the morning after."

"Hey, Adam Sandler holds a special place in my heart." I laughed again, sniffling, and he put one arm around my shoulders.

"Come on, baby."

We went to a little café down from my place where we bought sandwiches and coffee, and about eight minutes later, we were at Juliette's – Antoine had once again driven with his legendary skill, passing people on the right on the Ville-Marie Highway and parking in front of a fire hydrant.

"If there's a fire and they can't get to the hydrant because of you, I hope you're going to feel fucking awful," I said as I shut my door.

"There's not going to be any fire..."

"Yeah, well, that's easy to say. It's like that episode of Seinfeld where they park in the handicap spot and the handicapped guy ends up hurting himself and..."

"Chloé?"

"Yes?" I put one hand on my hip and looked at him defiantly. "What?"

"Get out of the way, you're blocking the sidewalk." I turned around: a woman in a wheelchair was trying to get by.

"Oh. Sorry. Sorry, sorry, sorry." I took three steps back, and shot a venomous look at Antoine, who was watching the scene and laughing.

"Nice. Very funny."

"Yes. Very funny," he said, lighting a cigarette.

"Jerk. Does Juliette know we're coming?"

"No. I didn't call. I just told her yesterday that we'd be by today, but I didn't say what time."

I rang once, then twice, but no one answered. "What

should we do?" I asked Antoine. "I'm hungry. I think I'm
going to eat a sandwich."

"Wait. We'll go around. Around back."

I followed him behind the old factory, to a rusty fire
escape, that could be pulled down with a metal rod that was
lying in a corner.

"*Après vous*," he said.

I glanced nervously at the steps. "Will you please tell me
why you go to all the trouble of going up this way?" I asked.

"It's just cool." He gave me a little slap on the ass, and I
started to climb. The stairs rocked a little too much for my
liking, but we still made it up to the top floor. Antoine
pulled the stairs back up, then he pushed the emergency exit
door – which was never locked – and we stepped into
Juliette's studio. It was dark – Juliette had hung big drapes
over the windows, and, after my eyes adjusted to the darkness, I noticed she'd hung them over her paintings, too.

"Look," I whispered to Antoine. I was whispering, like
we'd just come into a church or a museum. He was right
behind me. I could make out his silhouette, and the glow of
his cigarette.

"Let's go find Juliette," he said. "There's no way we can
look at this stuff without her."

I walked in front of him into the apartment, to Juliette's
room, which was empty.

"I'll go let them know we're here," I said to Antoine.

I'd only taken three steps when a stark naked man came
out of Marcus' room, and stopped right in front of me. He
was kind of short, completely hairless, and not very young.

"Errr…"

He blinked two or three times, then he saw me, and, as
natural as anything, he said, "Hello! Can I help you?"

"Um… No… I… I'm a friend of Juliette's." And since I
didn't really know what to do, I went to shake his hand.
"Chloé."

"Delighted. I'm Michel."

He extended a friendly hand and leaned forward. "And your friend?" he asked, looking at Antoine.

"Hi," said Antoine, extending a hand. "Antoine."

Michel slowly looked him over from head to toe – it was a perfectly absurd situation, but at the same time, it was disarmingly commonplace, we were all there, incredibly relaxed, how are you, fine and you, I see your penis, oh yes, and all the rest. After a few seemingly endless seconds, Michel finished his evaluation, went "hmmm" appreciatively, and said, "Excuse me. I was on my way to the bathroom."

"Oh," said Antoine. "It's that way."

"Oh, yes. Thank you. I'm still a little mixed up. It's quite some apartment, eh?" He turned on his heels and walked calmly towards the bathroom. Antoine and I stood there without saying a word for a good minute.

"Okay," I said finally. "What just happened?"

"I'm not really sure…"

"Are you always this cool, when you chat with naked people?"

"Hey, I played hockey for years."

"But… did you see his stick?" I was stunned. It was enormous – and not only lengthwise.

"Oh," said Antoine. "I didn't look. That's not something you do in a hockey locker room."

"I bet. And I'd like to point out that he wasn't shy in checking out your qualities."

"Yeah, but you were between us. It was like I was protected by the shield of your femininity."

"What?"

"If he tried anything, I'd have shoved you into him. That certainly would have confused him for a little while and…"

"Hey! Hello, you guys!" Marcus came out of his bedroom, stark naked as well, and I made an exasperated gesture. "Christ, Marcus!"

"Oh, sorry, sweetie. Hello, Tony Boy!"

"Whatever," Antoine grumbled.

"Your 'friend' is in the bathroom," I told Marcus.

"Michel? Did you meet him? He's good-looking, eh?"

"Yes, he was very… naked."

"Did you see his…"

"Marcus…" said Antoine.

"Oh, of course. And you're not interested in men!" His tone implied that Antoine was just pretending not to be interested in men.

"Okay," said Antoine. "Just you."

Marcus beamed. "Anyway, it's too late for you, Tony Boy." He clasped his hands like a teenage girl in love. "Michel… I think he's the one."

I raised a questioning eyebrow. "Really?"

"It's been three weeks, and… wow!"

"That's great!" I was happy for him. If there was anyone in the universe who deserved a good, hairless guy who was comfortable being naked, it was certainly Marcus.

"I'm going to slip into something more comfortable."

"Yeah, you do that…" Antoine sighed.

Juliette appeared at the end of the hallway, wrapped in a towel the colours of the Jamaican flag. She passed Michel, who was still as naked as ever.

"Michel."

"Juliette."

Michel went into Marcus' room, and, when she saw our stunned expressions, Juliette just said, "Yeah, well…"

"You really think he's the one?" I asked her when we were in her room.

"Listen, to tell the truth… it never lasts very long. But Michel is really very nice, I think. Not like the other little ninnies he's brought home."

"And, um, did you see his…"

"Yes," answered Juliette. "It's something else, isn't it?"

"My God… I'd think… I don't know… I'd think it would hurt, don't you?"

"Oh," said Juliette. "There are some questions I prefer not to ask."

"Thank you!" shouted Antoine, who was looking through the window while Juliette got dressed.

"Hey," she said. "Great party, last night."

"It was pretty good, wasn't it?"

"Quite a success," Antoine offered. "It almost took quite a header with your sister's situation, but... how did that turn out, anyway?"

"Stéphane left, and Daphné stayed at my parents'. But they talked for a long time – Daphné said she felt relieved."

"Are they going to keep the baby?"

"Of course they are. I always knew she'd keep it. Stéphane knew it, too, deep down. That's why it was a little dishonest when he said, 'We don't know if we're going to keep it.' What he should have said was, 'I don't know if I'm happy we're having this baby.' He ended up admitting it wasn't the financial implications that were worrying him the most – it was just that he thought that having two kids was already a lot."

"He could have said something sooner," Antoine said.

"He did mention it, but Daphné got hung up on the money question. That's what's bothering her the most. Because, as for the rest – the fact that they already have two, and all that – well, she'd thought of that, too. She was afraid she couldn't handle it either. But, she thought it over, and she came to the conclusion it really was worth it. Now she says it's just a matter of helping Stéphane do the same."

"Lord..." Juliette sighed. She hooked her bra, seemed to hesitate, then took it off before slipping on a big sweater. "And do you think he's ready to do that?" she asked me.

"He realized that Daphné wanted the baby. He said he'll work at it, he's sure he'll be able to get over his fears."

"What about Daphné?" asked Antoine. "Is she going to give Stéphane credit for working at it?"

"Of course," I answered.

"It's still not easy," said Juliette. "On my way home last night, I was thinking about them, and I said to myself that our problems are pretty lightweight."

"I know," I said. "It's awful, but ever since I found out about the whole thing, I can't stop telling myself, 'God, you're lucky!' at least ten times a day. And you have no idea how happy I am to have only absolutely meaningless problems."

Antoine turned his head a bit towards me. "Enjoy it. It could be your turn next…"

"Antoine, really."

"What, you'd make a good mother, Chloé."

"Come on…" I didn't add anything – I'd tried to imagine having children with Simon a few times, and I just couldn't do it. But I was flattered. "You really think so?" I asked Antoine.

"Of course," he answered with a laugh, still with his back turned. I smiled and I saw that Juliette was looking at me, with one eyebrow raised.

"Anyway," she said as if she wanted to change the subject. "It's safe to say the Moroccan Kasbah was a big success. But your big plan was absolutely awful!"

"Excuse me!" Antoine shouted, indignantly. "It would have worked perfectly if the brother-in-law hadn't opened his big mouth!"

"Okay, okay, Agent Bond," said Juliette. "Sorry."

She finished getting dressed, and gave me a nudge. "Oh, and Simon… Wow!"

"I know…"

"He's supernice," she said. "And funny. He really made me laugh. Chloé, I think you've got something there. And *mea culpa* for having pushed you in the other direction." I smiled. Juliette pointed her chin towards Antoine, and silently asked, "What about him?"

I waved my hand and mouthed, "I'll tell you later."

"You're always talking behind my back," said Antoine.

"Yep," said Juliette. "Exactly. Would you please step into the studio?"

"Right behind you," Antoine answered, finally turning around. "We saw the sheets you put over the canvases."

"I preferred not to take the chance. I never know with you. I did the right thing, didn't I?"

We followed her along the hallway. She stopped outside Marcus' door and gave three little knocks. "Time for the unveiling!" she said.

"Coming!" Marcus shouted.

"I haven't let him into the studio for six weeks," Juliette explained. "He deserves this."

Marcus came out, finally dressed (though somewhat precariously) and asked Juliette if Michel could come, too. "Of course," said Juliette.

The five of us headed towards the studio, and I realized my heart was starting to beat faster. I looked at Antoine and we both smiled.

Once we were in the studio, Juliette asked us to turn around, and we heard her heavily removing the sheets from the paintings. The four of us were exchanging nervous looks – even Michel seemed excited. "It's a great honour," he said to me, and I noticed he rolled his *r*'s.

"Can someone get the lights?" asked Juliette.

Marcus stepped forward and flipped the big industrial switch. A flood of light fell upon us, and Juliette said, "You can turn around."

Which we did in perfect unison. Then there was silence. Tiny Juliette was next to a series of paintings, eight of them, to be exact, and it was like a shock. I think I took a deep breath, and so did the others – they weren't really paintings, they were more like collages. I had a hard time analyzing everything: there were strong, moving colours; organic pinks and powdery golds layered on top of each other; blues that were anything but cold; and yellows that seemed to leap

from their frames; strange silhouettes that were hidden at
first and then turned out to be leafless trees whose branches
got lost in the profusion of colours; round, happy Buddhas;
words; and a handprint.

It was so beautiful and sad it made you want to cry – I
could see Juliette in each colour, in each denuded tree, in
the solitary, mauve hand sprinkled with silver. I heard
Michel, to my left, say, "My God," and I realized my eyes
were full of tears. I tried to say something, but all I could do
was bring a hand up to my mouth – then I felt Antoine's
hand in mine, and I didn't move a muscle.

"Juliette," Antoine finally said. "It's… what have you
done?"

"It's amazing," sighed Marcus. "Amazing."

Juliette started to laugh nervously. "You… what do you
think?"

For a moment, we were all lost in a symphony of ono-
matopoeias, superlatives, oohs, ahs, and remarks of
"extraordinary," "magnificent," "incredible," and a whole
bunch of words about art that we undoubtedly used incor-
rectly, but sincerely. I was saying things like, "The canvases
look like they're alive," while Marcus clapped his hands and
laughed, and, after stepping up to each work and then stepping back to kiss Juliette, Antoine said, "It's unbelievable.
I'm so proud to know you… it's unbelievable."

I took Juliette in my arms – she was shaking – and she
said, "I worked so hard… I'm so happy."

"Happy? Ju, you have the right to be a lot more than
happy."

Michel stepped forward, with one hand on his chest. "I
don't know anything about art," he said to Juliette. "I didn't
know you could be moved by a piece of art. I'm bowled
over."

"Giulietta," Marcus shouted. "I think we're going to be rich!"
That relaxed the atmosphere and everyone started to laugh.
"We should have brought champagne," I said to Antoine.

"It's not even one o'clock," Marcus pointed out. Then he paused and added, "Oh, who am I kidding, we should have champagne!"

"I'll go get some," Michel offered.

"I'll come with you, my love," Marcus said to him, and they left together, Marcus with one arm around Michel's waist and a finger in the back pocket of his jeans.

We turned back to the paintings and the three of us stood there for a moment, without speaking. I stepped over to one of them and studied it – there was paint, but there was also crepe paper or something similar stuck on top of the drawings which, in some cases were almost perfectly exact, and in others nothing more than simple sketches. The third and fifth ones were covered with text, and I recognized Juliette's delicate, slanted handwriting. It wasn't possible to read all the words, but, on the third one, on the multi-coloured background, I could make out bits of the Apocalypse, "*Je suis l'Alpha et l'Omega*" in French, and then, in English, "And I heard as if it were the NOISE of thunder, one of the four beasts saying, come and see and I saw" and further along "and I looked and beheld a PALE horse, and its rider's name was Death... And hell followed with him."

Beneath a drawing of a colourful turtle shell covered with gems, there was a quote from Huysmans' *À rebours*, and then, further along on the right, a passage from Rimbaud's *Une Saison en enfer (j'ai de mes ancêtres gaulois l'oeil bleu blanc...)* and other sentences whose origins I couldn't identify. Antoine, who was standing in front of the fifth painting, read out loud, "Will it be me? The girl forever ambling the grey twilights? Will it be me? Will it be me?"

He turned towards Juliette. "What happened?"

"It just came to me," answered Juliette. "Spontaneously. All the sentences – the ones I wrote myself, and the other ones, too. They insisted, I thought they were essential..."

"Why in English?"

"Because that's how they appeared in my head. Everything you see just came to me, and then I couldn't get them out of my mind. I'd finished the third painting and then I started thinking about des Esseintes' turtle in *À rebours* and it became kind of an obsession."

"It's so… serious," I whispered.

"Hey," said Juliette. "I'm fine."

I leaned towards the painting once again, and I read, "*Je suis dans la nuit, et j'essaie d'y voir clair. Il y a longtemps que j'ai cessé de trouver ça original.*"

"Is that Céline?"

"No," said Antoine, studying the fifth painting. "Camus."

"That's right," said Juliette.

"Listen to this," Antoine said to me. "*17 septembre – deux frites, un coke – est-ce que vous êtes de Savannah?*"

"I'll explain that to you later!" Juliette said, laughing. She pointed out a delicate line at the top of the third painting that said, "Legolas! What do your elf eyes see?"

"Oh!" I shouted. "From *The Lord of the Rings!*" It was a line from the film that always made us laugh, and that we enjoyed repeating as seriously as possible when one of us was off in space, "What do your elf eyes see?"

"That day I was thinking of you," she said to me.

"Oh…" I felt all warm inside.

"What about me?" asked Antoine. "Do I have a line?"

She showed him a sentence just below the quote from *Une Saison en enfer: "et sur cette pierre je bâtirais mon église.*"

"I've always thought of you as my foundation," she told Antoine, with her eyes lowered.

Leaning in, he continued to study the painting, and I was bitterly thinking that his sentence was quite a bit prettier than mine. When he straightened back up, I saw he was deeply touched. And Antoine was not the kind of guy who was easily touched. He took Juliette's face in his hands, and gave her a big smile before saying, "You are extraordinary."

Juliette's eyes were sparkling and her cheeks were flushed –
she was proud of herself, and that was absolutely marvellous: in ten years, I'd never seen her so proud.

"Tell us about it," Antoine requested.

"What?"

"Everything. How you did them. The order you did
them. Everything."

"It's a long story," said Juliette. "And not very clear."

"We don't care. Are you in a hurry, Chloé?"

"I've got all day." I took out a sandwich, handed another
to Antoine, and took a bite out of the first.

"You have any more of those?"

I tossed her half of mine, and she went and pulled the
old mattress over and put it in front of the paintings. "Bring
over the couch," she said to Antoine.

"There's a couch in here?"

"Yeah. Over there." She pointed to a pile of random
objects in a dark corner of the studio that included, I
noticed, one of the green shoes I'd loaned her months
before for an installation.

"Hey! My shoe!"

"Yesss," said Juliette, a little uncomfortably. "Anyway, it's
not really in style anymore, eh… think of it as a favour."

I looked understanding. "I see, you really saved me from
making a fashion faux pas."

"Those are exactly the words I was looking for."

Antoine pushed the couch over to us, and we all settled
down on it. Marcus and Michel came back a few minutes
later and we drank good champagne and asked Juliette
completely ridiculous questions (Marcus: "What's the…
message?") and listened to her patient replies. An autumn
wind was coming in through the emergency door, which no
one had closed, and the more I contemplated the paintings,
the more I thought we were looking at something that was
a lot bigger than all of us, and this made me both strangely
and deeply happy.

Michel was the one who finally had the good sense to ask Juliette when and where she was going to show them.

"Very soon," she said. "I've spoken to Florent…" She wagged an authoritative finger at Antoine and me, and didn't even give us time to trade a tired glance. "He's coming to see everything Monday, and we'll book a date at the gallery. It's just a little complicated because, well, there are only eight pieces, after all, but we're going to try to dig out some other things I've never shown. Can you come over this weekend? I'm going to go through everything."

"Oh, yes!" I said, and then I slapped myself on the forehead. "No. No, I can't, I'm going to Kingston."

"Kingston? Jamaica?" asked Marcus.

"No, Kingston, Ontario. It's almost as exciting…"

"Why are you going there?" asked Juliette. "Oh… the in-laws, eh?"

"Yep."

"Oh boy…"

"What, oh boy?"

"Oh, I don't know. Meeting your in-laws is always something pretty special, isn't it?"

"Not necessarily. If Simon could survive my family, I figure there really shouldn't be any problem."

"No," said Juliette. "I suppose not…"

We changed the subject – the imminent lack of champagne was a much more pressing issue – and I was still lost in Juliette's canvases. I was looking at the colours, the textures, and a smiling Buddha face, and I thought to myself, "Okay, Kingston. What could possibly go wrong?"

Chapter 16

"What do you mean, everything went wrong?" Juliette was sitting at my dining-room table, looking at a big bowl of sliced apples.

"What do you mean, what do I mean?" I answered. "Everything went wrong. It's simple enough, isn't it?"

"Yeah, but how?" Juliette asked carefully, as if she were talking to a crazy woman who could bite her head off if she looked at her the wrong way. She waited a few seconds for me to reply, then, seeing I wasn't going to comply, she settled for swallowing a piece of apple.

"Hey!" I shouted. "Don't eat my apples, I have just enough for my pies."

"One piece!"

"I said 'just enough'!"

Juliette opened her eyes wide and put the unbitten half of the piece of apple back in the bowl, without taking her eyes off me. I met her look briefly, and then I burst out laughing, just as she did. I collapsed onto the table in the middle of the apple peels and cores.

"I'm sorry, it's just that it was such a shitty weekend, you can't even imagine. And now, I have to make these fucking pies, and I really don't feel like it."

"Don't make them then," said Juliette, practical as ever.

"No… I start work again tomorrow, so I won't have time, and next weekend, I still won't feel like it, and if I don't make them, I'll feel guilty… I always make my pies."

"I know. I like your pies."

I chucked the paring knife on the table. "Stupid pies…"

"Okay," said Juliette as she picked up the knife and grabbed

an apple. "Don't go blaming your problems on these innocent apples. They didn't do anything wrong. So, take off your
apron and tell your buddy what happened in Windsor."

"Kingston."

"Whatever."

I sighed and took off my apron (a horrible denim thing
with big pink letters that proclaimed me "the coolest cook
in Coaticook" – a gag gift my father had given me that still
made him laugh).

"Where should I start…" I thought for an instant –
Siffleux was walking around the table, and I threw him an
apple skin, which he sniffed for quite a while before swallowing it whole.

"He even eats skins?" Juliette asked. She was just asking,
to make conversation – Siffleux's dietary habits hadn't surprised us in a long time.

"Mmmm," I said.

"And the cores?"

"Certainly. But I'm afraid he'll choke."

"Of course." She picked up another apple and started to
peel it. "So?"

"Well, you remember how I told you Simon thought his
mother was 'sad'?"

"Yes."

"Well, that's a bit of an understatement. She's not sad. She's
completely, absolutely, totally hopeless. Not hopeless like, 'Oh,
I live in intense, horrible hopelessness,' no, hopeless like, 'I
don't have, have never had, and never will have hope that
anything at all on this planet will ever be able to pull a smile
out of me.' And, in case that's not enough, it's like her sadness or her hopelessness, or whatever you want to call it, has
filtered out. Their house… their house is a tomb."

We arrived in Kingston on Saturday afternoon – I had
suggested to Simon we leave on Friday night, but he'd
declared that "one night would be plenty." The town was
nice. It was a clean, Ontarian – in the good sense of the word

– university town. Simon's parents lived in a little cottage in the suburbs – they'd returned to Kingston after living in Montreal and Paris, and had settled down a few streets from where Simon had grown up. We'd parked in front of the red-brick house, and I thought to myself that it was exactly the kind of light, calm neighbourhood where I'd imagined Simon had lived.

Then, I met his parents, who were nothing, and I mean nothing, like the way I'd imagined them – I'd envisioned an Irish mother with sparkling eyes and caustic humour, and a father as handsome as Simon, as exotic and mysterious as the Balkans were to me. As I got my bag out of the car, I suddenly realized I hadn't seen any pictures of them at Simon's.

Only his mother came outside to meet us, and she did so without even a hint of a smile – she was tiny and diaphanous, her hair was still blond and she had big, pale green eyes that were handsome, but so sad it was unbearable to look at them. She might have been very beautiful once, but I wasn't exactly sure: something told me she must have been born with the same bitter, resigned line she had in the corners of her mouth, the same look of a caged animal, and the same coldness in every move she made.

She barely spoke and seemed to still live in a mythical Ireland she'd never visited: her family had lived in Canada for three generations, but in her house were a number of ugly, nostalgic, Irish objects: tiny harps, felt clovers, the text of "Molly Malone" calligraphied onto a piece of fake parchment. When we got there, she hardly said hello to me – a cold handshake, a quick glance, and then she'd turned towards Simon and said, "Slobodan, my boy" – this, in my opinion, was the best moment of the weekend.

"Slobodan?" asked Juliette.

"That's exactly what I said! It seems that Simon was baptized Slobodan."

"But that's not Croatian, it's Serbian."

"It also seems that Mr. Markovic's father is Serbian, and that his father's name was Slobodan."

"Oh... and what's Mr. Markovic's name?"

"Elio. His mother was Italian."

"Complicated."

"You have no idea. I was treated to the whole Markovic family tree, which, honestly, I would have found fascinating if the guy hadn't been so sinister. Between the wars, moving and all the rest, their family trees are a lot more exciting than ours, you know?"

"Excuse me!" said Juliette. "My ancestor, the very distinguished François-Baptiste Beauchemin, left Trois Rivières in 1848, to settle in Saguenay. That took courage, you know."

"You're right."

"And then, my father the pioneer came all the way to Laval. Now that really took courage."

I laughed. "In my family, no one had left Quebec before my father. They'd been there for twelve generations, I think. My grandmother still hasn't forgiven him, either. Her oldest son, abandoning the family domain, I'm telling you..."

"But getting back to Slobodan," said Juliette, "why didn't he keep his name? It's nice."

"That's exactly what I asked him."

Simon had looked at me, as if he couldn't believe I could ask him such a question, and he'd answered, "Slobodan? It sounds like a trampoline."

Then he'd repeated, "Slobodan, Slobodan," and I had to agree – the name did carry some kind of musical elasticity that could be unpleasant. "And," Simon had added, "don't you think Slobodan Markovic sounds a little too much like Slobodan Milosevic? It would be like having Adolph Hatler for your name."

"Or Rudolph Hitler."

"I think we're on the same page," Simon had said.

He'd gone by Slobodan until he was fourteen. Then, in

1989, Milosevic had come to power, and his father had said it was out of the question for his only son to have a name that sounded like the name of the man he suspected was torturing Croatians. "And that was good," Simon had explained, "because we were moving to Montreal." And his mother, whose sense of practicality was up to any challenge, had stated that Simon would be perfect, because it was a name that sounded good in both official languages.

"Didn't that really confuse you?" I'd asked Simon. "Changing your name at fourteen?"

"Ehh. I was in a new town, a new school where they spoke a language I only half understood, I didn't know anybody: pretty much everything was confusing to me, so changing my name wasn't that big a deal."

That's when I understood that Simon had a superhuman capacity to resign himself to things. I didn't know if he'd gotten it from his father, who'd been through the war, Communism and hardships; or from his mother, who seemed to be resigned to enduring life on this planet, though, from all I could see, it depressed her immeasurably. It was a personality trait I didn't really like, and I didn't want to see it in Simon. But it was undeniably there, an urgency to accept anything without flinching, and, to my eyes, it was an incomprehensible weakness: if Simon got slapped, he'd turn the other cheek.

I'd gone to Kingston in the hope of learning a bit more about the man I loved. But with the exception of this initial discovery, which had depressed me somewhat, I couldn't find out a thing: his parents seemed completely closed to the idea of telling me about their son (the opposite of mine, I'd thought, who'd followed Simon around telling him vivid, embarrassing stories about me).

In fact, his parents hardly spoke to me all afternoon; all they did was ask Simon questions though they didn't really seem interested in his answers. His father was constantly asking him if he was making lots of money, how much

money he'd invested, how much he spent every week, and
Simon answered him diligently: he was obviously terrified
of his father.

While we were having a drink before dinner (some
Cinzano, instead of the Italian wine Simon had brought,
which his father refused to open on the pretext it would be
"a waste"), Simon's mother had finally gotten around to
asking me what I did for a living. She showed no reaction
at all when I told her I was a TV researcher (something told
me that even if I'd told her I was a trombone player or an
undertaker, her reaction would have been identical). She'd
then asked, "Are you a *séparatiste?*" and I didn't even have
time to open my mouth before Mr. Markovic said, "Of
course she is. All Frenchies are," which had made me want
to scream a sovereignist slogan before I walked out of the
house. Simon didn't say a word, didn't twitch, didn't raise
an eyebrow; he'd remained as impenetrable as his mother.

After that, came the Markovic family genealogy, which,
thanks to patient, fanatic research by Simon's father, went all
the way back to the thirteenth century. There was Dubrovnik,
of course, where Mr. Markovic had been born, along with
Zagreb and all of Croatia, ancestors from Montenegro and
Macedonia, some from Albania (but they were "Catholic
Albanians," he'd stressed several times). Mr. Markovic did
not even ask me once where my family was from.

"Well, Quebec, Quebec, Quebec…" Juliette pointed out.

"Okay, that may be true, but still. And I could have added
Normandy. Before Quebec, it was Normandy."

"Everybody here comes from Normandy."

"Excuse me! Some people come from Picardy!"

"Well, if you put it that way," Juliette said, "it's an end
of the world."

"Exactly. But, from all appearances, Mr. Markovic didn't
give a shit. The mother, on the other hand, showed some, oh,
I wouldn't say animation, but a teeny tiny bit of interest when
I said I'd been to Ireland. She said, 'My family's from

Limerick.' And I said, 'Oh, I went to Limerick.' I tried to describe the town for her, but she wasn't interested anymore."

"Why hasn't she ever been?"

"Search me. I felt like it would have been pretty awkward to ask her that. And they'd lived in France! It seems to me that once you're there, Ireland's not that far away! Simon's explanation is that his father doesn't want to go and his mother doesn't want to travel alone."

"Shit," Juliette muttered.

"Shit is right. And it was shit all weekend long. Not a word during the meals. I felt like they were making a huge effort to ask me things like my last name, what my parents did and where I'd gone to school. Separate bedrooms, of course."

"Separate bedrooms?"

"Yes, Chubby. And here's the best part: just before I went to bed, I told Simon I'd come meet him in his room and he answered with such a forceful 'no' that I wanted to come back to Montreal right then and there."

"Oh come on, that's normal," said Juliette. "It's his parents' house."

"Well, he could have laughed! Or made a joke, or I don't know what, but he reacted like I'd suggested we bump off his mother during the night. It's like he'd turned back into a repressed teenager at his parents'."

"Maybe that's exactly what happened," Juliette suggested.

"Maybe…"

I gave a long sigh. I didn't know why, but I'd been wounded by Simon's flaws. They bothered me, they hurt me. He's so perfect, I thought to myself, he doesn't deserve those little weaknesses.

"Anyway," I went on. "A really crappy weekend. It didn't stop. Church on Sunday, which could have been relatively interesting, or slightly amusing if the mother had quit shooting me indignant looks every ten seconds because I didn't know the damned prayer."

Juliette started to laugh. "Sorry... it's just that... it's kind of funny."

"That's right, you go ahead and laugh... I'm telling you, it was just hours of fun. After church, I figured, okay, maybe we'll go for a walk, Kingston is pretty, but no, back home and everyone sits down in the living room, and Simon starts playing cards with his mother while the old man takes his nap. The whole afternoon. And not once, not one single time, did Simon come to my rescue."

"That's strange," said Juliette. "He's so... so exactly the opposite of all that!"

"I know! I don't know how those two could have produced Simon but... in the car, on the way back, he said to me, 'Now do you know why I did so well in school?' 'Because your father beat you?' I asked, but he looked like that insulted him. Finally, he said, 'No, because I preferred spending all those hours studying than having to deal with them.'"

"Maybe," said Juliette, "he's so open and kind today as a reaction against them."

"Yes, obviously. Do you want a beer?"

"Of course." I got up, and went to the kitchen to get two beers. Siffleux was lying on the floor, in a puddle of sunshine, and he meowed lazily. Probably because he wants a beer, too, I thought.

"Anyway," I said as I came back into the living room. "I don't care if my boyfriend's parents are sad and stupid. But, we hadn't even gone a block before he dissolved in excuses. That means he knew I'd spent the longest twenty-four hours of my existence. But, even if you forget about that, he could have warned me in advance, don't you think?"

"Did you tell him that?"

"Yes. But then he looked so sad and sorry – he said: 'Well, I wasn't going to tell you that the best thing for you would be not to meet them'!"

"Good point," said Juliette.

"He said he also wanted me to meet them because they were part of him. I understand that, too. I wanted to meet them, too. Somehow, I'm glad I know where my Simon comes from. No, what I can't stand is that he didn't do anything. He didn't say a word when his damned father called me a Frenchie, like I was a pile of crap. Shit, in a family like his, I'd think he could be more open to other cultures."

Juliette shook her head. "I finished the apples," she said. "Come into the kitchen. I'm going to roll my crust." She followed me, taking off the apron and handing it back to me.

"Did you ask Simon why he didn't do anything?"

"He said that there was nothing he could do against his 'parents' will.' I suppose that's true. And that's also why he didn't try to make things a little warmer for me, or to describe his parents in a better light. All in all, I had the feeling he wanted to show me to them, even though he knew they wouldn't approve." I poured a little lemon juice on my apples, and got out the flour.

"I don't know... It was weird to see Simon like that... that there's a side of him that gave in to all that."

"Listen," Juliette said to me. "Really. You expect miracles from him. The guy's perfect, even if his relationship with his parents is rough."

"Oh, I know, I know. I'm not being fair. But it's like, it's like I'm having a harder time forgiving him his imperfections than anyone else. I didn't want to see him like that. It hurt me. And when we came back yesterday, he was discouraged, he was telling me he was always like that when he saw his family, and that bothered me, too. I wanted to tell him to stand up for himself..."

"Easier said than done, you know!"

"Stop it! I know there's no excuse."

"It'll pass," said Juliette. "You just got back. Plus, if there's any guy in the world who can make you forget he doesn't have a great family, it's Simon. Seriously, Chloé, he's too handsome to be true."

"Exactly."

"Okay," said Juliette. "That's enough. You're looking for problems. Simon's not a serial killer, right? He just has strict parents! That's all! And he grew up and he doesn't live under their thumb anymore, but he's also decent enough to keep seeing them once in a while."

"Oh... I know... I know, I know, I know, I know. I'm just a spoiled rotten kid, who's lucky enough to have a family like mine... I swear to you, I called all of them this morning and told them how great they are – my father asked me if I was dying or about to leave for Uganda for a year, or something like that. Poor Simon. When we got back, he said, 'Now do you know why I was so happy to meet your family?' And I answered, 'You have no idea.'"

"I think you've rolled it enough," Juliette pointed out.

"What?"

She pointed at my crust, which was now stretched out in an immense circle and looked more like a crepe than the bottom of a pie.

"Oh, shoot!" I fixed the problem, and thought about Simon, about how his face was closed when he was playing cards, in his parents' dark, brown living room. How could he have become such a being of light? For a few seconds, I loved him even more. I couldn't be mad at him, I had no right. Once again I realized how easy my whole life had been.

"What about you?" I finally asked Juliette as I put my pies into the oven. "Did you guys sort through your old pieces like you wanted to?"

"Yes. It was pretty cool, in fact. Florent came to take a look late Sunday afternoon, but Marcus, Michel and Antoine had finished most of the job. We'd spent all day Saturday and Sunday in my storage and my studio... they didn't take it too seriously at first, but we ended up doing quite a bit of sorting."

She smiled. "The guys were really too nice. At first, they didn't want to say anything, because they all said they didn't know anything so their opinion wasn't worth crap, but I managed to convince them. Honestly, they didn't do a bad job! Well, I finally found out my series of crying faces wasn't really a big success…"

"Oh. The crying faces…"

"Did you know that Antoine kept his in a closet?"

"Oh, the boor!"

Juliette gave me a questioning look.

"Okay," I said. "I knew. But not for very long! It's just that when you told us you thought you were completing the work of your life, we remembered the last time, and, well, that turned out to be the crying faces. So…"

"Oh, it's okay… Even I can't look at them anymore. We took two of them out and Marcus put his hands to his face and shouted, 'My eyes! No!' I had to admit that, well, let's say, they weren't my best paintings."

"Maybe not, no. But the other things you showed us last weekend… I don't know if we made it clear to you, but they're incredible, Chubby. Incredible."

"Listen. Florent liked them."

"Florent?" Even if he'd never produced anything anyone would ever want to look at, Florent was the prototype of the artistic snob. He always claimed to know, with one glance, what was "acceptable" and what was only "worthy of a high school art class." Obviously, according to him, ninety-nine percent of what he saw belonged in the second category, and this even included a number of masters like Picasso, Gauguin, all the Impressionists and "especially Pollock and Rothko," whom he described as "uselessly pretentious." And there was nothing about him that could justify his attitude, except, as he often repeated, a series of his paintings had been shown in New York – caricatures of women, with huge breasts and red, greedy lips. They were ugly, and completely lacking in originality: Antoine had already told him that if one or two of his paintings had been purchased, it was because some moron thought he'd found some work by Corno at bargain prices.

So, if he was saying he liked Juliette's paintings, it was a noteworthy event. Obviously, his taste meant nothing, but, still – a bitter, jealous snob had been unable to hide his admiration of Juliette's work.

"He was seriously impressed," Juliette went on. "He even offered to be my agent."

"No! No, Juliette, seriously…"

"No, I don't want an agent. It just means he thinks there's money to be made off them. And, in Florent's case, that's the biggest compliment there is."

"How much are you going to sell them for?"

"Florent said something about $2,500 or $3,000 apiece."

"Pardon?" I was flabbergasted. Juliette's other paintings had sold (when they had sold) for about $700 or $800, *maybe* $900.

"Yeah, I know," said Juliette. "It seems a little ridiculous to me for someone who's really unknown, but well… we have time, so we'll see. The problem is that if I don't have any other commissions, I'm afraid I won't be able to produce. I'm afraid all this was like… an accident."

"A fucking beautiful accident."

"Yeah, but still an accident."

"Maybe not."

"Maybe not," said Juliette opening another beer. "But since I finished them, I haven't felt like painting."

"Isn't that normal?"

She shrugged her shoulders and moved over towards the window. "I don't know. Honestly, these days, my definition of 'normal' doesn't mean much." There was no bitterness in what she was saying – it was just an observation – all there was in her voice was a bit of amused surprise.

"When are you going to show them?" I asked.

"In five weeks. The opening will be November 25th. Will you be there?"

"Are you kidding me? I'm there already."

Chapter 17

Antoine took me by the shoulders and gently shifted me to his right, so he'd be between me and the gutter – something he always did when we walked together. Someone (his mother, undoubtedly) had taught him that men must walk closer to the street, in case a passing car made a splash. He also opened doors, motioned for women to go ahead of him, picked up things they dropped, offered his arm when I had to go downstairs in high heels. They were gestures I hardly noticed anymore, but, when I happened to notice them, they still made me smile. Even though he talked about his conquests like other men talked about cars, Antoine was actually quite an old-fashioned gentleman.

I watched him and laughed, and he cocked his head towards me, "What?"

"Nothing. You're quite a gentleman, you know."

"Um, no, I am not a gentleman. I'm just a guy, that's all."

I ran a hand under his chin. "No… Antoine, you're a gentleman."

"NO!" He jerked back his head. "I was just brought up to be polite, that's all."

"Hmmph. Cute."

"Chloé!"

"Yes?"

"I'm not 'cute.'"

"Yes, Antoine, really, you're very cute." I took his arm. "I'd even say you're adorable."

"No one has ever called me adorable before."

"That's because they don't know you!" In a stupid, high voice, I said, "Oooh! Antoine, you're so hot! You're such a man! You're so cool, Tony Boy! Oooh! Take me, Antoine, you're sooooo masculine!"

He started to laugh.

"If they knew you," I said, in my own voice, "they'd all say you were adorable. On top of all the other things they say, of course, but adorable nonetheless."

"You're crazy."

"A-d-o-r-a-b-l-e," I spelled.

"Silly."

"You have to know yourself, cutie…"

We were walking towards Florent's gallery, where Juliette's opening was starting in just over an hour, and both of us were a little more nervous than we wanted to admit, which is why I was making such ridiculous small talk. He'd picked me up ten minutes earlier – the gallery wasn't far from my apartment, and, anyway, he'd had his licence taken away the week before, which had prompted me to repeat "ah HA!" and "I told you so" until just a little while earlier.

We were supposed to meet at the gallery exactly an hour before the opening – it was a tradition that went back to Juliette's first show, in a rather ugly bar in the Jean-Brillant building at the University of Montreal. Since then, whenever she had a show, even if it was nothing more than a ridiculous installation with my green shoes, the three of us got together to drink no less than one six-pack of Molson Export.

"You think we'll still be doing this in fifteen years, when Juliette's a big artist having shows in Paris and New York?" Antoine had asked as he helped me get my coat on.

"Oh, probably… And, if it's in Paris, it'll be all the more important. It won't be easy to find Molson Ex, you know. We'll have to bring it in our suitcases."

"Obviously. But still, we're starting to have an awful lot of traditions to uphold, don't we?"

"You getting sick of traditions?"

Antoine shrugged his shoulders and smiled. "No," he'd answered and we left.

Just as we arrived at Florent's gallery (which, in fact, was more like some space he rented on boulevard Saint-Laurent than an actual gallery), it started to rain – a cold drizzle that promised to turn into snow. Florent was waiting for us at the foot of the stairs, smoking a cigarette. He must have been about forty, but he looked fifty – he kept his dull, thinning hair long, never took off his jean jacket, and his nasty gaze had something undeniably slimy about it.

"It's on the second floor," he said. "Juliette's waiting for you. She kicked me out for a half-hour. Apparently you have to be alone…" He was winking at us, as if to imply he knew we weren't going to be drinking Molson Ex, but having a quick, traditional three-way.

"Um… right," I said. "See you in a bit, Florent." He let me by, then without even trying to keep me from hearing, he said to Antoine, "Hey, which one are you sleeping with? Hmm? We were wondering about that the other day. The short one? I figure it's both of them…" He laughed. Antoine stood there in front of him for several seconds. "Florent," he said, "don't give me an excuse to beat you up. I'd like it too much, and afterwards, I think I'd feel a little bit guilty."

Florent gave a meaningless little "pfff" and went out into the rain.

"You beat people up now?" I asked Antoine in disbelief. I had never imagined him beating people up – I didn't think it fit his personality at all, and that it would be more like him not to stoop to something like that. On the other hand, I had seen him get beaten up once by a jealous guy who'd come flying into a bar and given him such a punch in the jaw that he'd gone sprawling on the floor. Antoine simply smiled at him knowingly, and, while the bouncers kicked the other guy out, I thought to myself, "The jerk, he's proud he got hit by a jealous guy."

"No," Antoine answered, as he began to climb the stairs.

"I'm not into that, but I'd be happy to make an exception for Florent."

I imagined him kicking Florent's ass, and said, "Yeah, I suppose if I could do that, I'd consider it, too. You know how to do that?"

"Sweetie, how many times do I have to tell you, I played hockey for ten years."

"Okay, okay, okay. Ten years of hockey and Your Majesty is able to look at naked guys without blinking, and fight, too."

"A wealth of knowledge, I'm telling you. Can you mend a hockey jersey?"

"I can't even sew a button back on, Antoine." I started to climb the stairs again, but I turned around, "You, on the other hand, are fucking adorable, when you're mending a hockey jersey."

He smiled. "Let's go. March."

"Okay, cutie."

When we stepped into the gallery, I couldn't hold back an "Ohmygo-od" worthy of an overexcited Valley Girl: the space was light and completely open and, on the wall opposite the door, Juliette's eight paintings were hung in all their splendour. The simplicity of the décor showed them off perfectly, and far from the disorder of Juliette's studio, they looked even more vibrant and pure – they looked unreal, like sparkling islands: as you drew near to them, it seemed like the colours melted together and retained their own identity, and then the drawing would suddenly pop out, only to fade a second later, in a silver sparkle or a purple flash.

"Omigod!" I repeated, when I saw Juliette, standing next to a big window.

"Not bad, eh?" she said to me.

"Omigod!"

"Okay, that's enough..." she added with a laugh as she came to give me a hug. Behind me, Antoine said, "Holy shit," but I suspected he, too, felt like saying "Omigod."

"It's incredible," I said to Juliette. "A knockout."

"Florent wanted to put them on the back wall," she said. "He thought it would be better if the guests 'discovered' them, rather than being 'confronted' with them."

"Florent is an asshole. You know what he just asked Antoine? Which one of us he's sleeping with. With that ugly pig face of his... It must make him crazy to think about it."

"I hope," said Juliette, "that you told him you were sleeping with both of us. It would have killed him!"

"No," Antoine answered, from the other end of the room. "But I politely offered to beat him up."

"He's quite the gentleman today," I murmured to Juliette.

"This one is really beautiful," Antoine said. "I didn't see it when we were sorting through everything at your place." He was talking about an abstract painting – big red and pink lines rippled across the canvas. You could see faces, profiles, fruit, anything you wanted, really.

"Yeah," said Juliette. "I did that one a long time ago – it was in my bedroom, under my bed, to tell you the truth. I thought about it a couple of weeks ago and I dug it back out – I was sure I wouldn't like it, but then I said to myself, 'Why not?'"

On the same wall as the eight paintings, hung a few older and more recent pieces Juliette had never shown before. Their style had nothing to do with the series of eight, but the general effect was intriguing, stimulating even. Behind us, on the other wall, hung several small, very vivid paintings – one was in blue tones, another in oranges... they went from bubble-gum pink to lime green. "They're not much," Juliette said, "and they're not expensive. But they sell pretty well. People who don't want to invest in art are often happy to take a little something home."

Then she went to get the Molson Export, and we all stood in the middle of the room and clinked our bottles, without saying a word. Solemnly, we took the first sip, and then I said, "Ewww," and made Juliette laugh.

"You're such a snob," she said. "It's no worse than any other beer."

"No, no, that's just it: it is worse than any other beer."

"You still gonna drink it?" Antoine asked me.

"A girl's gotta do what a girl's gotta do," I answered as I took another swallow.

"Because there's another one on the way."

"I know, I know. After two sips, I get used to it." We started walking through the room, since it was still empty. It was peaceful – a nice, timeless moment. Rain was falling against the big windows, and we were talking in loud voices so we could hear each other from one end of the large room to the other.

"Doesn't it make you a little sad that they'll be split up?" I asked Juliette.

"No. No, not really. I like thinking they'll be in different places. They'll stay connected in my head. It'll be like an invisible network. Just for me, of course, but it'll still be there."

Antoine stepped over to the big paintings and he leaned close to the little card, next to the first one, that indicated the title of the work, the name of the artist, the medium and the asking price.

"You finally came up with a title," he said.

"Yeah. I thought *Untitled 1, 2, 3, 4, 5, 6, 7* and *8* was a little drab. But I had a really hard time. I'm no good at titles."

"What is it?" I asked, stepping closer.

"*Tonight, three times,*" Antoine read.

"You've got a lot of biblical references," I said.

"Well," Juliette answered, with a shrug, "I went to Catholic school."

Antoine walked over to another one of the paintings. "*That night, in the garden of olives.*"

"Who do you feel betrayed by?" I asked her.

"Besides you two? Lots of people." She smiled as she said it, as if she thought there was something particularly charming, almost pleasant, in that.

Antoine continued to read the titles of the paintings – the third, the one with the sentences Antoine and I were now calling "our sentences" – was entitled *Self-Portrait*.

"It's the first title that came to me," Juliette told us. "In fact, that one named itself."

I smiled at her. "I think it's perfect." She looked down, like a shy young girl being complimented.

"Ah-hem!" said Florent's big voice, as he entered the room. "Am I too early? Are you done with everything?" He grinned stupidly at Antoine, and, when nobody said anything, he came in.

"It looks good, doesn't it?" He was standing in front of the eight paintings. "It really looks good," he repeated. And for a few seconds (really just a few seconds) his gaze was a little less nasty, and seemed simply tender. Then he smiled and looked at his watch. "It's seven o'clock, kids. The guests will be here any minute."

The first ones to arrive were people I didn't know. They came in, and, without fail, they each stopped at the threshold, with a look of astonishment, and sometimes even wonder on their faces. Then they stepped inside, looked around for Juliette, and gave her a warm kiss. She looked comfortable, chatted in a lively way, laughed heartily. From our corner, Antoine and I watched the guests and entertained ourselves by guessing who would say what.

"Oh, he looks like he's going to say, 'Powerful! Very, very powerful!'" Antoine said, pointing a finger at a fat man with grey hair who seemed very knowledgeable.

"She's going to say something stupid like, 'What you've done here is very interesting,'" I added, indicating a tiny, angular woman with huge glasses and a perfect bun.

My father and Simon arrived at about seven-fifteen. They'd just come back from a farm in the Eastern Townships where, according to Simon, they produced the best *foie gras* in Quebec – this had piqued my father's curiosity, since, more and more often lately, he was looking for excuses not to go to the office. Like all the others, they stood before the paintings, stupefied or enchanted, until I walked over to them.

"Hey," I said, pressing against Simon.

"Hey," he said, kissing me distractedly, not taking his eyes off the paintings. "It's… Wow…"

"I know, everyone says the same thing."

I went and gave my father a kiss, as he nodded his head happily. "This is good, Chloé! It's very, very good, even." He stepped closer.

"You know," he whispered, "I've never really liked her work, but this I like. I really like it. Too bad your mother couldn't come. Where's Juliette?" He spotted her across the room and headed over, with his arms wide open shouting, "My dear Juliette!"

Simon, who was still standing quite near the door, said, "It's very, very impressive, eh?"

"Yes…" I looked at the paintings again – I was impressed every time, too.

"It's… it's not really my style, to tell you the truth," said Simon, "but… wow."

"Not your style?"

"No…" He laughed and finally leaned in close to me, "No, don't tell anyone, but… I have terrible taste in paintings. I don't know anything about it. I prefer representational things, it's… easier. Take Vermeer, for example. That I get."

"But Vermeer's work is beautiful!"

"Yes, I know. What I meant is that I prefer paintings I can understand easily. Vermeer, you look at it for a long time, hours, you observe the light and the shadows, you don't have to spend the whole time wondering, 'What did he mean?' It's the same reason I have trouble with some poets. Mallarmé, Emily Dickinson… I'd like to like them, but it doesn't work. It's not for me, I suppose. But Vermeer, on the other hand… oh… have you ever seen a Vermeer?"

"Yeah, in 2001, Juliette and I went to see an exhibit in New York..."

"At the Metropolitan?"

"Yes!"

"Hey!" said Simon. "I saw that, too!"

"Really?" I was disproportionately happy, like people always are when they discover they have something in common with someone else.

"Yes! Maybe we were there at the same time!" Simon said.

"We went in April"

"Me, too!"

We laughed in unison, with that silly laugh people in love often have. "I love you," Simon said.

"I love you, too." And we kissed in front of Juliette's big paintings.

"Well now!" said a voice behind me, "I heard about it, but I didn't believe it."

I turned around, still in Simon's arms, and I saw Stéphanie and Charles. I hadn't seen them since Stéphanie had announced their engagement, three months earlier, and it seemed like a lifetime ago.

"Hi!" I was happy to see them. I hugged each of them – Charles, potbellied, in a brown tank top, smiled kindly and said, "I'm so happy for you, Chloé." And I remembered that, the night they announced they were getting married, I'd been almost unable to say the same thing to him.

I introduced Simon to them, and Stéphanie said, "This is great! You can come to our wedding together!" And I smiled, very happily, because I pictured myself with Simon, under a flower-covered canopy, surrounded by friends who would finally see my healthy, vital happiness (and, of course, my incredible boyfriend). I pictured us – I was in a light, sun-yellow dress, he was in a light grey jacket – dancing elegantly among the happy couples.

"So," I asked Stéphanie, "when's the big day?"

"August 20th – exactly one year to the day after the corn roast. You'll get the announcement soon…" she added with a wink. "Oh! But…" She pointed towards the paintings, which she'd just noticed. Charles had already moved on, to admire them. "My God… it doesn't look like anything Juliette's ever done before."

"No, eh?"

She tilted her head. "I don't know if I like it… but… do you like it?"

"It took my breath away."

"Oh, that's for sure," said Stéphanie, "it'll take your breath away, whether you like it or not. That must mean she did a really good job… Where is Juliette?"

She was at the back of the room, talking to the short, angular woman and my father.

"Has she changed sides, too?" Stéphanie asked.

"No. No, she's even more committed to staying single. Completely, this time, if you get what I mean."

"Like nothing, nil, *nada*?"

"Total *nada*. She says it's just her luck to be named Juliette and then give up on love."

"Oh, there is a certain irony to it, but… didn't she have a boyfriend before? A little blond guy who came to the corn roast?"

"Yeah, Samuel, but he turned out to be gay."

"Ouch," said Stéphanie.

At the same instant, I saw Samuel, though I hadn't noticed him come in. He looked at ease walking around among all the people he seemed to know, and he approached Juliette. She looked surprised, but happy, and they gave each other a kiss.

"Did you see who's here?" Antoine asked me as he came over and gave Stéphanie a kiss.

"Yes. Interesting."

I pointed him out to Stéphanie, who shouted, "Ah, yes!

I recognize him! And it's true that, well, he's not exactly the poster child for masculinity…" Antoine and I smiled knowingly.

"What about you?" Stéphanie asked, turning towards Antoine. "I suppose you're still holding down the fort… Still a serial dater?"

"Serial fucker," Antoine clarified. "I don't date much." Simon started to laugh and I elbowed him, for appearance's sake only.

"Oh, lord," Stéphanie sighed. "You don't know what you're missing, Antoine."

"Don't worry about me," Antoine told her. "I'm not bored."

"No, I don't doubt that. But you'll see, someday, I'm telling you, one of them's going to make you change your mind. Look at Chloé."

And that's what he did. He looked at me, though not for very long. Then he turned away and said, "Yep." I looked up at Simon, who seemed lost in observing a small canvas – something that looked like a yellow sun on a pale background.

Barely two hours later, several paintings had been purchased, including five of the eight big ones, at $2,500 each – and since Juliette had arranged with Florent to pay him a flat rate for the use of the space, he wasn't taking a cut. It wasn't huge, but it was excellent news for Juliette, who'd made a living the last few years off slim grants, an occasional sale of a painting and Antoine's generosity, since he paid for her just about everywhere we went – at first, pride made her protest, but she hadn't said anything about it in a long time.

"Can you imagine: $12,500," she said to me. "That's pretty much what I made last year for the whole year."

"Not bad."

"It's huge!" And she laughed, repeating, "I can't get over it, I can't get over it…"

At about nine o'clock, as some people were starting to leave, Marcus and Michel arrived, dressed to the nines. They'd spent the last two months living out their feverish, nudist love, and Marcus' natural exuberance had increased tenfold. Still, he was a handsome sight, in his elegant black suit, with his red shirt and wide smile. He was talking to everyone, and he kept lifting Juliette up in his strong arms – she didn't protest, but she laughed and waved her feet, which were about a metre off the floor.

"I've never seen her like this," Antoine came and whispered to me. She was in the centre of a group of people who were listening to her attentively.

"I know… Really, the 12,500 bucks is great, but it's nothing compared to this. She's changed since she painted those pieces."

"I hope it lasts," Antoine said. "I think she fucking deserves it."

"Fucking right."

And the two of us stood there, sipping glasses of Caballero, looking at Juliette, and smiling.

The exhibit lasted a week. The eight big paintings all sold finally, to my great distress – it seemed to me that the third one, the one Juliette had called *Self-Portrait*, should have come back to us. I'd thought about buying it, but I waited too long. When I finally made up my mind, it had been sold, and I'd almost chewed out Juliette, who spent the whole day apologizing and repeating, "If I'd only known…" But she was on the verge of ecstasy: in the end, the show had earned her almost $30,000, of which, as Antoine kept telling her, she deserved every cent.

Simon had bought two pieces from another series for his restaurant, and, once in a while, his customers asked where they'd come from. Proudly, he'd tell them that they were by a friend of his, and he could put them in touch with her.

There was also a good deal of word-of-mouth – gallery owners started calling Florent about Juliette, or phoning her directly, to mention their interest in seeing her "new pieces." By mid-December, Juliette had gotten enough requests to be convinced she should start painting again, and she'd even had some business cards printed, which really made us laugh ("I'll call you tomorrow," Antoine would say to her. "Do you, do you have a card?").

I was still happy with Simon – now it seemed like I'd been with him for years, which, according to Daphné, was "marvellous." I agreed – I told myself there had to be something marvellous here, and I silently wondered if this was it, if there wasn't anything better, and I'd get mad at myself. I couldn't have said what I wanted, or what that "more" was that I sometimes wanted. Often, when I was lying next to him, I'd worry that my heart didn't beat fast enough, and that, sometimes, it seemed he wanted more. But I didn't say anything about it. Not to Juliette, not to Daphné – I didn't want to tell them I was nothing but a spoiled brat.

Then, on December 15th, I managed to convince Simon to take a vacation and come with me to Belize. He'd hesitated for a long time, but I reminded him I'd agreed to go to his parents' house for two days and he finally agreed. I was happy – ten days in Belize, walking on the warm sand and in quiet villages, eating lobster and *lambis*, making love several times a day – maybe that would be what I sometimes called "more."

We had gone to bed rather early that night, after spending a peaceful afternoon looking at travel brochures on Belize and talking about what we'd do there. It must have been one in the morning when my phone started to ring. Simon muttered something and I mechanically got up to answer it, thinking Antoine had forgotten his keys again. It happened at least twice a year and, generally, he slipped into Juliette's through the emergency exit and then slept in the studio. But when he had a girl with him, the problem was more delicate, and he'd gotten into the habit of calling me, because I had a spare set of his keys.

"Hmmm?" I answered, too sleepy to pretend to be mad.

"Chloé?" It wasn't Antoine.

"Chloé, it's Stéphane." I bolted upright.

"What is it?" I said. "Daphné? What is it?"

"Daphné had a miscarriage."

I tried to chase away the last fog of sleep. A miscarriage, I thought. Was it serious? I didn't think it was too serious – I mean, Daphné wasn't in danger of dying.

"Chloé?" Stéphane asked.

"Yes. Yes, I'm here."

"Daphné's at the hospital. Nothing serious, they're doing a D & C."

"Is she all right?"

"Yes, yes. She'll be all right."

"Stéphane? What happened?"

"These things happen, Chloé. These things just happen."

"I… Where are you, now?"

"At home, with the girls."

"And Daphné's alone at the hospital?"

"Yes, that's why I'm calling."

"You want me to come and stay with the girls?" I wondered why he hadn't simply called his mother, since she lived near them. "I'm on my way."

"No," said Stéphane. "I want you to go to the hospital. Daphné would prefer it if you went."

"Oh. Okay, I'll go. I'll leave right now. You want me to call when I get there?"

"Yes, please."

"Okay. Bye, Steph."

"Chloé?"

"Yes?"

"She's at Sacré-Coeur."

"Oh, yes. Good to know. Thank you."

I hung up and started to get dressed.

"What's going on?" asked Simon. When he was tired, he automatically talked to me in English.

"My sister had a miscarriage. I have to go to the hospital."

He propped himself up on his elbows. "I... I'll drive you."

"No. No, thank you. It's our business." I kissed him on the forehead, and I left.

Chapter 18

I got to the hospital a half-hour later and Daphné, I was told, was already in a room – she'd been admitted two hours earlier and a nurse with a tired but very kind smile told me there was no reason to worry. She also indicated that visiting hours were long over, and, since Daphné's condition was stable, she couldn't let me go up. I just stood there, devastated, and asked myself, "What would Mom have done?" I started to harangue the tired nurse. I told her about my poor sister, all alone, without even her husband, with her empty belly, and well, I was on quite a roll when she gestured for me to stop and told me her room number.

" Oh! You're wonderful!" I said.

"You do what you can. You are a very good sister."

"You do what you can."

She smiled again. "I'll tell you how to get there."

I thanked her profusely and left, following her directions, making two wrong turns, turning back around, passing the same sleepless patients who were slowly walking the hall with their IV poles.

I like hospitals. That always made me a little mad at myself, because I knew they were places with more sorrow than happiness, but I thought that, whether there was cause for tears or for joy, everything was reduced to the most essential. There was no pretence – even in the chaos of Emerg – and I always found this fact strangely calming. Poor Daphné, who thought the exact opposite, had only agreed to give birth in a hospital because her midwife had convinced her that, with twins, it was by far a preferable location.

I finally found her room and saw her in the far bed, lit

by a lamp that was giving off what had to be the palest light in the world. There were three other beds, hidden by pale green curtains – a woman's soft snoring could be heard.

"Hey," I whispered as I came closer to the bed. Daphné turned over on her pillow – there were dark circles under her eyes, but when she saw me, I thought I noticed an almost joyful spark in her gaze – and I started to cry.

"Come on now," said Daphné, "I'm not even crying."

"Oh… Dadi! How did it happen?"

"What do you mean how did it happen? I lost my baby, that's all."

"Oh…" And I sat down next to her, took her hand, and cried even harder.

"Chloé, I'm not dying." Practical even in a hospital bed, I thought. "There's a lady over there, in the bed on the left, who just had a brain tumour removed." She shivered, though I don't know if it was out of disgust or fear. "So, really, I don't think I have any right to complain."

"You do have the right, you know."

She stared at me, but didn't say anything.

"Do you want me to call Mom?" I asked her.

"No. Not right away. Tomorrow morning, okay?"

"Whenever you want. I'm not going anywhere."

"Are you allowed to be here?"

"No, but I made myself a friend at the reception desk downstairs. She wasn't going to let me come up, so I said to myself, 'What would Mom do?'"

Daphné laughed weakly, "So you bugged her until she let you come up?"

"No. I just talked to her, that's all."

"You're right," said Daphné. "Mom would have done the same thing."

I ran a hand over her forehead. "You're hot."

"Yeah. It's okay now, but when I woke up at eleven… listen, I thought I was going to die. I was having these contractions – the doctor who saw me said that was normal, since I was already at four months." She sighed and, for the first time since I'd gotten there, she looked like she wanted to cry. "Four months! I always heard that at four months, there's no more danger!"

I gently stroked her head, without speaking. After a few minutes, I asked, "Does it still hurt?"

"Not too much. I'm okay. They gave me something when I came in, I don't even know what, it hurt so much I couldn't even see straight. The… the fetus came out in the ambulance, just before we got here. A doctor examined me. They're going to do a D & C, you know, just to be sure. But he seemed to think everything looked okay."

"The… the fetus, eh?" I couldn't help but say it, as if the word were still there, next to our heads, waiting for someone to do something.

"Hmmm," said Daphné, gritting her teeth. "I saw it."

"Oh! Oh… how?"

"A stupid reflex. I raised my head."

"Oh…"

Daphné lifted one hand, spread out her thumb and first finger – the size of the fetus.

"You know what?" she asked.

"What?"

"I thought of Auntie Ursule."

"What?" We both started to laugh. Auntie Ursule was my mother's aunt, but we never knew her. She was the family crazy woman we'd heard about the whole time we were growing up. She heard voices in the sink pipes, she got all dressed up to watch Pierre Trudeau on TV, convinced he could see her, and she claimed she was the illegitimate daughter of an Indian witch. My mother had a thousand and one stories about her, and I suspected she'd made about half of them up herself, but, nonetheless, Ursule had become a kind of legend for Daphné and me, and I'd named my first cat in her honour.

Ursule's craziness, my mother had told us, had been

brought on by a miscarriage when she was eighteen years old. She'd locked herself in the bathroom, alone, and had saved the fetus, which she then kept in alcohol on the fireplace mantle. "She'd talk to it," my mother told us. "When we went to her house, she told us to go say hello to it. A little two-inch thing in a jelly jar…" Daphné and I were fascinated by the sordid story, and we imagined Ursule with long black hair and old-fashioned dresses, living in a big gothic mansion with gargoyles and pointed turrets (she actually lived in Kamouraska, in a pretty pink and green house – a very ungothic locale, indeed, which had disappointed us greatly).

"I thought of Ursule," Daphné said with a sad laugh, "and I thought, my God, she picked it up… I swear to you, in situations like that, the things that go through your mind are unbelievable."

"Poor, sweet Dadi…" I kissed her right hand. "And Stéphane?" I asked.

"Oh, Stéphane. Poor Stéphane. He was panicking. He's a doctor, and he was panicking."

"Yes, well, he's a gastroenterologist, right. Maybe he's more comfortable with duodenums than with miscarriages."

"Especially when it's his wife who's having one."

"Especially."

"And he feels guilty."

"Why?"

"Because it took him almost four months to want the baby." Poor Stéphane. He'd even consulted a psychologist, without telling Daphné, who'd helped him "open up to the idea of a new baby." The last time I'd seen him, about two weeks earlier, he finally seemed to have gotten over his worries and was talking about the baby, something he hadn't been able to do before that.

"You should have seen him," said Daphné. "He was crushed. He kept saying it was his fault because he'd stressed me out too much with everything."

"Yeah, but…"

"I know. But you understand…"

"Yes. Yes, I understand."

There was a long silence, punctuated by the other woman's snoring and the beeping of the monitor. I was holding Daphné's hand, she'd turned her head away, towards the window – in the glow of a streetlight, we could see snowflakes falling; they were heavy and silent, too. It was twenty after two, and I wondered if Daphné was sleeping – she was breathing regularly, without making any noise, and I realized I wasn't tired at all. Someone was walking down the hall, with a firm step, possibly a nurse. I pulled the green curtain around Daphné's bed and backed my chair into the triangle of shadow it created between the nightstand and the wall. I didn't have a book, or a magazine – so I watched Daphné, and the peaceful room, our little isle of light in the sleeping hospital.

I tried to imagine what could have happened – the pain, waking up, the surprise, the realization. She'd been so happy the last few weeks, she kept repeating "everything is back to normal," and "everything is going the way it should." Daphné had always had strange ideas like that, and she honestly believed that there was an order to things and that this order was good and that we should try to attain it. More than anything, the absence of order frightened her. I thought maybe that was why she'd wanted to see me. Because I was always in disorder, I'd never known how to appreciate the calm beauty of motionless things, and I got calm when everything else wasn't.

After a half-hour, Daphné started to stir. She opened her eyes, and then she sat up with difficulty and asked me for the glass of water on the nightstand.

"I can't sleep," she murmured. "And I'm exhausted." She took a little drink and then handed the glass back to me.

"Why did you want me to come?"

"Because…" Daphné answered. "I know it's not fair, but

I'm mad at him... And don't tell me it's not right," she added before I could even say a word, "I know that. He made such an effort, the poor thing. But I didn't want to see him. And I didn't want to be here with him either. And besides, there's the practical side of things, too, it's better for him to stay with the girls."

"Of course."

"Oh, I'm an awful person, aren't I?"

"No. No, stop it, Daphné. It's normal."

"I don't know," she said. "Lately I don't really know what's normal."

She punched her mattress weakly. "I feel so helpless!"

"You are helpless, Daphné. It's okay."

"No! It's not okay! I don't know how to deal with all this. I don't know how and it's traumatizing me! How do you do it? You've always been able to accept this kind of situation."

"What are you talking about? I've never gone through anything like what you're going through, Daphné."

"No, I mean when everything's up in the air. Exams at school, the times when we were waiting for important answers, when Mom and Dad almost broke up... You were always calm..."

"I don't know. The more everyone around me gets upset, the less I get upset. I think a lot of people are like that. It's no big deal."

"But it's a good start," said Daphné. And I thought to myself, that's true, it is a good start. But I nonetheless conducted my own life with all the assurance of a chicken with its head cut off.

Daphné looked at me, "When are you going to do it?"

"Have babies?" I said "babies" in an astonished, amused tone that surprised even me – it sounded like I meant emus or dromedaries – something completely unlikely.

"Yes," answered Daphné.

"I don't know. Sometime. Not right away."

"You'd make a good mother."

"Pardon? They gave you too much medication, Daphné." I couldn't believe she'd just said that to me. Coming from Antoine, the compliment was somehow charming and gratuitous – he didn't know anything about these things, after all. But, coming from Daphné, it was completely disarming.

"No," she said, "I've always thought that. Not right away, obviously, but someday. I'm telling you. The way you listen to people, and talk to children. Your patience."

"I'm anything but patient!"

"You are for important things."

"You think so?" I was smiling in spite of myself. I was immensely flattered.

"I think so," said Daphné. "And plus, with Simon, I can really see it."

"Stop it with that! Mom said something about it the other day. We haven't been together long enough."

"Haven't you ever talked about it?"

"No."

"But you do want kids, right?"

"Yeah, but it's vague. I want kids, sure, but not here, not now! I don't see why I have to plan it all out already."

"Don't get mad," Daphné said. "One last question."

"What?"

"If you don't have kids, will you feel like you wasted your life?"

I leaned on her mattress: "Daphné, I. Don't. Know. I think I'd be disappointed, sure, but I'm not going to go having a baby with the first guy who comes along just to have one. I don't want to be the kind of girl who, at forty-five, finds herself climbing the walls cause it's her last chance. I also don't want to be an overwhelmed, unhappy mother, wandering around Disney World in Birkenstocks, with dirty hair, looking like she's on the edge of a nervous breakdown, and yelling at her kids. I don't want to lose myself in all that, you understand? It may be selfish, or unnatural, or whatever, but whenever I think about it, I say, 'I want to have kids,' not, 'I want to be a mommy at any cost.' Do you see the difference?"

I was afraid Daphné would be insulted, that she'd think I was accusing her, of being one of those women who wants to be a mommy at all costs, but she answered, "Yes, I can clearly see the difference. I have friends who are like that – they were more obsessed by the idea of being a mommy than by the idea of the kids they were going to have. But you shouldn't look down on them."

"No, I know, I know. Sorry. But do you see what I mean? Not that I believe in destiny, but if it works out for me to have kids, then I'll have kids, that's all. I'm not going to force it."

"Okay," said Daphné. "We'll see."

She gave me a little wink, something I'd never seen her do before and she patted my hand like a grandmother.

"You know what?" she asked me.

"No, what?"

"For a long time, I didn't think you were as smart as me."

"Pardon?"

She repeated what she'd said.

"Okay, what's going on here?" I asked, "Are you playing 'I'm in a hospital bed, the two of us are all alone in the night, so I'm going to tell you what I really think'?"

"Maybe," Daphné answered.

"Okay, but before you go on, for a long time, *I* thought *I* was smarter than you."

"But I got better marks than you at school!" Daphné said, so genuinely she made me giggle.

"Exactly. I figured all you had was school smarts. That's it."

"Well, I thought you were always making bad choices."

"Same here."

"Pardon?" With that, she sat straight up.

"When you got married, when you had the girls... I said

to myself, she's burying herself. I thought you'd really chosen an easy, predictable life."

"You're the one who chose the easy, predictable life."

"Yes," I said to her. "I know."

She slowly lay back down.

"But it's not all black or all white," she said.

"No, it's not all black or all white."

A few minutes later, she fell asleep.

I still wasn't sleepy, so I went for a walk around the hospital. In a waiting room, I finally found a pile of old
magazines and a coffee machine, and I went back up to
Daphné's room with copies of *People* and *L'Actualité* that
were a year old, and a tea. At around four o'clock, a nurse
came in and made the rounds of the beds. When she got to
us, she said, "You're not allowed to be here now." I pointed
out that I wasn't bothering anyone, and she said those were
the rules, and that was it. Then she left without even looking
at me.

I thought about horror movies like *Twenty-eight Days
Later*, and I imagined that, maybe, one of the other occu-
pants of the room was suffering from a rare and terribly
contagious disease and that I was going to catch it and
spread it through the city – then there would be the army,
helicopters, panic in the street, people running in every
direction, and trampling each other; then, inevitably, a tidal
wave would swallow up New York – all because a tired, dis-
illusioned nurse hadn't insisted on getting me out of the
room in time.

A little before six o'clock, Daphné woke up with a start.
She saw me, immediately stretched out a hand, and said,
"Oh my God," then she started to cry; so I climbed up on
the bed next to her and took her in my arms – I'd never held
anyone like that, like a child. I gently rocked her and she just
let me, which was quite astonishing in itself since this was,
after all, Daphné. With her head resting on my chest, she
said, "I really wanted it."

"I know."

"But for a little while, I thought maybe I didn't want it! Maybe the baby felt that, maybe..."

"Daphné. You, as the world's greatest pragmatist, you know that has nothing to do with it. And you know you'll have another one, right? You're only twenty-six."

"I don't know," said Daphné. "Stéphane was ready to accept this one, but what about now, now that we have the choice again? What if he suddenly decides he doesn't want more children? I don't know..." She started to cry again. I couldn't feel my left arm anymore, and one of her elbows was pushed rather painfully into my ribs – collateral damage, I thought. She calmed down, slowly, and she finally stretched, reaching for the copy of *People* I'd been reading, which triumphantly announced Ben Affleck and Jennifer Lopez's new relationship.

"Didn't they break up?" Daphné asked. "Even I know that."

"Yeah, but that's the most recent magazine I could find."

She read the article with almost comical interest, then she said, "Fascinating. Do you have any more?" I handed her my pile.

For a little while, we flipped through the magazines – Daphné was constantly interrupting me, to say things like, "I suppose you also knew that Tom Cruise isn't with Penelope Cruz anymore?" and then, "Cruise, Cruz, it sounds the same!" She read the magazine from cover to cover, rubbing her eyes and yawning her head off, then she closed it and, with sudden surprise, asked me, "Aren't you tired?"

I shrugged. "No. I don't know. Strange, isn't it?"

"You didn't even doze off a bit while I was sleeping?"

"No. To tell you the truth, I am starting to feel a little tired now, but I'm okay."

"Were you sleeping when Stéphane called?"

"Yeah. Since about eleven."

"Eleven..." said Daphné. "I think it's been years since I

went to bed after ten. Ever since the girls started sleeping through the night."

"For me, it's just the opposite. Before, I never went to bed before midnight. Even when I was home alone. I'd read, or watch reruns of *Law & Order* or old movies. It was like…"

"You're wising up now that you have a boyfriend," said Daphné.

"Yeah, I know."

"You don't have to say it like it's a bad thing."

"No, it's just that sometimes I get a little nostalgic. Just like you predicted on Mom's birthday. I remember the good old days, and think to myself, 'Those really were the good old days.'" I looked out the window. It had stopped snowing and the sky was starting to turn blue above the rooftops.

"Everything going okay with Simon?" Daphné asked me.

"Super."

"Super?"

"Yes, super. There's nothing to add."

"Nothing to add?"

"No. Nothing to add."

"Well, good, then."

I thought that if I didn't say it to her, right now, before the sun came up, and before it was too late to play "I'm sitting by your hospital bed, in the middle of the night, and we're having a real heart-to-heart," I'd never say it. So I put my magazine down on Daphné's bed, and I said, "Okay. I know it makes me Queen of the Idiots to talk to you about this now, while you're in that bed, but honestly, I'm just going to say it because if I don't do it now, I never will, but honestly, I don't know, Daphné."

"Don't know what, Chloé?"

"I go to bed every night and I think to myself 'This can't be it.' Simon. This can't be all there is. There has to be more."

"Like what?"

"I don't know! Otherwise, I'd be looking for it. I'm just eternally dissatisfied. A spoiled brat."

Daphné rolled over on her side, towards me. "Maybe there is more."

"Okay, coming from you, that's very weird."

She smiled. "I told you I don't know what's normal anymore." She extended a hand towards me, and I took it.

"Seriously," I continued, "I think it's just in my nature not to be able to be happy with what I have. Simon is perfect. Literally. There's no reason on this earth for me not to be happy."

"Are you staying with him because it's reasonable?"

"No! I'm staying with him because I love him."

"Sure, but at the same time, you think what you're doing is reasonable."

"No! Well, yes, but it's just it's all the same thing, that's all. But listen, Daphné, I don't want to talk about it. It's too trivial."

"Whatever you say. But like I told you, I've always found it easier to be reasonable."

She turned over on her back. I almost said something, but I stopped myself – it would have come out all twisted, in a stupid, childish sentence like, "But I'm not reasonable, I don't choose the easy solutions." I've spent my life doing what didn't require any effort at all, and now, for the first time, I was working to make a relationship work. It certainly wasn't a thankless task, but I was still working at it. It wasn't a big deal, I thought, and it didn't necessarily make me a "reasonable" person. I so didn't want to be reasonable. I thought it was a small, sad word that had nothing to do with my dream of immense, pure love.

I was in the midst of all these pointless thoughts, when a long moan arose from one of the beds that was opposite Daphné's.

"What's wrong with her?" Daphné asked.

"How should I know?"

The woman continued to moan long enough for me to decide to go ask if she needed something.

"No!" said Daphné, who was as afraid of sick people as she was of hospitals. "Go get a nurse."

"Good idea."

I walked out of the room, and walked towards the nurses' station that I'd noticed earlier. Day had now completely broken – it was a tiny, greyish day I could make out through the big windows. I finally found a nurse, who was apparently a lot more energetic than the one who did the nightshift, and who started to yell at me because I wasn't supposed to be there, and that it certainly wasn't my job to come get her, and, anyway, she was on her way. Pitifully, I followed her into the room, where the sick woman had stopped moaning. She opened the curtain that had hidden the bed, exposing a woman who must have been about eighty years old, and who was sleeping, with her mouth open.

"My God," said Daphné. "She's dead."

"No, she's not dead," said the nurse. "She's sleeping."

"But a little while ago, she was shouting."

The nurse leaned over the old woman for barely even a minute, and then she stood up, saying there was nothing wrong. "As for you," she said to me, "you come with me. I don't know who let you in here, but it's absolutely against the rules."

"But she's my sister…"

"No. Listen, we're not going to play this game, okay. Come on. Anyway, the doctor will be by in an hour. You're have a D & C, aren't you?"

"Yes," said Daphné.

"It won't take very long. Your sister can wait downstairs if she wants, but not here."

"All right, all right, Nurse Ratched," I said. "I'm coming. I'll call Mom, Daphné."

"Okay," she answered.

I hugged her and she looked at me with her little girl eyes.

"It's just a D & C," she said, to reassure herself.

"It's just a D & C," I repeated. "If it looks like it won't take too long, I'll stay here."

"No, go get some rest."

"Daphné…"

"Okay." She lay back down and I left with the nurse. I followed her to the emergency waiting room, where a few tired people were waiting, staring at the wall. A little boy was running among the rows of chairs, laughing and shouting, and no one seemed to notice him.

"It's quiet," I said to Nurse Ratched.

"It's that time. The people who were here tonight have stopped being afraid, they've gone home. The others are still sleeping, or they'll be waking up and they'll be here soon. I have to ask you to move along."

"Move along?" I repeated, doing my best not to laugh.

"Yes, this is an emergency room."

"I just need to make one call."

"In the main entrance."

I turned on my heel, thinking I'd soon be able to draw a map of the hospital from memory, and I headed off towards the main entrance, which smelled cold, and like an old ashtray, because of the people who were constantly coming in and going out, and because of the people who smoked between the two doors. I put on my coat and I called my parents.

"Hello!" answered my father's happy, morning voice.

"Dad? It's Chloé."

"Oh, good morning, sweetie."

"I have a little bit of bad news, Dad." It wasn't really "a little bit of bad news," but I didn't want to make him panic for no reason, and "a medium-sized bit of bad news" sounded pretty awkward.

"What's going on?"

"Daphné's lost the baby."

"Oh!..." There was a distressed silence at the end of the line. "Oh, how sad… when?"

"During the night."

"But she's all right?"

"Yes, yes. I'm at the hospital, now, with her. Well, I'm not with her anymore because I got kicked out of her room, but everything's okay."

"Is she in good spirits?"

"Hmpff... you know. She's not in too bad shape. She's strong, you know."

"Of course, of course..." He seemed to be thinking for a moment, and then asked, "Where's Stéphane?"

"With the twins. I think Daphné preferred to have me here."

My father went "hmm, hmm," in an understanding way, and I could feel he guessed that Daphné was blaming Stéphane.

"That's why," I said to him, "it would be better if you wake up Mom. You know, in situations like this, I think a girl needs her mother."

"Yes, yes, of course. Exactly. What hospital are you at?"

"Sacré-Coeur. Tell Mom I'll wait for her at the main entrance."

"Okay, sweetheart. I love you."

"Me, too, Dad."

I hung up with a smile and went to buy a muffin.

My mother arrived barely a half-hour later, which was something like a miracle, since it usually took her at least an hour to pull herself out of bed. She was wearing jeans, with a big, red cashmere sweater, and a long coat – an outfit which, for her, was extremely eccentric.

"Oh, sweetheart!" she said as soon as she saw me. She opened up her arms and hugged me like I was the one who'd just had a miscarriage. "Are you okay?"

"Well... yes," I said. "I'm okay."

"Oh, sweetie. It was so nice of you to come. Why didn't you call sooner?"

"I don't know. There was nothing to do during the night except wait. So I waited."

My mother ran a hand through my hair. "Lord… Where's Daphné? How is she?"

"She's okay. We can't go see her right away. I talked to a nurse before you got here. They're going to do a D & C, but not for another two hours. I should have called you to tell you to come later, but I'm starting to have a pretty sleepy brain."

"No! No! I'm going to go up and see her."

"We can't. It's not visiting hours."

My mother gave me a look I knew very well – it meant, "They don't know who they're dealing with."

I laughed and added, "Yeah, you'll manage. You know, last night, they didn't want to let me up either, so I asked myself, 'What would Mom do?' So I pulled out all my charm and my pigheadedness, and it was a great success."

"Ah… you see, your old mother can still teach you a thing or two."

"I know…" I pressed against her. "But now, you go and see Daphné. She's all alone, poor thing. You know how she hates hospitals. Go cheer her up."

"I'll do my best. I had two miscarriages myself, you know."

"What?" I summoned the last bit of energy I still had left so I could look appropriately shocked – and I really was: my mother had never told us that.

"Yes," she said. "One before you, and another between you and Daphné."

"Really? I didn't know!"

"It happens," my mother said. "Poor little Daphné. Maybe she got it from me."

"Is it hereditary?"

My mother shrugged. "No idea. But I'm sure it won't do her any harm to talk to someone who's already been through the same thing."

"I agree completely." I gave a long yawn. "Okay, then…
I'm going to go get an hour or two of sleep, because I'm
starting to get pretty fuzzy."

"I'll call you as soon as they're done with the D & C."

"There's nothing to worry about with a D & C, right?"

My mother gave me her reassuring mom smile,
"Nothing at all. But I'll call you anyway."

"Thank you."

We kissed each other good-bye, and as I watched her go
down the big hallway, with her coat floating behind her, I
thought that the nurse who was going to be able to stand
between her and her daughter still hadn't been born.

On the wall, a big clock said it was seven-forty. I yawned
again. Next to me, a man who looked completely exhausted
raised his cup of coffee in recognition. "Hey," I said, and I
dragged myself over to the phones.

I lifted the receiver and mechanically dialled Antoine's
number. A woman's voice answered, "Hello?" I racked my
brain to try and figure out who it could be. A woman
answering Antoine's phone. I thought of Julie, the little
florist he saw from time to time. He'd introduced her to us,
and she was a charming, young twenty-two year old who'd
started working in a flower shop to pay for school, and then
ended up falling in love with the job. Also, she was not at all
impressed by Antoine, which really amused Juliette and
made her like her right away.

"Julie?" I tried.

"No. It's Miko."

"Ah! Oh. Miko. Hi, Miko." I made a face: Miko was a
Japanese woman whose beauty and grace were so stellar that
I always became temporarily stupid when I saw her. She and
Antoine had dated a few years earlier – in my opinion, she
was the only girl he'd almost fallen for. But she was as
unbearable as she was beautiful, which is a lot, and they'd
stopped seeing each other regularly, and settled for sleeping

together once in a while. I always imagined torrid sex scenes, and, especially since, according to Antoine, Miko was even more beautiful naked than in the pretty, clingy dresses she always wore.

"Miko. It's Chloé."

"Oh. Hi, Chloé." She waited. I remembered she never spoke, except to complain to Antoine and ask when they were going to leave.

"Can I talk to Antoine, Miko?"

There was silence, and then Antoine came on the line.

"Chloé? It's not even eight o'clock, what are you doing up?"

"What are you doing with Miko?"

"I'll give you three guesses."

"Never mind. I hope I'm not bothering you."

"No, I was just getting out of the shower. Is everything okay?"

"Mmmm. I'm at the hospital. Daphné lost her baby last night."

"Oh, fuck."

"That's right." I looked at the rotary dial on the phone and was rather astonished to realize there were still rotary phones in existence.

"Chloé?"

"Sorry. I was in the clouds."

"Didn't you sleep?"

"No. But I'm all right."

"Do you want me to come get you?"

I suddenly remembered he'd lost his driver's licence.

"You don't have a licence anymore," I said.

"I'll take a cab."

"No, come on, now. I can take a taxi by myself."

"Don't be ridiculous. I'll be right there. Where are you?"

"Sacré-Coeur."

"Okay. I'm on my way."

He hung up and I thought of Simon, who must be worried. I shook my head, a bit surprised – the idea of calling him instead of Antoine hadn't even occurred to me.

He answered after the first ring. Obviously, he hadn't slept well, and he was happy to hear that Daphné was out of danger. I apologized for not having called sooner, and he repeated I had nothing to apologize for.

"I'll come get you," he said.

"No. My father's coming. I think the family needs to be together. He'll give me a ride." Simon said he understood.

It was the first time I'd lied to him.

Chapter 19

Sitting outside on one of the steps leading to the entrance, I waited for Antoine. It was cold out, but there's no doubt I would have fallen asleep if I'd stayed inside. I still couldn't believe I'd lied to Simon, over such a stupid thing – and, at the same time, I couldn't see how I could have told him I'd called Antoine first. Besides, why had I called him? I rubbed my head and thought about Daphné, and said to myself, "At least she won't be able to say I was being reasonable." And I smiled in spite of myself, just before I realized I was a complete idiot.

"You look good." I looked up. Antoine was standing there in front of me, and I hadn't even seen him coming.

"I'm okay," I grumbled. He held out a hand, and I got up with difficulty – I felt like I weighed about two hundred kilos. "Come on," he said to me. "Let's get you to bed."

Once we were in the taxi, he asked me, "Simon couldn't come?"

"I didn't call Simon."

"Why not?"

"I didn't think of it." I was so tired, I started to laugh. Antoine didn't say anything – he smiled sweetly and pulled me close into him. I leaned against his chest, and closed my eyes – he smelled good, just like always.

"What happened?" Antoine asked. I told him the whole story – the fetus in the ambulance, getting to the hospital, the old issues of *People*, the conversation in the sleepy room, everything, except what I'd told Daphné about Simon.

"You're so nice," I finally said. "It's kind of ridiculous; really, I should have taken a taxi on my own. Sorry."

"Do you mind? You know I'd go all the way to Iqaluit to get you."

"Iqaluit, eh?"

"Well, okay, maybe as far as Sainte-Thérèse, or Blainville, even."

"Blainville! Wow, I must be dreaming!"

Antoine laughed and kissed me on the head.

"And just what were you doing with Evil Miko?"

"I repeat, what do you think?"

"Oh, I know... even I'd consider sleeping with Miko."

"Really? Because I can set a little something up for us, if you want."

I slapped him on the thigh. "Shut up. You don't even like three-ways." I remembered refusing to believe it the first time he'd told me, but he'd insisted, assuring me that three-ways were seriously overrated. "The first time, it's pretty impressive," he'd said. "Because, well, just for the kick, just because you can say, 'I'm screwing two girls at the same time,' it's pretty remarkable. But after that, it's almost inevitably a disappointment." He had a rather logical theory about it, which stated that "the idea you have of a threesome is always more exciting than the thing itself. But with just one person, you never know."

The taxi was getting close to my house.

"Yeah, but Miko," I said to Antoine. "She's unbearable."

"Every second spent with her doing anything but screwing is a real nightmare."

"But why do you..." I didn't finish my sentence. It would have been like asking an alcoholic why he hadn't refused the best bottle of whiskey in the world.

"It's an aesthetic thing," said Antoine, laughing.

"You can be a real jerk when you want to... Anyway, I really liked Julie."

"I like Julie, too."

"Wow, Antoine." I patted his hand. I could see trees going past the window – from where I was, I could only see the naked tops of them, and the highest floor of the brick houses on boulevard Saint-Joseph. The clouds had cleared, exposing a blue, perfectly pure sky: the kind of sky that comes with very cold weather, which made me smile at the thought of soon being under my comforter. I snuggled against Antoine.

"Do you think I'm too reasonable?" I asked him.

"Reasonable?" He gave a little laugh. "No. Really, Chloé, I don't think that's the most appropriate word to describe you."

"Have you ever wanted to be reasonable?"

"What are you talking about?"

"It's Daphné," I said. "She claims that, at lots of times, for certain people, it's easier to be reasonable."

"Easier? I don't know, Chloé. It depends on what you mean by reasonable. If you think it means having reason rule your instinct or your desires… it seems like it's harder, that it requires you to constantly do battle with yourself, but, all in all, for some people, it is easier to live that way."

"Hmmm. You really can't criticize yourself if you've followed reason. There's something reassuring about that."

"Maybe that's what Daphné meant. And there are lots of people who prefer to have a code. Like a code of ethics. It simplifies a lot of things. Like they say, being completely free is the hardest thing in the world."

"That sounds sad to me," I said.

"No. It's not sad. It's a damned beautiful challenge, if you want my opinion."

"Easy for you to say, Mr. 'All I want out of life is pleasure, the rest is not for me.'"

"That's not true," said Antoine. "I'll have you know I live by a very specific code. It has lots of principles."

"Right, principles like 'pleasure first' and 'only live in the moment.'"

"They're still principles." He paused and then added. "Don't kid yourself, Chloé. I'm a lot less free than I look."

I looked up to see what he meant, but we'd arrived. The taxi stopped. "You want me to come up?" Antoine asked me. "I've still got forty-five minutes before I have to be at work." "No. Simon's still here. I told him my father was giving me a ride."

He shook his head.

"I know," I said. "It was pretty crappy of me."

"No."

"Yes. Besides, you have Miko at your place."

"Oh, Miko told me to fuck off in Japanese."

"You like that, anyway. You get excited when she yells at you."

"Oh… it's true, there's something about her when she's mad…"

I leaned over to give him a kiss. He turned his head and I hit the corner of his lips – I felt a little shock, a slight jolt, and I got mad at myself for it. But it was uncontrollable – it was the way he smelled, I told myself. Or just a reflex. I was trying to find an excuse, which seemed absolutely ridiculous. Antoine put one hand under my face and asked, "You going to be all right?"

"Of course." I looked down. "I'll be fine."

"You'll let me know how Daphné's doing?"

"Of course. You're really fantastic, Antoine."

"I know, sweetie." He winked at me, and I got out of the taxi.

Simon was already up. He was sitting at the dining-room table, reading the newspaper and having his coffee. He immediately got up and came towards me, full of concern and a kindness I was sure I'd never possess, and he took me in his arms.

"How's it going?"

"My mother's with Daphné and…"

"No, how are you?"

I smiled at him. How could I complain, even implicitly, about him? I thought about my stupid lie, and I felt ridiculous, and small. Often, even as I wondered if there was a bigger love than the one we shared, I would tell myself I didn't deserve a man like Simon.

"I'm okay," I answered.

"Come to bed."

"I want to take a shower first. I smell like the hospital. If I'm not out in an hour, it's 'cause I fell asleep in the tub."

"I'll come get you," Simon said laughing. "I can stay till noon if you want. In case your mother calls while you're sleeping."

"That would be nice," I said, feeling three times more ungrateful.

My mother called at around eleven. I was sleeping so deeply, I didn't even hear the phone ringing. Simon didn't wake me up until noon.

"Everything's okay," he said. "Daphné's gone home."

"What? Hmmm?" I was still half asleep – I'd had a series of strange dreams that had seemed quite real: I could see myself wandering around the hospital entrance, again and again, the rotary phone, the tired man with his coffee, like I was watching a TV program that kept showing a loop of the same images. I had the distinct impression I was waiting – I kept repeating, "It's coming."

"What?" I repeated.

"Daphné," Simon said gently. "She's gone home."

I sat up. "Already?"

"Yes. I guess it was surprising they even kept her overnight."

"I'll call her."

"She's sleeping. But your mother is with her if you want to call her." He handed me the phone with a smile.

"Chloé?" answered my mother.

"You knew it was me?"

"They have a call display unit here. Very interesting gadget. I have to tell your father to get a phone that has that."

"How's Daphné?"

"She's asleep. She's okay. The D & C just took a few minutes. Everything's good."

"That's it? That's all of it?"

"Well, yes," answered my mother. "That's all. At least for the physical part."

"And the rest?"

"Oh, it'll be all right. She's only twenty-six, you know. I'm more worried about her relationship with Stéphane."

"Come on, Mom. No one gets divorced over a miscarriage."

"No, no, I don't think they're going to get divorced, Chloé. But they've got some work to do, I think. They're both mad, at themselves and at each other. They hardly talk to each other, you know. Stéphane is the kind of guy who would rather talk to a shrink than to his own wife. It can help, but still... Those two don't communicate."

She had said "communicate" as if it were a magic word, possibly even a slightly dangerous word, that shouldn't be used lightly.

"Is Stéphane there?" I asked.

"No. He went to work."

"Do you want me to come over? I can spend two or three days helping or cheering her up."

"Tonight," my mother said, "I think it's better for them to be alone. I'll talk to Daphné when she wakes up, but I think I'll take the twins home with me. To give Daphné and Stéphane some space. So they can communicate."

"Right, communicate," I said with the same mystic intonation.

"Don't laugh at me. You know what I mean."

"Of course, I know. Listen, ask Daphné to call me. If she

wants me to come over, I'll be there. Today, or tomorrow or whenever."

"Why don't you stop by the house tonight? Come give me a hand with the girls."

"Yes, that would be fun."

"Perfect," said Mom, very happy. "I'll call you."

At seven-thirty, I was at their place, cooking veal cutlets, while my mother was looking after the twins in the living room. My father was hovering around me, a martini in his hand, laughing gently. "The last time she was alone with both of them at the same time, they weren't walking yet. I think she's a little overwhelmed."

"And the idea of helping her hasn't crossed your mind?"

"Sure it has," he said, without even pretending to go towards the living room. I smiled at him.

"You know," he continued, "when your mother had her miscarriages, she went through a lot of pain. The second time especially – she started to be afraid there was a problem, even if all the doctors told her otherwise. Well, I understood, but not enough. I had to keep an eye on myself constantly, telling myself it was far from being the end of the world."

"I understand," I said to him. "In my opinion, if something hasn't happened to you personally, you can't really get it."

"Really? You too? That makes me feel better. I was thinking maybe it was because I'm a man."

"No… I think there are three sexes on this planet: men, women and women who have had children."

My father laughed. "Maybe, yeah. Well, in any case, I thought I was terribly ungrateful. Ungrateful and helpless. So, I got mad."

"Like Agaguk, when he beats his wife while she's giving birth. Such a charming scene."

"Still… that may be a bit of an exaggerated example."

"I wasn't talking about the result, I was talking about the feeling. Anger in response to the helplessness."

"That's right. So, I'd get mad at myself and then I'd get mad at her 'cause I was mad at myself. You know, the good old vicious cycle?"

"You should talk to Stéphane about it," I told him.

"Yes. We'll see how they work things out. Your mother thinks the two of them are pretty stressed. And that they don't 'communicate.'"

"Yes. What's with her and 'communicating'? She must have said that word five hundred times since this morning, and every time, it's like a magic formula."

"That's another one of her books. You know, her personal growth stuff and all that. She's quoted Guy Corneau so much I don't even hear her anymore."

"It's better to hear that than to be deaf."

"It's still funny," said my father. We always made fun of my mother's penchant for New Age mysticism and pop psychology. Treatises on astrology, graphology and interpreting body language were side by side on her bookshelves with titles like *Feel the Fear, and Do It Anyway, Twelve Chapters to Happiness* and biographies of the Dalai-Lama.

"As long as she doesn't start writing herself," I said. My father burst out laughing – a big HA! – and he came closer to the dish the cutlets were soaking in. I watched him, thinking, "He's going to put his finger in the sauce in 5, 4, 3…" On 2, he did it and brought his finger to his mouth, with childish happiness. "Mmm. Cream. And what's that taste?"

"Port. I deglazed the pan with port, and then I'm going to put it in the oven with cheese. It's called *escalope à la Maria*. You'll see, it's fantastic. Simon showed me the recipe."

"Your mother's going to protest, you know. She's going to say it's not good for our cholesterol."

"Because you think you can get me to believe the two of you are looking after your health?"

"Your mother is. She looks after hers and mine."

At that moment, my mother's head popped through the doorway. "Darling," she sighed. "Bring me a dry martini, please. These kids are going to drive me crazy."

"There's no more vermouth."

"Doesn't matter, doesn't matter. Just some vodka. It'll be perfect."

I waited till she was gone, and then I smiled at my father, "She's watching your health, eh?"

"Pfff. One little martini…"

I stroked his back, and went to see my mother in the living room. She was sitting on the couch, bent over towards the twins, who were playing with misshapen, multicoloured dolls: a Barbie with one leg, a Barbie with no head, and a kind of baby with half-burned-off hair and a punched-in eye.

"My God," I said. "They're really hard on their dolls."

My mother looked up at me. "Those are *your* dolls. The Barbies were yours and the baby doll was Daphné's."

"We mutilated our dolls?"

"For hours on end. I don't ever remember seeing one Barbie with her clothes on. You used to give them tattoos. Piercings, too. Very avant-garde, now that I think about it. Piercings really weren't in style then."

I picked up the baby doll. "It's been burned!"

"Yes, Daphné was gentler with her dolls. But one day, she wanted to try something and it almost turned into a catastrophe. If she'd been alone in her room, I'm not sure what would have happened. Luckily, she was in the kitchen with me. She lit the hair on fire with a candle and she looked at me with a very proud smile, while the doll flamed in her hand – it smelled like burnt plastic in there for days, don't you remember?"

"Not in the least…" I imagined Daphné, as a child, with her René Simard haircut, and a burning doll in one hand, and I started to laugh.

"Tapou!" shouted Mya, reaching towards me. In the girls'

language (which my father had named "twinspeak"), "tapou" meant "doll," just like "apanne" meant "what is it?" – those were two of the rare words in their language I understood. Daphné did pretty well with it, "I'm almost bilingual," she often said.

"Dolly?" I said to Mya.

She looked at me with big, wide eyes, "Tapou!"

"Tapou!" repeated Rosalie.

"Okay, tapou." I handed the doll to Mya, and she took it carefully and brought it over to her sister.

"When are you going to have some?"

"Some what?"

"Children?"

"Oh, Mom…"

"You want kids, don't you?" She sounded almost desperate.

"Yes, I want kids. I'm just not in a hurry, that's all…" I tried to sound casual.

"Anyway," my mother said, "Simon would make such a wonderful father."

I clenched my teeth. I still couldn't imagine myself starting a family with Simon: no matter what I did, it didn't come together. Still, Simon was everything a woman looking for a father for her children could dream of. He had terrible parents, of course, which was a concern, but I figured if I was bubbling over with enthusiasm at the idea of having kids with him, I would have made do with a cantankerous Irish woman, and a bitter Croatian man.

"Of course," said my mother, "it's a huge step. Would it scare you?"

"I suppose."

"That's normal. But it changes your life, eh. Look." Rosalie and Mya were now fighting over the doll. My mother separated them and took out a shaved puppy dog to create a diversion, but the only result was that the twins started fighting over the puppy dog. She smiled and let them go.

"I don't know how Daphné does it," she added. "And now, they're sitting down. But when they start running everywhere… I don't know how she does it. She impresses me sometimes."

"Me, too. More and more often."

My mother smiled. "You've changed, my girl."

"Yes. I know."

"Are you happy?"

"Well yes. I think so." I thought about the bright, dazzling happiness of a few years ago. "Things change, eh?"

"What?"

"Happiness."

"I don't know. I think we're the ones who change."

"Sometimes…" I looked at the twins, pulling with all their might on the one-legged Barbie. "Sometimes, I miss the old days."

"I know," said my mother, and I could see in her eyes that she really did. She turned back towards the twins and my father came in with her martini.

"I used the shaker," he announced proudly.

"But it's just vodka…"

"I know, but it's a nice gesture." He handed it to my mother, who blew him a kiss.

"I have to go check my cutlets," I said.

It was a nice evening. I was exhausted, but happy to be with them. All in all, the twins were pretty calm, and they went quietly to bed at eight-thirty. The three of us stayed there in the dining room, finishing the port that hadn't gone into the recipe and talking like old friends. My mother was worried about Daphné and Stéphane, and she kept on about their "communication," and my father made fun of her, but tenderly. They got a little excited when I told them about the trip Simon and I planned to Belize, and they reminded me they'd been there themselves, ten years before. My mother started giving me all kinds of advice – they were holding hands and making each other laugh, and I thought that was exactly what I was dreaming of: love anchored in time, made up of memories and years spent together, that the passing of the hours hadn't worn out. Love that was still alive and enriching, with a nice patina.

My mother often repeated that there was no more beautiful love than an old love. I'd always found that idea a little depressing; the only way I ever imagined love was as something flamboyant and ephemeral, with fireworks. I was just barely starting to understand that certain things could be flamboyant and durable. Daphné had asked my father if he still loved my mother like when they first met, and he replied, "Of course not, I love her much more. What good do you think it does to go through so much together?"

They'd almost split up when I was twelve. My mother had developed a very strong attraction for another man, and, out of spite, my father had taken a mistress twenty years younger than he was – a sad and, all in all, quite ordinary story. There had been shouting in the house, but nothing awful: my parents got along too well to rip each other apart. We never found out the details (which, honestly, suited me just fine), but they'd finally made up. For a long time, Daphné had claimed it was just because of us, but she eventually had to admit it was really for them.

And that night, I could see, better than I ever had before, the permanency and endurance of true love. As I was going to go to bed in the room they still kept for Daphné and me, I thought to myself that they were lucky, really lucky, and I wondered how I'd managed not to see it the whole time I'd lived under their roof, and even during all the years since then, when, to me, love looked like Antoine and Juliette laughing in the muted light of a bar.

I spent the next day at Daphné's – she and Stéphane had finally managed to "communicate." A series of abscesses had been burst, in fact: Stéphane had admitted he'd felt helpless for a long time, long before the miscarriage, that he thought he was a bad father and he blamed Daphné, because she was always everywhere and never gave him the time and space, really, to be a father. He knew he was wrong to feel that way, but he wanted to be honest with her; and she wanted to be, too – she told him that she was afraid about having no other identity than her role as a mother and that was why she couldn't leave any room for him. They'd also talked about the third child that Daphné wanted and they decided to give themselves a year to make a decision. Daphné told me she was ready for anything, and that what counted was the twins and Stéphane, and they already had that.

She looked relieved, and calmer than I'd seen her in months, since before the whole matter of the pregnancy and the miscarriage. "It's like I finally understand myself," she'd told me. She was getting back to the order she liked so much, the certainty that each thing and each person was in its place, and that our lives really were a logical series of events. "That's the way I am," she'd said with a smile. "What do you want, that's the way I am."

It hadn't stopped snowing for four days, and for the first time this year, the snow was piling up – first a thin layer, then big banks that made drivers curse and children laugh. We'd gone for a walk with the twins, who were discovering the joys of winter. They took three steps, bent down, touched the snow and burst out laughing. Once, twice, twenty times. I'd pick one of them up, and, for a few seconds, imagine I was a suburban mom, taking her walk, and telling her children to make sure there was no ice in the snowballs they were throwing. "I don't want a little life like that," I'd said to Antoine two days later. "You won't have one," he'd answered me. "Not you."

Simon was working like crazy – the holiday season was always intense, an uninterrupted series of office parties and family dinners that left him exhausted and a little glum. Antoine was in a bad mood, too – Christmas in his family was a sad story: even though she had a new husband, his mother was always nostalgic about long ago Christmases, when Antoine's father was alive.

Antoine said that dinner on December 25th depressed him in advance, then on the day itself, and the days that came after. His sisters, a single mother who didn't say much and an old maid who talked so much she made you dizzy, still treated him like a little boy, and harassed him with questions about his matrimonial future, which irritated him beyond belief. He usually left at about ten o'clock and spent the rest of the evening at my parents', where he spent a long time complaining about his family to my mother, who rubbed his back and made him martinis. She'd say to him, "I should have adopted you, Antoine," and he'd laugh almost shyly. He looked like a child at those moments, and I knew he didn't really like people to see him that way. But he came back every year, like clockwork, and we always expected him.

Juliette, on the other hand, was in the clutches of another attack of creativity, but this one was joyful and lighter: the paintings she was working on, and that she'd agreed to show me before they were finished, were somewhat like the first series – I could see the same pure, vibrant colours, but all the sadness you could see in the others was gone. Since Simon was working almost every night, we had lots of girls' nights out, just the two of us, or with Marcus and Michel (which, we'd decided, was still a girls' night). We'd have movie nights, just the two of us, drinking Chardonnay, and watching *The Lord of the Rings* for the umpteenth time, shouting, "Legolas! What do your elf eyes see?" and we thought we were hilarious.

I, too, was in a joyful mood. Not only had I purchased all my gifts by December 20th, which was something of a miracle, but the idea of spending two days at Simon's parents' was bothering me less and less. I'd convinced myself it would just be some sort of endurance test, and that the days would go by slowly, for sure, but afterwards, there would be Christmas dinner at my parents' and the New Year's Eve party, which was always festive and generally a decadent little affair that had started at Antoine's, though we'd moved it to Juliette's so we'd have more room.

I was waiting for all this anxiously, even a little feverishly, and I had a hard time understanding it. One night, a little before the end of *The Fellowship of the Ring*, I'd talked to Juliette about Simon, and the fact that I had the feeling there had to be something "more." She'd listened to me, patiently, and then asked, "More what?"

"I don't know. But it's like I'm waiting for something. The feeling's not always there, sometimes it disappears for days, I don't think about it, I feel good and light, and then it comes back. Like something urgent. And I don't know what it is. I don't know what I'm waiting for."

"You can't wait forever," Juliette had said.

"No, I know."

But that's what I was doing. I was waiting, with this weird feverishness deep inside me – I was waiting for something, someone, a moment. And, without knowing why, I had the same feeling I'd had in that dream, after I'd spent the night at the hospital with Daphné. I thought to myself, "It's coming."

Chapter 20

On December 31st, I was still waiting. I had arrived at Juliette and Marcus' at about two o'clock, to help them decorate the apartment: Marcus had gotten out his collection of boas and we were hanging them all over the place – on the door frames, from the pipes that ran along the ceiling, around the toilet seats (this was an idea of Juliette's and she'd convinced Marcus to sacrifice three of his boas by saying, "Come on, how many times in life do you get the chance to shit with your ass sitting on feathers?").

Marcus and I were in charge of replacing all the white light bulbs with pink, yellow and red ones. I was sitting on his shoulders and he was carrying me from room to room, handing me light bulbs, and babbling on and on about Michel, whose mother he'd met for Christmas. "Can you imagine, sweetie? It's the first time in my life someone's introduced me to their parents, and I'm forty-one years old!"

"I thought you were only thirty-three," I said mischievously. "Or was it thirty-one? Didn't you tell us you were thirty-one on your last birthday?"

He laughed and explained, "I decided to face reality, sweetie. I'm forty-one and fabulous! Michel loves me just the way I am."

"That's wonderful, Marcus, really. It's wonderful. And, besides that, he's right." I bent down and kissed him on the head.

"You know something," he said, "I don't think I've ever been this close to a woman's crotch."

"The honour is all mine."

Marcus handed me a pink bulb and asked, "What about you? Christmas with the Markovics?"

"Honestly, it wasn't that bad. I expected to be so bored that, actually, it turned out to be almost a pleasant surprise. Okay, sure, I had to spend hours talking to Simon's mother about gravy, but still. She almost smiled at me when I gave her her gift."

"What was it?"

"An awful thing I bought in Limerick ten years ago. And not only is Mrs. Markovic, née O'Shea, from Limerick, she also likes awful things. So it was a huge success, I think." The gift was, in fact, a limerick, written on a piece of parchment whose four corners were decorated with green sequins.

"And how was Simon?" Marcus asked me.

"Exactly the same as last time. I don't know, it's like he switches off when he comes in contact with his parents. But at least this time, I knew what to expect."

"He's so nice."

"Mmhhmm." I was starting to get tired of my family and friends telling me that Simon was nice, handsome, kind, funny – each one of their comments reminded me that, despite this orgy of perfection, I still wasn't completely satisfied. Which meant I was probably difficult and spoiled, or, possibly even crazy.

"And besides," I added, to create a diversion, "I knew Kingston's boredom would be followed by Christmas dinner at my parents'. And that's always great."

"Did Antoine come this year?"

"Arrived at eight o'clock sharp."

Marcus laughed. "Poor Tony Boy… What about your sister? How's she?"

"Oh, a lot better. Really a lot better. You know what I was telling you about my mother's pop psychology books? And her obsession with the word *communicate*? Well I think she rubbed off on Daphné. Now she and Stéphane talk to each other, they tell each other everything… it's a little annoying, but, at least, they really look like things are going well. And they want to meet my parents in Vienna. They leave in two days, without the twins, for the first time."

"Oh, they're going to spend the whole time in bed!" said Marcus.

We'd gotten as far as the kitchen when Juliette and Michel came in, their arms filled with packages. "I got cheese," said Juliette, "smoked salmon, crackers, blinis, some kind of cheap caviar, celery, carrots, cherry tomatoes, five kinds of dip, at least twenty kinds of hard sausage, olives, pickles, liver pâté, smoked oysters, Matane shrimp… shit!"

"What?" asked Michel.

"We forgot the cocktail sauce."

"No, we didn't, my dear!" Michel started rooting around in one of the bags and pulled out two jars of horseradish sauce.

"Ta-da!"

"Oh! Wonderful," said Juliette. "I thought I was going to have to go back to the Atwater Market." She looked up at me – I was almost nine feet off the floor – and added, "There were about… my God, a hundred thousand people there." Then she looked at Marcus and said, "Hey! I bet you've never been that close to a hoo-ha in your life, eh?"

Marcus and I started to laugh. "That's exactly what we were just saying," Marcus answered. "This is a very special moment for me."

Michel laughed, too, and blew him a kiss. "We're almost done," Marcus told him. "Are you going to help me put the confetti in the balloons?"

"Oh, no!" shouted Juliette. "No confetti! Christ, I've just barely finished picking up the stuff from last year. And just the day before yesterday, I found a condom under the couch."

The condoms were from a piñata that Marcus had hung in the living room last year, after he'd filled it with candy,

joints and condoms: a source of undeniable pleasure, even
if one of the guests had almost gotten knocked out by a
hockey stick when someone who was a little too enthusiastic
missed the piñata by a couple of centimetres.

"Too late," Marcus answered her. "Even borrowed the
helium pump from the club I work at. It's going to be
absolutely fantastic! When the guests start arriving, the balloons will be up on the ceiling. Then they'll start to slowly
fall (he was making exaggerated, sweeping gestures to sym-
bolize the falling balloons). And then, we can grab them,
and throw them at each other, and, poof! Confetti!"

"Oh, lord," sighed Juliette.

"What, confetti's pretty. So festive. And I'll vacuum up
after. I promise."

"Ooookay," Juliette grumbled, as Marcus winked at
Michel.

Ten minutes later, they were in Marcus' room, where,
they said they were preparing the balloons, but I had my
doubts about that. They came out about two hours later,
wearing silly grins, but with no balloons. "A slight delay,"
Michel explained.

At eight o'clock, the four of us were sitting under a bal-
loon-covered ceiling, eating sandwiches and drinking beer.
The first guests usually arrived at about nine o'clock, in suc-
cessive waves – the DJ and emcee first, who was in fact a
friend of Antoine's who was crazy about music, and would
never let us pay him; then friends who'd been at family dinners; friends Juliette and I had known at university, and
who'd begun their evening in bars; Marcus' "colleagues,"
who always showed up a little before midnight, still in drag;
people who had to work that night, like Simon, in restaurants and clubs (Simon, whose restaurant had been rented
out by a big group, had made me a solemn promise not to
arrive any later than eleven-thirty, even if, he said, it wasn't
"particularly professional").

At about eight-thirty, Antoine appeared in the living

room, with a case of champagne in his arms. "There are two more of these downstairs," he said and Marcus and Michel jumped up to go down and get them. Antoine put down his case, walked over to the table in the living room, without saying a word, to get himself a beer.

"You okay?" asked Juliette.

"No. Not really. I was just at my sister Micheline's. They're all over there for tonight. It's going to be unbelievable: my mother, if you can believe it, just got dumped by her husband."

"Pardon?"

"Yes," said Antoine. "That fucking asshole left her."

"Between Christmas and New Year's?" Even I was rather horrified. "What kind of bastard does something like that?"

"A bastard," said Antoine, "who said he couldn't stay with someone who was that sad, and that if, thirty-three years later, my mother's still not over my father's death, she never will be."

"My God," sighed Juliette.

"And I mean," Antoine continued, "I mean, sure, it can't be super-cheerful living with my mother, and sometimes even *I* think she needs to move on, but Christ! He left her on December 30th! I swear to you, I was ready to head right over to his place to kick the crap out of him. He knew what he was getting into three years ago when he got married. My mother told him. She'd warned him that part of her had never gotten over... over the whole thing. He knew it! And now, His Majesty is tired of it, and he leaves. Nice mentality! Fucking nice mentality!"

"You probably would have done the same thing he did," said Juliette.

Antoine looked at her without saying a word, and then he pointed a finger at her. "I have *never* tried to make *anyone* believe *anything.*" Marcus and Michel, who'd just come into the room with their cases of champagne, rapidly turned on their heels and headed towards the kitchen.

"Sorry. I just meant that... his timing is definitely terrible, but..."

Antoine sat down on the couch and took his head in his hands. "No, I know what you mean. I'm aware that it's impossible to live with a woman who still loves a ghost, but the difference with me is that I never would have made the commitment, for Christ's sake. He made a commitment." He emphasized the word *commitment* and for the first time since I'd met him, I could see that, deep down, Antoine's values were somewhat traditional. He's afraid of hurting someone, I thought. That's why he's never wanted to promise anything.

"You want to know why I didn't head right over to that asshole's place?" he said. "Because, honestly, my mother didn't even look hurt."

"What do you mean?" I asked.

"I think, in a certain way, she doesn't care. She got really hurt, when my father died. As for the rest... Not much touches her. I don't even know why she got remarried."

"Maybe she wanted something to touch her again," I offered. "Maybe she thought if she got married again, it would happen."

Antoine didn't say anything. He raised his head, and then fell back against the couch. "Oh, I don't know," he said. "I lived my whole life with the guy, and even though he was dead, he was all over the house. When I was a teenager, there was nothing in the world I wanted more than for my mother to forget him. I was mad."

"At who?" asked Juliette. "At your mother or your father?"

"Mostly him. I'd look at the pictures she kept on the fireplace mantle and I'd think, 'Go away, you old bastard, once and for all. This is ridiculous.' Then, before at Micheline's, I saw my mother just looking a little more distressed than usual, and I felt the same way. I wish that she would've cried, that she'd really been affected by this, and I said to myself,

'The old bastard's haunting her again.' I'm thirty-six years old, girls, and I'm still mad at my father. Who's dead. Ridiculous."

"No," said Juliette. "It's kind of a delayed Oedipus complex."

Antoine turned towards her, half-smiling, "A delayed Oedipus complex? Do we really have to get into two-bit psychology? I get enough of that from your mother," he said turning to me. "She wanted me to read *Absent Fathers, Lost Sons.*"

"Oh, no, I don't believe it!" I started to laugh. "When was that?"

"Back in the beginning, when I first met her. I think she wanted to see us together, and she thought if I read that book, I'd understand things and, I don't know, ask you to marry me, or something like that."

It was Juliette's turn to laugh. "My God. The face of the planet would have been entirely different…" She gave Antoine an affectionate slap on the thigh. "Sorry again, about what I said before."

"It's okay," he said. "But, honestly, I've never tried to get anyone to believe anything. That detail is important to me."

"I know," said Juliette. He smiled at her.

"You didn't want to stay there?" I asked Antoine.

"Are you nuts? Micheline was crying, because it reminded her of when her husband left her, Elise wouldn't stop talking, the kids were fighting, my mother was looking out the window, and three of my obese aunts were smoking cigarettes and watching the news in the living room. No, really, I didn't think twice. And, I think I depress my mother more than anything because I remind her of my father. So, being there at midnight so she could say, 'Oh, son, you have your father's eyes…' " He looked up at the ceiling. "When I can be here surrounded by balloons and the two women of my dreams…"

"Pardon me! The three women of your dreams!"

exclaimed Marcus who, apparently, had been in the hallway the whole time, listening to our conversation.

"That's right," said Antoine. I looked at the little wrinkles that formed around his eyes when he laughed, and I kissed him on the cheek.

"Why don't we open a little champagne?" I asked. "Before everybody gets here?"

Three hours later, Juliette found me in the kitchen, "Okay, I just opened my closet to get a sweater, and two people were sitting in there, doing coke. What's the world coming to these days?"

"Why are they doing it in your closet?"

"I haven't got a clue."

I shrugged. "I guess they didn't want anyone to see them. So what the world is coming to is that you have to act like nothing's going on."

"I closed the door back on them," said Juliette.

"That makes sense."

I looked around us. The kitchen had been invaded by a hoard of people with the munchies who were devouring whatever they could get their hands on.

"It's a good thing I bought ten extra bags of chips," said Juliette. "You want some more champagne?"

"Please." The rhythm of the D & B that was playing was echoing through my whole body – it wasn't unpleasant, in fact, it was kind of bewitching. We grabbed another bottle and headed towards the living room, where some of Marcus' friends, of indeterminate gender, where dancing suggestively in the pink and orangey light. Every once in a while, a balloon would half-heartedly break away from the ceiling and someone would touch it with their cigarette, so they could laugh joyfully when a shower of confetti fell on their face. At the end of the room, near the big windows, Antoine, Michel, Florent and three of our other friends were playing poker, so seriously it was absolutely ridiculous.

I went and stood behind Antoine, and said, "Bluff."

"Bluff about what?" asked Florent.

"Bluff," I repeated.

"He's bluffing?"

"Maybe."

"What do you know about poker?" Florent asked me.

"Maybe more than you think…"

"Girls don't know anything about poker!"

"You don't know Chloé," Antoine said to him. "She thinks like a man." He said that to me a lot – coming from him it was a compliment. Florent looked worriedly at me, and then at the men he was playing with. "But anyway, you can't play without bluffing, right? Right?"

Michel shrugged. "I don't know… are we bluffing or not?"

"You can play without bluffing?" asked Denis, a tall, thin man from Rivière-du-Loup who'd gone to school with us and still dressed like Kurt Cobain. In a class on the nine-teenth-century French poets, he'd written a comparative essay on Rimbaud and Baudelaire, which he'd entitled "Rimbaudelaire" – the professor almost had a stroke, and the expression became a legend. Poor Denis never under-stood why we laughed so much when we heard it, "But it was great," he'd repeat. "A comparison! Between Rimbaud and Baudelaire. It studies their similarities! What they had in common! So I called it "Rimbaudelaire"! Why the hell does that make you laugh?"

"No, you can't play without bluffing!" said a voice behind me. I turned around: it was Simon, who'd just arrived. I gave a happy little shout and threw myself at him. "Eleven-thirty," he said. "On the dot. I abandoned my team like a coward to get here." I kissed him, while behind us arose a noisy debate about whether or not it was possible to play poker without bluffing. "To bluff or not to bluff," said Antoine.

"For Christ's sake," shouted Juliette, "not a one of you knows the rules, if I understand correctly?" Michel kept saying

that, in Vegas, he'd played without bluffing, and that if it could
be done in Vegas, it could be done anywhere.

"You're not too tired?" I asked Simon.

"I'm okay."

"Some champagne?"

"Oh, yes."

"Come on," I said. "There are glasses in the kitchen."

We crossed the smoky living room and went into the
kitchen, where a small group of people was finishing what
was left of the chips while they chatted peacefully.
"Seriously, man" said one girl who was completely stoned,
"Bush is going to go down in history as the worst president
the US ever had. But the problem is, sometimes, history
doesn't move fast enough. Because, that's just it, when he
goes down in history, it'll be history already. Get it? Like, it
won't be in the present, so no one's going to learn anything
from it." A fifty-year-old man who was playing with another girl's hair said, "Man…"

I got a glass for Simon, and, at the same time, a transves-
tite with the giggles came into the kitchen and opened the
fridge, wiggling his hips. He took a bottle of water and
knocked it back in a couple of seconds – I could see his
Adam's apple bobbing up and down between long locks of
pink hair – then, still laughing, he said "Oohoohoohoo! It
is hot in here!" and then he swished away.

"Man," said the fifty-year-old man. "It takes all kinds,
eh?"

"Diversity is beautiful," added someone else.

Simon gave me an amused smile, and we headed back
towards the living room. "Who are those people?" he asked
me.

"In the kitchen? Friends of Juliette's, I think. The girl
who was talking about Bush is a sculptress, if I'm not mis-
taken. As for the rest, as you can see, a lot of them are friends
of Marcus. Some are Antoine's friends – they came in the
beginning when the party was at his place, and then they

followed it here. Some friends of mine are here, too – but I wonder where they are. Oh, there's Frédéric Martel and Mathieu Tremblay, remember them? They went to school with us, and sold cigarettes? We still see each other once in a while. They're here with their girlfriends."

When we made it to the poker table, it had been abandoned. "They couldn't come to an agreement," said Juliette. "And when they finally decided to bluff, they realized they didn't remember whose turn it was, and nobody felt like playing anymore, anyway."

We went and sat on one of the yellow futons we'd shoved into the corner, along with big pillows, some chairs and two inflatable mattresses, to create what Marcus called a "boudoir." A mirror ball above the dancers was spinning and splashing light onto them and us.

Juliette was coming back with another bottle when the music stopped and Marcus appeared above the crowd. Standing on a table near the DJ, he wasn't wearing anything but his white briefs, and the two huge feather wings that usually hung on the wall at the head of his bed. He'd also put on makeup, silvery and white powders – he looked fantastic. "He must have been rehearsing this for a long time," I whispered to Simon. I saw Michel, next to me, looking at him with admiration. Marcus stood there for several seconds, with his arms stretched out, and then he glanced at the DJ and, in his loud, deep voice, he shouted, "Okay, people, in 10…"

Everyone joined in the countdown. In 3, 2, 1 – over our shouts of "Happy New Year!" the music started up again, even louder and more rhythmic than before. Simon was holding my face in his hands and kissing me. "I love you," he said to me. I read his lips, more than I actually heard him say it. "Me, too," I shouted and we kissed again. "For next year," he said to me, "all I wish for is you." I just smiled at him – he was so handsome, in the moving light, so good for me. For myself, I wished I would be happy with him.

Marcus came up to us – Michel threw himself into his
arms, and they gave each other a long kiss. Then he turned
towards me, radiant, and hugged me tight, lifting me off the
ground and half suffocating me. "Happy New Year, sweetie.
Happy, happy, happy, happy New Year." There was a round
of kisses and hugs, toasts and glasses of champagne drunk
in one swallow. Simon was stopped by a group of gay men,
some of them in drag, who wanted to kiss him and, according to a handsome man with greying temples, possibly
convert him. A good sport, he laughed, and good-naturedly
hugged the leather corsets and Paul Smith shirts. I grabbed
Juliette by the sleeve, "Where's Antoine?" She motioned that
she didn't know, and I went looking for him.

The long hallways were filled with people kissing and
laughing – I tripped over the legs of a girl who was sitting
on the floor and crying in another girl's arms. The same
people were still in the kitchen; they seemed to be unaware
of the time and were still talking the same way, punctuating
the distress caused by American politics by worriedly
repeating, "Man." I continued on towards Juliette's room,
and then I saw Antoine over by the studio door, where he
was laughing with some friends, guys who worked in advertising like him, and who I'd never really liked. I waved at
him from a distance, to say, "What are you doing?" and then
I went towards him.

"Excuse me," I said to one of his friends who was facing
him. He turned and smiled at me, and I gently moved him
out of the way so I could hug Antoine.

"What are you doing here?" I asked him.

"We were talking when we heard Marcus. It was too late.
I knew it would be a zoo in the living room, so I thought
I'd wait a little while."

I gave him a playful, reproachful look. I was still in his
arms, and I had to stand on tiptoe to get close to his height.
He had me by the waist – with one hand behind my back
and the other on my hip. I smiled at him. In the hallway,

next to us, I could see that his friends were moving away, and a constellation of soap bubbles came out of nowhere, reflecting the light of a pink bulb.

"Happy New Year," I said.

"Happy New Year, sweetheart."

"What shall I wish you?"

He smiled at me, staring at me, and I wondered if he was drunker than he looked. Then he ran a hand along my face, brushing it ever so lightly, and he stepped closer to me. I thought to myself, I have to get out of here. I couldn't hear much of anything, not the music, in the distance, or the far-off laughter, or the heavy beat of the bass, which I could barely feel. It seemed like I wasn't thinking about anything – I was motionless, in the eye of the storm – then Antoine kissed me, with infinite gentleness, and my heart leapt. I opened my lips, I wanted him so much my stomach almost hurt. I put my hand on his neck and then I kissed him, and everything came back: I thought of the hallway, of the people who were there, of Simon who was off somewhere kissing friends, of me, of Antoine, and I raised my head.

For just an instant, he looked surprised, as if he couldn't believe what I'd just done, then he put one hand behind him and the studio door opened. He took one step back and pulled me against him. When he was about to kiss me again, I put one hand on his chest – I remember feeling his heart beating, and that it was no longer the same rhythm as the bass.

"What are you doing?" I asked him.

He looked at me with an indefinable expression of mixed sadness, surprise and desire. I grabbed him by the shirt and pulled him close to me.

Chapter 21

Obviously, it was a very bad idea. It wasn't even an idea, to tell the truth, it was a reflex, unstoppably I fell against him. I'd had time to think, time to tell myself it was a bad idea, but I don't think that I spent even a second thinking I should leave. I wanted to fall, I wanted to give up everything, I wanted the sin – and above all, I wanted Antoine. I wanted him, and his dark eyes, his smile, his expert hands, his body, and the texture of his skin.

In the semidarkness of the studio, we started to kiss, gently at first, then with a sensuality I'd never known before – I felt like I was getting lost in him, in each move he made. And I could see. With my eyes shut, pressed up against Antoine, with his hands under my sweater, I could see. On my back, on my stomach, on the tips of my breasts, I could feel the light touch of his fingers, like an electric shock that left delicate waves of goosebumps along my skin.

I was leaning against the wall – a floor lamp had crashed against the ground when Antoine had pulled me into him, and I couldn't have cared less. He was holding my face in his hands, and we were kissing, and, over his shirt, I was stroking his chest, his flat stomach, his sides, which I knew were very soft. I thought to myself, I could just stay here, doing nothing but this, forever. Antoine leaned down to kiss my neck, and, behind him, I saw the red light of the exit sign that hung over the emergency door. Slowly, he lowered his hands, first to my waist – then one of them dropped down and wandered back up along my thigh, and I noticed he almost didn't dare to touch my breasts, he brushed along them, cautiously. This wasn't like Antoine: usually, he would have undone my bra, my underwear would be on the ground, and we would already be doing it.

This observation brought me out of myself. The outside world came back to me all at once, and I realized what we were doing made no sense. I put my hands on his shoulders and I said, "Antoine." He raised his head and looked at me without saying anything. I repeated his name and I lowered my eyes. I couldn't look at him and step back at the same time.

"I can't do this," I said. Those were the only words that came to mind. I almost felt like crying because I still wanted to kiss him so much. He raised my chin with his right hand – I kept looking down, and I said, "Stop. I can't do this." I pushed him. "Stop," I repeated. He took two or three steps back – behind him I could make out a painting Juliette was working on: puddles of golden paint were reflected in the exit sign. Antoine wasn't moving. I straightened my shirt and nodded towards the door, towards what was on the other side of it; Juliette knew I'd gone looking for him, Simon must have been wondering where I was.

I finally looked up and looked him in the eye. He stared at me for a moment, without speaking – it felt like he was trying to see inside me – and he ran a hand through his hair, something he often did when he had a decision to make. Then he raised an arm towards the door, like someone who's indicating an exit to someone else with an "after you." I brought one hand up to my forehead and I went out.

The hallway was filled with people who were laughing and shouting. A girl with a confetti-covered afro smiled at me, she had little diamonds stuck to her eyelids. I smiled back at her and went towards the living room, with the distinct impression I'd just come out of a dream. I ran into Frédéric, our old classmate, and he took me in his arms to wish me Happy New Year.

"I saw Simon Markovic!" he said to me. "I can't believe you two are together!"

"Yes…" I glanced around and thought, I'm in a lake of absurdity.

"Where is he, by the way?" I asked Frédéric.

"He was over by the DJ table a couple of seconds ago."

"Thanks, Fred."

I finally found him, sitting in the "boudoir" area with Juliette, Denis "Rimbaudelaire" and three completely drunk girls who were laughing really loud. Marcus was standing next to them, still wearing his big wings, and looking like he was telling them a hilarious story. Simon was laughing, too. He looked up at me, still smiling, and said, "Hey! Where were you?"

"Oh, I was looking for Antoine," I answered. "I found him, he was with his friends, so there was a whole round of 'Happy New Years!' and then I bumped into Frédéric."

Completely satisfied with my reply, Simon moved over and motioned for me to come sit next to him.

"Where is Tony Boy?" Juliette asked, leaning towards me. "I still haven't wished him Happy New Year."

"He was near your studio a little while ago." I was unable to look her in the eye.

"That I know," said Juliette. "He's probably trying to get some girl in there!" She got up and I snuggled up against Simon. I said almost nothing for the rest of the night, I just settled for sipping champagne and listening to Marcus, who was in fine form. He and Simon had invented a ridiculous game that was making them both die laughing – they were talking about their relationships, adding details little by little, imaging a rich, tender past. They were speaking English, which was logical, but with a Scottish accent, which was quite a bit less logical. But I was grateful to them for being so happy, and for not thinking too much about me – for covering my silence with their laughter.

Twice, Marcus came over to ask me if I was okay. "You look like you're off in space," he said. I answered that I was drunk, and he gave me a kind smile and a couple of big pats on the back – he himself was completely drunk and stoned. Once in a while, Simon would shoot me a worried little look, but then I'd sigh and hold up my glass and he'd laugh, then he'd shoot another quarter into the shot glass on the table (Michel's idea, really: he claimed, and rightly so, that the traditional bar game was always a great success: whoever got the coin in the glass had to do a shot of tequila, and the result was that everyone was drunk and beaming).

By five in the morning, more than half the people were gone. A small, courageous group was still dancing on the floor which was now strewn with confetti and deflated balloons, some people were kissing on the couches, some were asleep on the floor. We were in the kitchen, raiding the pantry, when Juliette came in, staggering and laughing: "You know those boas of yours that were on the toilets?" she asked Marcus. "Well... they're ruined. I think someone made a point of throwing up in every toilet."

"Charming," I said.

"Pfff," said Juliette, grabbing a box of Lu cookies. "It should be no surprise though, should it?"

"I'll come help you clean up, if you want."

"Really?"

"Noooo..."

We kept on eating and laughing, and finishing what was left in all the bottles lying around the kitchen. I looked at Simon and tried to find a trace of remorse inside me, or a vague regret, but there was nothing but the memory of Antoine, like a huge fire. I felt bad because I didn't feel bad, but I almost couldn't believe what had happened – I thought to myself that I'd wake up, realize it had only been a dream, and that you can't feel bad about a dream. You can only remember it.

It must have been about 6 a.m. when I said to Simon, "I have to go, or else I'll end up throwing up on Marcus' boas too." He took me by the waist and we went towards the door. In the living room, the drag queen with the pink hair was still dancing, all alone, under the disco ball. The DJ had gone and someone had put on a Coldplay album. She was dancing, with her eyes closed, to a slightly sad piano tune.

"Did Antoine leave?" I asked Juliette as she walked us out. I hadn't seen him since the studio.

"No, he's in the 'boudoir' with a girl. And I was right, they did have sex in my studio." Suddenly, my heart sank violently. "What a night," Juliette went on. "I open my closet and two people are in there doing coke on the floor, I open my studio, two more fucking. Sign of a successful party, I suppose."

I didn't answer – I was furious, or jealous, or hurt, or a bit of all three. I kept thinking, that's all he wanted, deep down; he's just doing it to be a pain in the ass; and I also thought that I shouldn't be thinking all those things. Simon held out my coat and helped me put it on, tenderly pulling up the zipper. Then he hugged me, gently rocking me in his arms while he said good-bye and thank you to Juliette. Then, over Simon's shoulder, I saw Antoine with a tall girl he had by the waist. They were leaning against one of the big cement pillars in the living room, and Antoine kissed her and said something to her that made her burst out laughing. Then he turned around, to come over to the door, and that's when he noticed me. He stopped and looked me right in the eyes, despite the girl who was hanging from his shoulder and trying to get him to turn his head. Then he simply raised a hand to say good-bye, while Simon kissed me on the head.

When we got to my place, Simon said, "What an incredible party! But you were pretty quiet tonight."

"Yeah, I know," I answered. "By about one o'clock, I just felt wiped out. I'm tired."

He kissed my neck. "Too tired to make love?"

I smiled, and said "No." It was a stupid, absurd challenge: I wanted to prove to Antoine that I could make love with someone else, without thinking about him. And that's what

I did – the two of them were so different, and Simon was a good lover – I didn't think about anything, in fact, except myself and my own pleasure.

But as I fell asleep next to Simon, I remembered Antoine, his kisses, and his touch, and I could still feel the electric trace of his fingers along my skin.

I woke up the next day, around noon, with a good, solid headache. Simon was still asleep. I got up quietly and went to get a Gatorade in the kitchen, then, with my cats trotting joyfully behind me, I took two Tylenols before I went and sat down in the living room. The weather was nice – bright sun was coming in the windows, and Siffleux, who now had a full tummy, came and lay down in a big pool of light at my feet. Puce followed him, and she jumped lightly up onto my lap. I scratched her little back, while I looked outside, and tried to find some meaning in what had happened.

I thought maybe I'd done it because of that vague dissatisfaction that had been haunting me for a while. Maybe I didn't understand myself anymore, maybe I was drunk, maybe I was trying to prove something to myself (what that something could be, however, I had no idea). I hadn't wanted to hurt Simon in any way, that much I was sure of. It wasn't just pointless revenge, an effort to make him jealous. I thought about what Antoine had said to me a few months earlier, "Everyone just wants to be surprised." And surprised, I was. Beautifully. And I loved it. It was an electric sensation, which was both invigorating and inebriating; the impression of being physically, mentally, totally awake. "Oh my God," I said in a very low voice – that's it, I'd just realized, that's what I'd been waiting for.

But what about Antoine… why him? Because, whispered a little voice I bravely tried to silence, he was the one I wanted. It's his fault, I thought. With his stupid bets and his "I never met another girl like you," he had put it in my head.

And since I'm not perfect, and unable to realize how lucky I really am, I couldn't stop myself from looking around even though I was in a stable relationship with an ideal man.

I reacted negatively to the thought of Simon: did he really have to be that ideal? All he did was emphasize my character flaws, my weaknesses, my desire for Antoine. I was still scratching Puce's back, and she was purring louder and louder, and I was telling myself that everything was Antoine and Simon's fault, and that maybe I wasn't made for love – maybe loving was too hard for me.

But images from the night before kept coming back to me, sensations – Antoine's mouth, his body, his cock against me – and I thought of his hands barely brushing my breasts, and murmured, "Just what was he up to?" I was dying to talk to Juliette about it, but I kept telling myself she couldn't find out about it, that no one could find out about it, that as long as everything remained a secret, I could still make myself believe that nothing had happened. Then I thought about Daphné and, for the first time in years, I wanted her advice. But she was in Vienna. I sighed and, since I had nothing better to do, let myself think about our hands on each other.

Simon made me jump when he came into the room.

"You okay?" he asked. He was holding his head in his hand.

"Not too bad," I answered him. He came toward me, stopped next to Siffleux, in the sunbeam. I could see the light playing on his naked body, and I reached a hand towards him, slowly tracing the shape of his back and his bum.

"Oh God," sighed Simon. "The game of quarters probably wasn't the brightest idea ever. Is there more Gatorade?"

"Of course. I'm always prepared."

He smiled and leaned down to kiss me. "Happy New Year, my love."

"Happy New Year."

He trusts me, I thought, as I watched him head towards the kitchen.

We spent the day in bed, making love, sleeping, and laughing when we remembered the night before. "You think we should go help them?" Simon asked me.

"Tomorrow. I don't think they'll do much cleaning today."

"No, that's probably true…"

We made up stupid games, games for people in love, riddles about our past and what we liked, what our favourite season was, our most embarrassing sexual experience, what we'd do with a million dollars…

"Okay," Simon said. He'd just told me about the first blow job he'd gotten, how he was almost afraid and had ejaculated after about eight seconds in the girl's mouth, how she'd slapped him and called him every name in the book. He was sitting in my bed, propped up against a pile of pillows, with the quilt up to his waist. "Okay, what about you? Your first time?"

"The first time someone gave me a blow job?"

"No, silly. The first time you made love."

"Oh…" And I realized I had never told him about it.

"Well," I started, "it wasn't anything fantastic. I was fourteen. At camp. It was a little ridiculous. I wanted it to happen so bad, I wanted to get it over and done with. Remember what I was like when you knew me at school? Kind of awkward, a little nerdy around the edges… I wanted to destroy that image, and, in my teenage head, the secret was to not be a virgin anymore. So that year, at camp, I did everything I could to get a boyfriend. When you've only got two weeks, I'm telling you, you don't have a second to spare. I uncovered my clever treasures and, especially, my breasts."

Simon started to laugh.

"It was ridiculous," I went on. "I was strutting around in tiny camisoles… it's funny, it was stuff I never would have had the courage to do at school, but there, in a different context, it was okay. Well, you know what teenagers are like; after a few days, I had a number of interested parties who all believed I had a lot of 'experience,'" – I put air quotes around the word. "And I chose the nicest one... well, that's not true, there were one or two others who were nicer, but they weren't as cute."

"Gotta keep your priorities straight," Simon said.

"Hey, what do you think I'm doing with you? All I want is your body, sweetheart."

He laughed again, and I continued, "So, this is it. One night, he came to pick me up in my tent, and we went and did it in the woods... it was awful. I had branches jabbing me in the back, I was terrified, but not as much as he was... we were done in less than ten minutes. He was radiant, I was devastated. I'd imagined something incredible, you know, really romantic, but, oh well... So that was it. My first time."

"Did you ever go into the woods with him again, after that?"

"Twice. When I got back to Montreal, he called because he wanted to see me again, but I didn't want to see him."

"Why?"

"Because it wasn't a very good memory, I suppose. I didn't want to think that I'd sacrificed my ideas of a super-romantic first love just to 'get it over and done with,' with a boy I didn't really care much about."

Simon nodded. "And did it work?"

"What?"

"At school? Were you more popular after that?"

"It's sad to say, but yes. I don't know if I'm the one who changed or if word got around, but, yeah, it worked. Stupid, eh? At fourteen I figured out that sex can give you a kind of power."

Simon pulled me close to him. "It's not stupid," he said. Then, licking one of my breasts, he added, "...and it's true."

Later on, he went to the fridge to get the *foie gras* and

caviar he'd hidden in one of the drawers. We drank champagne and watched reruns of the New Year's Eve specials from the night before – I hadn't set foot outside all day and I felt good, tired but good, and I thought to myself that life would be simpler like this, if it were just Simon and me, an apartment with three cats and an inexhaustible supply of champagne and gourmet food.

We arrived at Juliette's the next day around noon, with a case of beer and two extra-large pizzas. The apartment looked like a battlefield – the furniture was moved around, the floor was strewn with confetti, cigarette butts and empty bottles; it looked like a hurricane had hit the kitchen, dirty boas where hanging from pipes more or less everywhere; and deflated balloons sat in the corners and on the couches.

"It's not so bad," said Juliette. "You should have seen it yesterday. On the living-room floor, on top of the confetti and empty bottles, there was a completely wasted drag queen. Right there." She pointed towards a chalk outline of a body, like in a police investigation.

"What's that?" Simon asked, laughing.

"He wouldn't wake up," Marcus explained. "So we got a piece of chalk and did that. As tired as we were yesterday, we thought we were very funny."

"My God," Juliette added, "we were so tired, it was ridiculous. Then we were too lazy to change the light bulbs so we had dinner in the kitchen, with pink light shining on us."

"Groovy," Simon said.

"Exactly," Marcus replied.

Simon, Michel and I got busy on the living room, while Juliette and Marcus took the kitchen. Every once in a while, we heard a disgusting "ewwww!" from them, usually followed by laughter and a crash of objects. "There was smoked salmon stuck to the wall!" Juliette shouted, followed by Marcus who was waving around something that looked like paste. "It's wet bread!" she trilled as she passed us and hid behind me.

"Juliette has a wet-bread phobia," I explained to Simon who was trying to look understanding. Marcus finally threw his projectile towards us – I ducked just in time and Juliette got a good wad of it in her hair. We were then treated to a few sharp shrieks while she ran to the bathroom.

"Really," said Marcus, "I never get tired of that."

When the living room and the kitchen were cleaned up, we pulled straws to see who would clean the bathroom, which had been declared a disaster area. Marcus and Simon were selected and they marched off courageously, as we applauded solemnly. "History will remember you," I shouted to them as they turned the corner, and we burst out laughing.

"I'm going to go straighten up the hallway," Juliette said to me. "You going to help?"

I followed her – it was the same hallway I'd walked down, two days earlier, beside myself, to get back to Simon in the living room. I stared at the studio, as if Antoine and I were still in there, kissing like we thought it would stave off death.

"I'm going to go see what's in there," said Juliette. "I hope Antoine and his chicky didn't touch anything. I just opened the door yesterday to make sure my painting was okay, but I didn't really look around... I would not be thrilled to find a condom on the floor, you know."

I managed a smile, and I remembered the lamp that had fallen over when Antoine pushed me into the wall.

Juliette made a slow tour of the studio, while I watched, leaning against the door frame, not daring to go inside. She finally got to the wall and went "pfftttt," when she saw the lamp. "Really," she said, "he could have told me he'd broken something." She picked up the pieces of glass and lined them up one next to the other, to see if they could be glued back together. "Oh well," she sighed. "It wasn't worth much." Then she looked up at me and asked, "You okay?"

"Yeah, I'm okay."

"You look weird, Chloé."

"No, I'm still just a little tired, that's all."

Juliette raised one eyebrow, still holding a big piece of glass in each hand. "You sure?" she insisted.

"Yes, yes."

"Everything okay with Simon?"

"Yes, really. No, I'm telling you, I'm just tired. We're not that young anymore, eh? It takes me two days now to get over a night like that."

Juliette nodded her head and she went and put the pieces of the lamp down on a little bench. She thought something was up, I could see it, but she knew me well enough to know it was useless to push me now. Dear Juliette, I thought. She put a hand on my shoulder and we walked out of the studio.

Simon and Marcus came out of the bathroom an hour later – Michel immediately served them each a glass of wine, and we settled down in the kitchen to eat. "Oh," said Marcus looking at me, "we forgot to change the bulbs."

I looked up at the pink light that was shining about us: "Why don't we leave it like that? Just one more night?"

Marcus smiled at me, "Good idea, Chloécita."

While we were eating, I asked Juliette when Antoine had left. "Right after you," she answered. But she didn't specify if he'd been alone or not, and that's what I wanted to know. I kept thinking that I should tell her, that I had to tell some-one, but I didn't know how. I could imagine Juliette's reaction: "The day before yesterday, in your studio, furious necking with Antoine," and I almost wanted to laugh. But for the time being it was my secret. I was trying to keep myself from thinking: *our* secret.

I didn't hear from Antoine for the next few days. Simon had gone back to work on January 3rd, the poor guy, but I was still lazing around at home, since I'd refused a contract in order to go to Belize. Financially, it was a very bad decision, but I'd never been an ace at financial planning. I slept late, spent hours reading on the couch, with Puce lying on my belly, went to the movies with Juliette, who'd stopped asking questions, though once in a while she looked at me in a way that invited me to share. Not right away, I felt like telling her. And I'd think of Antoine. I wanted to know what had gotten into him. I wanted to understand. He should tell me if he was still thinking of the studio and what had happened there. But he wasn't calling me, and, obviously, I was too proud to call him.

After a week, though, I thought it didn't make any sense: Antoine never went a week without calling or coming over. And I kept repeating to myself, "What's he up to?" Besides, I wanted to see him. Because, I said to myself, he was my best friend. That was reason enough. I'd picked up the phone at least twenty times, intending to call him and leave a message which was becoming more and more complicated. When one day I realized that I'd spent almost an hour repeating the message in question, I decided the whole thing was getting ridiculous. I slipped on a pair of jeans and a little top, put on my coat and left for his place.

Chapter 22

When I arrived in front of his apartment, for a second I thought about using my set of keys. Normally, that's what I would have done, and that's exactly why I wanted to do it now, so everything would still be normal. I took out my key ring, hesitated and then rang the bell, swearing under my breath. After a minute I was just about to ring again, when the door opened up. I held my breath and tried to look as casual as possible. And I looked up at him – he was barefoot, in jeans and a tee-shirt and he was looking at me without saying a word. There was a brief moment of suspense – a moment of expectation. I realized I'd taken a step back when he'd opened the door, and that I didn't dare come closer.

"You're wearing jeans," I said, "and a tee-shirt." I couldn't remember ever seeing him wearing anything but a button-down shirt.

He shrugged. "It happens sometimes. Didn't have time to go to the cleaners." He looked up at the sky and squinted because of the sun, though it was already going down at the end of the street. I was waiting for him to smile at me, to ask me in, but he didn't do anything, except blink his eyes in the light.

"Antoine," I said. "How are you?"

"Okay."

"Can I come in?"

"Of course. Come in." He turned his back and I followed him to the living room – he'd put on a Stone Roses album that I liked and I smiled behind his back. Everything was pretty tidy, as usual – piles of magazines on the table, the

CDs all lined up on the shelves, the two big bookcases with their orderly books, one on each side of the fireplace. The kitchen, which opened up onto the living room, and the dining room were spotless – the only utensils that were ever used, of course, were the shaker and the corkscrew. On the dining-room table, and on the one in the kitchen, I noticed two big pots of flowers with vibrant colours. Julie, the florist, must have been by during the week.

"Did Julie come over?" I asked him.

"Yes." He sat in a chair and stared right into my eyes, with a persistence I wasn't used to. I took off my coat and settled down on the couch opposite him. There was a glass of wine on the table, and an open book, Gide's *Les Nourritures terrestres*.

"I read that," I told him.

"I know, it's yours. You loaned it to me, three or four years ago. I still hadn't read it."

"Oh." I didn't remember anymore, and I was having a hard time thinking, because he wouldn't take his eyes off of me.

"You want a glass?" he asked me.

"Please."

He got up, and I watched him walk. Usually, I thought, I would have told him his jeans made his ass look good. But I kept quiet and picked up a copy of *Vanity Fair* from the table.

Silently, Antoine served me the wine – I was disoriented, I didn't recognize him and, for the first time since I'd left my house, I wondered what I was doing there. When he sat back down, I said, "Antoine."

"What?" He had one arm stretched out on the armrest of the chair, the other arm bent, and he was still staring at me, with his chin on his fist.

"What do you mean, 'what'?" I said to him. "What, 'what'? Juliette's studio…" I made an exasperated gesture.

"What, Juliette's studio? We were drunk, that's all."

I was flabbergasted. I wanted to shout, "Excuse me? That's all you can think of to say?" but I didn't want to look too upset.

"Okay," I said. "All right. I don't know, I didn't hear from you and I was wondering."

"I was busy. I saw my mother." I managed not to add, "And Julie." His chin was still resting on his fist, and he wasn't saying a word. I turned the pages of the magazine, without really seeing them, for what seemed like an eternity: I didn't know what to say, where to start – I was too proud to point out that we weren't *only* drunk. I knew he knew that, too, and I cursed, more than ever, the bad faith he sometimes showed. In fact, I was about to point out his bad faith, when he said, "Leave him."

I looked up at him. He was sitting in the same position and still staring at me with the same intensity. I asked, "Pardon?" in a voice that was so weak, it surprised even me.

"Leave him," he repeated.

I wanted to say, "For you?" but I couldn't do it. I could hear my heart pounding in my ear, and I felt almost out of breath.

"Antoine, what are you talking about?"

"Simon. You don't love him."

I pursed my lips. His gaze was still as intense and cold, and I remembered that he could be very hard sometimes with some of his lovers – to one overly insistent girl I'd actually heard him say, "Go play somewhere else." But I'd never been on the receiving end of that dark, concentrated stare, which was like an accusation, a warning to keep quiet. He's not letting me get close, I thought. If he wasn't like that, maybe I'd do something. But I was getting madder and madder at him. So I said, "I do too love him," and, in his eyes, I could see he didn't believe me. "What are you doing?"

He dropped the hand he'd had under his chin, and sat back deeper in his chair, "Do you really want to know?"

I threw the magazine on the ground. "What are you doing? Why are you being like this?"

"I don't know, Chloé. Why don't you tell me?" His tone was perfectly calm, perfectly cold, and it made me want to slap or kick him.

"You're just pissed off because I left," I said, standing up. "You can't take it when someone says 'no,' can you? That's it, isn't it?" Now I was acting in bad faith: I knew that wasn't it. But as I said it, I realized there might be a little bit of truth in it. "Nobody's ever told you 'no' before, Antoine. And because of your stupid macho pride, I have to put up with this shit!"

"You know why nobody ever tells me 'no'?" He leaned forward in his chair, then, very slowly, he said, "Because I never act until I'm sure the girl is dying to do it. You wanted it, Chloé. It's the only thing you wanted, Chloé. The. Only. Thing."

"Fuck you."

"That's right."

"No, fuck you! You're the one, Antoine. You and your fucking bets and your declarations that come eight years too late, your damned pride, you're the one…" And to my chagrin, to my extreme chagrin, I began to cry. I wiped away a tear, and then another, and I closed my eyes, with one hand on my mouth.

"Chloé…" said Antoine.

"No." I heard him get up and I opened my eyes – his eyes weren't cold anymore, and I remembered what I'd thought on December 31: he's afraid of hurting other people. He reached out a hand to me, but I pushed it away, abruptly, as if he'd burned me. "Don't touch me!" I said. I was too afraid of his hands and my own desire. In his eyes, I could see he'd understood, but it didn't seem to make him happy, or even a little proud. He looked sad, and a little angry – but not at me.

"Listen," he said. "I… I'm sorry. I didn't want… I'm sorry."

I took a deep breath and wiped my cheeks with my sleeve.

"I didn't want to make you cry."

"But why then? Why did you look at me like that? It's like I wiped out your family! What did you think, that you were going to win me over like that?"

"I don't know, I…"

"Stop saying you don't know!"

"Okay." He turned around and put both of his hands behind his neck. "I can't have this conversation."

"Why?"

He ran one hand through his hair. "Because," he said, "I thought about it all week. All week, Chloé. And it makes me… I don't understand myself anymore, okay? And it makes me mad to be the guy who makes you cry and who says things like, 'You don't love him,' it makes me mad. Maybe you love him, maybe you don't. I don't know."

I wanted to say a thousand things to him. I wanted to talk about the studio, about the almost shy way he touched me, about everything that had just been said, and what was between the lines. To tell him that I couldn't take the first step towards him, even though I wanted to because I was risking a lot more than being unfaithful. To tell him that, despite everything he might be afraid of, a man like him couldn't hurt women.

"Chloé?" He came closer, but not too close. "Why did you come here?"

He wasn't challenging me with his question – he wanted to know. And I couldn't tell him I didn't really know myself, that I had too many questions, that I needed him, so I said, "I wanted to see you," and that's all.

We were both standing there, in the middle of the living room, and Antoine was going to say something when I heard a woman's voice, in the entryway, shouting, "Hello?" I turned around, and Julie was in the living room, with an enormous bouquet of white roses, and she said, "The door was unlocked, so I let myself in. And look at what they were going to throw away! They're already open, so they won't last long, but still… Oh! Hi, Chloé!"

She put the bouquet down on the little bench near the door, and came over to me, gave me a kiss, and wished me Happy New Year. I thought she'd notice I'd been crying, but she didn't look like she thought anything was up, and she just asked me how I was, if I'd had good holidays, if I'd made any resolutions. My answers were mechanical, and I couldn't believe she was there, that Antoine was expecting her and hadn't said anything about it to me. He looked at her, without saying anything, and she finally turned towards him, "Well, of course, macho men can't say hello when their friends come in, but 'Hi' anyway!" She gave him a kiss on the cheek and a little pat on the shoulder, as she laughed lightly to let him know she wasn't impressed at all. She knows how to deal with him, I thought.

"Do you want to have dinner with us?" she asked, and I felt my heart sink heavily.

"No," I said, "I was just about to leave." I picked up my coat and gave her a kiss, showering her with pointless wishes for the New Year, and then I stepped over to Antoine. "I'll walk you out," he said.

At the door, I looked up at him. "I'm sorry," he repeated. "I should have told you…"

"No, why?"

"Chloé…" I shook my head and I opened the door. He took me by the shoulder and gently turned me to face him. I put one hand on his chest – I was making a superhuman effort not to cry. Antoine said, "I'll call you tomorrow, okay?" I nodded yes before I slipped out the door. I heard him repeat my name, but I didn't turn around.

I quickly walked towards the corner of the street, in the crisp, cold air, with my arms crossed over my chest, listening to my steps as they crunched in the snow, and trying not to think about anything. It really was awfully, terribly cold, and my eyes hurt, because of the tears that were freezing in them. I finally found a taxi and sat down in the back seat, still shivering.

"Where to, miss?"

"Hmmm?"

"Where are we going?"

I had no idea. I thought about Daphné – I really wanted to see her, but she wasn't coming home until after I left for Belize in two days, and I thought of my mother and Juliette. I didn't want to be alone, especially not alone with the image of Antoine and Julie's roses. The driver asked, "So?" and I told him to go ahead and put the meter on, but that I had to think. He said, "Whatever you say," and I put a hand over my eyes.

Juliette is going to think I'm ridiculous, I thought, she'll think I'm completely ridiculous. I must have already run to her place crying about a dozen times, usually because of a man, sometimes for other reasons, some of them serious, some completely idiotic. Then I thought to myself if there was one person in the world who would welcome me, with open arms, it was certainly Juliette. So I gave her address to the driver and I smiled, it had become such a habit to go find warmth and comfort in the old Saint-Henri factory.

We'd only gone two blocks when my cell phone started to ring ("Jingle Bells," which Antoine had set on Christmas night, and I still hadn't changed). I nervously took it out of my bag and I saw it was him. I made a face at the phone, and threw it back in my bag, then, I grabbed it and answered. "What do you want?"

"For you to come back," Antoine said.

"I don't think so, my boy."

"Chloé…"

"No, you know what? You're going to think I'm a party pooper but I don't really feel like having dinner with you and Julie."

"Julie left."

"Pardon?"

"It was all ridiculous. She's not stupid, you know, when she saw me standing there like a moron and that, well, there was some tension..."

"Tension? Antoine, I don't care if you kicked Julie out, although it's not very nice, but, really, I don't care."

Obviously, it was a lot easier to be mad at him when he wasn't in the same room as me. "And, I'll have you know, I don't feel like having you stare at me like I'm some kind of slut."

"Chloé, I said I was sorry."

"Well, I don't care about that, either." I stopped: I wanted to hurt him, it was a pointless desire for revenge.

"Please come back," he repeated.

"No."

"But I'm telling you I'm sorry. I acted like a jerk. I don't understand myself anymore, Chloé."

"Yeah, nobody knows what they're doing anymore. I must have heard that same remark from just about everyone I know in the last few months. My sister didn't understand herself anymore, Juliette didn't understand herself anymore – and me, too, I've been having a bit of a hard time lately, too."

"Come back."

"Stop saying that! What are we going to do?" There was silence – I knew he was thinking the same thing as me.

"I can't go back there. It won't work."

"Okay, okay. We can go get a drink, or something to eat somewhere."

"No, Antoine, I... not now, I'm too mad, I'll say something stupid." That was completely false: the only thing I was afraid of was giving into temptation – I wanted him too much.

"Oh, Chloé..." It's impossible to lie to him, I thought. He must hear my pheromones.

"Please," I said to him. "I just need to sit and not think about anything, okay? Please."

338   RAFAËLE GERMAIN

He paused for a moment and then said, "But are you
okay?"

"Yes, yes, I'm fine. Really."

"Chloé…"

"No, look, I'm just pulling up to my house."

He sighed. "I'll call you."

"Sure. I have to go. Okay? Please."

"Okay. Bye then."

"Bye." I hung up and leaned my head back, sighing loudly and rubbing my face. I didn't know where to start, how
to tackle the situation – but I knew I was upset and, especially, terribly excited, and that was the worst of it. My
phone, which I was still holding in my right hand, rang
again, making me jump unreasonably. It was Simon, calling
from the restaurant. I took a deep breath and answered.

"Hello."

"Hi, my love." I closed my eyes: his voice always calmed
me down, his presence, even at the other end of the line,
reassured me. He's everything that's good and solid in my
life, I thought.

"How are you?" he asked.

"Not bad. I'm on my way to Juliette's. How are you?"

"Good. It's my last day before the trip."

"That's true…"

"I feel a little bad about leaving the team, but, well, let's
just say I'm having a hard time convincing them it's breaking my heart to take off for ten days down south with the
woman I love."

I smiled. We were far from Antoine and his dark eyes that
stirred me up so violently. Simon, with his soft voice and
his eyes that were blue as the night, was a safe haven. I
thought about Belize and said to myself, wanting to believe,
that maybe everything would work out there, that, in
Simon's love, and in the heat and the rhythm of the ocean,
I'd find something like certainty.

"I can't wait to leave," I said to him.

"Me neither." The taxi stopped in front of the old factory.
"I'm here, sweetheart."
"I just wanted to tell you to have a good evening."
"Okay. I love you, you know."
"Me, too, my love."
I hung up, smiling even wider, and bent forward to pay
the driver. He took the money and said, "Eventful life, eh?"
I gave him a dirty look: "Mind your own business."
"Hey, don't get angry, honey! Can't help but hear, eh?"
"Yeah, yeah." I slammed the door and ran all the way to
Juliette's.

Marcus, in his underwear and flip-flops, came and opened
the door.
"Oh, Chloé! Chloé! Chloé!"
"Marcus... don't you ever wear clothes? It's minus 35!"
"Not in here, sweetie," and he swivelled his hips, lasciviously.
"Okay, okay," I said. "Is Juliette here? I really have to see
her."
"In the studio." He pointed to the back of the apartment,
with a gesture that looked so gay, I started to laugh.
"Thanks, Marcus." I walked in not bothering to take off
my coat, and I almost ran to the studio. Juliette was standing
in front of one of her paintings, doing something I couldn't
name – she was wearing surgical gloves and, from where I
was standing, it looked like she was stroking the canvas.
"Hi!" I said. I stood in the middle of the doorway, and
looked purposefully to my left, where Antoine and I had been
more than a week before. I stared at the wall, the floor, the
lamp, which had been put back in its place, as if I was expecting them to give me some kind of answer, or explanation.
"There," I said to Juliette, pointing to the exact spot.
Ideas and words were tripping over each other so fast in my
head, that I decided it would be easier to give them free rein.
"There, what?" Juliette asked me.

"December 31, with Antoine. Oh… Furious necking."

"What?"

"Against the wall. At midnight. When I found him. He kissed me. I kissed him. And, oh… Juliette, I have a problem."

"Okay, whoa, whoa, whoa, hang on a minute." She took off her gloves and put her hands on her hips. "Because I saw him there," she pointed to a shelving unit about two metres from where I was standing, "having sex with a girl who wasn't you."

"Oh, we kissed, we didn't have sex. Juliette," I repeated, "I have a problem."

"Oh, my God," said a little voice behind me.

"Marcus!" shouted Juliette. "Can you stop listening to other people's conversations?"

He ignored her and repeated, "Oh, my God."

"Marcus, I need to talk to Juliette, and…"

"I'll go get the drinks," was all he said, and I heard him run down the hallway. Juliette took a step to close the door, but I motioned for her to let it go. "At the point I'm at," I said.

"Okay. Let's start at the beginning. You and Antoine kissed."

"Yes."

Juliette nodded, with a big smile on her face. "I knew it," she said. "I knew that would happen! And if you think I didn't notice that you've been all upside-down since New Year's Eve… I've been wondering what could have happened. I thought maybe that was it, or that maybe you two had talked…" She clapped her hands, looking delighted. "Ha! I can't get over it! Incredible. Hey! You're the ones who broke my lamp!"

"Yep."

"Son-of-a-bitch…" She looked like she thought the whole thing was very funny. "Oh, it doesn't matter! No one cares! It's incredible."

"No, it's not incredible, Juliette. It's a problem."

Marcus came in just then, a little out of breath, with a bottle of Jamaican rum under one arm, a carton of papaya juice under the other, three glasses in one hand, and a few limes in the other. "Okay!" he said, getting started on his mixture right away. "Details, details, details! Oh... I wouldn't mind getting kissed by Antoine."

"No," I answered. "You would mind getting kissed by Antoine because you love Michel, remember?"

"Oh, of course, of course," he said. "I'd feel guilty, terribly guilty. But..." He smiled dreamily. "... mmmm. It must have been good, wasn't it? Antoine's a good kisser, right?"

"Of course, he's a good kisser!" I shouted. "He's a divine kisser! That's my problem!"

"Too hot?" asked Marcus.

"Oh, my God," I sighed. "Juliette, it was..." I still hadn't formulated it, not even in my thoughts. "It's the dirtiest thing that ever happened to me in my life."

"And you didn't have sex?"

"No sex. Nothing."

"Not even a little..." Marcus successively and rapidly imitated a hand job, a blow job, and then something unidentifiable – he snapped his fingers which, according to him, must be how to stroke a clitoris.

"No," I said. "No-thing." We were all sitting around cross-legged, with the bottle of rum in the centre of our little circle, and I realized I was smiling happily at the memory of what had happened, and also because I could finally talk about it.

"He didn't even touch my breasts," I added.

"Are you sure it was Antoine?" Juliette asked, making us all laugh. I told them more details, until Marcus asked, "What about after that? After that?"

"After that, nothing. Until this afternoon. I just came from his place."

Two overexcited "Oh my Gods" came out of them and I smiled, rather proud of the effect I'd created.

"You did it," said Juliette.

"Oh no. We so didn't do it." I told them all about his cold gaze, his saying, "Leave him," my tears, the arrival of Julie, the phone call in the car. They were hanging on my every word, and Marcus was constantly adding rum to my glass, as, flabbergasted, he just kept saying "my, my, my."

"Yes, well," said Juliette when I'd finished, "I think it's clear, isn't it?"

"What?"

"He's in love with you, Chloé. He's in love with you."

"No, no. This is Antoine, it's not…"

"Chloé…" Juliette insisted. Then she started to count on her fingers: "He didn't touch your breasts. He didn't push you against the wall, like he would have with any other girl."

"A punishment fuck," Marcus interrupted.

"Pardon?"

"Punishment fuck," Juliette repeated. "You never heard that expression? Antoine said it to us the other day. When you take a girl, standing up, against a wall, bang, bang, bang, he said it's called a punishment fuck."

"I loooooove that expression," Marcus sighed.

"Isn't it a little… violent?" Juliette asked.

"Yeah, well, it's not really a punishment, Juliette, as long as you get off, too," I said. "It's certainly not a tender screw, but…"

"A tender screw?"

"That's an expression my sister came up with. When you do it slowly, so tenderly that the sheet on top of you doesn't even move. But, a punishment fuck has its own charm, too. You know, bang, bang, bang."

Marcus started to laugh and Juliette said, "Yes, yes, okay… I have done it before, I'd like to remind you, in the not so distant past. If I can get back to what I was saying…" Again, she raised her hand, and started counting again. "So. Antoine didn't touch your breasts. He didn't give you a 'punishment fuck.' He looked hurt when you left. He told you he thought about you all week. He said, 'Leave him.' Could it be any more clear?"

"Oh, I don't know. We're talking about Antoine, after all..."

"I've always thought he was in love with you."

"Oh, Juliette, honestly..." I waved my hand, but I had to work to keep from laughing – I didn't really believe it, but it was an idea that made me really happy.

"I'm telling you," Juliette insisted. "He's just realizing it now, that's all!"

"Yes, but THE question," said Marcus, "is: Do you love him?"

"Well..." I realized that, up till then, I'd been so shocked, so upset, that I'd been unable to distinguish between love and desire. I didn't know if I was really mixing them up or if I refused to see that the one was hiding behind the other.

"But," I repeated, "I can't love Antoine." It was, at that moment, the only constructive thought I had. "I can't love Antoine. I have Simon. Simon!" I repeated, trying to make them understand.

"Yes," said Juliette, "there's no doubt you've got the best guy in the world, but... that's not the question."

"No," I interrupted her. "I think I'm just obsessed with Antoine, because now I have someone else, and I'm attracted by what's forbidden, like a stupid teenager... And besides that, it's him, with his bets and declarations that come too late! He's not in love with me, Juliette, he's just turned on because he can't have me anymore."

Marcus nodded. "That would be just like him."

"No," said Juliette. "I'm telling you both: he loves you."

"Stop that already!" I shouted.

"Why does it bother you so much?" Juliette asked me. "Is it because if he loves you, you're going to have to make a decision? Is that it?"

"No! Juliette! *I can't* be with Antoine. I can't be with a guy who'll screw anything on two legs! Come on!"

"That's just it, then: you're afraid."

"No!"

"Chloé," said Juliette. "I know you. It's what you were waiting for. Subconsciously, maybe, but…"

"Oh, I know!" I moaned. "I know! The rush was…" I put my face in my hands. "Oh, it's awful…"

"It's not just the rush you were waiting for," said Juliette. "It was Antoine."

I pointed a finger at her. "Don't say that."

"I saw you," Juliette went on. "When he had that stupid idea of a bet. I saw you."

"Stop. Stop. That's not it, I… I'm just all mixed up. Completely, completely, completely. I know two things: Simon is the most marvellous man I know, and, I want Antoine. I'm sure of those two things. As for the rest, I don't understand a thing."

"What about Simon?" asked Marcus. "Do you love him?"

"I said, 'As for the rest, I don't understand a thing.' Can I have another rum?"

Marcus made me another drink, while Juliette rubbed my back and said, "Oh, poor, sweet baby." I smiled at her. That was what she called me when she wanted to gently make fun of my existential dramas. I got up and walked towards her paintings. They were magnificent and imposing, and I still thought there was something religious, almost sacred, about them.

"You know," I said to Juliette, "I'd like to have that kind of gift, too, to express myself like this. To have this kind of refuge."

Juliette was getting up to come join me when the emergency door opened up and there was Antoine, without a coat, standing in an icy draft.

Chapter 23

I heard Marcus say, "Oh, God. He's back," and I would have laughed, if I hadn't been so astounded. Antoine gave him a quick hello, closed the door, and turned first to Juliette, then to me. He smiled, "I figured you'd be here," but I was too astonished to say anything at all. Then he came down the iron steps and looked at each of us in turn – Marcus, half-naked and still sitting cross-legged in front of the bottle of rum; Juliette, standing in the middle of the room; and me, near the big painting.

"What?" he said. "Are you really that surprised to see me here?" Quickly, I thought, if I were thinking rationally, I'd say no, it's not really surprising. But, let's say, I was having trouble being rational, then and there, with my rum, in front of a newly arrived Antoine.

"Yes," Juliette finally said. "I should have expected that."

"I should think so," said Antoine. "Well, I don't know what Chloé has told you, but, judging by looking at you, I think you're up to speed on a thing or two."

Marcus hitched his thumb at the wall, behind himself, where I'd told them we'd kissed. Antoine ran a hand over his face, then he smiled, looking almost embarrassed, and he asked me, "Does everyone think I'm a bastard now?"

"No!" I answered. "No way. No way. Right? I didn't say he was a bastard, did I?"

"Oh, no way!" shouted Marcus. I opened my eyes wide at him, and he put a hand over his mouth.

"I went by your place," Antoine went on. "Because, remember, you told me you were going home."

"Yes, well…"

"Anyway. Obviously, you weren't there, and then I told myself I couldn't follow you all over the town like a psychopath, but I didn't feel like going back to my place either, so I came here. I was on my way over when I realized you must have done the same thing."

"Oh..." That was the most concrete thought I could formulate. Antoine, on the other hand, was perfectly cool, like nothing had happened, like, earlier in the afternoon, his cold stares and his unspoken thoughts.

Marcus got up, then, as he winked exaggeratedly at Juliette, he said "Yes, well, we'll just go finish our rum somewhere else, okey-dokey?"

"No!" I shrieked.

"No," said Antoine, stepping closer to Marcus. "Chloé doesn't trust me." The truth was that I didn't trust *me*, and everyone knew it, but they had the decency not to say it. "However," he added, "I might have a glass if you have any left."

"Oh, of course! Of course!" Marcus gave him a flirty little smile and walked out of the studio.

"Okay," said Juliette. "I don't want to get mixed up in something that doesn't concern me, but it seems to me the two of you might need to talk, right?"

"What did she tell you?" Antoine asked her.

"Just what happened," I answered. "Here. And at your place this afternoon. Antoine, I couldn't not talk to someone. You know me."

"I know, sweetheart." I shivered when he called me "sweetheart," even if he always called me that. "Besides, that's exactly why I'm here, too."

"Oh, great," Juliette sighed. "If you don't mind, I'm going to go get my psychologist's couch, and my fake Sigmund Freud beard." I smiled and, behind Juliette, I could see Antoine rolling his eyes: we both knew Juliette loved to play psychologist.

"It's okay," said Antoine. "I'll spare you. Chloé already

told you everything, right?" I could see that Juliette was a little disappointed. Marcus, who'd just come in with another glass, looked absolutely devastated.

"No," Juliette told Antoine. "You must have your own version of the facts, don't you?"

He smiled. "You can't resist, can you?"

"No!" answered Marcus. "We want to know! Details, details, details!"

Antoine was laughing, with his hands in his pant pockets. How could he have gone from the state he was in earlier to the state he was in now? Either he's very strong, I thought, or he doesn't give a shit. And I realized I would have preferred it if he was still mad, still upset, even if I had to face that dark look – it wasn't as hard as this cheerful nonchalance. I thought he was so handsome, too sexy; I felt like when I'd met him and he made my head spin, only now, eight years had gone by, and there was Simon, complicating everything.

"Come on!" Marcus repeated. "Details!"

I put my glass down on the edge of an easel and spread my arms wide, "Excuse me, but am I the only one who thinks this whole situation is completely fucked up?"

"Well…" said Juliette, "you know, I always said…"

"What?" asked Antoine.

"That…" She looked down at the floor, gesturing back and forth between Antoine and me. "…that the two of you… at one point… something…"

"Well, that's nice and clear!" said Antoine laughing.

"Okay, that's enough!" I shouted. "I'm sorry, but I'm not going to stand here while you discuss all this, it's ridiculous. Antoine, it's your turn, there's more rum, tell them what you want to tell them, I'm getting the fuck out of here."

"No, don't go," said Antoine. For the first time since he'd come in, he looked at me like he had on the doorstep, before I left him, a few hours earlier, and it made me feel so good that I repeated, almost curtly, "No, I'm leaving."

He came over to me. Immobile, I watched him until he was almost right up against me. "Stay," he asked. "Please."

"No…"

He stroked my face, gently and pushed a lock of hair back behind my ear. If he kisses me, I thought, if he leans down, I won't be able to say no. I turned my head, without conviction, and I saw Marcus, over by the door, following the scene with such interest that I wouldn't have been surprised to see him take out a bag of popcorn. I said, "I think this is the most absurd situation I've ever had to deal with," and that made Antoine smile.

"Okay," said Juliette. "I'm going to leave you alone for a couple of minutes, okay? Come on, Marcus."

"But…" said Marcus, as Juliette grabbed him by the arm. They left the studio, without shutting the door – my guess would be they were right outside, eavesdropping like they never had before.

"Listen," said Antoine.

"No, Antoine… I'm leaving. Really."

"Okay, okay." He was talking in a low voice. "I just wanted to say I was sorry again. I thought again about everything I said to you, Chloé, and it was really awful."

"No, stop it…" He was still right next to me, with one hand on my right arm.

"You're right. It's my pride." I looked up at him. "Hey," he said. "I just admitted I committed the sin of pride. Me. I hope you took note of the date and time." I laughed weakly.

"It's okay," I said. "It's all right."

"I had no right to say all that. I had no right to do all that either."

"No, Antoine. It's not like you twisted my arm or anything." He smiled, and I saw the little light I knew so well flicker in his eyes. "It's not just me, eh? It was really…"

"No, shut up!" I raised an authoritative finger in front of him – and for the first time since the beginning of our conversation, I was able to smile freely. "Shut up," I repeated.

"Okay," he said, laughing. "Your wish is my command, my darling."

"In fact, that was a command, Antoine."

"Then your commands are my wishes, that's even prettier."

I love him so much, I thought.

"Don't you want to go for dinner tomorrow?" he asked me. "Just to see if I can dissolve in excuses again for hours on end?"

"No, I can't, I…" I was almost uncomfortable telling him. "…I'm leaving for Belize the day after tomorrow, at four in the morning." He looked hurt, but so briefly I didn't know if what I'd seen was what I wanted to see or what had really been there.

"That's right," he said. "I'd forgotten. So why don't you stay tonight, then?"

"I don't know."

"Come on, we'll drink rum, we'll listen to Marcus' dirty stories, come on. You can't take off for Belize and leave me with all this guilt."

"But you wanted to talk to Juliette…"

"I wanted to see you, silly. And I'll have all the time in the world to talk to her while you're in Belize." I smiled, and wondered if one night with him could be considered cheating – I wanted him so badly and I wanted him to tell me he wanted me, too, that it was all he was thinking of, too, but that he was holding himself back, out of nobility and love for me.

"So, you'll stay?" he asked.

"Yeah… Okay."

"Come on then. Those two idiots must be listening to us anyway, so we may as well talk in front of them."

Juliette and Marcus were standing in front of Marcus' bedroom door, looking perfectly innocent as they chatted.

"Oh, there you are!" Marcus shouted.

"Yeah, that's good," Antoine said. "You had enough time

to get from the studio door to your bedroom door. That's good, because we didn't notice a thing."

"I don't know what you're talking about," said Juliette, faking anger. "So, were you able to talk?"

"We talked," I said. "And if you don't mind, I might stay for dinner."

"Who said you were invited to stay for dinner?" Juliette asked.

"Very funny," said Antoine, taking her by the shoulders and dragging her towards the kitchen, as Marcus whispered to me, "He's so hot... and so nice. He played it right, I think."

"Marcus!" shouted Juliette.

"Yes, yes, sorry. Hey! You want me to make my rotisserie chicken?"

Sitting on tall stools around the centre island in the kitchen, we watched Marcus lovingly marinate his chicken, then spice it with scientific precision, then put it on the skewers so he could cook it Creole-style over the grill on one of the stoves. He'd made the set-up himself, a skewer and two poles, and he patiently and regularly turned the chicken, drinking Alsatian wine and explaining how he could cook five at once, which seemed impressive, but hardly useful.

Antoine sat next to me, and from time to time, he touched my shoulder or my arm, but as naturally as ever – sometimes I thought I could make something out in his gaze, the reflection of a memory, maybe, or a regret. I thought to myself that my regrets must be visible, too, and that Juliette and Antoine could undoubtedly see that, once again, I wanted to abandon myself in his arms. But I was happy, too – I couldn't have tolerated the idea of seeing my friendship with him be altered in any way. And there we all were, like before, like always, and I kept telling myself that was all that mattered.

Marcus' chicken, like almost everything he made, was

marvellous. He served it with rice and green beans, and in the middle of the island he placed a sauce he'd made himself, from Jamaican peppers, which, according to Antoine, was a weapon of mass destruction. We ate it anyway, to show off, and make Marcus laugh, and we laughed, with red cheeks, and watering eyes, slapping each other on the back and grabbing our throats. Marcus took tiny spoonfuls and swallowed them proudly, shaking his head and saying, "Bunch of amateurs…"

I would have liked to have talked some more to Juliette, tell her absolutely everything – just for the pleasure of talking about Antoine. But, for the time being, I had to wait. We'll see, was what I was thinking. We'll see when I get back from Belize, we'll see in Belize – I told myself, maybe everything would magically return to normal, leaving nothing but a delicious, painless memory that had nothing to do with the images that were still tormenting my libido.

I left at about one in the morning – we'd finished the chicken, finished the Alsatian wine, finished the little honey cakes. I'd hugged Juliette and Marcus, and Juliette looked me straight in the eyes, "We'll talk when you get back, eh? You have to do what you have to do." Which would have been very useful if I'd known, exactly, what I had to do.

The four of us were standing at the door. I was putting on my coat, making the usual promises of "I'll drink to you all," and "I'll drink a piña colada and think of you."

"Bye," I said to Antoine.

"My princess." He took me in his arms and hugged me tight. I nuzzled the hollow of his neck, breathing it in one last time before I left, and I was about to step back when he kissed me on the cheek. Then he leaned towards my ear and whispered, "You make me dizzy, Chloé."

"You make me dizzy?" Juliette repeated at the other end of the phone. "Wow."

It was eight-thirty, the day after our little dinner party –

I'd already packed my bags and was waiting for Simon, who'd decided to do a last shift at the restaurant, to ease his conscience. He was supposed to be back around nine, and I was bored, hoping for a call from Antoine – which wasn't happening – and finishing a bottle of wine that was in the fridge. When I couldn't take it anymore, I finally called Juliette – I wanted to know if Antoine had talked to her after I'd left, and, especially, tell her about his dizziness.

"That's nice," said Juliette.

"Yes. Unless you take it more literally and it means that I make him slightly nauseous."

"I really doubt that."

"Yeah, I know." I smiled, and I took a handful of pretzels from a bowl that was sitting near me on the sofa.

"What are you eating?" Juliette asked.

"Pretzels. Did you know I hate pretzels? I don't enjoy them at all. But when there are pretzels around, I can't stop eating them."

"It's like the crusts on some cheese," said Juliette.

"No, I like cheese crusts. It's different with pretzels. There's a rather interesting relationship between disgust and compulsion. I don't know if any psychoanalysts have already studied the question or not."

"Of pretzels in particular? I would guess probably not."

"Still. It's a very interesting metaphor. Or a more superficial manifestation of a kind of internal conflict."

"What do you mean by that exactly?" asked Juliette.

"No idea. I'd like to connect it to what's going on with Antoine, but it doesn't really work. Simply because, obviously, I don't hate Antoine, so I can't really compare him to pretzels."

"Obviously," said Juliette.

I broke off the end of a pretzel and threw it to Siffleux, who sniffed it briefly before biting into it.

"You know what," I said to Juliette. "I think he's flirting with me."

"Antoine?"

"Yes. I just had that weird impression, last night. He's flirting with me."

"That's normal," said Juliette. "Simply because he's trying to pick you up…"

"…first of all," I interrupted her, "we're not sure of that."

"Oh, come on, Chloé! It's obvious! And, by the way, you're flirting with him, too."

"Pardon?" I shouted like an offended virgin.

"Not flirting like, 'Hey, baby!'" Juliette continued, "but you're flirting, in your own way. The way you look at him, the fact that you touch him less than before…"

"Hang on, you're telling me that touching him less is flirting? You're pretty twisted, you know."

"Not at all. Hang on two seconds." She was gone for a minute, and then came back with a "Sorry," and a mouth full of food.

"What are you eating?"

"Pretzels, you gave me a craving. So, getting back to what I was saying, yes, it's flirting. Just like the fact that he didn't try to kiss you last night in the studio. Touching each other, kissing each other – those are predictable things. He's paying attention to you. And, by not touching him, you're showing you're afraid to touch him."

"That might be stretching it a little, Juliette."

"Tsk, tsk, tsk. I'm telling you. Since I've been single, I've been noticing stuff like that. It's like monks, you know. They're more sensitive to the movement of other people's souls…"

"Okay, Ju. Whether or not you're right, it's a little surprising, don't you think? It seems like we're in another place now, doesn't it? We've known each other for eight years. We had sex on a sink in a bar bathroom. Does he really have to flirt with me? Now?"

Juliette thought it over for a moment. "That's Antoine," she said. "It's his principal means of expression. You can't forget that. That's how he approaches other people. He charms them. Even men, even your parents, even girls he's not the least bit interested in."

"Yes, that's true. Still, it's weird."

"Deep down, he's always been courting you," Juliette said.

"I know, but now there's like another layer to it…" I stopped and shook my head, "Or, it's just that I want to see it like that?"

"That may be true, too," said Juliette, which bugged me a little. "You're going to have to make up your mind, Chloé. You can't keep hoping that he'll keep on flirting with you, and wanting to drag you off to a dark corner while you keep telling him no and saying you love Simon."

"I know, I know…"

Juliette laughed and said, "The two of you are so much alike! You both want to go on with your lives, but you also want to know the other one is there waiting for you when you feel like it. And, to top it off, you're both enjoying the whole thing."

I didn't say anything: again, she was completely right.

"Juliette?"

"What?"

"Did he say anything to you last night? After I left."

"I asked him if he was in love with you."

My heart leapt – I grabbed another handful of pretzels and stuffed them all in my mouth. "What did he say?"

"That he didn't understand himself anymore."

"Oh, Christ!" I shouted through my huge mouthful of pretzels. I was really starting to get sick and tired of everyone not understanding themselves anymore! "What does that mean, he doesn't understand himself anymore? That's what he told me yesterday, 'I don't understand myself anymore'! That doesn't mean anything!"

"Do *you* understand yourself?"

I was stuck. "Okay, okay," I grumbled. "Don't be a smart ass. No, I don't understand myself. But I'd like it if someone, somewhere, understood themself. It would be nice for a change."

"Well, I'll tell you one thing," said Juliette. "When Antoine says he doesn't understand himself anymore, it means, yes, he's in love. It's never happened to him before, don't forget. So, there's no doubt it's a little upsetting. Especially since it concerns his best friend. And it looks like he's afraid he'll hurt you."

"But of course, he'd hurt me! Christ, I love Antoine, but you know as well as I do that the guy is toxic!"

"He can change."

"Oh, that would surprise me. And besides, it doesn't matter," I said. "I've got Simon."

"You have Simon." There was a bit of sarcasm in Juliette's voice.

"Why do you say it like that?" I asked.

"Because… it's not my place to say this, and it'll probably come back and bite me on the butt, but you don't love Simon. I'm not even sure you're in love with Antoine. I wonder. I don't know if it's just a desire for something else, but it shows for sure that you're not in love with Simon. You're looking for ways out."

I rubbed my eyes. I had considered this possibility. In a confused way, but, still, I had considered it. In the solitude of my room, I had told myself the same things, and they had hurt me. But I couldn't manage to formulate any certainty about it. And then, Juliette didn't know Simon like I knew him. She didn't know how sweet and gentle he was; she didn't know that sometimes, when I was with him, it seemed like I had some answers.

"You know," I said, "that really is going to come back to bite you if I stay with Simon."

"You said, 'if.' You don't say 'if' when you're head over heels in love."

"Oh, stop…" I threw a little piece of pretzel to Siffleux. "Isn't that kind of stretching things a bit?"

"Stretching things…" said Juliette. "I'm not sure that's the best expression in this conversation."

I laughed. "You know what I mean."

"If you say so," said Juliette.

"I should just shut the hell up and wait to see what happens."

"You can't do that, Chloé. There are other people involved."

"Oh, shit… I know. I owe Simon more than that."

"And Antoine."

"Oh, yeah, well, he's another story! Let me remind you that eight years ago, he wasn't interested. So, I'm not going to start feeling all guilty today."

Juliette laughed, "Well, you could get revenge on behalf of the hundreds of girls he's pissed off since he was sixteen…"

"Sixteen? Thirteen! He started when he was thirteen – with his big sisters' friends."

"Oh, boy…" said Juliette. "That makes twenty-three years. How many girls do you think he's had in twenty-three years?"

"Okay, see, that's exactly the kind of thing I'd rather not know. Would you like to be number 978 on his list of conquests?"

"Well, that didn't seem to bother you eight years ago. Although back then, you were probably only 743, which is nothing. Seriously, have you ever asked him how many girls he's been with?"

"No! I don't want to know!" I shouted. "And besides, I'm not even sure he knows himself."

"I think that's kind of attractive."

"What?"

"I know it's kind of retro, but I've always found that attractive – guys who've had, like, a thousand lovers."

"Hmph. A thousand's an awful lot. And, sure, it might be attractive, but it doesn't really inspire confidence."

"No," said Juliette. "That's true." I heard her open a beer. "How many guys have you been with?"

"Me? I don't know. Thirty or so."

"Oh, come on!" exclaimed Juliette. "I know you know the exact number. If I know you, you've made lists."

"Okay, okay…" I answered laughing. "Thirty-four. And I remember all their first names."

"Congratulations."

"You're one to talk! Did you ever remember the name of that Indian guy in London even?" Juliette burst out laughing, and we started talking about the "guys from London," a series of young men of a variety of ethnic origins whom we'd met during an extended stay at a youth hostel: Frederico from Italy, who was not to be confused with Frederico from Spain, Nicolas from France, Ross from South Africa, David from Israel, Curtis from America and a number of guys from Australia… and one guy from India.

There had been a lot of movement between rooms and beds, and, one night, Juliette ended up on the terrace with an Indian guy who was passing through. They spent the night there, and, the next day, the Indian guy was gone, leaving behind a happy, fulfilled Juliette – until she realized she'd forgotten his name. Despite our searching through the hostel's registration book, we didn't find a thing, except his signature, in Hindi (or, according to Ross from South Africa, who'd been to India, in Marathe, since the Indian guy was from Mumbai. Then someone pointed out that maybe the same alphabet was used in Hindi and Marathe – there followed a long discussion on semiotics, which was anything but conclusive, and Juliette came home with nothing but a lover identified by a passport number, a signature in Hindi, and two initials: a G, that could have easily been an S or a J, and an M. We invented a ton of possible identities with the names and Indian words we knew: Gandhi

Maharaja, Sanskrit Masala, Ganesh Madras – and we finally settled on Johnny Michaud, which was very unlikely, but had the advantage of being funny).

We reminisced about those good memories for quite a while, and finally ended up, like always, with "We'll have to go back, eh?" though we believed less and less we would. I was going to get back to the topic of Antoine when I heard Simon's key in the lock.

"I have to go, Chubby."

"Your man home?" asked Juliette.

"Yep. You'll come look after the cats, right?"

"No problem. Diet for Siffleux, regular for the girls, right?"

"That's it. Every two days'll be okay. But it would be nice if you stayed a little sometimes, to…"

"I know," Juliette interrupted. "To snuggle with Puce. Don't worry."

"It's just that… she was emotionally deprived."

"I know. Have a good trip, Stretch."

"Thanks."

"And good luck. With everything."

"Thanks, Chubby."

I hung up and looked at Simon, who was smiling at me.

"What do you say I cook us up a little something?" he asked me. He glanced at the bowl and the last half-pretzel in it. "If you're still hungry."

"Of course. I'm always hungry."

We kissed and he said to me, "I think we're going to have a wonderful trip."

"I think so, too, my love."

And I really believed it.

Chapter 24

My mother handed each of us a martini.

"I can't get over how tanned you are, Chloé. Are you sure you put on lotion?"

"Yes, Mom."

"Because the sun in Belize is a lot stronger than here, you know, and…"

"Mom!" shouted Daphné. "Will you please leave her alone? She's not red, she doesn't have blisters, and she's not writhing in pain in the burn unit, she's just tanned."

"I know," said our mother, "it's just that…"

"MOM!" Daphné and I shouted in unison, which made all three of us laugh. My father's head appeared in the doorway, and he asked, "Everything okay?"

"Yes, yes," my mother shouted. "I'm just so happy the four of us are together."

"Me, too," I told her. "It must have been at least six months since we've done this. It was a good idea, Daphné."

I'd gotten back from Belize three days earlier, and I'd called Daphné right away; she'd immediately proposed a little "nuclear family" evening – an opportunity that came up less and less since she'd had the girls, which might be why it always seemed a little festive to us.

My father came into the living room, with a tremendous bowl of guacamole and a bag of Tostitos. "Tell me what you think," he said. "I've been working on this recipe for a long time, and I think it's finally perfect." He did the honours himself, and then sat down next to my mother and asked, "So, Chloé! Belize! Sun! Eh! How was it?"

"It was super," I answered. "Super, super."

"Super, super," said Daphné, "super, super, *super?*"

I laughed and told them, in detail, about Belize City, the little hotel on the beach, the wooden huts, the hammocks hanging on the porches, the tall trees and leisurely days, the fresh fish, the *Caipirinhas* that started at four in the afternoon, playing Scrabble and drinking cocktails, the sun and the sea, the wind and the sound of the waves.

And Simon. Simon had been perfect, like always, only this time, I didn't get tired of his perfection. It hadn't reminded me of my faults and my shortcomings, it had simply calmed and reassured me, and I'd told myself a thousand times a day, as I watched him reading in his hammock or as we shared long kisses in the waves, that I loved him. It was a series of clear, beautiful days; I almost completely managed to not think about being afraid of this love, seeing the little huts, the beach and the sea as a little bubble that was protecting it. I was delighted not to realize that the almost victorious joy I felt about my love was possibly the proof of how fragile it was.

I'd thought of Antoine, a little, furtively, when we'd first arrived – but I hadn't had to force myself, like I did in Montreal, to keep from seeing him everywhere. He was in my dreams, however, but most of my dreams were innocent. Just one night, I dreamed about long, tender kisses, hugs with just enough reserve to be intoxicating, and I woke up at dawn with his image in my head – I went for a walk alone on the beach and tried to figure everything out, but I kept coming up with the same answers as always, which really weren't answers at all: I loved Simon, I dreamed about Antoine, I didn't know what I wanted. Then I sat down in the sand, facing the horizon, which was still sunrise pink, and I thought about Antoine, and I imagined him with me on the beach, I closed my eyes and watched us make love near the sea – I could allow myself to cheat in this way, while I was here, so far away from him, where we were momentarily unassailable.

"What about Simon?" asked Daphné.

"Simon," I said with a smile, "was himself."

"He's such a marvellous boy," my mother sighed.

I told them about the sea, and how we read and happily did nothing, how we giggled, and they told me about their trip, Vienna, the cafés, the museums, the bright, chic restaurants, the incredibly clean, beautiful city. Daphné hadn't looked so radiant in ten years – "Just ten days without the girls… I don't want to seem like a bad mother, but shit, that did me some good! And was it ever good for our relationship!" She and Stéphane had really "found each other again," she said – my mother added that it was because they'd finally "communicated," and Daphné laughed, as she recognized that she was more or less right. The plans for another baby were still up in the air, but the tension and pressure had disappeared, and that was visible on Daphné's face, which had reclaimed its twenty-six-year-old softness and movement.

A little before dessert, the two of us got up to wash the pans; like when we were little we took advantage of the forced chore to bug each other, or, sometimes, tell each other secrets. I was washing and Daphné was drying, like always, and she asked, "What about Simon?"

"Like I told you…"

"Chloé, I wasn't that stoned in the hospital. I still remember our conversation. The questions you had. You told me you wondered if there wasn't 'more.'"

"Everything's okay."

"Okay?"

"Yeah… the trip really did me some good."

Out of the corner of my eye, I could see Daphné nodding her head, although she didn't really look satisfied by what I'd said.

"What's wrong?" I asked.

"No, no. It just looks to me like you're not sure."

"Oh, Daphné…"

"Listen, maybe I'm wrong."

"Yes, you are wrong. He's wonderful, Daphné. And the trip was idyllic."

"Idyllic?" she laughed.

"Yes, idyllic." It was my turn to laugh. "You have something against that word?"

"No, not at all. It's very expressive."

I flung a few soap suds in her face, and she swung her hip into me, and I thought, after fifteen years, I've got my sister back.

"I'm really happy for you," she finally said.

"Me, too. Really."

I didn't tell her about the flight back when Simon asked me if I wanted children and I almost swallowed my little bottle of vodka, and I do mean the bottle along with the vodka. I muttered "yes," and he smiled and we started playing that little lovers' game where you make up names for your future children and then say things like, "He'll have my nose and your mouth, your eyes and my hair, your sense of humour and my talent for conversation." I'd played along, of course, because I hadn't had a choice, even if I couldn't, absolutely couldn't, imagine myself having children with him. It wasn't him, it wasn't me, it wasn't the fact of having children – I wanted them and I knew it – it was a simple, yet complete inability to picture having them with him.

I didn't say anything about the night before either, when it seemed like my heart had burst when I saw Antoine again. He was as cool as ever, saying I was beautiful and tanned, and when he told me about his week, and his stupid advertising ideas, he made me laugh – not once did he mention the trip, except to ask, "was it good?" to which he accepted a reply of, "Super." It took me a really long time to get back to a normal heart rhythm; then, when what Juliette called his contagious "coolness" got to me, I relaxed, I made jokes, too, I teased him, and I told him about the books I'd read just like always, just like always.

I kept quiet about all this, because I'd decided I wanted
to be with Simon, that he was the one I loved, and that,
maybe, it was normal for love to sometimes encounter a few
troubles. I'd decided I didn't want to keep being the spoiled
little girl dreaming of what she can't have – I was a responsible woman, nearly thirty years old, and I'd spent ten idyllic
days with a marvellous man: there was no way I was going
to screw it all up for teenage desires. I wanted to be happy,
and I thought I'd finally figured out that happiness was no
longer something easy and changing that came and went,
carried along by beer and friendship, that you didn't have
to think about. Happiness was earned – it was something
you had to work on, and I wanted mine to be successful.

And that's how I spent weeks patiently and attentively
building the happiness I now wanted more than anything
and which had, at its centre, the people I loved. I'd accepted
a contract that would take me to June – I was working days,
and Simon nights, so we saw each other a little less, which
was pleasant: I realized I missed him, and that I liked missing him, during the week, and sometimes I'd go surprise
him at the restaurant. We spent our weekends together, and
I liked this simple, gentle rhythm, it rocked me, like Simon
and his sea blue eyes – he was so attentive that sometimes I
wondered if he suspected something, if he hadn't sensed all
the questions I'd been asking myself. But if that was the case,
he didn't let it show, though I thought that it was possible,
that he was delicate and thoughtful enough to do that.

As for Antoine, he kept floating from girl to girl, eternally
carefree, and no one brought up what had happened in
Juliette's studio, or everything that hadn't been said. He'd gone
back to being the friend I'd always had, the one I knew better
than anyone and the one who knew me like the back of his
hand, and I'd come to believe that what had happened at the
beginning of the year was nothing but an episode, a charming
detail in the history of our friendship. I was, however, jealous

of his conquests – but, of course, it would have been inappropriate to mention it, and I would also champ at the bit when
I'd imagine him making love to them, and what he whispered
to them at the crucial moment just before.

There where still as many dinners, parties, impromptu
and pointless celebrations, sometimes at my parents', sometimes at the old factory, sometimes at Simon's restaurant.
That's where, at the end of March, my birthday dinner was
held, when Simon closed the shop one Friday night and
invited all my friends and all my family – a noisy, festive
affair that almost turned bad when someone, for some
unfathomable reason, started making Russian toasts: at ten
o'clock, at least fifteen shot glasses had been shattered
against the brick wall, though this didn't seem to bother
Simon in the least.

"It's not like it happens every day," he said to me as he
kissed my neck. I leaned into him, and I was happy. The
night before, he'd given me an original edition of *Voyage au
bout de la nuit* he'd discovered on the Internet. It was the
book he'd seen me reading on my lap back in math class,
fifteen years before, and he'd spent weeks looking for it. I
was still touched by it the next day, as the glasses smashed
against the red brick, and I kept telling him, as I looked him
in the eye, that I loved him a little more every day.

That night I got a mountain of gifts, some were completely charming (Juliette's was a pair of green shoes that
were "in style"), others ridiculous (some Chinese balls from
Marcus who was afraid I was bored during the week when
I couldn't see Simon). As the wrapping paper lying on the
floor crinkled, and someone kept shouting "vodka!"
Antoine came over to tell me that he didn't have my gift
with him. He smiled and added, "You'll have to come get it
at my place. I couldn't bring it here." He refused to give me
any hints at all, but he seemed particularly pleased with his
idea, which made me even more curious.

"When can you come over?" Antoine asked me. I wanted to say, "First thing tomorrow," but Simon had taken the weekend off to be with me.

"Monday?" I asked.

"Perfect. Come meet me at the office at six. We'll go to my place together."

At six o'clock the next Monday night I was at his office, an open space where there were a number of big tables for brainstorming, colourful computers all over the place and perpetual clutter that said, "Here, people are paid to have ideas." Antoine was sitting at a table with two other people, a young man who looked like he'd come straight from a rave, and another young man I remembered meeting on New Year's Eve. I walked over to them and noticed Antoine was playing with a Rubik's Cube.

"Very retro," I said to him. He leaned his head back and laughed. "Not bad, eh? We got a case of them last month. It was the thirtieth anniversary of the Rubik's Cube." He was always getting things like that, sent by the manufacturers who must have thought that ad creators always needed to keep their hands busy while they thought about how to sell electric shavers.

He introduced me to his two co-workers, got up, said good-bye to a few people who were still lingering, gave a young woman with a pile of folders one or two recommendations, and then said to me, "Shall we go?" as he gently placed one hand on the small of my back.

When we got to his house, he took my coat, and said, "You can't look."

"At least give me a clue!"

"Nope. Shut your eyes."

"Antoine..."

"I said, 'shut your eyes.'"

"Okay, okay..."

I closed my eyelids and he put his hands on my waist. I was still a little feverish when I was alone with him and I felt slight goosebumps rise on my back and my breasts.

"Go ahead," said Antoine, and I took several cautious steps.

"What is it, a cat? Why couldn't you bring it to the restaurant? Is it big? Did you buy me a car? It had better not be obscene, you know…" I could sense we were going into the living room, because we walked around the whole room, before we stopped just about in front of the bookshelves.

"That's good," he said. I opened my eyes, and froze. Leaning against the fireplace mantle and completely hiding the hearth was *Self-Portrait*, Juliette's painting that had "our sentences" on it, the one whose sale had upset me so much. I put one hand on my mouth, and I looked up at Antoine. He was smiling at me, visibly pleased with what he'd pulled off, and I heard myself say, "It can't be…"

"I knew you liked it," he said. "And it didn't seem right to me for it to go to anyone besides you or me. So, I…"

"But, Antoine!… It's incredible, I don't know what to say!" I placed a hand on his chest, gently holding his shirt. "Antoine!" I repeated. "It cost twenty-five hundred bucks!"

He shrugged. "But it's worth it. And honestly, if I'm spending money, I'd just as soon have it go into Juliette's pockets."

I nodded, but I still couldn't believe it. He was in the habit of giving me gifts that were too extravagant – designer handbags he got in Europe, clothes that always fit perfectly, a plane ticket to New York – but the painting took the cake.

"But, Juliette!" I finally said. "She's known this whole time?"

"No," answered Antoine. "I only told her the day before yesterday. Otherwise, you know her, she's no good with secrets; there's no doubt she would have let it slip. No, I'm not crazy, I just told a friend of mine you don't know to come by the night of the opening and buy it. Very clever. In exchange, he had the pleasure of keeping it at his place for four months. I thought I'd bring it over to your place one day when you were working, but I'm kind of a baby – I wanted to see your reaction."

I realized that I was still holding onto his shirt. I let go, and, with one hand still over my mouth, I stepped closer to the painting. I touched it lightly with one finger and was again taken aback by the colours, the delicate hues that mixed together and opposed each other, by the gold that sometimes looked like it had been breathed onto the canvas and that disappeared under a blue and reappeared on a pink. I reread the words we'd already noticed, saw others for the first time, and thought to myself I had all the time in the world to study it, to slowly, patiently dissect it.

"I'll be able to spend hours looking at it," I said.

"I know. It's been here for a week. That's exactly what I've been doing." He approached the painting, too, and leaned in close to the bottom of it.

"Look," he said.

He pointed a finger at a golden patch that extended to the left corner. I bent down and, in characters that were so fine and pale they looked like they'd been engraved with a needle, I read: "Just a fool's hope." I looked up at Antoine.

"Isn't that from your *Lord of the Rings*?"

"Yes. 'There's always hope. Just a fool's hope.'"

Antoine laughed, "You two really know that movie by heart, don't you?"

"Of course, you know that… But the fact that she wrote that, like that…"

"I know." He didn't need to say anything more and we were both quiet for a moment – I thought of Juliette, who'd written the sentence so lightly, so that it had to be found, so that it was barely there, so that some people wouldn't even see it. That was her, she was in there, in that fragile, stubborn hope, and she'd made the sentence her own and had flowed with it out onto the gold of the canvas. I wanted to take

Juliette in my arms, and I touched the sentence again, very gently. I'm in there, too, I thought, I have a hold of a fragile hope inside me, too – it's a different hope, but it's there, and I've felt it, hazy but real, deep inside me, and I wondered if Antoine felt it, too, and what his was like. I looked up at him and I could see the sentence was resonating in him, too.

I straightened up and hugged him, very tight. "I don't know how to thank you," I said. "It doesn't make any sense. It's the nicest gift anyone's ever given me."

"No…"

"Yes, it is!" I kissed him on the cheek, and I looked up, with my arms still around his neck. "Yes, it is," I repeated. And I felt like I hadn't felt in weeks, I wanted to give myself over to him, to close my eyes and let myself go. But he smiled, and said, "Okay, okay." Then he added, "In fact, it's a bit of a selfish present – I really like this painting, so knowing it's at your house, instead of with some jerk like Florent, really makes me happy, too."

I tenderly nodded. "You know you're wonderful, right?"

"Only with you, sweetheart."

He ran his hands along my back, then took my face in them – then he softly kissed me on the right temple, and then moved away, still holding onto a lock of my hair that slowly slipped from his fingers. "Only with you," he repeated flashing me the little grin I loved so much.

"It's an incredible gift," I said.

"Come on, stop. You're the one who's incredible." He was dramatizing everything. For the last two weeks, he'd been working hard to neutralize our silences, make our glances meaningless. Paradoxically, it was something that both hurt me, and also made me completely grateful to him. I gave him an affectionate little pat on the arm. "You're silly, Antoine."

"Come have dinner with me. There's a nice little restaurant right next door. After, if you want, you can bring your painting home."

"No, I can't take it home in a taxi."

"Yeah, that's true…"

He thought for a moment, and then said, "Why don't you come over with Simon when he has time?"

"Of course," I answered. I didn't like hearing Simon's name mentioned – it was too much for me. He helped me put my coat on, and we left, amid the big springtime snowflakes that were tumbling from the sky, and headed to the restaurant near his place.

That night, when I got home, I told Puce about the gift I'd received. I was taking off my makeup, looked in the mirror at her attentive little face gazing at me, and said to her, "It's incredible, Puce. It's no ordinary gift. Don't you think it's special that he gave that painting to Mommy? Hmmm?" I bent down to kiss her and she purred gently – another of her cryptic replies. It was only later, when I was lying in the darkness of my room that, out loud, I again said, "Puce, it makes no sense!"

I couldn't sleep, and I thought of the idea of fragile hope that Juliette had breathed into her painting – I was thinking of mine, what I hoped for, and I kept telling myself it was happiness, this happiness I'd seen as the Holy Grail, a treasure hunt, and a gratifying task to accomplish. It's ridiculous, I thought. You couldn't hope for happiness the same way other people hoped for a good return from their company at the end of the year, or an improvement in their golf handicap. I couldn't run after prefabricated happiness with Simon, when I was happy to be with Antoine in a restaurant on a Monday night.

"Oh, my God," I said out loud. I rolled over onto my stomach, and added, "Puce, Mommy has a problem."

I spent the next few days trying to organize all these thoughts – organization, I must say, has never been my strong suit, and I was going around in circles, I fretted, I chewed on my pencils at work, and at night, I harassed Juliette with worried and repetitive phone calls – she listened patiently, but she'd let me know that she wanted nothing more to do with the situation. "All I can tell you," she said, "is you should break up with Simon." I'd hung up with a moan, telling myself that for someone who wanted nothing more to do with the situation, her comment was rather direct.

Simon, who I saw twice since then, was constantly asking me what was wrong, and, like an idiot who absolutely wanted to avoid the conversation, I kept answering, "Nothing! Everything's fine! Great!" I could see I was hurting him, and it made me sad. The next Saturday, we went to Antoine's to pick up the painting – he and Simon chatted in a friendly way while they had a beer, and, in distressed silence, I watched the two of them. When Simon went to the bathroom before we left, Antoine came over to me: "What's wrong?"

"Nothing. Nothing. I'm not feeling up to par."

"Chloé." He pointed a finger at the bathroom and whispered, "Does it have something to do with him?"

I shook my head and said, "No… I don't know. It doesn't make any sense, Antoine."

I couldn't lie to him – it would have been pointless, he would have known right away. I remembered his eyes when he'd said, "Leave him," but now, he smiled at me sweetly and took me by the shoulder. "It'll be all right, sweetheart. It'll work out." He gave me a quick hug, and went back and stood behind the kitchen counter. When we were leaving, while Simon was putting the back seats down to make room for the painting, he said to me, "Call me anytime," and I smiled awkwardly. I didn't know what I could say to him, since, one way or another, he was the source of all my questions.

The next day, at two o'clock, I got a call from Daphné.

"What are you doing?"

"Nothing, just reading…"

"We've been waiting for you since noon!"

"What?" I slapped my forehead, "Oh shit!" It was the twins' birthday – they were turning two and Daphné had organized a brunch at her place – the plans had been made a couple of weeks ago, and, obviously, I'd forgotten. Simon, who was also on the guest list, had left that morning for Kingston, but he'd been kind enough not to invite me. I grumbled something and jumped in a taxi.

My parents were at Daphné's, of course, but there were also some neighbourhood moms – it was a kids' party, with balloons and goody bags; the children, all under the age of five, were crawling around on the floor, fighting, screaming, running between our legs, and pulling on their mothers' pants shouting, "Mommy! Mommy! MOMMY! Mommmmyyyy!" *ad nauseam*, until a patient and slightly tired face bent down towards them.

"I'm sorry," I said to Daphné. "Really sorry." I handed her my gifts – two identical dolls and an educational game which I knew Daphné would really like.

"Where's Simon?"

"In Kingtson. I forgot... I'm sorry..."

"No, no." She looked at me sideways. "You okay?"

"Oh," I waved my hand in discouragement, "I'll tell you later."

It was rather difficult to talk about a quest for happiness and relationship worries when children were attacking on all sides, grabbing you by the hand and shouting, "Come play!" or climbing on your lap, like Coralie, the little three-year-old neighbour, a little girl from Guatemala who'd been adopted and seemed to have an all-consuming passion for me. I carried her around a good part of the afternoon until, at about four o'clock, her mother came to relieve me – Coralie screamed and clung to my neck. I literally fled to the kitchen, where I found my father, sitting at the table. "I'm taking a little break," he said. "All these kids are unbelievable. It's like a hurricane."

"I know…" I slumped down next to him and took a piece of cauliflower from a half-empty veggie tray.

"What's going on with you, Chloé?"

"I don't know…" I turned towards him and saw his big brown eyes, his white hair and the kind face I loved so much, and I finally said, "I have doubts, about Simon."

"Why?" asked my father. "I hope he hasn't hurt you?" I smiled – my father was always afraid that the men that went through my life might hurt me, which insulted me greatly when I was younger ("What? Me? Hurt because of a guy?"), so I always answered no, even when I cried myself to sleep.

"No," I answered. "You know Simon. He could never hurt me. He's too good, too kind" – and I thought for the first time since I'd met him that I didn't like how good he was, that his kindness weighed on me.

"No," I went on, "I just have doubts, that's all."

"What kind of questions?"

"Well, I don't know, and that's the problem. For a while now, I haven't been able to stop wondering if there isn't more than this… I'd managed to push it out of my mind, you know, I told myself, a guy like this doesn't come along twice in a lifetime, but now…"

"It's normal," said my father, "to have doubts."

"Did you ever have doubts, about Mom?"

"We almost split up, when you were twelve."

"Yeah, I know, but did you ever doubt your love for her?"

My father smiled. "No, but there are several kinds of love, Chloé."

"I know, that's what I keep telling myself. But can I spend my whole life telling myself that?"

"Telling yourself what?" I looked up. My mother, in a long pink and black tunic, had just come into the kitchen, with a martini in her hand.

"You even drink martinis at children's parties?"

"I can put it in a bottle, if you prefer." I smiled and reached out my hand to take a sip.

"What can't you keep asking yourself for the rest of your life?" my mother asked.

"Oh, if Simon… It's like for the last six months, I've been trying to convince myself this is it, true love. Seems to me that's not a good sign, is it?" My mother looked at me for an instant – I must have looked pretty pitiful to her, because she ran a hand over my face with the distressed look mothers get when their children face their first failures.

"Oh, my sweetie. Do you remember when you were little? You were always asking me that: Will I find true love, Mommy? And I would answer…"

"*Qué será, será…*" my father and I sang in unison.

My mother laughed. "So you do remember. You were talking about incredible love, fairy-tale love. You weren't even ten yet and you had already made up your mind, and there was no changing it, that you were going to find true love. And then one day, that was it."

"I was sure a boy had hurt you," my father said.

"We asked ourselves a lot of questions," my mother continued. "Our little girl had been dreaming about Prince Charming and fireworks, and then suddenly, at fourteen, she decided to turn her heart to stone."

"I didn't turn my heart to stone!"

"Oh yes you did," said my father. "The poor boys you would see… you'd be interested in them for a couple of weeks, and then you'd drop them."

I nodded and laughed a little – they were both right. At fifteen, I discovered the pleasure of using my charms on boys, and I practised on all the cute boys at school and in the neighbourhood.

"I really was a tease," I said.

"An awful tease," said my mother, laughing. "Really awful."

I remembered that she'd tried to lecture me about it, telling me men didn't like teases, but I simply hadn't believed her. "And you never let a single one of them off the hook," she went on.

"I know. I think that's why I stopped talking about true love. I was with all these boys and I asked myself, is this all there is? Just this? Two or three butterflies in my stomach, and that's it? I liked it, I had a lot of fun, but it seemed like it didn't have much to do with what I thought true love was all about."

"Fifteen years old and already disenchanted," my father sighed.

I laughed a little, "No, no, I wasn't disenchanted. I was just a little disappointed, in fact. But I figured it wasn't that bad and that I sure wasn't bored... I don't know. It wasn't annoying or anything, it was just a little dull for me."

"No, I know you," said my mother. "You never accepted how dull it was."

"That's easy for you to say, you read my diary!"

They both burst out laughing. "Okay," my mother continued. "But still. I could see you were still hoping for something, or someone. Vaguely or unconsciously. Even when you completely stopped talking about it in your diary. Even when you wrote your stupid manifesto."

"I think you're right," I said. "More or less unconsciously."

"I was starting to get excited about you finding it, though!" And she got up to make herself another martini. "At twenty-eight, nonetheless... You know what I was thinking. That your problem is always having Antoine around." I jumped when she mentioned Antoine. "My theory, well, our theory," she added, pointing to my father, "is that you were in love with him. Or at least that he kept you from seeing the other men around you. He's pretty fantastic, that Antoine."

"Mom, that had nothing to do with it," but I thought they were probably right.

"I don't know," my mother continued. "But, well, you met Simon. And now you have doubts. I can see that, sweetie. You're not as happy as you'd like to be." She sat next to me, and, looking at me very seriously, added, "You can't be mad at yourself for it, Chloé. For not wanting to settle for second-rate happiness. It's better for you to realize it now, than in a few years, isn't it?"

"But, Mom, Simon is so perfect! He's so... ideal! I can't just let him go! I keep telling myself that if I let him go, I'll regret it my whole life and..."

My mother took my face in her hands, tenderly, and said, "My poor girl. There are so many things I could never explain to you." She wasn't talking condescendingly, or lecturing – in her voice, I could just hear the sincere regret of a mother who, like all mothers, would have liked to have managed to better equip her child for life. "Oh, Mom," I said and I fell into her arms and she held me tight, I was crying a little, but I finally felt good, perfectly good, against her chest, in her arms, where nothing could get me. Thank you, God, for Moms, I thought.

She rocked me for a few seconds, then, in a suddenly professional tone, said, "So, what are you going to do now?"

"I don't know!"

"Yes, you do know." I turned towards my father, who, nodding his head, looked like he was saying, "Yes, you certainly do know."

I buried my head in my hands. "I can't do that..."

"Is there someone else?" my mother asked.

I straightened up, "What?"

"Is there another man?"

"No! No!" I answered hurriedly – and I told myself it was true. I had realized I didn't love Simon the way I wanted to, and that it had nothing to do with Antoine. It was the most reassuring thought I'd had in days: I'd tried, with all my might, to love Simon the way he deserved, but I hadn't succeeded. And even if Antoine hadn't been in the picture, it would have been the same story – he was just the catalyst. I thought it all over, very quickly, and I murmured, "Oh! My God!"

"Chloé," said my father, rubbing my back, "I think you've got some work to do."

The children and their moms started to leave a little while later – Coralie, in tears, hung desperately onto my hair – and then we had a quiet dinner, with Daphné, Stéphane and his parents. I couldn't sit still anymore – I wanted something to happen, I wanted to do something, but I didn't really want to admit what I had to do.

My parents drove me home. Before we left, Daphné took my hand. "You going to be all right?"

"I think so," I answered. "I think I waited too long, Dadi. I think I've been ridiculous. I thought that if I forced myself, it would turn into what I wanted. But, shit... have you seen Simon? Why can't I love a guy like him?"

"Come on, Clo. There are no answers to questions like that."

"I know, I know. You were right, you know. I thought I was doing the reasonable thing."

"Yes," said Daphné with a smile. "But reason is my field, not yours."

"It's still funny. I'm starting to think that sometimes what seems to be the least reasonable is actually the most reasonable. You know what I mean?"

"Yes..." said Daphné. "It's deep..."

I gave her a little tap on the arm. "Don't laugh at me."

"No, I understand," she said. "You know, when I got married at twenty-three, and decided to give up the idea of a career for the children... it didn't feel like it was a super-reasonable decision. I thought maybe I was screwing up my whole life, and I was terrified."

"You had doubts?"

"Yep. The cat's out of the bag."

"Honestly," I said to her, "I always thought you had doubts. Because if you didn't, you would have been down-right abnormal. But I swear, you hid it damn well."

"And yet... You see, I did the right thing. I have two girls who are my whole life, and I have Stéphane, who I wouldn't trade for anyone in the world. It's true it's not always easy, and it's actually quite hard sometimes, but honestly, I've never regretted my decision. Even this fall, before my miscarriage. I did ask myself all kinds of questions, but I never regretted a thing."

I nodded my head, and took my sister in my arms. It was her way of giving me advice, and of encouraging me, without having it seem like it. "Thank you, Dadi."

"Come now," she said.

I kissed her and called "Bye, Stéphane!" towards the living room. He appeared and gave me a big smile. "Bye, Sister-in-law."

"Ciao, Brother-in-law." I smiled, and I left.

On the way home, we talked about this and that – my mother gave way too many details about the Klimt paintings she'd seen in Vienna: she couldn't remember a single title and her descriptions were more or less incomprehensible, but her enthusiasm was contagious, and, for the whole ride, I managed to think of something besides Simon and the words I was going to use to tell him I was sorry, so sorry.

My parents dropped me off outside my place. I was sitting in the back seat of the car, and they both turned back towards me.

"Good luck," said my father.

"Call us," my mother added. "And Chloé? Do what makes you happy."

It was a vague bit of advice, but I was starting to have a clear enough idea of what that might be. I went up to my place and sat down in front of Juliette's painting, which I hadn't yet hung, so it was leaning against one of the living-room walls.

"It's so beautiful..." I said to the cats, who were lying here and there around the room. "It's so beautiful!" I looked at it for a moment, from a distance, so I could consider it as a whole, and then I picked up the phone, with a sigh. I had messages, and I was going to listen to them right away, but I wanted to call Simon first. I knew he had a big week ahead, but I didn't want to wait, out of respect for him – I decided I'd go by the restaurant the next day. Sadly, I dialled the number and got his voicemail, so, in as natural a voice as possible, I said, "It's me. I don't know if you're going to pick up your messages or not, but I just wanted to tell you good-night and that I'll come by the restaurant tomorrow at the end of the night. Call me if that doesn't work for you, otherwise I'll see you then. Good-night, sweetie." I made a little face when I heard myself say "sweetie," and I added, "love you."

I put the phone down on the sofa, and rubbed my forehead, sighing even louder. Then I thought about the messages, and picked the phone back up. The recorded voice told me I had eight new messages. Astonished, I frowned and listened to the first one.

"Chloé! Shit! It's Ju! You'll never believe it! It's crazy! Okay, listen, there's a gallery in Montreal..."

She stood back from the receiver and shrieked excitedly. "A gallery in Montreal that's interested in taking some of my paintings and in... in?..."

"In what, for Christ's sake?" I shouted into the phone.

"... in showing them in a contemporary art fair that's happening in New York! New York! Eeeeee!"

Then she hung up. She'd said the last sentence so quickly, I wasn't even sure I'd understood. I saved the message and listened to the others – Juliette; then Juliette again, doing nothing but shouting, "I'm flipping out!" Then there was my disagreeable neighbour who wanted to organize a renters' meeting (there were five of us) to discuss how we were going to "negotiate with the owner"; Antoine, who wanted to know if I'd heard the news and who, apparently, was also flipping out; then Juliette again, telling me the fair was happening in two weeks, that it was confirmed and that I had to come; Juliette yet again asking what she should wear; and finally, Antoine saying, "Okay, sweetie. Take off the 12th, 13th and 14th, we're going to New York."

Chapter 25

"You know, I bet forty dollars with Juliette you wouldn't be ready." Antoine was lying on my bed, and distractedly petting Puce, who was purring on his chest.

"Shut up," I said. "If you hadn't had the stupid idea of driving, we could have left a lot later."

He looked up, "Oh, please. You wanted to drive as much as I did." I threw a pillow at him, and I said, "Two minutes. I have to figure out something for my suitcase."

"It's 8:48," said Antoine. "If you're not ready by nine o'clock, I'm leaving without you."

"I think…"

He'd had the idea of driving to New York the week before, because, as I quickly understood, he'd just gotten his licence back. At first, I rebelled against the idea, until, on his knees, he promised me he'd drive carefully, adding that, he really didn't want to lose his licence again, anyway – an argument I found rather convincing. Then he'd brought up the call of the road trip ("A six-hour road trip?" I'd asked, confused), but I'd already made up my mind. I liked the idea of driving down slowly, with him.

Juliette had flown down two days before, and, since then, she'd called each of us at least twenty times to tell us, in great detail, about every hour of her day. She was overly excited, and rightly so, and told us about the big art centre where the fair was taking place, the other artists she'd met, the city, the restaurants where she'd eaten, the little soaps at the hotel that smelled like peaches – we really were over-informed, and almost as excited as she was.

"I'm ready," I said to Antoine. He got up and gently put Puce down on the bed. "Who's going to feed them?"

"Marcus. Michel doesn't live very far away, so he's glad to do it."

"Things are really going well for those two, eh?"

"True love."

"That's so great," said Antoine, as he took my huge suitcase. "Oh, Christ, Chloé! We're coming back on Saturday! It's only four and a half days!"

"Imagine what it's like when I go to London for two weeks."

"I don't even want to think about it."

He was about to go out, when I grabbed his sleeve, "Oh, wait, I almost forgot!"

"Now what?"

"Wait!" I ran towards the kitchen, and came back, triumphantly, with a case of Molson Export.

"You can't be serious," Antoine laughed.

"Hey, a tradition is a tradition."

"Yeah, but... don't you think they have Molson Ex in New York?"

"I wasn't sure. Are you sure?"

He shrugged.

"Exactly," I said. "And I didn't want to spend a whole day running all over the city looking for Molson Ex. So I'm taking it with me."

"Are we allowed to take it across the border?"

"Of course, silly. What are they going to say, 'No, don't invade our country with your bad beer'?"

"Yeah, I guess you're right. Okay, then, let's go. Can you please carry the beer yourself? I have a two-hundred-pound suitcase to take down."

"I know, but you're sooooo strong..."

"Chloé..."

I closed the door behind us, and followed him down the

stairs, telling myself I was really going to have to tell him about Simon. The day after the twins' birthday my mother had called, to tell me she was afraid she'd gone too far, that she hoped it hadn't seemed like she'd been putting Simon down. "It's just that," she added, "I see you with him, and as marvellous as he is… I could really feel that it wasn't really right." We'd talked a little more, and I'd hung up, sad as could be, with her advice, "not to fool around with it, out of respect for such a nice boy," still ringing in my ears.

At the end of the night, at about 11:30, I'd dragged myself to Simon's restaurant. I had a thousand clichés running through my head, stupid things, like "It's not you, it's me," sentences that began with, "You're really wonderful, but…" not to mention the ridiculous classics like, "You deserve so much better than me" – that one, however, I thought was true. I didn't want to serve him these empty words that were already overused. I wanted to find my own words, but they weren't coming. I didn't have the words to tell someone like Simon I didn't love him.

When he saw me come in, he'd immediately noticed how serious I looked, and I realized I wouldn't really need many words, because it would be much simpler, and undoubtedly much more brutal than I had imagined. I sat down at the bar and he came and sat next to me. I only had time to say, "Listen," before he'd raised a hand and shook his head.

"I know," he said.

"What?"

"Chloé, I'm not stupid. I've seen you the last few days; I heard your voice yesterday on my machine. Maybe I'm paranoid, but I don't think so."

"Simon…"

"You've come to tell me it's over, right?"

"It's not…"

"For fuck's sake, Chloé." He dropped his hand down on the bar and turned towards me. In the restaurant's filtered lighting, his eyes looked positively black, and I thought of

Antoine, when he'd said, "Leave him." It's just that Simon's gaze wasn't cold, it was fiery. He looked at me for an instant, it was long enough for me to examine his handsome features, his bottom lip which I loved so much – long enough for me to realize, to my great surprise, that I was sure this was what I wanted – and, in an even harsher tone, he'd repeated, "Did you come to tell me it's over? Yes or no?"

I took a deep breath and answered, "Yes."

"Okay, it's done. You can go, now."

"But, Simon…"

"No, that wasn't a suggestion, Chloé. Go. Now." Then, when he saw my shocked face, he added, "Get out," in English, and I went out into the cool night, both dismayed and amazed. I turned back towards the restaurant and saw he was no longer there, and I stood there on the sidewalk, too stunned to do anything. I'd imagined a long conversation – him suggesting we talk about it the next day, asking me questions, maybe trying to convince me. I'd finally started to walk – it took me three blocks to realize there was a whole part of Simon I'd never known that had just surfaced in the restaurant. Obviously, I'd thought about going to Juliette's but I went home and sat down in front of the painting. I was sad and confused – but despite my best efforts, I felt liberated and a bit happy.

I hadn't talked to Simon in four days – he wasn't returning my calls, and he refused to talk to me when I tried to get in touch with him at the restaurant. He finally called me one night to tell me, in that same extremely harsh tone, that I could stop by his place one night during the week to get the things I'd left there because he'd be out. "You can leave your key on the table in the living room," he'd said. I'd started to cry, in silence, because his harshness hurt and worried me, and I'd tried to say something, something trivial no doubt, but he'd stopped me. "I don't want to know your reasons, Chloé. And, honestly, I don't really want to hear your voice right now. I would imagine even you can understand that." And I'd hung up, slightly hurt and vaguely insulted, but unable to blame him.

I'd gone by the next week and spent a few minutes walking through the apartment when he wasn't there. I felt a bit of remorse, I felt nostalgic, but mostly sad – what had happened, I asked myself. All that love. I didn't want to believe I'd simply made a mistake, that I'd thought I'd loved him, but never really had. There had been something, I was sure of it, but that something had disappeared, and all I felt now was a gentle sadness that wasn't even worthy of what had been there. I'd thought about leaving a note on the living-room table, but, obviously, I had nothing to write, and I knew Simon wouldn't have liked it. So I put down my keys, and I left.

Almost two weeks later, I still hadn't said anything to Antoine, and it was starting to get ridiculous. The official reason was that I'd only seen him once – we'd both been pretty busy because of the time off we were taking to go to New York, and Antoine had been to Toronto three times in the last week and a half.

The real reason was that I was scared – scared he'd think I'd done it for him, scared of what he might do, and of my reaction. Juliette had pointed out, when I'd asked her not to say anything to Antoine, that I'd unconsciously used Simon, these last four months, as a shield between myself and Antoine. I still wasn't sure she was right, but now, with four days in New York ahead us, I realized I was concerned about this free space between us. I was afraid I'd give in to his advances (if he even made any) and that I'd fall in love, or back in love, with him – I knew it wouldn't take much, I was already very close to falling, and that is exactly what one part of me wanted. But I also knew Antoine, and I knew it wasn't a good thing to love someone like him.

Besides that, after such a long delay, I had no idea how to bring the subject out in the open. "It'll come naturally," I said to myself, as I placed the case of Molson in the trunk of his car.

It was nice out, and very mild – a beautiful April day, perfect for driving and we stopped in Little Italy to get two coffees before we really got on the road. Antoine was making jokes, he was obviously in a very good mood and very happy about this trip. Better yet, he was driving at a relatively reasonable speed, and seemed committed to learning the rules of the road. Beside him, with my feet on the glovebox and a copy of *The New Yorker* in my hands, I was completely happy. I realized it a little after we'd crossed the border – we were talking about movies (he said he'd loved *Dogville*, which I considered unbearably smug) and I was laughing and suddenly, I thought everything was right, the car, the fields along the highway, the empty Styrofoam cups, Suzanne Vega's voice singing "In Liverpool" on the radio, Antoine's smile when he said, "Shut up, it's a great film!" and his hand on the steering wheel – everything was in its place, and, in the midst of all of it, I was in mine.

A half-hour past Albany, Antoine headed for a little village where almost every house had an American flag in front of it, and we went into the diner on the main street, a place like you'd see in movies, with pink plastic booths, a long counter with stools on single metal legs and a waitress in a pink uniform with a name tag that said, "Hi! I'm Darlene!"

"Hello, Darlene," said Antoine.

"And how are you doin' today?" she asked us. She must have been about sixty, with a grandmotherly smile. We each ordered a hamburger and a beer, and we both sat back in our booth, happy.

"This place is unbelievable," I stated. "It's like being in an *Archie* comic."

"I know," said Antoine, "it's damn retro."

"I expect James Dean to walk in at any minute."

"After lunch, I'm going to play 'Love Me Tender' on the jukebox and ask you to dance. If James makes one wrong move, I'll challenge him to a drag race."

I smiled, and looked around us, attentively examined every corner of the room.

"You know," he said, "the only memory I have of my father is in a place exactly like this."

"Your father?" I asked. He'd told me before he had no memories of his father.

"Yes. It was the summer before his accident."

"But you were barely even four..."

"Yeah, but I remember, really. It's just an image. Every year, we went to Kennebunkport – my mother told me that part, I don't remember any of it, but one year, my mother and my sisters left before us, with my aunts, and my father and I drove out, 'just us guys.' We stopped in a place just like this. I remember the pink plastic booths." He gradually smiled – he looked happy to be remembering it. "It's crazy, eh? I remember the moment very clearly..." He waved his hand to underline how very clear it was. "For dessert, he'd ordered me a banana split, and I can see myself, looking at a mountain of ice cream, superexcited, and, at the same time, already knowing I wouldn't be able to finish it. Then my father looked at me and he seemed to think it was damn hilarious."

"You never told me that."

"No?"

"No."

He shrugged his shoulders. "It's just a memory."

"You want a banana split?"

"What?" He looked amused and a little uncomfortable. "No..."

"Come on. For old times' sake."

"They're really not that good," said Antoine.

"Come on..."

He laughed, "No!"

"What if I want a banana split?"

"You want a banana split?"

"Since we're in a place like this."

"Since we're…" He leaned both elbows on the table. "You're unbelievable, you know that? Okay, we'll have a banana split."

When it came, at the end of the meal, we both recoiled from the ice cream monster we had just been served.

"My God," said Antoine. "This is for one person?"

"It looks that way…" I dug my spoon into the ice cream and took the first bite. "Oh, boy." Antoine imitated me and started to laugh.

"It's awful," he said, "but it's not bad. The last time I ate one of these, I think, was that time with my father."

"Do you miss him sometimes?"

Antoine frowned imperceptibly – he'd never liked talking about his father. I thought he wasn't going to answer, but he took a bite and, looking more at the banana split than at me, he said, "I don't know… no. I mean, yes, sure, I would have liked to have had a father, but him? I didn't know him, so how can I say if I miss him…" He paused, and then added, "But I do wonder a lot. What it would have been like, you know."

"You think you would have been different?"

"Maybe. Certainly." He finally looked at me. "Okay, what do you mean, like I would have been less macho?" He pointed a finger at me, "I know that's what you're thinking, Chloé Cinq-Mars."

"I'm not thinking anything," I said with my most angelic look. "I suppose, that's all. I question. I wonder. I explore. I suspect."

"Okay, one more verb, and I'm throwing a scoop of ice cream down your cleavage."

He planted his spoon in the banana split and added, "Besides which, I'm not macho."

I giggled through a mouthful of ice cream, "Are you kidding me?"

"No, I'm not macho. I'm telling you that because I know you think I am."

"And does that surprise you?"

He laughed again, very slowly, like he was looking for the right words. "There's no doubt... sometimes... I act in a way that could lead you to believe that..."

"Lead me to believe? That's even lighter than a euphemism, Antoine."

"Listen. I like women. A lot. But that doesn't mean I don't have a heart."

I simply crossed my arms over my chest and looked at him mockingly. "Hey," he insisted, giving me a little kick under the table, "I have a heart. You know that, don't you?"

I wanted to climb over the banana split to kiss him. I nodded yes, and smiled.

"Yeah," I answered. "I suppose I do know that."

"Because if there's one person in the world who knows it, it's you."

I took his right hand. "I know." And I wouldn't have been able to tell him how I knew because God only knew he'd often gone to great lengths to prove the opposite, but instinctively I knew it. Then I thought of Juliette, Marcus and my mother, all of whom cared so much for him, and I added, "For your information, I'm not the only one who knows it. That little heart of yours is not that well hidden... in fact, you know what I think?"

"What do you think?"

"That you'd like us to think you don't have one. Or that it's really hard to find beneath that tough-as-nails exterior of yours."

"That's not true!"

"Oh yes it is!" I pointed a victorious finger at him. "You like people to think you're macho."

"Whatever."

"I'm right, Antoine, you like your image as a lady killer." And as I said it, I thought, I am right.

"What are you talking about?" Antoine asked me.

"You love it. You want to look like a heartless lady killer."

"No! I…" For a couple of seconds, I thought he was going to come out with something stupid like, "But I *am* a heartless lady killer," but he just took a big spoonful of ice cream. "Okay," he said, waving his full spoon. "This is going right between your two scoops." He lunged towards me and grabbed my arm. I shrieked like a little girl, and, as I laughed, I shouted, "Don't even try it, Antoine! I'm right. You want to pass for the biggest macho man ever, but your secret is out! Everybody knows your heart is as big as… Eeee!" A big glob of ice cream landed right between my breasts – I had to give him that much, the guy had aim. Antoine laughed, while I tried to look outraged and wiped off the ice cream. Then he said, "Whatever you say, sweetheart. I can be whatever you want. You're the boss." I threw my napkin full of ice cream at him, but he caught it on the fly. He put it down on the table, and looked at me strangely.

"What?" I said. "What? Do I still have ice cream on me?"

"When were you going to tell me about Simon?"

I was speechless for several seconds – I was actually trying to come up with an excuse. "I… but we haven't seen each other, Antoine, that's all, and… how did you find out about it?"

He sat back in his seat and crossed his arms over his chest, giving me a cheeky little grin.

"Shit, Antoine. Did Juliette tell you?" He shook his head no, still smiling – he loved this kind of situation.

"You're such a pain in the ass when you do that! Who was it? Not my crazy mother again?"

"No." He mushed his banana split with one hand, and leaned towards me. "No," he said. "It was Simon."

"WHAT?"

"Yes, well, I was pretty surprised by it, too, don't you know. It was last week. I went to his restaurant…"

"Why did you go there?" I interrupted him.

"Because I go there quite often, what a question! It's a damn good restaurant, I'll have you know." I remembered that, rather regularly, Simon would tell me that Antoine had been by, sometimes with friends, often with a girl.

"So, I went to his restaurant, innocent as anything, because, since you hadn't brought me up to speed..."

I hid my face in my hands. "Oh, boy," I moaned.

"Yeah, that's pretty much it," Antoine said. "So, he had the pleasure of telling me the news."

"What did he tell you?"

"That you'd left him."

"That's all?"

Antoine smiled. "He added one or two other things."

"What?"

"You really want to know?" He was wearing that wicked expression that always made me want to slap him, but once again, I wanted to throw myself at him, and this time the desire may have been even stronger.

"Oh, you make me sick!" I said to him. I had a vague idea of what Simon might have told him and, to tell the truth, I wasn't too sure I did want to hear it, then, in that little diner, when I already had to justify the fact that I'd kept my break-up a secret this whole time.

"You couldn't have told me sooner that you knew?" I asked him.

"Well, now, sweetheart, I don't think you're in the best possible position to accuse me of hiding things."

"But we've hardly seen each other! You were in Toronto and..."

"I didn't ask you to apologize." He looked like he was having a whole lot of fun.

"You're a pain in the ass," I said. "And you're a fucking pain in the ass because I know you liked hearing me say it."

He grabbed one of my hands and he kissed it. He was happy, comfortable, on his home turf: he was flirting with me a little, teasing me, playing it *carefree*. And, I thought to myself, he can't be beat at this game.

We got back on the road, under the beautiful April sun – there were big white clouds in the sky, Juliette would have called it a *Simpsons* sky. I was taking turns looking at the rounded mountains of the Appalachians, and their trees which were just beginning to bud, and Antoine, sitting next to me, with his smoky sunglasses and the smile I knew so well. I would have liked to have been a little mad at him, just for appearance's sake, but I couldn't do it – I'd never been able to stay mad at him for very long. I thought about what Simon might have said to him, something about the fact that I loved Antoine, that I'd always loved him, and I wondered if maybe that wasn't true. What an idiot that would make me, I said to myself. Eight years of my life spent unconsciously loving a man who didn't want to hear about love.

Antoine continued to tease me a bit, about Simon, about my "unforgivable act of concealment." He said, "In fact, there may be a whole part of your existence you've never shared with me. I don't know, a lover who's a married man and the father of two children, a parallel career as a stripper, a secret interest in salmon fishing… nothing would surprise me."

"Well… I did have a married lover, although he only had one kid, but…"

Antoine laughed. "That's true," he said. "Marc, right? I'd forgotten about him. He didn't want to leave his wife for you?"

"Yes! Lord! And I was terrified at the idea he would. So I ended it. He was nice, but… oh boy. A little intense. I could already see myself as a stepmother in a house in Brossard. What a nightmare!"

"What about salmon fishing? Have you been hiding that from me, too?"

"Very funny."

"Well, you never know! Since what happened at Simon's restaurant, I don't know anymore."

"You're such an idiot. Anyway, I'm not playing anymore. It makes you too happy to get me mad, so I'm not playing anymore."

"Aw, come on… you're so pretty when you look indignant."

"I'm not looking indignant!"

"You're looking completely indignant. When you squint your eyes, like that, just a little…"

"Whatever!"

"Exactly like you're doing right now." He glanced at me and smiled. "Adorable. Adorable." He turned back towards the road, while I used the rear-view mirror to try to see what I looked like when I was indignant.

"How do you feel about Simon?" Antoine suddenly asked. I looked up at him, sure he was still teasing. "No, seriously," he said. "You okay?"

"Well… yes, I suppose. I feel a little guilty. But not too much, it seems I have no reason to feel sorry or anything else for him."

"No, that's true," said Antoine.

"He doesn't even want to talk to me, so it is a little weird, of course. We talked every day, though. I just feel like it's a waste. Every time I think about it, I say to myself, 'What a shame…' When I went by his place to get my stuff, I felt sad – a tiny sadness, you know? Like a duckling in a puddle of water."

Antoine shot me a look. "A duckling?"

"Yeah, you know, just something sad and pitiful and…"

"I know," said Antoine. "It's a funny image, but I know what you mean."

"And at the same time, I kept thinking he deserved better," I added with a sigh. "I was stupid, in fact. A spoiled brat. And he's the one who's paying. He was talking about having children together, you know."

"Yes," Antoine said. "I know." He was silent for a moment, and then added, "You can say I don't know much about this kind of thing, but you shouldn't blame yourself. The guy was crazy about you, and you liked him a lot, but not the way he wanted. You weren't in the same place. But it's not your fault."

I turned towards him and smiled – I couldn't believe he was talking to me like this. "What?" he said, looking a little uncomfortable. "I may not be an expert in male-female relationships, but I'm not stupid, either. It's just good sense, isn't it? How many times does it work out that two people love each other equally? Not often, I bet."

I didn't dare answer him. He shrugged and said, "Anyway. That's my humble opinion. For what it's worth."

"It's worth quite a bit," I said. Then, before he had a chance to add anything, "I'm sorry, Antoine. I should have told you about what happened with Simon. It's just that…" Just what, I wondered. I wasn't sure myself.

"No, no," said Antoine, staring at the highway. Then he added, "It's okay," and I thought, he knows. He may even know better than me where my heart's ended up.

We arrived in front of the Soho Grand Hotel at about four o'clock. Antoine stopped the car and looked at me. "What?"

"Isn't Juliette at the Holiday Inn?" I asked.

"Yes, but the Chinatown Holiday Inn isn't that hot. So I made a reservation here."

"Oh." He crossed his arms and turned around completely in his seat to face me. "I reserved two rooms, if that's what you're trying to insinuate with that look like a scared virgin."

"I didn't insinuate a thing!"

"Oh!" He pointed a finger at me. "Little indignant look, right here."

I made a face at him, and we got out of the car. I immediately felt the wind, a light, warm breeze, like May in Montreal. I smiled at Antoine. "Nice, eh?"

"Nice indeed."

When I got to my room, I stretched out on the big bed, thinking of Antoine's face when he'd said, "Do you really want to know?" and wondering why, after all, he hadn't told me. Maybe he just didn't want to tell me. Maybe he thought it was better for me not to know. But that smile of his! There was hidden joy in his smile. A secret he was glad to have.

I ran my hands over my face, trying to stop thinking such pointless thoughts, and I looked at the time – it was four-fifteen and Antoine had asked me to meet him in the restaurant bar at five. I took a shower, explored the contents of the minibar, thought again about what Simon might have said to Antoine, and I sat down on the bed, with one towel around my head and another one around my body, when someone knocked on the door. He's unbelievable, I thought. I just have to be undressed, and he shows up. I opened the door, holding my towel, and saw Juliette.

"Eeeeee!" I shrieked, as if I hadn't seen her in years.

"Eeeeee!" she replied, and we fell into each other's arms, hopping around like teenagers.

"Come in, come in!" I said to her. "I'm just getting dressed. So? So? So? So?"

"Chloé, it's incredible. In – fucking – credible. Listen, there are six hundred artists."

"My God."

"Yeah, I said the same thing as you in the beginning, then I met a guy from Philadelphia who had pieces in last year's show and he explained to me that there are so many people, so many ideas exchanged, that everything really does get seen. There's some really conventional stuff, completely crazy sculptures, bad imitations of the Impressionists, magnificent paintings... You're coming tomorrow?"

"Of course. Oh, and look at this." I reached under the bed and pulled out the case of Molson Export.

"Shit, you're crazy!" Juliette shouted.

"The fair opens tomorrow, right?"

"Yes."

"And I suppose it would be a little awkward to drink it there, right?"

"Just a little," answered Juliette.

"Perfect."

I called Antoine. "It's me."

"Is Juliette with you?"

"Yes – did you call her?"

"Yep."

"Good plan, Tony Boy. Listen, instead of meeting in the bar, why don't you come down in fifteen minutes? We have a six-pack to finish."

I heard a laugh at the other end of the line. "Okay."

I hung up and turned towards Juliette, "Okay, before he gets here…"

"Did you tell him about Simon?" Juliette asked me.

"No, I didn't have to, he knew."

"No!"

"And do you know how he knew? He happened to stop by Simon's restaurant."

"No!" Juliette put one hand against her cheek. "I can't believe it. And Simon's the one who told him?"

"Yes."

"Ouch. How did he tell him?" Juliette asked me.

"Well, now, that's a different matter. All Antoine would tell me is that Simon explained to him that I'd left him, and then he added 'and two or three other things.'"

"What?"

"Shit, I don't know. When I asked Antoine, he gave me that teasing look, and asked, 'Do you really want to know?'"

"Oh," said Juliette. "Hmm." She thought for a minute in an almost comical pose – with a frown and one finger on her mouth, like in a comedy – and asked, "Do you think Simon told him you left him for him?"

"I don't know! I don't know! Every time I think about it, I get dizzy. Shit, can you imagine?"

"Hmmm. But, did you leave Simon for Antoine?"

"No! I thought we'd already worked this out. Antoine was just the catalyst."

"Yeah…" She didn't look convinced.

"Juliette!"

"Okay, okay! I believe you. Still…"

She didn't have time to finish her sentence – someone was knocking on the door. I looked at Juliette, amazed. "It can't be. It can't fucking be! *Every* time he shows up somewhere, I'm in my bra." I went to open the door, without even bothering to put a top on, and Antoine smiled: "Once again, I have excellent timing."

"Yeah, yeah." I let him in and he went and gave Juliette a hug.

"Oh, I'm so happy to see you!" I heard him say as I slipped on a top.

Julie started telling him about the fair, and I put our six beers on the little desk. "Kids," I said, "cocktails are served." We spent a good hour, sitting on my bed, laughing at ourselves ("We had to come all the way to New York to drink Molson Ex in a hotel room!") and remembering all Juliette's shows we'd been to, the good and the bad, the one where she didn't sell a single thing, the one where a painting fell off the wall onto Florent's foot, breaking two of his toes.

Outside, it was a nice, warm evening, and people were laughing and smoking on improvised terraces that were spilling out into the streets. We went for dinner in a little restaurant Antoine knew, where we stayed till almost 1 a.m. eating meringues and drinking white wine. "Just like the good old days," Juliette said – and it really was the good old days. I don't know if it was because all three of us were afraid it wouldn't last or because we knew how fleeting and precious it could be, but I could feel we were enjoying it purposefully, that we were enjoying it like never before.

Later, when we came home through the still busy streets, I could hear the two of them, walking just behind me – Antoine was saying to Juliette, "*Dogville* was fantastic!" – and I smiled to myself, thinking they really were everything I loved, and looking up at the fire escapes hanging from the buildings.

We left Juliette at her hotel, and Antoine and I continued on together – he had an arm around my shoulders, and I had one around his waist, and we were talking about Juliette and the dreams she kept so secret. "She'd never admit it," Antoine was saying, "but her dream is to be a success, a big critical success, like she deserves."

"You're right. She'd be too afraid it would bring her bad luck."

When the elevator doors opened at my floor, Antoine took me by the waist and kissed me on the neck – I slipped between the doors and when I turned around, he was leaning against the back wall, with his hands in his pockets, and smiling at me.

The fair was even bigger than I'd imagined – there were stands everywhere, separated by movable walls, and they created a huge labyrinth where you could find totems, still lifes, watercolours of flowerpots, electrical installations, abstract paintings and a huge polished metal cube that balanced on one corner.

We spent the day walking from stand to stand, with Juliette, who was asking questions, shaking hands, talking about her own art – she was showing me paintings, sculptures and all sorts of things I never would have seen, details, sometimes, but the ideas behind the work, too.

She didn't sell anything that first day, but seemed happy and still overexcited. That night we went to dinner with the Montreal gallery owner who'd brought Juliette, a beautiful woman of about forty, who, from what we could see, was just waiting for a sign from Antoine to go back to his room with him. A sign which, to our great surprise, never came ("Not my type," Antoine had explained to us while she was in the washroom. Juliette and I looked at each other: we thought she looked just his type).

The next day, after a visit to the fair, Antoine and I went shopping – he'd always been what I called "an excellent shopper": he walked through the summer dresses and $300 tank tops at Saks and Bergdorf Goodman, and brought me what he liked, what he thought would look good on me. And he loved doing it – I was almost always the one who got tired before him. "When I see you shop," I would tell him, "if I didn't have a ton of proof otherwise, I'd wonder if you weren't gay."

"No, of course not. I like nice things, that's all." And off he went to study the aisles of ladies' shoes.

At the end of the day, he went to meet a friend of his who now lived in New York, and Juliette and I went to have a girls' dinner, which we were delighted about. We settled in at a quiet table, in a pretty restaurant and Juliette told me about how she'd finally sold three paintings to an interior decorator who'd said she was very interested in anything she had, and who'd gotten her number.

"Can you believe it? It's incredible. Just six months ago, I never would have imagined this could happen to me. Never. I'm so happy, Chloé."

"I'm so happy, too… you really deserve it, Chubs; there are no words to describe it." We clinked glasses and Juliette leaned her chin on her right hand.

"You know," she said, "I never thought I'd be able to make a living from my art. Never. In my head, it was like paradise, a nice dream. And I'd accepted it, that's the worst part. I was resigned to it… And now… well, sure, I'm not making millions, but still. Plus, people are interested in my work, you know, it's not vanity, but my God! It feels like it gives meaning to everything I do."

"That it gives *you* meaning." She never would have admitted it, but I'd known for a long time what she was looking for in her work – no need to be a great psychologist to figure it out, but I think that Juliette secretly hoped it didn't show too much.

"Yes, that, too," she said. "It's ridiculous, but when people are interested in my paintings, it flatters me as much as if they were interested in me. I shouldn't think like that, but..."

"No," I interrupted her. "You're completely right. I know you, and your paintings are you. Absolutely you."

She smiled shyly.

"The *Self-Portrait* Antoine gave me," I said.

"Yes."

"He found the sentence."

"What sentence?"

"Just a fool's hope." I hadn't told her yet that I'd seen it. Without knowing why, I'd been waiting for a moment like this one.

"That one's your sentence," Juliette said. "The other one was just a little wink. This one is really yours."

"Mine? But you're in it, too."

"A bit, for sure. But when I wrote it, I was thinking about you. You, you and Simon, you when we wrote the *Manifesto*. I was thinking that in your own way, in your own funny way, you always had hope... I don't know how to say it..." She thought for a moment. "For a long time, I thought you had an absolutely naïve side – even in the *Manifesto* days. You were good at hiding it, but I could see that you thought there was something like true love, the kind of love that knocks you off your feet, changes your life, consumes you. And I said to myself, 'The poor girl's completely crazy, she's going to waste all her time chasing after it...' Today, you still believe it, and I know it. That something's going to happen someday, and that it'll knock you off your feet."

I smiled. "Yeah, I guess so. It's ridiculous, eh?"

"No," answered Juliette. "That's just it. What would be ridiculous would be your days moping because it hasn't happened yet."

"Maybe," I said. "We'll see. You know, I have considered the possibility it may never happen. I'm not that crazy."

"Yes, but you believe in the possibility. That's what I think is great about you. That you'd rather believe in the one percent possibility it'll happen than the other ninety-nine percent."

"You really don't believe that, too?"

Juliette shook her head. "Not for me. And I don't mean that bitterly, or anything else – I'm good now. Listen, if, by some miracle, it happened, I'd be the first one to be delighted, but I'm not looking for it. I've never felt better in my life than since I stopped getting mixed up with all those absurd guys. It's not true that without a man in my life, my existence is crap." She took a swallow of wine. "Love is wonderful, but not at any price. I feel good single. I understand myself better. I'm working. I even finally stopped thinking about my ex." She smiled and repeated, "I feel good," and, in her big blue eyes, I could see she was telling the truth.

"But as for you," she said, pointing a finger at me, "if you still think you're going to find true love, maybe you should stop acting like an ostrich."

"What are you talking about?"

"Antoine."

"Oh, Juliette… I thought you said you weren't going to get involved in that anymore."

She gestured powerlessly, "What can I say, when I'm in a good mood, the expert psychologist in me comes out."

"Yeah, but, Juliette… Antoine."

"What, Antoine? Chloé, you'd have to be blind not to see that there's something… huge between the two of you. And not just friendship."

I thought about Simon, who'd said it was like there was an invisible thread between Antoine and me, "as if, in a room, you could find one of you just by looking at the other."

"Oh, I don't know," I answered Juliette. "Honestly, would you go out with a guy like Antoine?"

"If I were you, yes. In an instant."

"Come on! It's a one-way ticket to disaster! He can't even be faithful!"

"How do you know that?"

"Come on, Juliette. You know Antoine."

"Yes. And I think he was just waiting to fall in love. I already told you that, but you didn't believe me. He was just waiting for that. Only, he didn't know it."

I sighed in exasperation. "Juliette, that makes no sense. Imagining he was going to wake up one morning and say, 'Okay, time to settle down.' No, it's not…"

"Are you in love with him? Honestly, Chloé."

I closed my eyes, and I thought – honestly. "I think… I think part of me will always love part of Antoine. But that's not enough to…"

"No," said Juliette. "All together. Because the parts count. What are you going to do, Chloé? Let something phenomenal pass you by because you're afraid you'll get hurt? I got hurt. And you know what? If I had to do it over again…"

"Oh, Juliette, please. You say so yourself, it was ten years ago and you're still not over it yet."

"Yes, but I'd still do it all over again. Because that was it! For as long as it lasted, that was it, see?"

"Juliette, it's fine to say that, but the tears! How many times have you cried because of that guy? How many times have you told me he made you lose faith in love?"

Juliette shook her head, looking around as if searching for inspiration. "I know," she finally said. "I know, but…" She sighed and smiled at me. "It was worth it, Chloé. When push comes to shove, it was worth it."

I looked at her in silence – I had a hard time believing her – I'd heard her say so many times that that particular love had destroyed her. But she shrugged her shoulders and repeated, in the same, slightly surprised voice, "It was worth it."

"Maybe for you, Ju, but…"

"What do you have to lose?"

What did I have to lose? Antoine? My happiness? I shook my head. "No, really, Ju. It doesn't make any sense."

I spent the next day going over what Juliette had said and trying to see if, in the end, she was right. I watched Antoine, the gestures I knew so well, his smiles, his looks, the way he frowned when he read something, and I thought, yes, I loved him, and not only part of him, but really all of him, even with his pride, his passion for women, his boyish selfishness, his habit of thinking everything was owed to him – I loved all of him. But he scared me too much, and, despite what Juliette had said, I had too much to lose. So I pushed those ideas out of my head, and told myself that if, in a few months, this affection felt like more than friendship, "I'd see."

We spent our last evening in a little bar in the Village, sitting on big pillows near a fire, celebrating Juliette's success at being approached by a local gallery. It was warmer out than when we'd arrived. Antoine and I had spent the whole day walking, stopping at the Frick Collection, then strolling through Central Park, where people were jogging in shorts and girls were tanning in tank tops. We came out of the bar at about two and walked to Juliette's Holiday Inn. I was a little tipsy – just enough to feel unhurried and happy, and to welcome the April breeze with open arms.

Antoine and I continued towards our hotel – I watched him walk near me, I watched him watch me, thinking it wasn't possible, Juliette was wrong, when he stopped, barely a block from our hotel.

"What are you doing?" I asked him. He just looked at me, with his eternal grin.

"Oh, boy," I said. "That smile never precedes anything good." I was in a good mood. It was nice out, the night was beautiful, the streets of New York delighted me. I took two little steps and stood directly in front of him. "What is it, Antoine?"

"Why don't you ask me what Simon said to me?"

I raised one eyebrow. So, he wants to play, I thought. Okay. "I didn't ask you because that's what you wanted me to do."

Antoine laughed. "Okay. Maybe. I've been waiting for four days."

"And you want me to feel sorry for you?"

"A little."

"And you really want me to ask you?" I said, imitating his tone of voice.

"I want you to want to know."

"Okay, okay, all right." I realized my heart was beating at its regular speed, but very hard. "Okay, then. What did Simon tell you?"

"He started off by asking me if I was sleeping with you."

"What?" I'd imagined so many possibly explosive sentences that that one almost disappointed me. I felt like asking, "Is that all?"

"Yes," Antoine continued. "That's what he said, but without beating around the bush like that. What he said was, 'Are you fucking her?'"

"Oh. That's... that's not like him." Then I remembered his reaction in the restaurant when I'd told him I was leaving him, and I thought maybe I hadn't really known him that well, after all.

"No," said Antoine. "It surprised me a bit, too, but whatever. I could understand the guy was kind of upset."

"What did you say?"

"What do you mean, what did I say? I said no, of course! Would you prefer it if I'd said yes?"

"No. Obviously." I turned and walked a little ways along the sidewalk. "So? That was it?" I asked. "That's what he said to you?"

"No. He said something else." I spun around and saw this was the moment he'd been waiting for, the one he'd conjured up, four days ago, with his smiles. Why did he do stuff like that, I wondered. He exasperated me – and I loved it.

"Okay," I said, sighing. "What is it? What did he say to you?"

He came closer to me, so close that I had to look up a little to look him in the eye.

"He said you were in love with me." I knew it, I said to myself. And still, I was out of breath, I could feel my heart, in my chest, in my neck, against my temples, everywhere. I thought I should say something, but I was silent. I looked at Antoine, and I waited.

He put one hand on my cheek, and it was like an electric shock. "Antoine," I heard myself say. Then he raised his other hand, and, in an incredibly delicate way, he took my face – it's like he's holding porcelain, I thought – and he kissed me. His lips, against mine, and my heart was almost hurting me. I closed my eyes and I placed one hand against his chest. "Don't do that," I ordered with a sigh.

He hesitated for an instant, his lips parted, then he looked up before he leaned back towards me again, looking almost helpless.

"I'm in love with you, Chloé."

For just a second, I thought I was going to faint. I heard myself breathe out, and then I stood there, breathless, thinking it was impossible, that I must have misunderstood, my only thought was, "It can't be."

"Pardon?" I finally said.

"I'm in love with you."

"Oh, my God." I took a step back and put a hand to my forehead. "Antoine, what are you talking about?"

"What do you mean, what am I talking about? I love you." He again stepped closer and I stretched out a hand to hold him back. I was too afraid, and I wanted him too much.

"You're not in love with me, Antoine, it's…"

"Oh no? Chloé, it took me eight years to figure it out. I think I know."

"Oh, my God." I couldn't say anything else – I felt like I was sinking into the cement, right there on the sidewalk, with people bumping into us, one arm keeping Antoine and I apart. He took my hand, squeezed it in his own, and said, "Look at me."

I looked up at him, and in his dark eyes, I could see a flame and an agitation I was unfamiliar with. "Simon," said Antoine.

"What?"

"What he said."

"Antoine."

"Tell me it's not true and I'll drop it." For just a second, I thought about tumbling into his arms, closing my eyes and listening to nothing but my desire. I shook my head. "Don't do this," I said to him.

"Why?"

"Because I can't." I thought I was going to cry.

"You can't what? I love you, Chloé. I've never been sure about something like this in my whole life. Never. And I know you love me. I know it." Then he added, "I know you better than anyone."

"Stop it!" I shouted. "You don't love me, Antoine, you just flipped out 'cause I had a boyfriend, and your hunting instinct, or I don't know what, made you believe you loved me…"

"But do you think I'm an idiot or what? You think I didn't think of that? I've been asking myself these questions for at least eight months! I thought I was going to go crazy, Chloé! So don't go telling me I'm kidding myself."

I shook my head no, and I brought a hand to my chest, to my heart, which was beating so hard, I was almost out of breath.

"Antoine, I can't be with you."

"Why?"

"Girls, Antoine!" I raised one hand. "You!"

"I don't give a shit about girls. Any girls."

"Christ, Antoine. You can't change. I know you."

He ran a hand through his hair and looked up. "Chloé. Don't tell me I can't change. I'm here, on a New York street, telling you I'm in love with you. And this has never happened in my life, I'll have you know, so, it's not like I didn't really, really think this whole thing over. For eight months. Chloé, I only feel like this when I'm near you. It's like I can see better, it's like, suddenly, everything makes sense. Do you understand what I'm saying?"

I could only nod – when I was with him, I felt like I could see the world better, too.

"When you come into a room... even if you're not near me, even if you're talking to someone else, everything is clearer."

"Stop, Antoine. Please."

"No! Christ, Chloé, when I think about my life, about all that, it's not my job, it's not the money I make, it's not Miko or Julie or any of the other girls I've had sex with, it's you. You give meaning to everything, you make all the difference. Otherwise, I'm just another guy, get it? It's your presence, in my life, that makes me someone extraordinary."

I wanted to say no, that it was the other way around, that he was the one who coloured my whole existence, but I was unable to speak.

"You had to fall in love with someone else to get me to wake up," Antoine went on, "and maybe that makes me a jerk or an asshole or whatever, but I can live with that, and I'm ready to accept it, it won't be the first time. But for you to say you don't love me... no."

"I didn't say that," I whispered, and I realized my hands were shaking. Antoine took me by the waist.

"Then what are you doing?"

"I can't!" I shouted, freeing myself. "I can't, Antoine! It sounds clear enough to me!" He turned around, with both hands behind his neck, and I heard him sigh in exasperation. "I can't," I repeated.

He came back towards me. "What do you want to do then? Just stay here? Because you're afraid? You think I wasn't afraid? I was doing fine, you know, having all the sex I wanted and not giving a shit about anything. But Stéphanie was right, Chloé. What are we going to do? Spend our lives afraid of everything and making ourselves think we're not afraid of anything? Is that what you want?"

"You don't understand, Antoine."

"No, I understand just fine. I should have kept my mouth shut, and you should have stayed with Simon. No danger, no problem."

"Fuck you."

"No, fuck *you*." He pointed a finger at me. "I don't know how many times you've said that to me, but now, that's enough. Let it go." He turned on his heels and started to walk towards the hotel – I wanted to say his name, call him, but I stayed silent and immobile on the sidewalk. After a few seconds, I leaned against the brick wall of the building I was standing in front of, and closed my eyes. I was completely out of breath, as if I'd been swimming underwater and had just come up.

I stayed there for five minutes, ten minutes maybe, until I realized what I had just done didn't make any sense. "Oh, my God," I said out loud, and a woman who was walking by turned and smiled at me. Antoine was right, completely right, and so was Juliette, and I was an idiot. I repeated, "Oh, my God," and took off running towards the hotel.

The lobby and the bar were filled with magnificent, cool people who looked like they'd never had a care in the world, just like Antoine had when I met him. I was convinced he'd be in the bar – when he was upset, he always looked for crowds, and martinis. I walked around the place, twice, three times, feeling like my heart was going to burst out of my chest every time I saw a man in a black jacket. Oh, my God, I was saying to myself, Omigod, omigod, omigod – I think I even prayed, vaguely; I was ready to invoke any deity

at all to find him, to go a few minutes back in time, to have
him with me, near me, to be able to see him again and stop
feeling like I was drowning.

But Antoine wasn't in the bar, or the lobby, and I thought
he must be somewhere else, that we were in a city of ten
thousand inhabitants, that he was certainly with a woman,
undoubtedly the over-forty gallery owner that had tried to
pick him up two days before. I ended up sitting in one of
the big chairs in the lobby, without really knowing why – I
was so lost, I could hardly think.

"Okay, okay, okay, okay…" I muttered, trying to take deep
breaths. It was urgent for me to calm down. But I was being
attacked by hundreds of images, the two of us in the street a
few minutes earlier, in Juliette's studio, the diner near Albany,
images that went back a few years – all our laugh attacks, all
our conversations, all the looks we'd exchanged, images of
Antoine, who wasn't here, not anymore.

That's what I deserve, I said to myself. It's exactly what I
deserve. I vaguely thought of staying there until he came
back, but I thought there was a possibility he wouldn't come
back, that he'd gone to spend the night with another
woman, and I almost felt sick. The lobby was still full of
smiling people who were coming and going, and I almost
wanted to scream at them, "Why aren't you helping me?
Why aren't we all organizing a search party to find him?" I
thought if I had been in a movie like *Notting Hill*, I would
have been surrounded by a group of eccentric but endearing
friends who would have feverishly helped me look for
Antoine. But I wasn't in *Notting Hill*, I was alone, in a hotel
lobby, and I felt like I was falling, sinking. It was a catastrophe, I said to myself – I won't find him, it's too late, he's
gone, I've ruined everything, he won't be back, and any second, a tidal wave was going to swallow up the city. Good.

I finally gave up – I felt tired and empty, and I went to
the reception desk to ask for a paper and pencil. Then I went
upstairs to Antoine's floor, and I stood there in front of his

door, wondering what I could possibly write. Every word, every sentence seemed so pointless that I felt like I was going to cry. I stood there for a minute, then I knocked – even if he isn't there, I thought, at least I'll have made a sound, in his room, where he would be again later. It was ridiculous, a little childish, but I couldn't keep from doing it, and then I placed my palm against the door.

I heard myself take a breath, and then Antoine was there, in front of me. I don't remember if I smiled, or even if I said anything. He was looking at me, in silence, one hand still holding the door, and I could see he was waiting. I closed my eyes, for a moment, and when I opened them up again, I realized I couldn't lie anymore, to anyone, especially not myself.

"You have to understand something," I said. I was shaking, I was beside myself, above myself, hanging somewhere above us, with the firm conviction that if I didn't now say the words that had been haunting me for so long, that I'd regret it forever. "I've loved you for eight years. Only you. Completely. And I was too stupid to admit it even to myself. Eight years, Antoine."

I stopped, a little shaken up from finally admitting it, to myself and to him. Antoine remained impassive, to such a degree I wondered if he'd even heard me – his eyes were just shining and seemed full of words. It was my turn to wait – I could have waited hours, days, I was nailed to the spot, glued to his gaze. Then he spoke.

"Simon added one other thing, you know."

"Oh yes?" I could hardly hear my own voice. It sounded like a puff of air.

"He said it was ridiculous."

"It was ridiculous?"

"Yes, you and I. It was ridiculous because neither one of us was doing anything about it and we deserved each other."

He's right, I thought. I looked down – I could hear my heart, and the regular rhythm of my breathing. Once again,

I felt like I was in the eye of the storm, in that perfectly calm, immobile place that exists there. But I couldn't stay there anymore, I knew that now. I looked up.

"You could break my heart, Antoine."

"No. No, I can't. Because I love you."

I smiled, and so did he, finally, finally, I could throw myself into his arms. He hugged me tight, so tight I thought I'd lose the little breath I had left, then his hands travelled up my back, to my hair, and, holding my face, he kissed me, and again, I thought of porcelain, his touch was that gentle and delicate.

"Antoine," I said between two kisses. "If I fall…"

"If you fall, I'll fall with you." I couldn't help but smile, and he said, "I know, I can't believe I just said that either. But it's true, you know. It's true."

I lightly stroked his cheek and lips. I had the impression – which was both terrifying and intoxicating – that I was on the edge of a cliff. What if I do fall, I thought. Yes, what if I fall? I could see Daphné telling me about reasons and regrets, I heard my father telling me I was afraid of love, telling me to "take a chance," I thought about Juliette's painting, and the hope I carried in spite of myself and everything else, I could even see my mother, in her silk housecoat, singing "Qué será, será." I could see all that and more, calmly, clearly: the absurdity of a life without Antoine, the beauty of the risk, the inescapable desire, and I saw Antoine's face, the face that I had been looking for for so long without knowing it – and joyfully, voluptuously, I fell.

Epilogue

Juliette leaned forward between the front seats. "We'll never make it on time. The wedding's at four o'clock." She sat back, and then leaned forward again. "By the way, I told you it would take almost two hours to get to Saint-Donat."

"Yes, but Stéphanie said it took less than an hour and a half!" said Antoine. "Christ, that's where she's from! What kind of person doesn't know how long it takes to get to their hometown? Hey, shit… Look at that, all those idiots are getting off at Saint-Sauveur."

"Can't you go a little faster?" Juliette asked him.

"I can't just drive over the other cars, Ju."

Juliette stuck her head out the window and shouted, "Hey! We have a wedding in a half-hour!" Then she sat back down.

"That was helpful," Antoine said. "Really, really helpful."

Marcus, who was sitting next to Juliette, started to laugh. "This is so much fun. A real adventure." I looked at Juliette in the rear-view mirror, and we smiled at each other. Marcus was her date for the evening – Michel had agreed to lend him to her for the occasion, to Marcus' great delight, because he "looooooved" weddings, and had warned us about a hundred times that he was going to cry like a baby.

"We should have gotten dressed in Montreal," I said. "Why didn't we get dressed in Montreal?"

"You were afraid to get your dress wrinkled," Antoine answered.

"So was I, I'll have you know!" shouted Marcus, making us all laugh. "Hey, I've got an idea. Why don't we get dressed in the car?"

"In the car?" I echoed, laughing.

"We should have tied him to the roof," Antoine said. "I told you I should have tied him to the roof!" Marcus laughed and leaned forward to kiss Antoine on the cheek. "Don't even try it, Tony Boy. I know you love me… Chloé, find us a good song. Something that'll pump us up!"

I turned on the radio, and a very official Radio-Canada news voice came out. "Chloé, I said pump us up!"

"I'll put in a CD."

"No! Change the channel!"

Exasperated, I pushed "Tune," and "Like a Virgin" exploded from the speakers, provoking a concert of "Eeeee! Leave it on! Madonna!" from the back seat. Juliette and Marcus started clapping their hands and singing at the top of their lungs, "You make me feel, so shiny and newwwww…" and I joined right in, shooting amused looks at Antoine, who was shaking his head and looking discouraged.

We'd gotten to the second verse when he shouted, "Shit, finally!" The lane had cleared and he'd immediately begun to accelerate. "Sorry," he said to me, "but these are extraordinary circumstances."

"Woo hoo!" shouted Marcus. Then he added, "Oh, God! He's doing 160 km/h. We're gonna die."

But, not only did we arrive at the hotel parking lot alive, Antoine didn't even get a single ticket, which, according to Juliette and I, was the result of divine intervention.

"Now do you know what I meant?" I asked Marcus as we got out of the car. "About the way he drives?"

"Hey, we made it, didn't we?" said Antoine.

"You're lucky we didn't run into any cops, though."

"Yeah, well, you know my famous sense of denial…"

"We don't have time for this!" Juliette interrupted. "We have fifteen minutes! So, we'll register, change and meet in the parking lot in ten minutes. Is that clear?"

"Sir, yes, sir!" said Marcus.

Juliette made a face at him and pointed a finger at Antoine and me. "Is that clear?"

"Yeah, yeah, okay!" And the three of us ran towards our rooms laughing.

"We'll never make it in time," I said battling with the zipper on my dress. "This is ridiculous."

Antoine started to laugh. "It's completely ridiculous. Stéphanie is going to come in carrying her bouquet and we'll probably be right behind her. The people will turn around towards the doors and there will be Stéphanie and her father, two little flower girls, and four late idiots."

I finally got my zipper up and I looked at Antoine, whose back was turned towards me, in nothing but pants, as he undid the buttons on the shirt he was about to put on. I crossed over to him, taking him by the waist, so I could kiss him right on the tattoo he had on his right shoulder blade – a Celtic cross he'd had done at the age of nineteen ("I thought I was pretty smart then, but now there are about 20,000 morons in Montreal with the same stupid drawing!"). He turned around and put his arms around me.

"You look handsome, my love." He smiled and kissed me. His mouth, his tongue, the texture of his skin – I loved everything about him, more and more every day.

"Mmm," he said. "We really only have ten minutes, right?"

I laughed and ran a hand along his chest. I kissed him between the pecs – the way he smelled always made me lightheaded. "I bet now," I said, "we must have about four minutes."

"That's a little short," Antoine answered, stroking my right breast and then my stomach through my dress.

"It's very short," I said. We kissed again, and then I ran laughing to the bathroom, so I could try to put my hair in a bun in record time.

Obviously, despite our heroic efforts, we arrived at the church late – we had time to see Stéphanie go into the church, and then we slipped into one of the back pews, laughing and elbowing each other like schoolchildren. The ceremony was unending, punctuated from time to time by Marcus' tears, and by our giggles (the priest, a very nice man, unfortunately took himself for a singer – his sung version of the *Letter to the Corinthians* plunged us into an abyss of hilarity we almost never recovered from).

Afterwards, a honking parade of cars left for Stéphanie's parents' house, near a lake, where the reception was being held. It was nice out – they'd set up little white tables all over the yard and the tree trunks were wrapped with white Christmas lights.

"It's charming," said Juliette, taking the glass of champagne a server offered.

"It's touching," said Marcus.

The sun was making the surface of the lake sparkle and as it shone through the trees, it made pretty little spots of moving light on the grass. Squinting, I walked to the edge of the water, and for a moment I got lost in the contemplation of the ripples.

"What a year, eh?" said Juliette's voice behind me. I turned and reached an arm around her shoulders. "What a fucking year!" Day for day, exactly one year had passed since Stéphanie's corn roast.

"It's pretty incredible, isn't it?" Juliette insisted. "I mean... I never would have believed it."

"Believed what?" asked Antoine, who was leaning against a tree a few feet away from us.

"Everything! The two of you, Marcus in love, my paintings selling in New York..." Only four canvases, but that had been enough to get a local agent to contact her and start managing her affairs. "Honestly," she repeated, "I never would have believed it."

"No, me neither," said Antoine. He shook his head and

laughed softly. "It really is unbelievable. When we get old, can you imagine how many stories we're going to have about this year?"

"My God," I said. "If I'm like my mother and her stories about when she was an actress, our children will go nuts from hearing about the famous year their parents fell in love and Auntie Juliette became a star…"

"…and wore a dress," Antoine interrupted me. Laughing, I squeezed Juliette's shoulder, as she muttered something and tugged awkwardly on the bottom of her skirt – in ten years it was the first time I'd seen her in a dress. Right up until the last minute she'd said she was going to wear pants, but Marcus and I convinced her, and she looked really cute, in a simple, little, blue and white dress that looked perfect on her.

"That's enough," she said. "I feel uncomfortable enough as it is…"

"You look really pretty," Antoine said to her, making her blush all the way up to the roots of her hair.

"Anyway," she continued, "I'll sure remember it. The year I wore a skirt… It will go down in the record books. And you better tell your kids, Chloé, because they won't see me in one very often."

I smiled at Antoine, who gave me a little wink – we talked about our children a lot, joking a little – neither one of us ready to have them right away, but I could see myself, with him, in a few years, with a baby in my arms.

"You know," Marcus said, coming over to Juliette and me, and putting an arm around each of our waists, "this has been the best year of my life. No contest."

"Aww…" said Juliette, teasing a little.

"Stop," Marcus replied. "I'm serious."

"I know, sweetie." She patted him on the hand, and I raised my head to give him a kiss – Juliette was looking at the lake, and Antoine, still leaning against the tree, smiled at me, and I could see perfectly that we were all thinking the same thing. I was about to go over and stand with Antoine, when applause broke out around us – the bride and groom had just arrived and were walking hand in hand among the old maple trees.

The evening went by in a flash – *mechoui*, good wine, knives clinking against glasses and kisses. When I'd asked Charles how he was he said, "Oh, I don't know. I'm hyper-ventilating, my heart's pounding, I'm hot, I'm dizzy, and I may faint any minute. It's happiness." Stéphanie flitted from table to table like a beautiful white butterfly. When night fell, they turned the Christmas lights on – the result was magical and charming. "I'm totally going to steal this idea for the apartment," Marcus said as we finished our dessert. "Don't you think so, Guilietta? Around the pillars in the living room?"

"We'll see," Juliette answered him. Then, she turned to me and said, "He has one idea like that every week. Last time, he wanted to hang diaphanous drapes behind all the pipes running along the ceiling. Can you imagine how ugly that would have been... Christ, diaphanous drapes. You want to tell me what that means, diaphanous drapes?" Marcus made a sweeping gesture. "No, no, sweetie! Diaphanous drapes are totally out. No, no, now, it's Christmas lights. I'm all about the lights."

We were sitting at one table with Denis "Rimbaudelaire" and his girlfriend, a slightly chubby blond girl who was always laughing and seemed to think Marcus was the funniest person to ever walk the earth. The white tablecloth was covered with wine and grease stains; there were at least six empty bottles on it, along with crumpled napkins, and plates strewn with cake crumbs. People were dancing on the grass, amid the tables that had been rapidly pushed out of the way to make room for an improvised dance floor where the young and young at heart were dancing the *Macarena*. In the middle of them, I saw Stéphanie do a few of the steps, and then she slipped away and came towards us. "She looks wonderful," said Marcus. He laid one hand across his chest, and gave a long, sentimental sigh. "Oh, my God. I think I'm going to start crying again."

"No!" I said. "You can't be serious? That would make only, what, twelve times?"

Marcus gave me a deadly look. "Laugh all you want, you heartless thing... Oh, Stéphanie, sweetie! You look so beautiful!" And he shed a few tears as he hugged her, while, all around the table, we smiled at each other.

"Finally!" said Stéphanie, sitting down heavily just behind Antoine and me. "I'm sorry, there are so many people to see! It never stops! Are you at least having a good time?"

"Super," Antoine told her, giving her a kiss. "And you look magnificent."

"Oh, you," Stéphanie said. "You, you, you... When did you plan to tell me you were together? If I hadn't run into Juliette last month, I would have fainted at my own wedding." She looked at us, one at a time. "I can't believe it. I absolutely can't believe it. Doesn't it knock you all right off your feet?" she asked Juliette and Marcus, who both shook their heads no.

"No?" Stéphanie asked. "My God, I guess you do know them better than me, but, Juliette, when you told me, I seriously thought I was going to fall over."

"I know!" Juliette said. She turned towards us. "Shit, she was shrieking so much the people around us looked like they thought I was stealing her purse."

"Yeah, but, lord!" said Stéphanie. "First, you got a boyfriend, Chloé, that was unbelievable enough, then Antoine? Honestly, my boy, I thought you were a lost cause. I was sure that even if one day love came and slapped you in the face, you'd be too stubborn or proud to do anything about it."

"It almost turned out that way," Antoine told her. "But I'm not the only one, I'll have you know. Miss Chloé was not exactly easy to convince."

"Well, I don't want to offend you, but that's pretty understandable."

"Okay, okay, okay…" Antoine gave a little smile of resignation. "In fact, you know what?" he said just for Stéphanie. "You helped me convince her. You were quoted at a very critical point in our relationship."

"What do you mean?" Stéphanie asked, visibly delighted.

So we told her – about Juliette's studio, our buried desires, the love that had slept for so long, the streets of New York, the April breeze and the Soho Grand Hotel room we didn't leave for forty-eight hours, how we both phoned our offices to tell them we'd run into "insurmountable difficulties" and called room service twenty times a day to get more champagne and fresh fruit.

"Really," Stéphanie said, "that makes you quite an idiot, Antoine. She had to get a boyfriend to wake you up."

"Well… I had to wake up in order to wake her up, so…"

"Hey!" I shouted. "I'll have you know I woke up eight years ago, and you didn't want to hear about it. So there…"

"Isn't she adorable when she makes that little indignant face?" Antoine asked Denis "Rimbaudelaire."

"They're so cute," said Marcus, with one palm pressed against his cheek. "I could listen to them squabble all day long."

Stéphanie looked at us one after the other, and laughed. "What about your ex?" she asked me. "He's not too bitter about having to play Cupid for you two?"

"Excuse me!" shouted Marcus before I could answer. "There's only one person who played Cupid here. In this story, Stéphanie, Cupido is black."

"What do you mean?" asked Stéphanie, as Juliette, Antoine and I sighed tiredly – Marcus must have told the story about twenty times in the last four months, and, generally, we were there. First, he bragged about being the only one to have encouraged me to look for love – the fact that love first appeared as Simon didn't seem to matter at all to him. He then claimed another exploit, which I'd only recently learned of, as his own: the day before I left for Belize, when we'd had dinner at his and Juliette's place, Antoine had stayed very late. Juliette had gone to bed and Marcus (and another bottle of rum) had explained "certain things" to Antoine.

"Can you believe it?" Antoine said to Stéphanie. "Me, of all people. I got a lesson about love from a drag queen. He started by telling me I was in love with Chloé – I didn't want to believe him, I was still hanging onto the idea I was only interested because she had a boyfriend… In fact, I couldn't even believe I was having that conversation. It's not like I've spent my whole life talking about my feelings, you know."

"Yes, we know," said Juliette.

"And that night," Antoine continued, "it went on for hours!" He started to laugh. "He couldn't quite get me to admit I was in love, that was too far out of the question for me, but he did make me realize I was obsessed with her. He said, and I quote, 'Right now, you're not seeing straight, Tony Boy. You're just obsessed with her. But she's going to leave Simon soon, you'll see.'"

"I was right," said Marcus.

"You were right about everything," Antoine answered. "But, Chloé looked happy with Simon and I didn't want to be the guy to spoil it, you know?" I smiled, this last gesture of Antoine's before we got together always moved me. "But, when I found out you'd left Simon… my God. It's completely ridiculous, Stéphanie, but I came out of Simon's restaurant and I said to myself, 'Okay, what would Marcus tell me to do?'"

Marcus clapped his hands, visibly delighted. "You see?" he said. "You see? Black Cupid, baby! Black Cupid."

Antoine rolled his eyes. "Okay, obviously, for the last four months he's been running behind us yelling, 'Black Cupid, baby!' But I guess it was worth it." He smiled at me and ran a hand along the small of my back. Personally, I love the idea of Black Cupid, if only because it put even more distance between me and Croatian Cupid, who I still felt a little bad about. I hadn't seen Simon since we'd broken up – we'd only spoken on the phone twice, and he'd been cold and polite and he'd told me that, to be honest, he still hadn't completely come to terms with the fact that it was indirectly because of him that Antoine and I had finally gotten together. But Simon, being Simon, had gone to the trouble of telling me no one was to blame, and I'd hung up feeling even more guilty, because deep down I wanted him to blame me – it was easier than doing it myself.

Daphné had bumped into him once, when she was shopping downtown. He'd been nice, of course, and they'd gone for coffee in a completely ridiculous place, like the basement of the Eaton Centre. Daphné had gotten him to talk a little – she hadn't told me everything and I was grateful for that. But she had told me that he'd been particularly hurt because early on he'd agreed not to worry about my relationship with Antoine, though it would have "scared off any other guy." He was mad at himself and he was mad at us for being too ridiculous, as he'd told Antoine, to do anything about it sooner, back before he was even in the picture.

Stéphanie nodded her head. "Well, as far as your ex is concerned, I'm not too worried. A handsome guy like that…"

"That's what I keep saying," I answered. "And besides, he's not just handsome, he's perfect, literally."

"What about me?" Antoine asked.

"You? You're full of character flaws. Why do you think I love you?"

That was the first thing my mother had said to me. Well, first, she'd actually shouted, "Finally!" We were at their house, with Daphné and Stéphane, the day I told them the news – I'd wanted to wait for the right moment, but after the first martini, right there in the living room, I'd shouted, "I'm in love with Antoine, and he feels the same way, it's been five days, and we spent two of them having sex in New York, and now we're doing the same thing, but in Montreal, and I love him, I love him, I love him." Then I stopped talking and I looked at them one after the other. "Oops?" I said. I was expecting a few worries, a few recommendations, at least a dozen frowns, and all I got was a "Finally!" from my mother and a burst of laughter from Daphné, who said, "It's super! It's fantastic! And, if it makes you feel any better, it's absolutely not reasonable." She was in a very good mood, she and Stéphane had decided to "try again" in the fall.

My father had expressed a few doubts – he was, of course, afraid that Antoine would hurt me, but all I could tell him was that I wasn't scared of anything, not anything at all, and that I'd never before been so sure of something. He'd tilted his head, given me his nice smile, and taken my hand. "What matters, my girl, is that you're happy." And I didn't need to tell him that, he could see it.

"I really wondered what you'd been waiting for," my mother said with a giggle. "I would watch you and think, 'What children. Real children who are too stupid or proud to realize what they're looking for is right under their noses.' You really deserve each other, you know?" I'd nodded yes, happily – nothing in the world made me happier than deserving someone like Antoine, and being deserved by him.

"Antoine…" my mother had added. "He's not perfect, but he's perfect for you."

"I must add," Antoine specified, "that her mother warned me that if I ever cheated on Chloé or was even just a little unpleasant, she would emasculate me with a spoon."

"A plastic spoon," added Juliette.

"A plastic spoon," I repeated. "But it's just a figure of speech."

"Oh, no," said Antoine, "she was perfectly serious."

Stéphanie laughed. "You have an unbelievable family, Chloé."

"Yeah, I know." I couldn't help but smile – I felt like I'd gotten it back after a year. I had gotten closer to Daphné, of course, but to my parents, too, who I could finally appreciate for what they were worth. "I really am spoiled," I added. "And, Stéphanie, you should see my mother, since we've been together… she's in seventh heaven. She kept saying she felt like Antoine had been her son-in-law for years, and just because we were a couple, it doesn't mean he couldn't come over for martinis with her anymore."

"In fact," said Juliette, "I don't think she's completely forgotten her plan to seduce him."

"And here's to you, Mrs. Robinson…" sang Marcus, and I started to laugh.

Antoine was about to add something else when a pretty girl leaned in close to him. "Hi!" she said to him cheerfully.

"Hi…"

He looked like he was working really hard to remember who she was. Juliette gave me a little kick under the table – we smiled at each other, and I motioned to Stéphanie not to help him.

"Watch this," I whispered to Stéphanie.

Antoine asked the girl a question or two, and they started to chat, exchanging pleasantries, like people who'd known each other forever. "Does he remember her?" Stéphanie asked.

"Not in the least. But he has this theory that indicates it would be impolite to show a girl he doesn't remember her."

"So he prefers to make them believe he does."

"Yes."

"And it works?"

"Every time. I don't know how, but over the years, he's developed a technique that's more or less infallible. He says even if you don't remember someone's name, you can look at them in a way that convinces them you never forgot."

Stéphanie looked over her shoulder towards Antoine, as he continued to chat and make the girl laugh.

"Doesn't that bother you?" she asked, turning back towards me.

"No, not at all. Listen, it's not like I just found out my boyfriend's been sleeping around for twenty years. I knew that already."

"And you're not afraid? That he'll go back to his old ways?"

I smiled. Everyone kept asking me the same question, of course. "I was afraid right up to the last second," I said. "But once I let myself go... no. I can't explain it, but I trust him like I trust myself."

"And you trust yourself?"

"Of course, what a strange question!?"

"What, how should I know!" Stéphanie said, looking sly. "You did sign the *Manifesto*, after all..."

"No, really," I said with a smile. "Honestly, I can't even imagine anything that could make me want to stray. But him, on the other hand... he's funny. He's a little jealous."

"What do you mean?"

"When I bump into my old lovers. He gets jealous. He starts to pout."

"He pouts?" Stéphanie asked with a laugh.

"Yeah, he looks kind of stupid and detached... I love it."

The girl who was talking to Antoine finally got up and waved to us before she left the table. She didn't even have her back turned before Antoine quickly leaned in towards Stéphanie and me.

"Okay, exactly who was that?" Juliette giggled into her glass.

"It was the little redhead," I told him. "The one you left the corn roast with last year."

"Mélanie," said Stéphanie.

"Oh," said Antoine, holding his forehead. "She dyed her hair..."

"Well," I sighed. "I recognized her."

"Shit, you could have helped me!"

"And miss that show? Oh, sweetheart. You don't know me very well."

He laughed and leaned towards me, gave me a soft kiss, with one hand on my cheek. Smiling, Stéphanie watched us, still looking like she couldn't believe it.

"Yes, well, if, on the night of the corn roast, someone had told me that…" she began.

"…you never would have believed it," Juliette interrupted her, and we traded knowing little smiles.

"No, that's for sure," Stéphanie went on. "Still. Two of the signers of your super *Manifesto*…" She emphasized the word *manifesto*, like it was a joke.

"You never did like the *Manifesto*," I said to her.

"No, I never did like the *Manifesto*. I thought it was stupid. Besides, it looks like you've all tossed it out completely, haven't you?"

"Um, excuse me!" shouted Juliette. "I am now the incarnation of the *Manifesto*. Single and more fulfilled than ever. A little respect, please. Chloé gave it to me, and it's nicely framed in my studio."

Stéphanie bowed respectfully, and then she suddenly looked up at us, as if she'd gotten an electric shock. "Oh my God!" she said. "Are you going to get married?"

I looked at Antoine. "She doesn't want to," he said.

"You asked her?" cooed Stéphanie.

"And I got a flat out refusal."

"We'd been together for five days," I said. "Honestly."

"Oh, come on," said Antoine, kissing my neck. "We've been together for eight years."

"Yeah, but for seven of those eight years you were sleeping with the best the city of Montreal had to offer."

"But deep down, I was an empty man," Antoine said, feigning despair. "I was in the dark, far from you."

"I wouldn't mind being in that kind of darkness!" interjected Denis "Rimbaudelaire," making us all laugh.

"So, you're not going to get married?" Stéphanie asked.
"Not my style," I said. "Church, city hall… nah. Honestly,
I can't see myself doing it. We don't need it, do we?" Antoine
looked powerless, while Marcus held his head in his hands.
"You're crazy, Chloécita. He's handsome, he's rich, he wants
to… Antoine," he adding, taking his hand, "I'll say yes,
whenever you want."

"Just when I was thinking I couldn't get any luckier,"
Antoine said as he got up. "If you'll excuse me, our glasses
our empty." He kissed me on the shoulder and turned
towards the bar.

"A ring?" shouted Marcus. "Won't you at least buy me a
ring?"

"No! Ask Michel – gay marriage is legal, isn't it?"

"He doesn't want to get married…" Marcus answered in
a downright pitiful tone. "How about a dress then? Antoine?
Will you buy me a nice white dress?"

"Okay," said Antoine walking away. "I'll think about the
dress."

"Something pretty with lots of tulle!"

"All the tulle you want."

"Oh, he's so yummy…" sighed Marcus, turning back to
us. "A real gentleman."

"And he really looks like he's in love," Stéphanie said to
me.

"He is," Juliette cut in. "Believe me."

"Oh, I can see it, too," said Stéphanie. "What about you,
do you love him Chloé?"

I gave them a wide, involuntary smile – I'd never imagined, I felt like telling them, that it was possible to love so
much, and so well. Everything during the four months that
were now between us and New York, everything delighted
me. The love I was discovering, in myself and in him, the
intoxicating sweetness of his presence, the certainty that
grew day by day that everything was finally in its place. "Oh,

I love him," I said. "So much, Stéphanie, you have no idea. I feel like I've finally arrived, you know? Where I'm supposed to be."

Stephanie nodded and smiled. "I'm happy for you."

"Me, too," I said to her. "I'm happy for you."

"It's been a nice evening, eh?"

"A fantastic evening."

Stéphanie turned towards Charles who was sitting at another table with some friends of his, and she blew him a little kiss, which he caught on the fly. "It's still crazy though, isn't it?" she said. "Love works in mysterious ways. It's incredible."

"Pretty much, yes," answered Antoine as he put two bottles of wine down on the table. On the dance floor, in front of us, people were making the letters *YMCA* in the air with their arms, to the Village People song. It was uncommonly inelegant, but they looked like they were having so much fun I smiled. The song ended but the DJ followed it up with "Go West," by the same group. "What is this?" asked Marcus. "A gay wedding?" He looked at the crowd of dancers for a long minute, and then said, "Ttt, ttt, ttt. Those people don't know how to dance at all. I think they need to see a professional."

"Oh boy…" sighed Juliette.

"Oh boy?" said Marcus. "You come with me, Giulietta!" He grabbed her arm, practically making her fall off her chair, and dragged her with him to the dance floor, where he started to shake his hips with staggering energy. At first people just watched him in astonishment, then they formed a circle around him – I could see his face above their heads, he was laughing and waving his arms in the air, and occasionally, opposite him, I could make out Juliette's blond hair.

I tilted my head back towards Antoine, who was laughing at the show. Our eyes met, and he grabbed my left hand and kissed it, then held it in his own. "I love you," he mouthed. I smiled at us, and I could see us, in this garden of lights, sitting together near a bride, and I could see Marcus and Juliette who were now dancing close, Marcus had finally found love and Juliette had stopped looking for it, and I thought that maybe we had arrived someplace. I thought about the world around us, my parents, Daphné, all the dressed-up people dancing by the August lake, and, once again, I could see a certain order in it, a strange kind of harmony we were all part of. I got up – Antoine ran a hand along my leg and I sat on his lap, with my arms around his neck, and, as I looked at his face, I thought, it's here and it's now. I have arrived.